WHEN INHUMANS CLASH

"Do you ... with *that?* ... arrogantly.

Vulture st...gg... "I ... don't know. Let's find out." She fired a steady stream up to the head and back down again. The Earth-daughter was flung against the wall by the force, but dropped and then recovered. She launched herself at Vulture, who was not quick enough. The Earth-daughter was on her at the first opening, steely hands around Vulture's throat. She heard and felt the neck snap, saw the life drain out, and let Vulture's limp form fall to the floor.

The Earth-daughter made her way to a wall panel and was about to press an activator when laser fire again raked her body. She screamed an inhuman, electronic scream. Her blackened, burned face looked up ...and saw Vulture, still bloody, head dangling crazily to one side, firing, firing, coming on...

In a deep, strained voice the Earth-daughter said, *"What are you?"*

WARRIORS
OF THE
STORM

Jack L. Chalker

A Del Rey Book

BALLANTINE BOOKS • NEW YORK

A Del Rey Book
Published by Ballantine Books

Copyright © 1987 by Jack L. Chalker

Library of Congress Catalog Card Number: 87-91143

ISBN 0-345-32562-1

Manufactured in the United States of America

First Edition: August 1987
Third Printing: February 1988

Cover Art by Darrell K. Sweet

For Edward Elmer Smith, Ph.D.,
who first took us Out There . . .
Thanks, Doc!

TABLE OF CONTENTS

PROLOGUE: THE PRICE OF SUCCESS

GENERAL WHARFEN HAD JUST COMPLETED HIS MORN-ing prayers and was in his prebreakfast meditative state when an aide presumptuously entered the room, stood, and bowed slightly at attention.

The general sat there in the lotus position, then suddenly raised his head, and those large, black eyes opened in slow and dramatic fashion. The aide was quaking with fear and exuding respect and apology, but he stood his ground.

The general did not immediately speak; he thought first, which was why he was the general. Clearly the aide knew what intruding would mean, and he was extremely uncomfortable in doing so. Therefore, he was here because something terrified him more than the general's wrath. The general was the highest ranking officer in the entire System Peacekeeping Forces, Chief of Staff and above even the fleet admirals. So, the general did not ask why he had been disturbed.

1

"Who?" he asked softly.

"A thousand pardons, sir. I would not—"

"*Enough*! Snivel later on your own time if you have any left! Answer my question!"

"A Val, sir. With the highest possible code."

The general sighed, untangled himself, and slowly rose. "Very well. Ten minutes in my office. I assume I am allowed time to properly dress."

"Y-yes, sir. I will inform it. Permission to leave, sir!"

"Go." He got up and was at his dresser before the aide had managed to back out and close the door. The general was entitled to a valet, but he never used one within his personal quarters. Clean, press, and prepare, fine—but there was a certain level of privacy he would not surrender.

The general was a perfect specimen of humanity. He was, in fact, more than human, and he knew it. He, and all the forces under his command, had been genetically engineered and bred to be superior. Even the lowliest soldier, male or female, was a fighting machine who could not only accomplish great physical feats but was also of the highest intellect. They were born, bred, raised, and trained to be soldiers, absolutely dedicated, absolutely committed, and absolutely obedient—even he.

But, the fact was, he still didn't like the damned machines and Vals in particular. They were, for all their massive design and inhuman appearance, far too human inside, and yet they were faster, stronger and possibly smarter than any human could ever be, which was why he disliked them. When one is as perfect as humanity could be, one does not like to look at someone, or something, that is even slightly better.

Still, absolutely none of the Forces would think of disobeying a Val with the proper codes and clearances, nor any command from Master System. Such a thing would be tantamount to a Fall from Grace. Not that he or anyone considered the machines, even Master System, to be gods; they were just machines, created by ancient human beings.

Humanity's ancestors, back on Earth, had reached a point in their development where they could destroy all life, and the great minds who helped maintain their destructive system went to work building the greatest de fense computer in human history, a self-aware and self-evaluative creation. With the knowledge that no one else was aware of their actions, they dared to program their creation to work out ways, any ways, by which the de-struction of humanity could be prevented—and then to in-sure that humanity could never destroy itself again. And when that time came, and the computer seized control of all the Earth's weapons systems and neutralized them, it took command. To save themselves, the political and mili-tary leaders obeyed it and carried out its orders. To fail to do so meant political death, at the very least, and replace-ment by more tractable leaders.

Inside the vast data bases of what was known only as Master System were vast knowledge and incredible new discoveries. Humanity already had some interplanetary ca-pability; to that Master System added the impossible—in-terstellar travel by "punching" a hole through space–time, pushing a ship across countless light-years under natural laws far different from those in our universe, then "punch-ing" back through again. The computer flew the ships; the computer alone knew the charts and objectives.

In order to fulfill its primary program and still retain absolute control, Master System constructed great ships to take billions of humans to the stars, to worlds that had been partially or fully terraformed. The heart of the interstellar ships was a device known as a transmuter, the result of a failed theoretical attempt to design a matter transmitter. Tremendous energy was required to punch through space–time, and using huge ramjets, the transmuter could convert thousands of tons of rock from the solar systems they visited to energy and store it in adequate quantity. The transmuter however, could not use this fuel itself. The only fuel a transmuter could use was a complex compound based upon an ore that formed only under certain geophysical conditions in certain solar systems—the ore murylium.

Master System charted the universe and discovered sufficient quantities of murylium for its needs. It built automated mines and factories out in space, supplied by a network of automated interstellar freighters. With bigger and more efficient transmuters Master System partially terraformed all the worlds it needed, then matched a large group of Earth-humans with each world, and transmuted them to those forms that could survive there. It established four hundred and fifty-one "colony" worlds and in the moving process created four hundred and fifty-one new forms of humanity. Those millions left on Earth were relegated to museumlike reservations and held at a cultural and technological level approximating the year 1700. Certain individuals from each culture—the best, the brightest, the most ambitious and innovative—were given access to Master System's technology. Working from hidden communities called Centers, they were expected to maintain the cultural level of the masses as it was, ignorant of the existence of a Center, or Master System. Only a few who lived in the old ways knew the secret; these served as field agents for the Centers' administrators. The colonial worlds were also organized in this fashion, as were even the few alien worlds under Master System's control. The system worked, but it had an uncontrollable side effect. In pooling all the brightest and most ambitious and skillful in small Centers with access to technology, it was inevitable that they would also find ways to beat the system. Master System allowed the Center personnel to think they were putting one over on the system they still faithfully served but to keep them honest and in touch with their cultures, all personnel were required to return to their native cultures and live the primitive life for a period of at least three months each year.

Master System had reduced, changed, and reseeded the human race in just under two centuries, and during that period a very few clever humans somehow managed to take control of some automated interstellar spaceships and fly them into noncolonial regions. Their descendants, the freebooters, provided the only means of contact between colonial Centers of different worlds and exchanged murylium and other exotic materials for access to data and technology that was beyond their means. The freebooters were useful at times, so Master System made a convenant with them, promising to let them be if they, on occasion, would aid Master System with information on illicit human activities of its far-flung centers. In effect, the freebooters became the four hundred and fifty-second colony without realizing it.

But Master System did not trust the stability of its creation, and so it constructed the Vals: massive humanoid robots with incredible mental powers and all the built-in tools and weapons needed to enforce Master System's rule. There were, however, very few Vals, and they were generally person or mission specific; when their task was completed, they were erased and reprogrammed.

The supplementary force was the SPF: the System Peacekeeping Forces, human beings born and bred to be fanatically devoted soldiers and police—roughly a thousand troops for each race Master System ruled. All forces were under the command of the Supreme Chiefs of Staff, which now was headed by General Wharfen and which outranked any other Center. The SPF had been used many times in local situations but never on a massive scale—until now.

* * *

Vals could sit but they almost never did. They were more than two meters tall, made of glistening black alloy in vaguely human form, but thick and broad in all departments. Except for their blazing crimson eyes, they were featureless, all their sensitive equipment armored and protected, but they moved with the ease and fluidity of a human, and they spoke in very human tongues.

The general did not salute or otherwise show deference to the Val; he knew such gestures meant nothing to the great machine and he was prideful enough not to bow to anything not human-born. The Val was a messenger and a tool, nothing more.

"I first require knowledge about the campaign against the freebooters," the Val said in a pleasant baritone.

The general took his seat behind his desk and relaxed. Vals terrified many people but they were nothing to him. Only enemies of the system needed to be frightened of these creatures.

"We hit all three *ersatz* freebooter centers in a coordinated action. We had a few wounded and some equipment failures but no real casualties. Almost all humans present were either captured or, when that proved impossible, killed. We have thirty-four prisoners and they have undergone extensive mindprobes. From the Gulucha and Halinachi staffs we learned next to nothing, but Saarbin essentially surrendered without a shot and we have much information from them on the location of freebooter routes, camps, enclaves, and their capabilities."

"Why were Gulucha and Halinachi so unprofitable?"

The general shrugged. "Gulucha's entire staff blew itself up when it found its escape routes blocked and no other alternatives. The only ones left were mindless creatures—prostitutes, bartenders, that sort of thing. Mindless transmuter creatures, essentially. Halinachi—well, Fernando Savaphoong and his immediate aides escaped, and we have been unable to locate or trace them. It was inexcusable, although I must say this Savaphoong was very clever and seems to have been the only one to plan for such an eventuality as the collapse of the covenant. Colonel Wor Shu Op and his staff have apologized to God in any event."

Even the Val understood what that meant. They were not executed—there was no reason to waste people that way—and they were not suicides. Rather, they had surrendered themselves and had been reprogrammed as basic troops. It was the ultimate humiliation for such as these, and that they had done so voluntarily because they were ashamed of their failure reassured the system of their absolute devotion.

"There is no sign of this colonization ship they control?"

"We have signs, but you know how vast space is and how easy it is to hide virtually anything there. There are probably many whole planets within our Quarter that we've never found or looked at; what is a ship, then, even of that size? They took a hundred tons of murylium and the freighter that contained it. I would say that speaks more for their capabilities than merely hiding. They are not on the defensive, and that bothers me. If they took it and ran to somewhere far away from the Quarter, then there would be little to worry about, but they are here, somewhere, and we are dependent on them to make a move in order to catch them. We *will* catch them, sooner or later, if they remain bold and aggressive, unless they make a run for it."

"They will not make a run for it. We would not even bother with them if all they were doing was attempting to sidestep the system. Master System is patient. We would eventually find and co-opt their grandchildren. Until now, no one has been authorized to know their true objectives, but Master System has decided that certain of its most loyal commanders must be informed in order to do their jobs properly. They are after components—disassembled logic circuits—that when assembled could cause massive harm to Master System."

The general was fascinated, although he well knew that what he was being told was so secret that it might eventually cost him his own mind in a Master System mindprint. "So? Out here?"

"Yes. The device is quite ancient and was created by the same ones who created Master System. The circuits are in the form of large, impressive gold-and-black jewelry—rings, in fact. Needless to say, the rings are inconsequential in and of themselves; it is the circuitry and code contained in the settings that is the danger."

The general shook his head in wonder. "Why would the Makers even build such things?"

"There are always checks and redundancies in any system, and destruct hardware in the most reliable machinery. They did not really know or fully comprehend what they were building, remember, and the potential for abuse made them nervous."

"But—why weren't these rings or whatever they are gathered up and destroyed during colonization and pacification ages ago?"

"They are a part of the system. They can not be removed and their assignment and availability is also prescribed. The best Master System could do was to distribute them among the stars and suppress all knowledge of their existence. In spite of all that, these people found out, and they are after the rings. That makes them the most dangerous people Master System has ever faced."

"Then the things will work."

"Yes, if all five are assembled and then inserted into Master System's special interface."

"You know where they all are?"

"Yes—to an extent. We know on what worlds they are, but not in all cases who has them. They have passed through many hands, all ignorant of their purpose, over the centuries. One is controlled by chief administrator Lazlo Chen on Earth. We believe he knows exactly what its purpose is, but that in itself is useless without the other four and the interface. Another is in the Cochin Center on Janipur where it is on display and taken out only on ceremonial occasions. We know the worlds and probably the regions for the others, but not necessarily the exact locations or possessor."

"And these rebels know the locations as well?"

"We believe so."

"Then—it's simple. We simply have to locate and take the rings first, leaving dummy duplicates as bait, sit back, and capture them."

"It is not that simple. The system requires that the rings be in the possession of humans with authority. That means administrators and the like. It could redistribute them at the beginning, for reasons not explained to me, but it cannot touch them now. It could interfere only to reassign the rings, and since the rings tend to be main badges of office rather than personal possessions, to eliminate an administrator would simply confer ownership on his or her successor. My orders are quite explicit. No one from our own forces must take the rings from their owners. The best we can do is to use them as bait, as you said, and deal with whoever comes to steal them. It is an irony that were you not under the command of Master System, you would be fully qualified to take and hold one of the rings, but since you are, as are all our forces, this is impossible."

The general was appalled, although the information confirmed a suspicion he had always had about machines versus humans. "You mean—they are fully allowed to steal the things, but we are not allowed to requisiton them for security purposes?"

"That is correct."

The general sighed. "Well, if we know where they are, we can cover them so tightly nothing could get through."

"Not necessarily. The colony ship has one hundred and fourteen transmuters aboard, four of which are large enough to do ship's repair and augmentation, and the memory capacity built into its core is more than sufficient to use them in the most complex ways. These people are dedicated to overthrowing the system or dying in the attempt. They will be fanatic enough to use the transmuters on themselves and take whatever form they need to get the rings, no matter what the personal cost."

Wharfen shook his head. "You believe, then, they are fanatical enough to do that? And to train and learn how to be something quite alien well enough to fool the locals?"

"I do. Security then must be absolute, yet none beyond this room, including particularly those who now possess the rings, must be told of the rings' true nature and importance lest we breed a generation of fanatics who one day could do what these renegades now only dream of doing. Nor should you be confident. These people do not act alone or in a vacuum. They had help and they were assembled for this purpose."

"Help? Who?"

"The enemy. Master System fights a stalemate: a war of machine against machine, far removed from here. But the enemy's clever. They have infiltrated us as we have been unable to infiltrate them. This is no mere band of rebels, General. This is a deep thrust inside our lines, a flanking maneuver that attempts to score the decisive victory by proxy."

"Who *is* this enemy?" the general asked. "Where is it being fought?"

"We do not know who it is. Great power, as great as our own. As to where, Master System does not tell us. If we need to know or our participation in active battle is required, then we will be told. Otherwise it is not our concern. We are, however, now involved, for this is an enemy thrust and we are required to blunt it. After all this time they have found a weak spot."

"Between a half dozen and a dozen people, many from primitive holds, in a fourteen-kilometer-long spaceship can threaten the entire system? I cannot believe that."

"We don't know their numbers. Discovering Arnold Nagy, the former security chief of Melchior, sitting in a bar on Halinachi with an unknown and two fugitives was something of a shock. We know they have more than just the one ship and the captured freighter. We must find them, General. We must make them come to us and then take them."

"But there is so much we don't know . . ."

"We know this—we have the easier task. They must have all five rings and know how to use them. Thus we need only prevent them from obtaining any one of the five to win. If we fail, all humanity will suffer."

"If we fail," the general replied, "we probably deserve to."

1. THE PRICE OF SUCCESS

AFTER THEY HAD MADE THEIR DECISION, THE CHOWS
had more than a month to think about it and agonize over it
and have not only second, but third and fourth thoughts
about doing it at all.

For the crew of the *Thunder* the time had not been
wasted. Originally, the vast interior of the ship had been
designed for two purposes: to transport large numbers of
uprooted humans from old Earth in a sedated state, and to
link them directly to the transmuters through which they
could be changed into the form Master System had designed to tailor them to the planet. Most of that was gone
now; the enormous interior was almost planetlike, with
grass and artificial sunlight and trees and small personal
buildings for the inhabitants. About eight kilometers by
two were available, but only a bit over four kilometers had
been transformed into living space, first for the small
Earth-human crew who'd stolen her and then for the crew

of the freebooter ships who had joined her. Aft was a work area for the ship's maintenance robots to repair and build whatever was needed. Only the final row of transport tubes, set against the rear bulkhead, remained untouched.

While this work was in progress, the great computer pilot whom they called Star Eagle worked with China Nightingale, the blind and eternally pregnant genius, and Doctor Issac Clayben, the greatest human expert on forbidden technology. With the files from the freebooter freighter *Indrus*, they pooled their intellects to learn all they could about the strange people who inhabited the world called Janipur.

The diverse Hindu culture from which the ancestors of that world had been plucked fascinated all of them. Its many and complex deities, its theories about reincarnation and an expanding and collapsing universe, its art and music and literature were all new to the crew of the *Thunder* and quite wondrous.

There was also a dark side to it, in that it used its cosmology to impose a rigid class structure determined by birth. One began as some insignificant living thing and then grew over successive lives to become a more complex organism and ultimately human, with the power to reason and study and make conscious decisions. But even as a human one had to start at the bottom, the lowest of the low classes, and serve a life as both a male and a female in each class, excelling and learning from that experience and thereby progressing to a new life in the next highest class. The ultimate were the Brahman, the highest class of the society, beyond which there was a new state, perhaps a godlike one.

The idea of rebirth was appealing in a way, but most of them shared the view of the cigar-smoking Crow security man, Raven. "If you don't remember who you were then what's the difference between bein' really dead and bein' reincarnated? Me, I think you get one go and that's it. Look at me. Smart-ass fat kid from a primitive village high in the mountains who became a warrior, then a Center security man, and now—well, whatever this is. Down there, if you're born a dirt farmer you *stay* a dirt farmer, no matter how smart or skilled you are."

Both the Chows and China had been born and raised in a culture that also believed in reincarnation and thought it quite logical, but their system was not as rigid as the Hindus'. And though they were familiar with a number of variants of Buddhism, Taoism, and Confucianism, they would find Janipur to be quite different. Master System believed in stability; the cultures it created were carefully edited versions of old Earth cultures, pared of all extraneous material. The China that had bred the Chows and China Nightingale was not the culture of their ancestors any more than were the Crow or Hyiakutt societies that had produced Raven, Hawks, and Cloud Dancer. Hawks, historian, had known this from the start, but few others could appreciate his thoughts that the various reservations on Earth were not so much museums as free-form historical fictions.

Janipur had been the victim of a particularly ironic twist by Master System. There were no sacred cows in Janipurian society; the *people* were the cows. At least, that was how the crew of the *Thunder* thought of it when looking at the pair now in the aft transport tubes.

Vulture, the strange creature who was the creation of the distorted genius of Isaac Clayben, and who could absorb the physical form, personality, and memories of any organic being, had done his job well. After infiltrating Cochin Center on Janipur, he had consumed and then become the deputy chief of security, which gave him great power and access to the vast bulk of Center files. He had picked a pair of Janipurians from Awadi Center, on another continent from Cochin; Brahmans by their gray coloration. As middle-level bureaucrats, part of the inevitable faceless horde that kept all political organizations working, these two would have easy access to Cochin Center without being known there.

It was the first time any but the crew of the *Indrus* had ever seen a real Janipurian, and the forms made a major impression on them.

They were human sized; the female was noticeably smaller than the male. Lying on their sides in the tubes, they looked very much like hoofed animals. Their "hind legs" were mounted on either side of the torso on a swivel joint that allowed the body to actually stand upright. The lower calf was thicker than one would expect in a four-footed animal and seemed to end in a broad, thick, rock-hard hoof. The hoof, however, was actually mounted on the back of the ankle, and the major thickness of the lower calf was due in part to a broad, flat, padlike extension of muscle and bone on another swivel joint that could lock out of the way for running on all fours but was otherwise wide enough and powerful enough to serve as a foot when the creature stood erect.

The torso was broad and thick; the arms were the same length as the legs and constructed in much the same fashion, although the handlike extensions beyond the hooves were more specialized, each with four long fingers and an opposable thumb that folded up when the creature was standing on all fours. The necks were long and thick, and constructed to allow the head to face forward in both four- and two-legged positions.

The faces were expressive and very human-looking, with pushed-in noses and overly wide jaws that moved from side to side as well as up and down and contained only broad, flat teeth. These were herbivores.

Most of the body area, excluding the face, was covered in thick gray fur.

"The musculature and skeletal structure are amazing," Clayben told them, sounding like a kid with a new toy. "Upright they are as elastic and as able to twist and bend and perform as normal humans are. On all fours, they are far more rigid but can probably run, leap, and kick better than any human. The feet are better designed for standing than walking upright, but the heads are very well suited for even the most intricate work."

Sabira, the crewwoman from the *Indrus* who had volunteered to go along on the mission because she knew and understood the basic culture of Janipur, said nervously, "I suppose there are greater differences than would be immediately apparent to anyone from the outside. Still, I had not thought of them as all that different in spite of appearances. Such things would affect their whole culture and way of looking at things, their basic behavior. I had not considered that."

"There will be other surprises, I fear," Hawks told her. "But the transmutation is essential to our mission. Second thoughts?"

She gave a slight smile and shrugged. "Some . . . many. It is to be expected. But I am needed; I am the only one with experience who is willing to go."

And that, of course, was the crux of the matter.

"One thing does puzzle me," Clayben added. "On their heads, here, seem to be nubs representing incipient horns. I'd be curious to know whether they have a function or are merely ornamental."

Sabira nodded. "The horns are functional only on the female. The way in which the child must be carried in the womb to be fully protected and insulated is with the mother in the four-footed position. As term progresses, the mother finds it increasingly difficult to stand until it becomes impossible about the fifth month. The pivot joints in the hands and feet lock into position so they cannot be lowered, the breasts enlarge, and the mother grows a long and nasty pair of horns with sharp points. Without her usual speed, it is the only protection she has during the remaining time. A few weeks after birth the horns fall off, and she can return to normalcy. The horns are saved and usually fashioned into carvings that are given to the child upon gaining maturity. They are considered a part of the child. The children are breast-fed for only a couple of weeks; after that their digestive systems are fully formed and they can eat basically what the adults eat. Do not think of the women as helpless at this time, however. They are extremely aggressive and quite dangerous."

Clayben nodded. "Fascinating. And the children are born fully formed and able to get about? Not like our helpless lumps?"

"Their hands and feet are rudimentary, but their legs are strong and firm. They are quite imitative and learn the basics of survival early on. They are self-sufficient as animals, although mostly defenseless, by the first month. But they are well advanced in many ways and because of their mobility and independence learn at a far faster rate than our own children at that age. The hands and feet, however, take years to fully develop, and their use must be learned and practiced. They are intellectually humans but physically animals until about the age of seven or so. They mature sexually at about age twelve or thirteen."

Clayben nodded again. Clearly the old scientist, after long inactivity, was coming alive again. Hawks wondered how alive he would be if it became *his* turn to be transmuted into something else. He suspected it was far easier to do things to others in the name of research than to undergo the process yourself at someone else's hands.

"Have the Chows seen these yet?" Sabira asked.

Hawks shook his head negatively. "Not yet. Today, perhaps. Now that we have our two prototypes, the clock is running, as it were, to get things going. This pair is officially on leave and a cover story has been developed for them. However, their leave is one hundred days and already five are gone. You all must study their bodies and learn whatever else you can in order to pass as Janipurians. Part of that study time must be here, until you have learned the basics, and then we will send you all down to live for a period with the natives and polish up. If you cannot fool the natives, then you will not fool Cochin Center and you certainly will not fool the troops infiltrated down there. Thanks to Vulture, you will then be reassigned to Cochin Center. By then you will have passed the hard tests and be ready to attempt the impossible."

"It is a lot to ask, to get that far in ninety-five days," she responded worriedly. "There will be so much to learn."

"More than just your lives will depend on your learning well that quickly. Without this ring, the rest are meaningless. If you are caught, then it will be a thousand times more difficult for those who follow to try again."

There was usually very little need for Chow Mai and Chow Dai to talk to one another. As identical twins, they had been virtually inseparable for good and ill. Each knew the thoughts of the other—or so it seemed, even to them —which made their conversation after they saw the Janipurians all the more remarkable.

"I do not want to do this thing," Chow Mai, usually the quiet one of the pair said. "You saw them. You thought what I thought."

Chow Dai nodded. "More like cows than people, I think, and their ways are very strange, as well. I look at us and know that we are not things of beauty, yet we are still human."

"And yet there is honor and obligation. Our lives belong to these people who saved us for this purpose. My nightmares have never gone away, nor have I felt normal since . . ."

Chow Dai nodded once more, understanding completely. They had been caught in common burglary by China Center security, mindprinted, and determined to be neither spies nor traitors but simply childish and immature thieves with a remarkable talent for getting past the most sophisticated locks. Neither understood flush toilets, let alone computers, yet they had been given a gift, or a curse, by their ancestors and by their illusionist uncle long ago.

After their capture, they had been taken down to the biotech labs where they had been examined and, still virgins, had been rendered forever incapable of bearing children. Then they had been lightly drugged and taken to the place where the lowest guards stayed, and there, no longer regarded as people but as mere playthings of the brutish louts, they had been tormented, tortured, and raped, again and again, until they felt so low and so vile that they were no more than what their tormentors regarded them as. It had gone on and on and on; there were three shifts of guards and little food or rest. When they had fought they had been cut and burned and mutilated, scarred beyond recognition, so that they looked barely human at all when suddenly the order came to prepare them and ship them off to Melchior.

On Melchior, China Nightingale had been treated by transmuter but they had not, their scars and disfigurements treated by slower, more conventional means. At the time this did not seem odd or unusual, but now they realized that the security chief of Melchior had been one of those conspiring against Master System and had not wished to subject them to the machine that could only be used once. Only the prisoner tattoos on their cheeks were of the transmuter process, and those could be disguised by added skin layers and colorization.

"It is what the gods decreed for us from the start," Chow Dai said, and sighed. "It is what we were born to do."

Chow Mai nodded ruefully. "I am unhappy but reconciled. Better to become a monster than to deny our destiny and be damned, or remain here and watch others suffer in our place."

"Perhaps," Chow Dai responded wistfully, "this will be the end of suffering."

They were ready.

"The process itself is intricate and could not be done without the computers designed for it," Isaac Clayben told them, "but in actual practice it's rather simple, quick, and straightforward. The original physics of the transmuter was discovered in ancient times, we think by humans. The idea was to eventually disassemble anyone or anything into energy, stored and coded so that it could be reassembled as matter someplace else after being broadcast or transmitted. The process eventually worked to a limited degree over special wiring networks, but the energy could not be broadcast and thus the system was somewhat impractical. Even though it represented the answer to Earth's diminishing resources, the project was not fully believed or supported—we think because many died or worse in the final experiments, increasing public anger—and it was abandoned. It didn't matter anyway. Without murylium the system could have never worked in a wireless mode. Master System picked up the experiments and continued them. It discovered that murylium was the key and perfected the broadcast capability that we have used to get from *Thunder* to our original base world and back. It's quite limited, however, and not practical for distances, say, on an interplanetary scale."

Clayben, excited to be in his own area of action once again, seemed completely oblivious to the tension and nervousness of those around him. Hawks was not, but he understood the necessity. Clayben was being longwinded about it, but this was essential information.

"Now, when the *Thunder* was designed," the scientist continued, "it was designed to use it as a limited transport mechanism first and foremost, bringing up whole populations from a planet and storing them in the tubes we saw when we first arrived on board. Each was then analyzed and an individual formula for their transmutation was devised. A mass mindprinter device was also used to insure uniformity of the new colonial culture.

"The mindprinting and transmuting programs were worked out and stored inside the computer memory. We have access to the ship's computers, mechanisms, everything—but not those original programs. We have improvised as best we could. We have an advantage in that we must have exact duplicates of this pair of Janipurians to pass security. Their brain structure is nearly identical to ours, although some functions were added and others redirected to allow for the physiological changes. By simply comparing your brain structures with theirs and noting the differences we are able to retain your own mental patterns while making the adjustments necessary to handle the body. All we can do with the mindprinter, however, is feed in the basics of the culture from the *Indrus* data banks. It will give you a grounding, but not the finer points. Those you will have to learn by experience, and that will be your most dangerous period before going into Cochin Center itself."

"I am puzzled," Chow Dai said. "There are three of us and only two of . . . them. Also, one of them is male. We are all female. How will you do this?"

"Any two that met our specifications for fooling security

and getting you into the Center were the best we could
hope for, considering the time limitations. Although some
Brahman women in this society do hold high positions, the
basic family structure is more traditional, whether high or
low caste. This male is a bureaucrat; the female is married
to and dependent upon him. The marriage was arranged
and is less than two years old, which helps us. What helps
even more is that she came from the field, not a Center,
and is the daughter of the local equivalent of a judge. That
means her Center records are minimal. The marriage to a
Center official, no matter how minor, is a step up for the
family. It is not uncommon even on Earth for a high official of the general population to raise children to romance
officials on leave. One major danger is that even from the
field, one of her class would be expected to be literate. You
will have to fake that or learn the rudimentary elements of
literacy. No way around it."

"But the two—male and female . . ."

"I'm getting to that. Married two years and not yet with
child is unusual down there. The fact is, she's not totally
infertile but there are medical problems that make her
chances of pregnancy very remote. Since divorce is socially unthinkable down there, there's only one solution for
a bureaucrat who winds up this way, and it is socially ac-
ceptable and understood. A relative of the same sex as the
infertile one is brought in and given some job—maid,
clerk, whatever is appropriate—but her real function is to
produce a child for the couple. He had applied for permission to do this while on leave—it's what Vulture was
looking for in the security records, as such a request has to
be approved by top security at the chief administrator level.
One side effect of the transmuter is that we can fix the
infertility problem, which is caused by partially blocked
tubes. We will now create a sister from the field—an identical twin. I doubt that she actually has such a twin, but

Vulture assures me that he can create such a record. One psychological truth of using computers for all record keeping is that if you can somehow bypass the security codes and enter false data, it will be believed by anyone who looks without checking further—unless someone suspects you. The male is expected to report to his new post with his wife's sister. He will."

Sabira turned to them. "Because, I know my way around machines, am literate in Sanskrit, and I know their ways, I will become the man."

The Chows were both appalled. Even though they had often dreamed of the power men held in their society, neither had ever wanted to be a man. It seemed, somehow, a step down.

"You—you *want* this?" Chow Dai asked.

"None of us want any of this. It is our duty. I follow the basic beliefs of my ancestors. I believe I have been a man before and will be again before my human incarnations are completed. This will probably cause me to live an extra life, but to not do what is needed for our survival and the future of all humankind would be vastly immoral. I must learn to act and think like and be a man; you must steal the ring. The burden is equal."

"I will correct the fallopian tube problem in both of you," Clayben told them. "The defect is potentially life-threatening as there is a danger of ectopic pregnancy—outside the womb. The defect is difficult to spot or diagnose; I don't think a routine return-from-leave physical will have any chance of noticing the change and blowing the cover. After this is over I will also correct the problem in the original female, and we will use the mindprinter and hypnos to put them in a very cooperative frame of mind. They can never return down there as they are. Even if it was established later on that they were duplicated and not the perpetrators, they would most certainly be killed anyway just as insurance. Now, whenever you are ready we can begin. There will be no pain or other sensation. It will be no different from being transmitted down to the world."

Forever . . . like them *. . . forever . . .*

"Get it over with," the Chows said in unison. "Do it now."

The easiest and most efficient way for Star Eagle to work was to use the last remaining bank transport tubes and the local network transmuters built into them. In a sense, it was an echo of long ago, when Master System had determined that populating the stars was the only way to ever guarantee that humanity would survive. The tubes could be automatically sterilized before use, then loaded with their human cargo and sealed until the process was complete. Up on the bridge, Star Eagle allowed China to monitor but not to participate in the operation. It was too delicate. Still, she could comment to the computer and did so.

"Are you certain you can do this without the program for Janipur?" she asked, not for the first time.

"You know I only deal in probabilities," the computer responded. "The initial tests went well. I hesitate to say this, but Clayben has more experience in this sort of thing, and he feels confident. I do not like the man, but if he could make Vulture with far inferior equipment, he can do this. All three of us have done our best."

She sighed. "The poor Chows. They haven't had much of a life until now. I hope this doesn't condemn them to eternal misery."

"They may never be totally satisfied, but they will adjust," the computer assured her. "That is the one area in which the human mind is both superior and incomprehensible to me. You have an almost infinite capacity to adapt to almost anything. Freezing cold, boiling heat, eternal rain, desert . . . All these primitive conditions humans adapted to and thrived. You, too, have adapted, both to blindness and to your overpowering drives."

"Adapted—yes. I accept my conditions because there is no alternative. But content this way? No, that I will never be. I accept it, as one accepts and learns to live with disfigurement, handicaps of various sorts, and accidents of birth and fate. In my mind, though, I am always—envious. Always someone else."

There seemed no proper response to that. "Energizing," reported the ship's computer. "I now have them in three large files and I am doing a comparison check. It is fascinating in a way. No one, not even the Chows, have identical checksums, but those are the closest I have ever measured between two people. Now energizing the models. Done. Comparing male model file to file Sabira. Fascinating—in many ways there are far fewer differences than I would have expected. Now reading and comparing genetic codes. Fascinating. Again there are far fewer differences than anyone would have thought. It is almost trivial, yet the results are so different. There are millions of differences but they are so minor, so slight, that it shows how remarkable it was that humanity evolved the way it did. There are more common denominators than differences here. The ancestry of the Janipurians is quite clear."

"The body is not the problem. It is integrating body and mind that is the problem."

"Very slight. More difference in the spinal column than in organization of the brain. Different areas of the brain are used for some motor and autonomic functions, but personality and memory are stored the same way and in the same places. This should not be as difficult as I thought."

China wondered about that, considering that this was a computer that could read through and find specific data in a hundred encyclopedias in nanoseconds, yet it was taking several minutes to do this process. Star Eagle, however, was leaving nothing to chance—with this kind of transmutation, there was no margin for error, no tolerance for mistakes.

Still, she knew that what it was doing was astonishing, beyond human comprehension for speed and complexity. It was creating comparative computer models of the reformed Sabira and then stimulating various areas of the brain and central nervous system, checking out everything to make absolutely certain that there was no mistake. The entire psychogenetic and psychochemical makeup had to be correct or the body might not work right or "fit" right. The skeletal mechanics and the kinesiology of the exercise were the easy parts. Personality and memory had to be absolutely retained while the new body had to operate seamlessly with the different brain information. Cell memory learned by the mere act of being born and growing up Janipurian had to be retained and integrated with memory and personality formed in a completely different environment. Immunities gained from mother's milk and from a lifetime on Janipur also had to be maintained. Most microorganisms on colonial worlds had evolved into different enough forms that Earth-humans could not catch the diseases, but these people would be Janipurians going into a Janipurian world. It would not do to effect a perfect transmutation and then have them sicken and die from the lack of immunity to some common virus.

"They should check with their doctors more down there," Star Eagle remarked almost off-handedly. "The male had some incipient signs of early arthritis and a weak pancreas; the female has other things wrong including some small viral tumors. One wonders what the state of medicine is even at the Center level. I will correct those problems and flush the veins and arteries as well. Standing by. I have a new checksum validated by models. The male is completed. Sabira is completed. The female is completed. Chow Dai integrated. Chow Mai integrated. Stand by at the tubes. Reconverting . . . Done."

A small crowd had gathered at the tubes with Hawks and Clayben. The tube mouths had gone opaque when the humans had been energized; now they flicked to clear again. Inside, now, were no longer any Earth-humans. The two on top looked the same, but the three below now contained Janipurians.

For Chow Dai and the others it was almost as if nothing had taken place. She had crawled naked into the tube and lay flat, then watched as the machinery activated and the mouth clouded up. There was a slight disorientation as if the scene she was seeing had been suddenly altered, then strong hands reached in, grabbed her arms, and pulled her from the tube.

The first thing that struck her was the noise. There were sounds all around her that she could not place; *click*ing and *whirr*ing and *whoosh*ing, and there were voices, too, far off but if she concentrated, she could almost make out what they were saying even over the din created by the crowd at the tube.

"Try to stand," Clayben said, his voice sounding oddly distorted but still clear and a bit too loud. "Just on your hands and knees for now. Give it a try."

She managed, and it felt rather comfortable. Steady, anyway. She crawled completely out onto the catwalk and looked around. All the familiar faces were there, but they looked *different* somehow. There seemed less color, as if things were washed out, but those nearby—and even the catwalk itself—seemed far more detailed; by focusing she could count every thread in Hawks' pants or see the pores in Clayben's craggy face. She looked forward toward the building and maintenance area below and found it difficult to focus. Nothing down there, or beyond, seemed to register, yet when one of the spindly robots far away moved and picked up something she was able to not only focus in on it but see it clearly, almost isolated from its surroundings. A perfectly defined form almost suspended in space.

I cannot feel my hands or my feet! she thought suddenly, and looked down and saw her—forelegs. Even though she knew academically that it had happened, it wasn't until now that the reality of the situation sunk in.

She felt oddly distant from it. Later, perhaps, it would sink in but not now. Now she simply felt nothing deep inside. She looked over and saw the other two emerge from their tubes with the same aid.

They also had little trouble standing on all fours, and she remembered that Clayben had explained that this was in the design of the creatures. She stared at Chow Mai, both the form and the face, and knew that she was also staring at herself.

By the gods, we are hideously ugly! she thought, almost breaking but catching herself in time.

The catwalk was also an elevator system, and it slowly lowered them all down to the main deck level. None of the three had any trouble walking off; with arms and legs the same length it was easier than crawling.

"I'm going to remain and process the other two," Clayben told Hawks. "Let them get the feel of their bodies and give them some time. They must learn to use those bodies naturally, without thinking. Then we can give them what printer support we can."

Hawks nodded. "Now their burden begins."

When Star Eagle had first sent the thick bundles of grasses to them to eat, all three had recoiled. Finally, Sabira had decided that it had to be done and hoped that it would taste better to a Janipurian than to an Earth-human. It didn't. The stuff tasted like grass and straw, and the only positive thing to be said about it was that it was filling.

"We never ate with the Janipurians before," she noted. "I got the impression they prepared highly spiced food, both cooked and raw. Grazing was for the very young and the very poor. A survival skill, not a mark of civilization. No one needed to starve on Janipur."

"It is all we can furnish until you are down there, though," Star Eagle responded apologetically. "We do not really know their foods. I could only synthesize based upon logical deductions from the way the digestive system operates and traces of food in the systems of the pair we have. Their mindprinting will soon be finished, however, and they should be quite willing to help thereafter."

Mindprinting indeed, more than one of the crew thought. Brainwashing was the old term for it, when it was less subtle and more difficult to do.

None of the three felt extremely comfortable in their new forms, but they had no problem moving around so long as they were in, as Isaac Clayben called it, their "four-legged mode." Attempts to stand, or even unlock the hands and feet from their holding positions, met with frustration. Since they weren't much larger or heavier than Earth-humans, a couple of crewmembers of the *Thunder*'s complement tried lifting them into sitting positions in chairs. The three found themselves unbalanced, though, and tended to flail at the air with forelegs or fall over and out.

The addition of Jeruwahl Peshwar and his wife Madowa changed things a bit, but it wasn't easy. The two native Janipurians firmly believed their provided cover story, however, so they were friendly and cooperative if a bit taken aback and both awed and a little afraid of the strange forms now around them. As with the best cover stories, it contained more fact than fiction.

They now believed that Master System was attempting to eliminate the Centers of Janipur and reduce the population to limited, animal-like savagery. It was not known if Master System actually had this in mind for worlds other than Earth, but it was convincing enough, particularly since the pair knew that forces from Master System itself now roamed somewhat lordly over their land and Centers. They were impressed with the honor of the mission, although not a little bit unhappy that they were the ones chosen to be uprooted and their lives disrupted. This was ameliorated, somewhat, by the seriousness of the mission and most of all by the fact that three of the alien company should be willing to become like them. They were most touched, however, when shown evidence of their medical conditions and problems, particularly the dangerously malformed uterus, and the fact that these things had now been repaired.

"It is most confusing," Jeruwahl noted in his thick Janipurian accented English, "but we will do our part in this. I feel like I now have a twin, and I cannot tell my wife from the two others if all stand still."

It was Madowa who partially solved the food problem by providing a list of ingredients that turned the stomachs of those who understood what they were. Once equivalents were found for those ingredients that were native to Janipur, she was able to prepare very elaborate dishes for them all that had only one thing in common: one did not feel one's mouth after starting the dishes, but one felt the stomach for quite a while. All Janipurian food, it seemed, consisted of either the basic bland grasses or elaborate dishes spiced so hot they were almost on fire. The dishes could be eaten by the Earth-humans and many of the colonials on board, but few tolerated more than a taste. Only Sabira and the crew of the *Indrus* seemed immune; the captain of the ship proclaimed it was the first decently spiced food he'd had in many months.

Madowa worked with Chow Dai and Chow Mai on body movements and uses; Jeruwahl worked with Sabira, although he was more than a bit disconcerted by how effeminate this new male was. Sabira, shortening her name to Sabir, had thought it best for cultural reasons not to tell him that she was originally female.

There were tricks to making the body fulfill all its potential; subtle weight shifts, twists, and turns that someone born Janipurian took for granted but someone new to the body would never guess. It was startling and somewhat exciting to see Madowa, for example, simply stand up in a fluid motion with long hands and longer fingers looking very human indeed. Unexpectedly, they also walked upright—albeit very slowly and deliberately and for short distances. Upright was for civilized company, inside dwellings, and for social occasions. All fours was long-distance moving and speed. The combination of the two modes was smooth, effortless, and chosen almost without thinking.

The Chows were absolutely ecstatic when they stood erect, unsteadily, for the first time on their own, and falling over, almost breaking a few bones a number of times, did not daunt them. As on Janipur, the upright stance and use of hands and feet set human apart from animal in their minds, more than any other trait. They were determined, and they did it.

Only five days after they began their training, the Chows were standing up and even walking a bit with relative ease, and were talking with their hands as much as their mouths. By observing Madowa, they were now mastering the fine points of fluid and effortless natural motion.

Sabir was not as adept a pupil, even when helped by all the others. He could stand in a wobbly sort of way, but often failed miserably. It was Raven, in fact, who figured out part of the problem by just watching.

While Jeruwahl had been born with male anatomy and moved to accommodate it without thinking, Sabir was used to being female. Now, when Sabir tried to stand, he found that his mind was unaccustomed to directing the movement of his new male anatomy. It was slow and frustrating having to learn the basics of walking all over again.

The Chows, meanwhile, were already learning Janipurian cooking, at least partly out of self-defense. They wanted to prepare dishes that were merely volcanic rather than intolerable, and they finally found the right mix. Madowa Peshwar proclaimed the results "as bland as straw grass," though it was still fiery to everybody else.

Just when Sabir was willing to give up and accept the idea that he would never adapt, he did it—and had little trouble thereafter with movement. However, they now had only sixty-one days left before the leave was terminated and they were to report to Cochin Center.

The most profitable use of the time for the Chows, other than getting used to their new bodies, had been practicing with lock problems and traps rigged by Star Eagle in the office complex surrounding the central living area. There was no way to actually know the exact mechanisms used in the Center museum, but Star Eagle attempted to simulate the types of locks and traps reported by Vulture, attaining more and more complexity as they solved the easier ones. One of Sabir's predictions proved true—the eyes, at least in their near vision, and the hands were so superior that the Chows found themselves able to work successfully on very small, intricate traps. Their new physical attributes significantly enhanced that uncanny innate ability they had always had, but which even they really couldn't explain.

Their score was not perfect, however. In fact, in the most complex problems involving weights, cameras, and sound monitors they succeeded only four in ten times. But with the strict time limitation they hoped it would be enough. It *had* to be enough. They needed to get down to the planet almost immediately if they were to have time to interact with the natives while there was still a chance to survive any errors. And so they turned to China and Isaac Clayben, whose wizardry with the mindprinter and biochemical manipulations could best prepare them for their mission.

China had visited the Chows quite often during this period. Other than Sabir and each other, she was the only one they really felt comfortable around. It was, perhaps, the blindness as well as the shared past experiences. China could not see them as they were now, and even if their voices were slurred and they smelled a bit funny, her mental picture was still of their old selves.

"You are adjusting quite well," she told them. "I have seen the results through Star Eagle's interconnects, and you look and act quite natural. It is a fascinating human variation, in some ways superior to us and in no real way inferior."

"We are now used to it, yes," Chow Dai agreed, "but I am not certain we can ever fully accept ourselves this way. It is still wrong, strange, and we feel . . . ugly. At night we still dream our normal dreams, and when we wake up and see each other as we are, we feel it a nightmare."

China nodded and sighed. "I, too, have such dreams. Thanks to the bridge interface I have seen all this, all of you, but in my mind and in a different way than one truly sees. I was always so totally independent, so confident and arrogant, and now I am far less than you. I am totally, absolutely *dependent*. That, more than the loss of my sight, is my continuing curse. I am blind, my belly is swollen, my soul is filled with odd rushes and urges, and this is when I am at my best. During that period when I am not with child, I am degraded, and I hate myself later even though I know it is none of my doing. In a sense, I have become what my father intended: a breeding factory. In my youthful ignorance I cursed him, not for his intent or his contempt for me but because he would cost me my mind, my awareness, my knowledge, and turn me into a simpering little slave. I see that there was some mercy in the old man after all, for now I am in that exact situation, but with full mind and knowledge and it is far worse. I keep going only for the mission and victory. Perhaps, although I would like to think otherwise, I do it just for my father's reaction if we are able to win. You have merely changed to an alternate form. There are worse things that can be done to you, far worse. You must always remember that."

"We have been thinking that way," Chow Mai told her. "It may well be that Hawks is right—we all may pay a terrible price for this, and ours may not be the worst."

"You must remember that millions of people have been born and raised as you are now and have different standards. They will think of you as the only true human. Look at Jeruwahl and Madowa. It is a race far gentler and with kinder features than those of, say, *Chunhoifan*'s races—either one." The captain of that freebooter ship and two others had glistening black exoskeletons, terrible faces, and many features more appropriate to insects, and they ate stuff that made the rest sick just to look at. The two others of that crew, owlish, green humanoids with bulging eyes and winglike organs on their backs, were difficult even to talk to; it seemed as if they lived in a slightly different universe from the rest, and perhaps they did. When one heard in ranges far different from Earth-humans and ate a mixture of bloody meat and crushed rock and saw well into the infrared spectrum, different attitudes were to be expected. The point was well taken, and the Chows knew it, but the realization didn't lessen their own private agony.

"Tomorrow we will be using on you a mindprinter technique used by Centers all over Earth and perhaps all over the galaxy," China told them. "We have taken the pre-adjusted imprints of Jeruwahl and Madowa and added logical and expected experiences to account for their missing time. We were also able to edit a version of Madowa's recording to create a twin sister, Sedowa, and blend that into the Madowa experience sufficiently well so that the memories of the real Madowa will include our addition. It will fool the records computers. Such things always have. We were able to edit in memories of a minor brain dysfunction, a type of dyslexia that is not unknown in Earth-humans and possibly also is here. Vulture, who has created Sedowa's records to match our own, has added that to the files transferred from their old Center to Cochin. You will not be expected to read or write, and that will get you over a large hurdle. For the next sixty days you will *be* Jeruwahl and Madowa Peshwar and Sedowa Bhutto. You will truly believe this, just as I truly believed myself to be the boy Chu Li when first we met. It will remain consistent, your true selves inaccessible to mindprinter or your own will or knowledge, until Vulture brings you out of it."

"We are nervous and a bit scared of it, but we understand the routine," Chow Dai assured her. "We remember, however, that you were affected by Chu Li long after you reasserted control. After we . . . come out of it, will we still be ourselves, or something new?"

"You will remember all that you do now," China assured them. "However, none of the memories you had imprinted, including those of the sixty days, will vanish. You will be in complete control. Becoming fully yourself again is a slow process but a painless one; things will fade if not used or accessed. What memories of your experience you need, you will keep as long as you need it. What you do not need will fade. Even now there is a bit, a little bit, of Chu Li in

me, but it is not a bad thing. I treasure it. His rebellious-
ness helps keep me going. His spirit will not let me quit.
All I have truly lost is my overwhelming arrogance, and
that from my experience since and not through any mindprinter trick. We know they will check and spy on all newcomers with a thoroughness they never had before, so the
mindprint must be a perfect job, but you will gain from it
and lose nothing later. It is when you come out that the
danger will be great. Take care. We have had limited time
to get you this far, but there is no time limit, even if it be
years, to getting the rings. If we do not live to see the fifth
and final one in place, our children will do it. The only
thing you must not do is fail, and death will be failure, as
well."

"We will take care and we will return," Chow Dai
promised her. "We will do it because it is what we were
ordained to do. We were born in ignorance and fated, it
seemed like all those who grew up with us, to work the
paddies and have babies and die young. Instead the gods
worked in strange ways to make us part of a great thing.
We will not fail, and we will *personally* hand you the ring,
and if it is the will of the gods we, not our children, will
stand at the doors to Master System itself and see the great
thing we have helped bring about. *That* is what keeps *us*
going."

China hugged and kissed them, and for the first time in
her mature life felt tears come to her unseeing eyes. "I will
hold you to that," she said, "and I shall not forgive you if it
does not come out that way."

They were sedated after the mindprinter treatment, then
sent down to Janipur in coordination with Vulture's plan.
Because the odd creature had assumed the body, form, and
personality of the deputy chief of security for Cochin
Center, he had some freedom of movement and resources.

Master System's forces on Janipur might still have been suspicious of his moves and actions had they any idea that such a creature as Vulture existed, but they did not and the deputy chief of security was well known and above normal suspicion. Clayben had originally created Vulture as the prototype for a whole army of creatures designed specifically to avoid any trap Master System might lay, to penetrate any security, to become an invisible force, but his creation had proven too perfect: impossible for Clayben to control. It would never have occurred to the scientist to do what Hawks and Raven had done and simply treat the creature as a fellow human being and ask for its help.

Thus, Jeruwahl Peshwar awoke one morning in the large town on Janipur where he'd been born, as did his wife Madowa and her twin sister Sedowa, with memories of having visited the women's family and bargaining for Sedowa's participation in propagating the Peshwar name. Sedowa had been married at thirteen, of course, but her husband had died while experimenting with a new form of deep meditation that involved slow and supposedly controlled strangulation. *Suttee* had been outlawed long ago by her own tribe's progressive government, which happened to include her father, but not everyone agreed with this decision and Sedowa had been stigmatized and somewhat ostracized outside the family. She had been more than happy to comply with her sister's husband's request, and her father was particularly pleased that she had at last found a place.

None of this, of course, actually happened, but there was some distance between her family and his native city and *they* believed the scenes.

Skill was not transferable by mindprinter, but knowledge was. Jeruwahl was convincing enough that differences in movements and habits could be put down to changes made by his very alien Center lifestyle in the two years between visits; he was not suspected by the real Jeru-wahl's family. The twins cooked and cleaned and made clothing and jewelry. Clothing was not a basic of the race, but the genitals and rears and often the breasts were covered, and both men and women wore various jewelry appropriate to their caste level.

The women delighted in the sights and smells of the city, the huge markets, the bazaars, the street performers, and the general electricity even a small city provides those who live outside it.

Had they known they were in an environment even more alien than city versus Center or rural village, they might have gaped in wonder as a man on four legs pulled a small wheeled car to a building, then stood up, picked up the cart, and climbed a ladder straight up to the third floor. But such sights did not and should not seem wondrous to them under the mindprinter's hold.

Vulture had his men keep an eye on them, supposedly because they were about to be promoted and transferred at the end of leave to Cochin Center, but it allowed the trio to pass the closest inspection without raising suspicion. As they were newcomers, Vulture was required to put SPF personnel on them, as well. This was now an absolute requirement of Master System when anyone not already thoroughly checked was transferred to Cochin Center, and the risk and suspicion wouldn't stop even after they had entered and cleared all the usual checks. Master System, needless to say, knew about transmuters and mindprinter programs, as well. They would be only three of twenty new people coming in, which helped, and Vulture knew that he was dealing more with the SPF and a Val than with Master System directly and that the soldiers might not believe that the pirates of the *Thunder* would have such resources or go to such extremes. He hoped so.

Although there was nothing else it could do right now to

help or in any way interfere with the Janipur mission, *Thunder* was not idle during this period. Captain Paschitta-wal and the rest of the *Indrus* crew, along with *Pirate One*, were doing what they could to monitor, watch, and wait. The other crews, restless for some action, also had their chance. Star Eagle developed a separate recording system that would play back to *Thunder* from the freebooter ships giving a complete account of all that went on. It was in a code only Star Eagle knew, and he was certain it could not be broken or altered without him detecting it. There was no way to protect all the ships and crews from Master System and the SPF; that was up to them. What Star Eagle could do was guarantee, as much as anything could be guaran-teed, that no ship sent off into the void could be taken, turned, and made into a Trojan horse that might threaten the *Thunder*.

San Christobal, *Chunhoifan*, and *Bakakatan*, however, could now have freedom of movement and action. Since Janipur had been lightly defended, with Master System gambling more on preventing a theft and successful escape than preventing entry, it was probable that the same situa-tion existed in the solar systems of Chanchuk and Ma-triyeh, the two other places where rings were thought to exist. Security might tighten after the Janipur mission was finished so complete surveys of those worlds were ordered without any landings. This would at least identify the unique properties of the worlds they would eventually have to enter, give them basic information on the land and peo-ple and security arrangements.

After this, they could attempt to tap resources that might have escaped the pogrom against the freebooters. Sava-phoong was valuable here; the former ruler of Halinachi knew not only unlikely sources of information and material but also various codes for automated Master System de-vices, the result of gathering together the collective discoveries of a generation of freebooters who partook of his pleasure palace. The man himself remained mostly within his own ship, a semirecluse in a luxury yacht that supported him in the manner to which he felt entitled.

Kaotan was kept in reserve along with *Lightning*, although Takya Mudabur, the amphibian, was taken along on the *San Cristobal*. Discussions with the denizens of some of the water worlds she knew might give a clue to the location of the fourth ring, although it exposed both her and the ship to maximum danger.

Kaotan had been held in reserve at Vulture's request. They weren't yet certain what he had in mind, but it was possible that the ship would yet see action within the Janipur plan.

At the end of leave, Jeruwahl Peshwar, his wife, and his mistress bade good-bye to the city and journeyed four days northwest to the predetermined rendezvous point, where they were picked up by one of Janipur's few flyers and flown in a matter of hours to Cochin Center for entry processing.

The Center, a large, domed structure in an area remote from any pattern of settlement and in a region that would not support much of a local population, looked much like any other Center of Janipur or even on Earth. It was unobtrusive, nearly invisible except from the air, and most of it was actually underground.

As newcomers coming off leave, the trio were processed first by security; a mindprint was taken of each to be examined and evaluated by security computers that were not all that hard to fool. Then they were each given complete physicals that not only assessed their general condition but also would reveal any scars, birthmarks, evident of past medical procedures, and the like, all of which could be compared with their records before leave, to provide a check against tampering or possible imposters. Finally, they were started once again on the elite drugs that increased concentration, enhanced thinking, and also protected them against most common diseases; issued specially encoded clearance cards for the areas they were authorized to be in; and taken to their new quarters. All of their old belongings, including the art, the tapestries, and the other niceties of life in high position, had been shipped to Cochin from their old Center post.

As far as Vulture could see, they had passed their security screening with flying colors. He had no intention of bringing them out of their mindprinting any time soon; best they settle in and make new social contacts and betray nothing to the prying eyes of security and the SPF. He sat in a chair specially contoured for Janipurian shapes and went over their data, nodding to himself. It was part of the deputy chief's job to oversee and check on newcomers. He was looking for any flaws, holes, or minor details that he might have to balance out or rectify.

He almost missed it, and that would have been a tragedy. Even now, he wasn't certain what to do about it since it simply hadn't been thought of. The fact was, he couldn't think of *everything*, and apparently this had never occurred to Clayben and the rest, either. It was, however, a major problem, and one that could not be easily covered up. Things had been going along too smoothly; he and the rest had been lulled into a false sense of security and he knew it now. The question was, what to do about it?

He had an audio link with *Thunder* using a subcarrier of the regular transmissions between the orbital monitoring satellites and Cochin Center and a secure place to use it. That had been a major priority and was the one big risk he had taken. Now he used it to call to space.

The relay was first to the satellite, which was also being monitored by a drone fighter with a communications link. The fighter then sent it to *Indrus*, which relayed it to

Thunder, both of which were stationed many light-years from Janipur. There was some time delay between transmissions, but not enough to inhibit conversation.

"*Thunder*, we have a real problem," Vulture reported.

"Go ahead," Star Eagle responded. "I have Hawks and China tied in now."

"Stupid of us. We were so concerned with the mind-printing and computer security and all the rest that we overlooked the obvious. I almost didn't see it in the records because I wasn't looking for anything such as that. I've managed to cover up one part but I can't do it forever and then everything will hit the fan."

"What are you talking about?" Hawks asked worriedly.

"We made both the Chows fully functioning females and Sabir a fully functioning male, and then we mindprinted them so they thought they were the natives they're impersonating. It's quite natural, and I just don't understand how we could have overlooked it. According to their physicals, both women are pregnant—maybe five, six weeks."

"Damn!" Hawks swore, feeling like a fool. Then he thought of the other wrinkle. "But Madowa's on record as barren. This blows any reason for Sedowa."

"Not so much of a problem. She wasn't totally barren, it was just that the odds were against conception, and if it happened, the odds favored a nasty pregnancy. We can cover for that, but it really puts the heat on here. Either we let them go ahead and have the kids and wait a year or more—plus having to get two kids out—or we have to move very quickly on the ring. Too quick for my liking. The first three months, they'll be getting morning sickness and all that. At four and a half months, they'll start to show and feel more comfortable on all fours. By five and a half months they'll *be* on all fours and the horns will be growing. By six months, give or take, they won't have any more use of their hands or feet. *No hands*, Hawks—for four or five months, allowing for birth and recovery of the system. Hawks—you can't pick locks and steal things without hands!"

The leader of the group sighed. "Yes, I see. We'll have to run this through the group for a while here and make our decisions."

"The only positives from this are that the SPF and Master System sure as hell aren't gonna suspect two pregnant girls of being plants, and it's natural, even normal, to return from leave with child. We should'a thought that. It's the little things that kill you. Hawks—I can't guarantee getting the three of *them* out. Two four-legged kids with the minds of newborns—I can't see it. Not to mention they might not be so tolerant of having a mistress from the field here long if he's got a legitimate heir."

"The risks of waiting are worse than the risks of going too soon," Hawks said firmly. "I don't like it, but I see no alternative. We must go within the next ninety days. We will need every detail you can muster on that security system now. Your sleepers must be awakened. We go."

ᒥᒥᒥᒥᒥᒥᒥᒥᒥᒥᒥᒥᒥᒥᒥᒥᒥᒥᒥᒥᒥᒥᒥᒥᒥᒥᒥᒥᒥᒥᒥ

2. THE RING OF PEACE

THE FIRST FEW WEEKS AT COCHIN CENTER WERE really orientation—getting to know the layout of the place, the dos and don'ts specific to it, the social pecking order and one's place in it, and who was important, who was not, who was powerful, and who was to be feared above all. These were, in most respects, more important to long-term happiness at Center than learning a new job.

Barring emergencies, which were few, things worked slowly—most said leisurely—around Cochin Center as well as the other Centers on Janipur. Jeruwahl Peshwar was basically a statistician now promoted to low-level Evaluator. This meant he spent much of his time with computers and graphics projections looking for potential sources of long-term trouble for the system, identifying and classifying them, and then passing them along to higher specialists who would make the final decisions. It was not an ideal position for someone who didn't want any risks, since if some potential problem was not identified and passed on to the proper channels for action or was misidentified or sent to the wrong parties and things went badly, there was no one lower to blame for the results. It did, however, offer real potential for advancement if problems were identified that were not obvious and things ran smoothly for long periods in the areas under study. The right guesses made fewer problems for the higher-ups, so they looked good and tended to remember who made them the points.

His first job, really more of a placement test, was to examine the rate of population growth versus death rates in several major cities with high-density populations and project problems in food supply and other support systems as well as jobs for the new population and other such factors resulting from that growth. The bulk of Janipur's economy was still village-based subsistence farming, but a few cities, such as the one he'd just left, existed to supply a host of more elaborate products and services to legal and governmental centers, as well as religious centers. Cities needed to be supplied from the country, and cities attracted those people disillusioned with subsistence farming, simply down and out, or those looking for the end of the rainbow, and if a sufficient number came in and a poor underclass developed, there was potential for political ferment, violence, and challenges to the system. Children born to city natives could not easily be shifted to rural subsistence work. It was a tricky job keeping everything balanced without violating the technological limits.

Centers had odd top administrators, many with jobs that would horrify their own people. Administrators like the minister of plagues and pestilences, who could, surreptitiously, make very certain that a population was pared down to a manageable size, and the innocuous-sounding minister of meteorology, who could manage some very nasty tropical storms, floods, droughts, and the like as needed—or provide essential rain to an area where higher yields were needed. The offices of worthies like those received the reports of bureaucrats like Peshwar.

His was not a difficult or demanding job; the computers did most of the work. It would, however, have been far easier without the required Leave; it was hard to recommend a plague on people who you'd just lived with and really liked. That, in fact, was the official reason for the transfer; ones like him were not permitted to make such evaluations or decisions about their own native regions, and for obvious reasons.

They had been in their new homes for a bit over four weeks and things were going quite well. They had toured the Center—all the unclassified parts—and had even toured the museum in the center of the main level and seen the splendors of Janipurian crafts, the great gems and wondrous works in wood and metal from all over the planet. The central exhibit and artifact, however, was the chief administrator's Holy Ring of Peace, a grand ring of gold with a shiny black setting in which were two intricately carved birds looking at each other while sitting on a single stylized branch. One of the few objects in the museum displayed occasionally to the masses, it was known to all as an object of reverence and power, a great and mystical relic from Mother World itself, passed down from generation to generation.

Madowa of late had not been feeling at her best, however. She began by waking up feeling nauseous, and had dizzy spells and flushes now and then. It did not affect her appetite, however; if anything, she was eating far more than usual and including a fair amount of raw vegetables and extremely sweet confections, although she had not been a real sweets lover before. She shrugged it off, but when Sedowa began showing the same symptoms and both had missed two consecutive periods, they decided to go to the medical clinic and find out if there was some sort of contagious disease going around. The clinicians knew when the records came up what the situation was, but did far more thorough tests in light of Madowa's history of infertility. Madowa was about eleven weeks pregnant: Sedowa was perhaps eight and a half or nine. The news excited them, not to mention Jeruwahl, and more and more their thoughts turned to children and nothing else.

That made the invitation to visit Deputy Security Chief Nurim Boil all the more inexplicable. It was very unexpected, but they understood that an invitation from one such as this was not a request but a command.

Boil was a very large man for a Janipurian and had an enormous hawk nose and a facial expression that seemed locked in a permanent grimace. He looked mean and nasty without a gram of spirituality within him. He met them in a small, private office on the administrative rather than the security level, which was also odd but at least didn't generate unnecessary anxiety and require a hundred clearances. Boil locked the door, bade them be seated, and examined them for a moment. Then he said, strangely, "Vulture takes Clayben. Thunder and lightning result."

For a moment there was no effect, and then on all three of them it was like a cloud lifted from their minds and a whole enormous part of themselves that they never suspected was there was suddenly revealed and thrust forward. They were still Janipurian, but they now knew just who they really were and why they were there and who Boil must be.

Vulture continued in the Janipurian form of Hindi. It was more than adequate for what he had to say and was easier for them all. It wasn't safe for them to start thinking again in their old tongues. "This room is secure. We have a number of them about like this, feeding the monitors all sorts of distortions. With more than sixty SPF in the Center it's the only way to keep sane or do anything naughty. You are being monitored in your apartment and elsewhere, however. You're not under suspicion—it's just routine for new people. I'll take care of it when the time comes. Are you clear enough in the head now to go on with this?"

"Y-yes, I suppose," Jeruwahl-Sabir responded. "But surely you cannot consider doing anything at this point. Both of the women are with child."

"We are aware of that. That's why we have to rush this thing."

"We cannot do this! Not *now.* We must wait, however long it takes, until the timing is right."

"That is the protector and father talking," Vulture noted. "I'll give it to you straight. We have a plan, if the two women do their parts, that just might work. The getaway is tricky and probably messy, but it's the best we can come up with. Getting in is still a missing piece of the puzzle that you must fill in. The pregnancies are a good cover. Absolutely no one suspects any of you, that I assure you."

"But it is too far along. Already Madowa's body changes. In two weeks, three at best, the changes will come faster and faster and she will become unable to help. Sedowa is only two or three weeks behind." He stopped a moment, suddenly struck with a thought that horrified him. "We will not allow an abortion."

Vulture looked at the two women, who nodded in unison. "All right." He sighed. "I never even thought of that angle, since it would cause all sorts of problems and raise enormous suspicion. The bottom line: assuming we can steal the damned thing to begin with and get away from Center, all the forces of darkness will descend upon us like a horrible plague. We can't use any of the flyers for getaways since they're automatically tracked by the central security system. We will have to go overland, hiding out where we can and eluding the biggest manhunt this world has ever seen—with the technology of a Val and the SPF and Master System on top of us. I've been busy preparing that escape, but it won't be easy and it won't be quick. It is by no means certain that any or all of us can make it the whole way. It is absolutely certain, *dead* certain, that it will be impossible with two infants. And we can't leave them even if you were willing to—these people will use them against us. Torturing babies in public is just another means to an end for them. It's going to be tough enough handling two increasingly pregnant women."

"Then we wait until—"

"How long?" he challenged, not letting the potential father get the complete objection out. "Two years? Through the next Leave? I'd have to put you back under again, and then we'd have more babies most likely—and Sedowa would be sent home to a family that doesn't even know she exists. We cannot wait. We go now, or you three go back under permanently and are abandoned here and we will have to figure out a new way to send others in to do the job. What about you, young ladies? You're the key to this. What do *you* have to say?"

They looked at one another. The truth was, their minds were divided in this and they were having a great deal of trouble. A strong part of them resented this sudden nightmarish intrusion into what had been up until now the happiest time in their lives. The culture and attitudes not just of their Janipurian selves but of their original peasant upbringing on Earth told them that the child within overrode all other priorities and obligations. And yet the easy and desirable way was not the honorable way, and might not be the practical way, either.

"What do you mean I would be sent home?" Sedowa asked.

"I am not lying to you on this—your husband can check it out for himself. You are here on sufferance, to bear a child of Peshwar, and this you are doing. An unexpected extra is that his legal wife also now is pregnant after being declared barren—normally the one guarantee of getting pregnant, sort of like declaring a volcano extinct. Your term here is for two years, after which you must leave. They run you through a mindprinter and edit out all memories of the wonders of Center so you remember only living in a very big capital city of the normal type. The child is legally Madowa's, something you were supposedly told going in and agreed to. There's no legal challenge—your legal father's a judge, remember—because there was no coercion. You are a surrogate mother with no status beyond that. So you can't stay here, but you have no real home to go back to."

She was shocked and looked at Sabir. "He *is* just making that up to force us to go along. Isn't he?"

Sabir sighed. "No, I fear he tells the truth, but there are probably ways around it. There are ways around almost everything. Given what this man says is true, we still could give the *Thunder*'s great computer and its staff an extra year to figure out and allow for the extra problem. If we go into this in extreme haste, we will all probably die."

Vulture sat back and looked at them. He'd figured on something like this, but he wasn't terribly worried. Not yet. "Tell you what—just go back up to the museum in the next day or two and look it over again, this time from the point of view of the theft. I want to know *if* it can be done, and if so, *how* it can be done, and what would be required. This costs you nothing. Will you do that much for me?"

"We cannot refuse that much," Chow Dai-Madowa responded. "Give us three days from now to look it over and think it out, and give us some cover so we may discuss it without being overheard or recorded."

"I can't get you complete cover on that last one, but I'll activate your cards for this office. It's in a public area and isn't officially assigned. You can be relaxed here. Your surveillance may wonder what you're doing coming here so don't come here often, but take it easy and do it openly and confidently. I am pretty sure you two can lie your way convincingly out of a small encounter if you need to. We will talk again in three days, but not here. I'll arrange it and call for you. Good enough?"

That much none of them could object to.

The Chows were well experienced at casing a target and not looking or sounding like they were doing so. In other times they would have been natural bank robbers and probably very successful at it. Although they made a visit a day for three days to the museum, only one of them for any length of time, they made it seem a natural meeting place and did not raise any alarms. It was unlikely that they would in any event; a pregnant pair like this would have been dismissed from the overconfident and largely male security force's minds as no possible threat, no matter what their intent.

At the end of three days the two women were told to come down to the medical clinic for more follow-up tests, but when they got there they found themselves taken together to a small examination room and told to wait. Vulture arrived a few minutes later. They were mildly surprised.

"You speak to us while Jeruwahl is still at work," Chow Mai noted.

"I know. I'm not trying to separate you for any devious purposes, but the fact is that Sabir is only an excuse to get the two of you in here. I don't want amateurs in the actual operation if I can avoid it. Amateurs set off alarms. You have what you need?"

They nodded. "The great outer door appears to be a simple mechanical key lock, but it is not. The key actually must be turned to form a simple combination. With a wood or metal dummy key of the correct size it would not be difficult to open. Without them, using something for a pick, it might take some time."

"The guards make their rounds through there every five minutes after dark," Vulture told them. "Not much time. The hall monitors can be fooled, but I wouldn't like to do it for very long or somebody will notice. The key is locked in a case in Center security but I can see it. I know what it looks like and I think I can have a basic duplicate made. It might not touch all the sensors inside."

"No need. It is simply a matter of the turns. A simple mechanism. The inner door is computerized and encoded and appears to take a numeric code and a palm print. I 'stumbled' and by mere chance, of course, put my palm on the plate. The tiny sensors reacted to my hand and compared it to their records and flashed a red light. The comparison was there for a fraction of a second. The bypass appears to be the cut-out trace of a hand. It will take a few minutes and a few tools but I do not believe it's a problem. It is not nearly as elaborate as Clayben's on Melchior."

He nodded. "All right. I have recordings of the audio and visual sweeps of the areas that can be patched in to provide a continuous record for the computers. You are inside. Now what?"

"There are some kind of light beams all over the place," Chow told him. "They cover the main room like a spider's web. I could not see them but I recognized the pattern in the little holes in the walls and ceiling. China Center used some like that. To bypass that would take a special thing made of some thin, light, perfectly reflective material, and it must go all the way not only to the ring but beyond it. I have a drawing of the necessary shape. It will also have to be supported by sticks or rods somehow from the entrance. This *we* cannot make, but it will have to be made."

He took the drawing, studied it, and got the idea immediately, although he had to admit he never would have thought of it himself.

"We will need some sort of light source under it," Chow Mai put in, "but it cannot interfere. We will sew velvet pads for our hooves, so we may walk in silence. You will have to take care of the sweeping cameras."

"That's the same as the entry and corridor. I don't think we have to worry about them, though. I think they are automatic—turned on if any other alarms go off. If any other alarms are set off, then we're in a lot more trouble anyway. Continue."

"The case itself is not difficult to open, although the locks on both sides must be turned within seconds of each other to both unlock the case and avoid setting off the alarms. It takes two people to turn the locks. The problem is that they are simple spring locks that must be held in place while the case is open. This means the two must operate the locks while a third opens the case and takes the ring."

"You're sure there's nothing on the ring itself? No weight traps, no extra locks?"

"We think not. Remember, this is a ceremonial ring. It is taken out and used very often. The case is good enough. It is a lot of trouble and takes three to open properly, but if the chief administrator needs the ring, he need only walk down with two assistants with the keys, have the assistants turn the keys and hold them while the case lid pops up and he reaches in and takes it. He would not care about the *museum*'s security, which is for when it is closed. He just needs to come down when it is open, and that is probably whenever he wants."

Vulture nodded. "He takes the ring during the day, with all sorts of people around. If it had elaborate precautions, they would be observed. I think you're right—what they have is enough."

"They *do* add one extra thing when the museum is closed," Chow Mai said. "The long piece of tile in front of the case that is covered by the rug is on some kind of scale. It is locked down by day and unlocked, I suppose, when they close. We could see it outlined where it stretched and strained the carpeting."

"They said something about a weight trap when they briefed me on the museum's security, and I assumed it was there. It is not connected to the computer center, however. Not directly, anyway. It probably triggers gas or stun fields of some kind that would keep you unconscious until they opened up the next day and found you. I hadn't really noticed the details. Does it also cover the key locks?"

"Yes, but that is not a problem. Anyone can turn the key from the side. But it puts the ring out of reach of anyone also operating a key. The ring, on its stand and under its magnifier, would have to be lifted carefully and then removed to the back of the case and then up and out. Easy enough if you are standing right in front of it, but otherwise very hard. The top and front of the case are a single piece, so there is no way to put someone on top to reach down." Chow Dai sighed. "It would be easier to steal it from the chief administrator when he had it out."

"Yeah, sure—with all those SPF and regular Center security people around. I toyed with the idea of *becoming* the chief administrator and then I found that there was just no point at which he and I could possibly be alone and unmonitored for enough time to do it and cover up the mess. He is never really alone, and when he removes the ring, he always keeps it on his finger until the ceremony or function is over, then puts it back. I will get this information up to *Thunder*. The bottom line is, I suspect, that we can get to the ring but we cannot remove it. A way will have to be found to get around that weight sensor. I wish I knew how much it took to depress it. Only the chief administrator and chief of security can gain access to the details of the museum security system, and for one reason or another both are out of reach to me. You give me a precise list of what you need that you can't make for yourself, and I'll get on it."

"It is odd," Chow Dai said, "that with them suspecting, at least, that we're going after this ring and having that whole army here and all, they didn't put in all sorts of extra security, extra systems it'd take Star Eagle to beat."

"No. I already know the answer to that one, and it works in our favor this time. They believe their measures are adequate, that the ring is safe, but they really do not care if it is not. They are convinced that we cannot escape with it if we steal it. I think the plan is that if we do manage to steal it they will shadow but not apprehend us—at least not all of us, and not the one with the ring. The one ring is unimportant—useless without the other four. But out there in space, somewhere, are automated fighting ships and perhaps a ship or two of SPF forces, as well, under more than one Val. They want, they *need*, the *Thunder* and all of us pirates."

"If that is the case, then why do they not make this easier to steal?"

He chuckled. "If they did that, we'd smell a rat and would not lead them where they want to be led. That does not mean that they leave it all to chance and our overconfidence . . ." He snapped his fingers. "In fact, I think I know what they did. What *I* would do. If I am right, then we can use it against them. The getaway will not be easy, and not without peril, but we might manage it. You steal it. I'll get you out—if it is at all possible."

"We are still uncertain of what to do ourselves," Chow Dai admitted. "We—we find our thoughts confused and muddied, our loyalties mixed."

"Not too long ago you considered yourselves monsters," he pointed out. "Has this changed?"

They looked at each other, then back at him. "No, not deep down, although when we do not think of ourselves and allow Madowa and Sedowa to take over, we are content. But, unlike you, we will always be this way. On Janipur everyone is a monster of the same sort as we. It is—comforting. Back out there—we and our children will be monsters."

"We are all monsters, in a way," the shapechanger said. "You are at least something, someone. You know who you are and what you are. I do not. I can never be one person, one thing, no matter how long I live or how content I am. It would be nice to be human, to have children, to look forward to the future and to some inner peace. I can never have that. Never. There will be five of you on *Thunder* if we all survive this, then seven soon after, and perhaps more. You might well become the dominant race of the pirates. Your future, your children's future, might be bright and happy depending on our success. For me, the game is the goal. I enjoy playing this game, but I have nothing to win at the end of it. Master System or no Master System, I will not change, or gain."

His statement hit them with great impact. They had never thought of that before, and it made their own problems and situation seem far less important. Vulture in fact had no stake in all this; he was playing the game for its own sake.

"For now, say nothing of this meeting to your husband unless he asks where you can answer. I will get to work on the problems and get back to all of you. Now—go."

Madowa-Chow Dai stood and reached into her neck purse. She removed three small objects from it, each wrapped in cloth, then unwrapped them. "These are fragile," she warned. "Do not break or mishandle them."

He stared at them, suddenly realizing what he was seeing. "Impressions. You took impressions of all the mechanical keys! How?..."

"It was not too difficult," she responded, although he knew that it must have been. "Just make the keys."

He touched them. They were hard as a rock. "What did you use to get them?"

She grinned, which meant, for a Janipurian, showing all the teeth. "Bread dough. Very thick bread dough. It is a very convenient medium if it is not set too long."

He began to appreciate the level of genius he was dealing with.

Vulture had much to do, and contacting the *Thunder* was an early priority.

Hawks and the others listened intently to the details, and Star Eagle immediately put his robots to work creating what was needed from the digital data sent by Vulture on Janipur. They could arrange a drop far easier than Vulture could risk getting the items made himself, and take advantage of a higher technological level.

Working out the full details of the plan, however, was more difficult. Star Eagle was not of great help in this area; the computer could allow for all the unknowns and come up with predictions of success in the range of point three to about seventeen percent. The only contributions of real value the pilot could make were estimates of how Master System, its Vals, and its forces might react at any given level, but even these had to be only approximations. Vals and Master System might be eighty or ninety percent predictable, but the SPF and its leadership were humans with a great deal of autonomy. Those freebooters who had ever had dealings with the SPF could only vouch for their unswerving loyalty to the system and their love of action. Whether or not their officers could overrule a Val in the field was questionable, but certainly a good general could freely interpret orders and directives to his liking. Rewards were great if he was right; the penalty for failure was severe, but no general convinced of the righteousness of his or her decisions would let fear of punishment sway them. They were fanatics.

All of this information was gathered and compiled by those of the *Thunder*'s crew who had experience in such matters, and they began to formulate a new plan.

"All right," Raven sighed. "So we get 'em the equipment and we get 'em in with the skeleton keys and dummy stuff they want. Vulture has to be on duty in security during the whole operation to cover the alarms. Sabir—well, that's one to worry about, but maybe we can use this sudden infusion of male chauvinism on the part of our former Hindu lady to good effect. If he knows what's going to happen, you can bet we'll have a dedicated gun and watchdog. So they get in, use Star Eagle's gadget, get to the case, and flip the keys. Now we got a pressure plate that somebody's *got* to stand on to get the ring out. How much pressure?"

"Rats," Manka Warlock said.

"Beg pardon?"

"The vast bulk of that Center's population are still the distilled classical Hindu types with a real reverence for all lower life forms. I always thought Hindus were fascinating in that they disliked killing flies yet they killed each other in about the same numbers as everybody else in the world. Center has rats and a few other pests. Not the usual rats, either, although they're bad enough. I asked. These are large, hairy things but rats all the same. They live in the air ducts and ventilation shafts too narrow and winding for Janipurians to use. They don't kill them. They just try to feed them at designated spots to keep them out of real harm. They run from people unless concerned or in large groups, but they are big."

Raven followed her thinking. "In the museum?"

"It has air ducts and ventilation shafts, I am certain. It is in the middle of Center's main level. There are probably gratings but I will wager that sooner or later a few get in and have to be shooed out. They would break those light beams, would they not?"

He thought about it. "Yeah, sure. They'd have to. And that'd trigger the alarms—no. Probably not. A class-one security alert would result and all hell would break loose at regular intervals. Even if it was originally set up that way, they'd have gone nuts and changed it by now."

"Precisely. In fact, they are a nice little security backup in case someone tried a robot tentacle, let us say, down the shafts. You couldn't use those shafts without disturbing the rat colonies and that would result in alarms and an investigation or perhaps a horde of rats being dumped into whatever room you were trying to break into. Now *that* is a thought. Make such a commotion the night before you break in, it would cause them to assume any new signals were just more rats breaking through the unrepaired areas."

"Uh uh. Some of these people are as crooked as the next guy. You don't leave your museum vulnerable that way. You either post a lot of nasty human guards as supplements or you work through the night repairing it. Too risky. But I see what you mean about the rat problem. I missed that in the reports. If they're big and they do occasionally get in, then those light beams can't trigger a general alarm. Then what *do* they trigger?"

"The cameras and audio sensors. They *must*. A break turns them on and sounds an alarm in the security center. They check their screens, pan around, and see and hear rats, so they—what?"

Raven thought a moment. "Well, either they'd have to

come in and get them, or they'd have to switch off the beams . . . *Say!* We'll have to ask Vulture what the procedure is. If he can patch the outside video he can patch that as well. A lot easier than moving some cockeyed mirror contraption in that might not work and in a place where we don't have the precise angles to make sure it does. Good girl!"

"But what does that say about the pressure platform under the carpet as well?" she asked him, very pleased with herself.

"Uh huh. I wonder how much one of those suckers weighs? Or several? A kilo? Two? And they're pack animals. Almost never travel alone. Figure there might be as many as three running across at one time. Allow some margin—some *real* margin—and you might have a fair amount of weight required to trigger that sucker." He paused a moment. "Nope. Forget it. They have some monkeylike creatures and a number of other pets down there. You can bet the designer allowed for someone sending in small trained animals. Even if we allow six or seven kilos, it's not enough. Besides, somebody's got to close that case. Odds are it has some kind of time delay if it's open too long, whether they spotted it or not. It might sound an alarm when opened anyway. That's the way *I'd* design it."

"But this is a lower level of security than we are accustomed to. A lower technological level, Center or not. This was designed by humans, not machines, and built by humans to stop humans. It might sound a buzzer or ring a bell when opened, but if it did it would probably have the effect of turning on the audio and visual system so the duty officer could see if it were a real problem or a false alarm. A lot of this boils down to a very few true security systems. Almost everything except the pressure platform and the locks themselves is designed to turn on the audio-visual to see what is going on before a general alarm is sounded. Block those channels and the security center is blind, deaf, and dumb. It is a key weak point. They must not have much of a true criminal element there."

He nodded. "I don't know about their crooks, but clearly the system's designed to discourage somebody from trying. Beyond that, the thing really isn't all that hot. They seem pretty confident that nobody could escape even if they did take the crown jewels, and they'd normally be right. I mean, it's a *Center*, damn it! Strict computer-controlled access in and out. Codings, trackings, you name it. Let's face it—without Vulture we could steal this sucker but we could never get it out. Having the deputy chief of security on your side makes all the difference, and nobody is gonna plan for that. The more you look at our group the more you realize how much thought went into it. We're supposed to have a fighting chance to win, after all."

"All right. But that doesn't get us around the pressure-plate problem."

"Vulture has an idea on that. I don't like it much, but it might be the only alternative. We're gonna run some tests with that Janipurian pair and see if it works. Let's go on to the getaway. If they trip any alarms, even silent ones, it's all over."

She nodded. "I think our deputy chief of security can be counted on there. He will, after all, be in the security center and will probably outrank anyone there. Either of us in his situation could cover for quite a while if we had to. He can't hide a major exposure or alarm trip, though. All right—that has to be their problem. Now they get out and head for a prearranged meet. Where?"

"The clinic. He has some secure areas there, and it wouldn't be considered at all strange for folks to go there at any hour."

"Good. We will have to have some provisional diversions ready—just in case. Some nasties Vulture could set off by remote control if he needed to." She smiled. "Ones designed for maximum damage and casualties."

"Vulture's developed a whole line of hideouts along his route, but that whole place will be swarming with searchers once the theft is discovered. We can't get to them until they're clear: Security'll be looking for anything coming in for a pickup. They're gonna hav'ta lay low a long time, but maybe we can buy 'em a little breathing space. After Vulture gets this equipment from us, he won't need the fighter he's got down there now, and anyway it's too far to reach. If we time it right, we might convince Center that the fighter we take off has them aboard. They might even drop everything to chase it and blow it away."

She nodded. "We will try it, but if they do not buy it, or are the least suspicious, there will be only one way to save them."

He sighed. "Yeah. Space battle. Ship to ship. They might underestimate our strength, though."

"Or they might *overestimate* it. We must recall and out-fit the freebooter ships and practice with our whole fleet, such as it is. These freebooters are very good at running and hiding. I wonder how good they are in a fight."

Vulture had met privately with Jeruwahl-Sabir after the planning had been firmed up. The "husband," acting very much that role, had been more than just upset that Vulture had met secretly with both women earlier, and it had taken some politicking to mollify him. Vulture, in fact, was as worried about Sabir as he was the actual operation. This was someone he didn't really know well and was still having some problems understanding. It wouldn't take much to expose their whole plan and at the very least abort the mission, perhaps at the cost of three lives.

"I do not like this one bit," Sabir said coolly. "Already it has been awhile since you first brought us out from under the mindprint, and Madowa's horns are beginning to sprout. I do not think this is possible any more."

Vulture gave a slight shrug. "It is possible. Willpower can do a lot, and we aren't out of time yet. They want to do this thing, Sabir, and they are ready. I think now so are we. The only question left for me is you."

"What do you mean by that?"

"When this started, you weren't all thrilled about becoming Janipurian, I'm told, but you saw it as your duty and a chance to participate and help in a great undertaking. If you'd been a man at the start—say, Captain Paschitta-wal—I might have followed your subsequent behavior a bit better, but you weren't. If you'd had a past like the women had—stepped on, pushed around, raped, tortured —I might understand. But I think you knew coming in that the mission is everything. We—all of us—are at tremendous risk and expendable. Only the mission matters in the end. Not being the martyr types, we will all try to survive, but there are no guarantees. You were born a freebooter, not a colonial dirtcrawler. You *must* decide."

"That is easier for you to say, and perhaps easier for you to decide," responded Sabir. "You may have little to gain except satisfaction in your personal war against the whole system, but you have nothing to lose. I did not expect this, although we all should have allowed it. You see, up until now I have had nothing. I was born the last of eleven children to parents who looked a hundred when they were in their forties and scratched out the bare necessities on a small rocky claim in the middle of nowhere. When I was but thirteen, I came on to a mechanic on a freebooter tramp ship just to get out of there, to have some sort of freedom and life. When he was done with me, stupid and naive as I was, he abandoned me in a small settlement. I was but a defiled child, and I did whatever was necessary to survive and to get what learning I could. I sold my labor when possible and my body when it was not, but each time I learned something that was useful later on. I was an extra hand on twenty different ships, one trip at a time. I finally found the *Indrus*, which was owned and operated by distant cousins, and they took me on although they did not need me. I would not have remained, but it was comforting for a while to be with my own kind. Both men are married and devoted to their wives, and the only other crew member is Ravi's daughter. I had nothing. I have never had anything. That is why I volunteered for this. Why not?"

He nodded. "I see. And now, all of a sudden, you have some status, some responsibility, and two children on the way. You have blended into a society when you never had one before. Never mind the others, the mission, even the women. It is selfishness, is it not?"

Sabir bristled. "And why should I not be selfish? Who has ever given me anything? What do I owe you or them or anyone?"

"I don't give a damn what you owe to whom, and I don't give a damn what you want or think. Those two women have had it far worse than even you and they are committed. If you turned us in, they would not reward you and you know it. They would pick your mind to pieces for information on us, and the others' minds, as well. Your body might live, as some simpleton building his house out of his own dung and plowing someone else's fields, but your mind would die and your soul would bear the burden of your crimes. You can do nothing, but that buys you two years at most. When the time comes to take the next mindprint—assuming they don't catch you before that—there will be no deputy chief of security to launder your truths or protect your wife and children, and you don't have the rank to have it managed otherwise. If you wish to protect what is yours and play your petty games, you are better off

going along with me. The real Peshwar is very loyal and
dedicated to his wife. You will have both the Chows, and
the children, if we make it out, and you will have a position of authority and power. You are comfortable in this
society. It is too bad you were not born to it, but you were
not. So, be selfish—see it through."

Sabir thought that over and saw that Vulture spoke the
truth. "What you say is all well and good—if I thought we
could get away with it. I cannot believe that we will,
though."

"You haven't seen it all, nor will I show you now," he
replied, "but I think it's possible. Let's go for it. Let's take
a chance on life."

"When—if I agree?"

"The 'when'—when you agree."

He sighed. "Very well. If the Chows go along, I will not
stand in the way and will be what help I can."

"Excellent!" Vulture responded. "Tomorrow begins
Holi. The chief administrator will need the ring but has not
taken it as yet. It will probably be far too late for him to
put it back tomorrow night, but it will be on his finger and
he will be surrounded by guards. He might wear it the
whole festival, but I think not. In past years he has returned it after opening an *utsava* so people who come in
from the field for the festivals can see it on display. When
he removes it, I will be there, and this will give me a
chance to see just how the case is normally opened and the
ring removed. No matter what night he returns the ring,
that night we will take it."

Just because the Brahman class was privileged to know
of Master System, the wider universe, and some of its
technology did not make them any less people of their own
culture. In point of fact, Hinduism was particularly suited
to the hierarchical Center leadership, especially as that

structure had been reframed and reemphasized by Master
System. *Rta*, the balance of forces, the natural order, was
supreme. Vedic prayers were to the maintenance of order;
to watch the natural order carefully, imitate and perpetuate
it. It was a short, perhaps heretical step, but an easy one, to
see one's self as the maintainer of order, stability, and balance. The order had been disrupted in Mother India and the
people had been corrupted, but now Indra had given them
another chance, on a new world, in a new form, and set the
highest of humans, the Brahmans, the holy task of maintaining the *Rta* at all costs so that the chosen ones of Janipur could find their own paths to salvation and immortality
unencumbered by external forces.

The role of the Center Brahmans, then, was to do just
what Centers were designed for—maintain the balance and
eliminate anything that might change the way the people
and culture worked. It was a system tailor-made for Master
System's own goals, and it worked well, far better than in
many other places where it had been imposed. Unlike the
cynical Centers of Earth and many colonial worlds where
knowledge destroyed faith, here the Center elect were true
believers. Until the SPF had landed, the only contact Janipurian Centers allowed was with a few ships like the
Indrus, peopled by crew who shared much of their beliefs
and understood and respected them. To maintain stability
and balance, no matter what the cost, was a sacred duty.

They had the duty of *dharma*, of keeping the world and
its people on the right path, of maintaining things.

This was also a people who felt the necessity of *Bhakti*,
of devotion to and relationship with individual and often
personal gods; they placed enormous store in rituals and
ceremonies and had many deities. Their very form was a
matter of pride; on Earth it had been this part of Hinduism
that had brought the cow to a status of near or actual wor-

ship; on Janipur, they had some of the form and characteristics of the sacred animal.

The *Holi utsava*, or Spring Festival, was an ancient ritual devoted to Krishna, but it was also a time of joy and produced a near-carnival atmosphere punctuated with spectacular public ceremonies and rites open to all. Although it was Krishna's festival, the god Soma, and the fiery liquor named for him, would not be ignored. It was one of the few religious observances where all but the bare minimum of Brahmans from the entire continent could come and enjoy a bit of Cochin Center's comforts. Many would come to join in the celebrations by the masses, leaving only the ascetics and those leaders with strong local ties and not much love for Center or its comforts.

This was also the time when security had nightmares and the SPF had fits. As members of the ruling caste, those from outside had the right to enter Center and see it and visit their departmental chiefs as well as look at the museums, libraries, and shops that were outside the limits of normal purview. Security areas were still off-limits, of course, but with such crowds, the mere task of keeping them from unauthorized areas, breaking things or tapping on terminals kept all the security force busy.

The SPF, with its own modernized religion compelling and vesting them with the god-given responsibility of keeping order on pain of their immortal souls, had a hard time dealing with this idea of relatively open access to Center, even for a limited period of time. They simply couldn't check out everyone who arrived with their families and cousins, since nobody actually had to be invited and those who could showed up, often at the last minute. Center could not accommodate or maintain such a crowd, so they camped outside in what became a huge, temporary tent city.

Vulture balanced the increased security against the ben-

efits of the crowd and its confusion and anonymity. The
festival lasted several days, however; he no longer had
those days to spare, even if he would have preferred to
have dealt with an exhausted security force and an even
more exhausted and frustrated SPF. He decided he could
use the confusion of the festival far more than he could
afford to wait a week—if the C.A. put the damned ring
back.

The Brahmans in Hindu society controlled the spiritual
levers of power and authority, not the secular, but in practice the Brahmans of Centers were more secular than they
would have liked to admit. Still, they saw their roles as
purely spiritual. In the field, most were affiliated with religious orders, but a few were involved in the professions
and everyday life. Some were doctors and some lawyers or
judges; often they earned their livings this way while on
call as duty priests when needed. Each Hindu was his or
her own church, so there were no formal churches on Janipur, but ceremonies and rituals required priests, and the
professional service class of Brahmans was there to serve.
Even those who weren't needed or had had their turns before were at the festival, as well.

Vulture couldn't help but wonder what some of the
twice-born of lower castes would think if they could see
how unsaintly some of these secularized Brahmans acted
when they were entirely among their own. One of the security men remarked his relief that so few ascetics had
come this year; they were usually trouble, since they spent
most of their time berating and cursing their more material-
istic brethren. On those occasions, it took a fair amount of
soma in the belly to wash away the guilt that always lin-
gered in the back of the minds of even security personnel.
It was, in fact one of the most spartan of Centers, the
technology used only when it was essential to the holy
mission, but, still, when one was in an enclosed city with

its own climate control, electric lights, and computerized kitchen, it was hard to convince yourself you were striving to go beyond material things. There was little that could be done, though; fires, tents, and the like would not be practical at Center, and they would most certainly interfere with the computers and communications networks.

And, of course, somebody had to clean up the place, stock it, run the stores, and do all the other jobs that were beneath a Brahman. In other circumstances, the lower castes would have done it, but they were not permitted here, so a high degree of automation was required to maintain Brahman purity.

To Vulture, who was a product of no culture and an amalgam of many, it was just more proof that people would rationalize almost anything in the name of religion.

The plain outside on the morning of the start of the festival was a colorful sea of tents and a mobile sea of grayish-tan bodies. It was impossible to judge immediately, but it was possible that there were three or four thousand people in the temporary city. There were firewalkers—on feet, not hooves—and demonstrations of yoga and other powers of the mind and much more.

Shortly after nine in the morning, Chief Administrator Namur walked down the hall of the main level of the Center with his wife and retinue. He was dressed simply in a white loincloth and his wife in plain white silk, but what was impressive was that they *walked*, upright, the entire distance of more than three hundred meters that they were in public view, and they walked rather well. Since such a thing required not only great practice but great concentration and force of will, it was a gesture that impressed even Vulture, who was one of the retinue.

They stopped at the great red doors to the museum. The curator stood there, made obeisance in the time-honored way, then removed the large key from around her neck and stuck it in the lock. Vulture watched. One right, one left, another left, then right, then left again. There was a *click*, the curator pushed on the golden door latch, and the two doors swung inward. The C.A. and his wife followed the curator inside to the second and more modern security door, which opened when the curator inserted a small card and then presented her right palm to the plate. The inner door moved back silently, and they proceeded inside.

Vulture was several steps in back of the chief administrator, but his eyes took in everything. He decided they needn't worry about the light beams; either they were switched off when the inner door opened or they just turned on the monitors, as suspected. What was more interesting was that the carpeted area in front of the ring's case was bulging upward perhaps fifteen centimeters. Whatever it triggered was automatically turned off somehow, but he couldn't see how. Not the door. Why have the damned thing at all if it's turned off by springing the door? A thief would have to do that just to get in. Then it struck him— the combination! The palm opened the doors, but the numerical code deactivated the pressure plate. Neither he nor the Chows knew that combination, and the panel was recessed so that no one could see what numbers the curator punched. It was a standard enough system that it had been easy to figure out how to temporarily circumvent it, but that wouldn't deactivate the plate. Clever.

The curator and an assistant went to the plate. When the curator set one foot on the plate it depressed and wiggled but nothing happened, but in the split second when the other foot came down a bell began to ring. The assistant stepped on the other side, adding enough weight to depress and lock it, and the bell stopped sounding. There was no way to be certain, but he felt the bell was important for the delay before it rang—that split second when just part of the body weight was on the platform. Raven had been right; the thing had been designed to halt a Janipurian thief and to allow for Janipurian rats and other critters that might get in. The bell did not worry him; if it went off they'd know immediately that they'd blown it and then it would be time to try to shoot their way out.

Vulture, as deputy chief of security, had been handed one of the two keys to the case and told to take the left side. The chief would take the right, and the C.A. would remove the ring. He had been given the key only when he joined the party and would have to surrender it almost immediately. It had been hell figuring out how to take an impression of it but he'd managed. The impression wouldn't do much good at this stage, but, matched against the key made from Chow's Dai's dough impression, it would tell him before they were committed if they'd blown it.

On a nod from the chief administrator, both Vulture and the chief of security inserted their keys and then turned, he to the left and the other to the right. He had been instructed to hold it there. There was a *click*, and the case, fully four meters long and containing much more than just the ring, opened, the lid comprising the entire transparent area moving back electrically and merging with its back wall. There were solenoids along the sides, he noted, although the Chows already had figured this out. Interrupt one, by trying to reach in or climb into the case from the side, and the lid snapped shut. Vulture figured about half of the person who tried it that way would become a bloody part of the permanent exhibit.

The C.A. leaned over, approached the ring with his right hand from the back, carefully lifted it up off its peg mount and brought it back, up, then out. He seemed to examine it, then turned to his wife, smiled, and gave it to her. She nodded and as he held out his hand she placed the

ring on the third finger. It was a good fit, which indicated
that it had been relined in some way.

The chief administrator moved away, and with a nod
from his immediate boss, Vulture slowly turned the key
back to straight again. A mechanism clicked in, and the
case lid moved forward and clicked back into place. He
then removed the key, placed it back around his neck, and
followed the boss back out the doors. He reflected that it
was almost a pity that the ring wasn't still there today,
since the museum would have a couple of staff people on
but would be closed to the public. A perfect time for a
robbery—if he'd wanted anything other than the ring.

The ceremony and rites themselves were indeed impressive and quite solemn, lasting most of the day. This was a
rare occasion for communal worship, and much of it was
spent fasting and chanting, over and over, in unison,
"Krishna . . . Krishna . . . Krishna . . ." The chief administrator served as high priest for the rites, before a massive
statue of Krishna.

There was no physically possible way that a Janipurian
could accomplish the lotus position, but they could bend
themselves into incredible and impossible positions all the
same.

The ceremony concluded late in the day, and the crowd
broke up into random groups listening to teachers relate
various parables, lessons, or philosophies, or participated
in rites of faith including firewalking and demonstrations
of the power of the mind over the body. This would continue for days—although not with the chief administrator
leading—to a steadily diminishing number of the pious.
Some would spend the whole time in prayer, meditation,
and learning, but for most, one day was enough.

The chief administrator walked among them, though,
and at various points demonstrated his own great mental
control and at other times his humility by sitting at the feet

of a yogi or other teacher, and occasionally by stopping to talk with this person or that on an informal basis regardless of job or status. Vulture couldn't help but think how easy it would be to simply take the ring at this point. Unfortunately, anyone who did so would be brought down by several hidden but expert and well-armed SPF forces, by security forces themselves, or, if that failed, by the crowd. Stealing that ring was just about the most blasphemous thing you could do around this crowd of faithful; they would all consider it an attack on themselves.

By nightfall, it was clear that the chief administrator was not going to return the ring that night, but Vulture hadn't thought he would. Tomorrow would be soon enough. By then some of the holiest would have miraculously changed into tourists, and others into bureaucrats trying to score points with their superiors. It was a much better crowd to work with, anyway.

But the next day the museum opened without the ring. By the close of the third day, Vulture was beginning to worry that something in fact was wrong. Chow Dai-Madowa's horns were already out around a hundred centimeters and seemed to be growing so fast one could almost see them grow, and she was complaining of how tiring it was to stand for any length of time; Chow Mai-Sedowa was in much better shape but her own horns had started to appear and she was eating heavily. Those horns grew at an average of almost ten centimeters a day, judging by Chow Dai. Time was running out.

Worse, the chief administrator continued his public appearances—with the ring nowhere to be seen. Finally, five days later, when Vulture was already talking with *Thunder* about improvising and making alternate plans, perhaps taking the trio out of Center and getting them back up to *Thunder* somehow for the births—hard but not impossible if the ring was not in their hands and there was no hue and cry—when the call came to attend the chief administrator and replace the ring. It was done privately, quietly, near the end of the day and with none of the fanfare that taking it out had occasioned. Still, Vulture was reassured to see that the combinations and procedures didn't seem to have changed.

Nick of time, he thought, and sent signals to the trio and to *Thunder*. He was all prepared—in fact, he felt *over-prepared*. It was frustrating to have to wait until night.

3. Plot, Counterplot

IN SOME CENTERS, THEY WERE CALLED THE CATACOMBS: those endless miles of maintenance corridors, air shafts, storage areas, and the like hidden behind the smooth and polished exterior walls.

Vulture walked down a narrow corridor and stopped at a small door with a press-plate. He lightly rapped three times, then opened the door. "It is time," he said softly to the creature within.

"About time," Ikira Sukotae snapped irritatedly. "I feel like I've been cooped up in this thing forever."

To the eyes of an Earth-human, she looked much like a young, extremely voluptuous woman—beautiful, sexy, and overbuilt. She was not Earth-human, however, which was made clear by the fact that she was not quite four hundred centimeters tall. Her eyes, which looked more Earth-human than Vulture's, caught the added light of the corridor and seemed to flash like diamonds in the sun.

Closer inspection would reveal tiny, shell-like ears with pointed tips, two tiny hornlike protuberances sticking up out of her short hair, and other subtle differences. She was a colonial and, like Janipurians, her ancestors had been designed for a particular kind of world.

Normally she was nude, since her natural defenses included the ability to change her skin color to blend in with almost any background, but that was less relevant here. Unlike the predators of her own world, Janipurians could see into the infrared; although her body temperature was constantly being adjusted to match that of her surroundings, she always gave off heat and, while she might not be noticed in a grove of trees or a field, to a Janipurian eye she would stand out like a flaming candle against sterile walls. Still, she had real advantages on this world: the Janipurian brain would not recognize stationary objects a few meters but could zero in on any motion, and Ikira could be still as death for hours if need be. Hers was a rough world.

Vulture thought that to Janipurians she would appear at a distance like a monkey, and there were a lot of those about. Close up, however, her hairless body and curvaceous shape would mark her as an alien.

With a little help, she climbed onto Vulture's back and rode him, clinging low as he made his way to a different assembly point. He knew all the corridors and catacombs well, and although they passed a great deal of automated machinery and countless robots, nothing paid attention to them. Vulture had the right security clearances, and, matching her temperature and color to his and riding low, a Janipurian would have to be closer than three or four meters to even notice that something was on his back.

Getting Ikira to Janipur with the aid of the transmuter hadn't been all that difficult; getting back out might be. Vulture had kept the *Thunder*'s fighter that contained the transmuter in the mountains well away from Center, but his access to flyers would be useless now. Center's sophisticated tracking could pinpoint any flyer anywhere on the continent and, if necessary, seize control and bring it down wherever security wanted it.

The alien captain was essential to Vulture's plan, not only in the theft but also in the getaway. Janipurians could see in the infrared, but at night they could see little else; Ikira, on the other hand, had some trouble with direct bright light but could see perfectly well in the dark so long as there was any light source, however dim. Her people lived underground.

Neither Vulture nor Hawks had ever had the intention of sending anyone else down on this mission unless it failed, but Ikira Sukotae had proven to be the easiest solution to some of their problems. At least the captain hadn't had to be transmuted into Janipurian form; she would have had to have been transmuted as about a year-old Janipurian, which would have been no help at all.

Sabir and the Chows were waiting. Although they now all knew the plan intimately, they had not had any contact with the captain until now and there was little time for reunions. Vulture wore a small watch strapped to his lower arm, as did Sabir.

"It is now eleven past one," Vulture whispered. "I will need twenty minutes to get down to security central and in monitoring position. Give me the four extra minutes to activate my patches into the audio-visual system. You can observe the door from this service exit, but be careful not to be seen. Any time after one thirty-five, then, wait for the guard to make his rounds and get clear, then go. You must all cross the common, unlock the main door, get through, and close it behind you in three minutes. If there's any doubt, stay here or get back here and try again a couple of guard cycles later. Once inside, if you don't trip any alarms, take all the time you need. When you've got it,

come back to the main door, close the others, and press the
watch stud. That will send a little shock to me through my
watch, and I'll come up and clear things for you to get out.
If the alarm doesn't work or I'm not there within one hour,
I will come for you at, let's say, three-thirty."

Ikira looked at him. "And if you don't come for us?"

"I'll come. Now, you all know what to do and how to
do it. Let's give it a shot!" He turned and left down the
corridor.

"The wait is the hard part," Chow Dai sighed.

For Ikira, it was worse, although after five days down
on this world, most of them cooped up in what was little
more than a closet, she was ready to get it over with, as
well. While the Janipurians were oblivious to it, to the
alien captain the place stank. It smelled, in fact, like a
barnyard, and even five days had not dimmed its unpleas-
antness. And she would have to endure it for some time to
come. She wished, at least, that they'd let her have a cigar.

They couldn't even talk, since there were guards about
and possibly unjammed sensors as well. She had been
somewhat surprised that these catacombs common to all
Centers were not heavily monitored by security, but the
fact was that they opened only onto monitored public
areas, the main power room, and three service exits that
were well covered. This was a largely nonviolent culture
that experienced much petty crime but little more than that.
The museum was guarded only becasue it provided too
much potential temptation to someone on the downward
path of reincarnation. Still, it was clear security hadn't
changed the combinations, modified the locks or in any
way varied the system since it had been built centuries
earlier. That was working to their advantage.

They took peeks at their destination through a grating.
There was only one guard, as usual, but there was definitely something different about him. To the Janipurian

women, he was almost an idealized male, with thick muscles, an unnaturally handsome face, and a powerful and confident walk—and he wore a very nasty-looking laser pistol that was beyond Janipurian technology. He was most certainly SPF. The regular guards didn't look that good and weren't in that kind of condition, and tended to carry only a ceremonial dagger.

This guard was also military in his precision. Such discipline and organization was not characteristic of the Janipurian race. Exactly five minutes later another guard appeared looking just as perfect, and five minutes after him another. Then, at twenty minutes, the first guard was back. It was somewhat unnerving, but it actually served their ends. If any guard didn't show up on the dot, they would know something was wrong. If they did, all was clear.

"Sedowa—you have the main key?" Sabir whispered.

"Here. We go now?"

"One minute after the next guard leaves."

Down in security center, the duty CQ was sitting back reading and barely glanced at the monitors. Had he been staring at them, he would have noticed that, one at a time, their images shifted just a bit before showing the old familiar scene. Had he or his colleagues playing chess in the back been as militarily precise as the SPF, they might have noticed that the guard's rounds were now almost a minute off. There *was*, in fact, an SPF sergeant who might have noticed this as well, but he was busy arguing with Deputy Chief of Security Boil, who was duty officer.

Up on the main level, their hooves masked in velvet pads, and with Ikira atop Chow Dai, the four pirates watched the guard around the corner, then they all seemed to take a collective deep breath and emerged and made for the great red door to the museum. Chow Mai stood up and, seeming very calm and professional, inserted the duplicate key and turned it in the right-left combination. They held their breath but the door *click*ed, and they hurried inside, quietly closing it behind them. It was now locked once again, but as a safety measure there was an override bar on the inside.

There was absolutely no light in the space between the outer and inner doors, but they had to feel confident that Vulture had bypassed the audio and visual monitors with his own recordings. Sabir, the gadget-bearer, stood up and reached into the bag and felt for the light. It was unnerving being totally in the dark, and he felt a real sense of relief when he flicked on the light.

Because she was more mobile, Chow Mai was doing as much of the work as possible, allowing her sister to over-see and comment but mainly to stay on all fours. A small rectangular magnetic stone, procured locally and shaped by the two women, was removed and placed over the keypad. The entire switch was magnetic, including the alarm. All of the keys were now stuck in their raised position, along with the switches. The Chows had seen this switch many times before and wondered why nobody ever varied it. It was very easy to bypass.

The door itself, however, required a proper handprint I.D. A piece of stiff, coated paper was removed from the bag and brought very close to the handprint plate itself, until it was mere centimeters away. The pixels in the door plate began to glow, activated by the weak magnetic field on the coated paper Chow Mai held much as they were activated by a hand pressing on the plate. Centuries of palms pressed into the plate had smoothed the area and revealed the pattern they were looking for. Chow Mai, without actually contacting the plate itself, used a thin marker to outline the print pattern, then, using scissors, cut the pattern out of the coated paper. They had learned this trick at China Center from a junior security man who was on the make and wanted to impress them.

Now she carefully lined up the paper, with the hand cutout, steadied herself, and pressed it onto the plate. The incredibly good close-up vision of the Janipurian eye was paying off.

The door hissed slightly but did not move. Sabir was disturbed by that. "It didn't work!"

"Yes it did," Chow Dai whispered back. "Push it—push hard to the right."

He got up, put both hands on the door, and pushed. It was harder than he'd expected, but the door moved, slowly, into its recess until it was open wide enough for them to get through.

The museum lay before them, vast treasures on all sides and a direct corridor to the big main case in the back. It was not totally dark, although they had expected it might be, but the main lights were off leaving only dim emergency lighting on. It was more than adequate.

Ikira, however, saw far more. Her eyes saw the criss-crossed beams of light that went at angles from the walls and ceiling. The grid they created was not dense; she could have avoided them, but no Janipurian-sized body more than five years old could have.

"If those beams turn on anything more than the cameras we're sunk," she said in a low whisper.

"You can *see* them?"

"Yes. But you can't get around them. I can, though. Let's test out the main plan while you're still outside the room. I'm going to go and step on that pressure plate. If the bell goes, don't worry about me—just get back out the front door."

Sabir reached into the bag and removed a semiautomatic security machine pistol provided by Vulture. There would be no time to wait for a guard to pass; the bell would be heard. If it went off, they would have to shoot anything that moved outside.

The captain climbed down from Chow Dai's back and walked into the room. She dodged the light beams even though it was unnecessary; she had more sense than to test two systems at once. If the plate didn't work, the rest didn't matter.

Watching the tiny alien, Chow Dai remarked, "She moves like a hundred-yen prostitute."

Ikira reached the edge of the plate, examined it, wished she could see under the carpeting as to whether edge contact also would set it off, then stepped up and on. It went down a bit, but there were no bells. She simply didn't have enough weight to trip it, although she was determined to walk softly and slowly to avoid any excessive vibration.

Sabir was to remain in the doorway and cover the outer door as well as watch the time. Now it was the Chow sisters' turn to enter and test the light beams.

The moment the first one entered there was a *click* and the four security cameras came on. There was no attempt to conceal them; they were there as a deterrent. They fixed on the pair and followed them in, but there were still no alarms. Down in security, the monitors *did* come on, and the duty CQ gave a cry that brought the others there. He manipulated some of the camera controls and finally they saw it.

Two large, hairy shapes darted across the field of vision and they all laughed and relaxed. Some rats had gotten in again.

"This'll be all night unless somebody wants to go up and in there and chase 'em out," the CQ said in disgust. "Any volunteers?"

Nobody seemed particularly eager to go chasing rats after midnight.

Deputy Chief Boil sighed. "All right, then. Since we have no mighty hunters, I don't want to look at that all night." He reached over and flipped the cameras and monitoring system tied to the beams off. Nobody, not even the SPF sergeant, objected. The event was standard procedure these days, common enough that Vulture's tapped-in recorders had had no trouble at all getting a copy of a previous rat invasion.

"You should fumigate this damned place and get rid of those monsters," the SPF sergeant said.

The others viewed him with contempt. "They don't harm us, we don't harm them," one of the duty officers responded. "They might well be your relatives, sarge."

The sergeant fumed but knew better than to argue with these people. The more he saw of the ancient culture of his ancestors, the more thankful he was that he was SPF and not Janipurian, even if he was racially the same. The cultural contempt was mutual.

In the museum, the Chows were now on either side of the case. They could see the ring in the darkened case but there was no way to turn both keys and also reach it. That was Ikira's job.

Chow Dai got up on her feet with obvious effort, took the key, and nodded to her sister. They both inserted their keys as one, then the two were turned in opposite directions. The case clicked, then rolled back just as it should.

Although the case was low, Ikira took hold of the edge and pulled herself up and into it. She was now standing amid the richest splendor of Janipur—precious jewels, intricate sculptures of gold and other precious metals, and other valuable artifacts. She bent down, grasped the ring, lifted it off its peg and then back into her hand. It was heavier than she'd thought, and large for her tiny hands. "I will have to toss it on the floor and get it later," she whispered. "I have to lower myself back down carefully without bumping the platform."

She picked a spot, then threw the ring underhanded with

all her strength, which was not great. It struck the edge of the platform, then rolled off it and under a display case.

She turned her back and, grabbing the sides of the case, lowered herself gently back onto the platform. She then turned and very softly and slowly walked away and off the raised area. The Chows released their keys and waited until the case lid whirred back down and clicked once again into place.

Ikira went to the spot where the ring had rolled and wound up on the floor reaching under the case. For a moment, she was afraid that the thing had rolled too far under the case, which had only ten centimeters or so of clearance, but she managed. Even so, it took her more than a minute to finally locate it and bring it back out.

She got up and looked at it. It was a beautiful work of art, pure gleaming gold with a shiny jet-black stone of some sort, on which were embossed in gold the two birds on a branch. The interior had been coated with some sort of lining, apparently to make it fit a specific finger. The lining did not look original to the ring.

All three made their way back to the entrance and into the passage between inner and outer door where Sabir waited. "You have it?"

"We have it," Chow Dai responded, feeling very satisfied. "Any trouble here?"

"One of the guards might have been suspicious or just extra dutiful. He tried the door and almost gave me a heart attack, but he seemed satisfied."

"It was almost *too* easy," the captain noted. "If I hadn't almost lost it under that case, it would have been perfect. I would not have expected a harder time if it were just Janipur involved, but I am very surprised that Master System and the SPF didn't add to the system. They *do* tend to be arrogantly overconfident, but I still think we missed something."

"If they knew, they would be here by now," Chow Dai pointed out.

"Maybe. But perhaps we haven't fallen into the trap yet. Perhaps they want us to get away and lead them to the *Thunder*. We will see."

It had taken them less than an hour and a quarter. They spent much of the time resetting the locks, removing the coated paper and the magnet, and making certain the inner door shut tight once again. Now they had only to wait for Vulture. Sabir triggered his signal, and down in security central Vulture stiffened.

"Something wrong, Chief?" one of the deputy officers asked.

He rubbed his arm. "No, nothing wrong. Just a muscle pain, I guess." He sighed. "I'm going to go and make my rounds," he told them, a phrase that was a well-known euphemism among higher-ups for goofing off. "I'll be back in an hour or so. Call me if there are any problems."

"Yeah, sure, Chief," the SPF sergeant growled. He'd been there six months and in that time not a single actual event requiring security action had occurred, only a couple of false alarms such as the rats. This had to be the most boring duty station in the entire universe.

Vulture made his way back up to the main level. He didn't care if anyone spotted him; the deputy chief could go anywhere he wanted to. He passed one of the guards just before turning into the corridor for the museum and they exchanged nods. "Any problems?" he asked.

"Yes, sir. Terminal boredom," was the response, and the guard continued on. After all, he had a schedule to keep.

Vulture went immediately to the red door and knocked twice, then once. The door opened from within, causing a louder sound than any of them would have liked, and he held it open while those inside scampered back across the corridor and into the service area. He then gently closed the door and joined them.

"Any problems?" he asked.

"None. Piece of cake," Ikira responded. "Too easy."

"You'll never know how much work and sweat and technology went into making it that way," he responded. "Still, let me see it."

Sabir reached into the bag, brought out the ring, and handed it to him. He inspected it carefully, close up. "So that's what one of the buggers looks like. Fancy, but somehow I expected more. Hmmm . . . This lining looks new. I don't like that. I wish there was a way to test this sucker and make sure we haven't stolen a ringer."

That startled all of them. "Is that possible?"

"Sure. Always was. I didn't like the fact that it was missing for four days, and there are a lot of really fine craftsmen on this world. The stone looks right, though. I can't think of any way they could duplicate that synthetic stuff here. Well, if this *is* the real one, that suggests something else."

Janipurian nails were almost like claws, thick and nasty unless trimmed for detail work. Vulture never trimmed his unless it was to sharpen them. He dug into the lining, straining, and finally got it slightly open. He then just as carefully began prying up the tiny clasps that held it and removed the insert. "Let's move down the corridor a bit. I want to check this out under a strong light."

They reached a branch of the tunnel, and Vulture took the electric light from the gadget bag and held the insert against it. The insert appeared to be polished obsidian, but it was not. As the light shone through, Vulture could see a tiny mass in the insert, no larger than the head of a pin, with three or four hairlike extensions. "So *that's* what they're up to!"

"What?" they all asked almost at once.

"A tiny transmitter. Very clever. They took out the old lining and got their SPF shops or whatever to replace it with this one. Looks the same. They could follow us anywhere with this, even into space. It doesn't look very powerful but it's probably specifically tuned."

"Then they could track us here now," Sabir said nervously. "This must mean they know we're here."

"I doubt it. They don't know it's stolen yet. They'll have it on automatic monitoring so if we take it out of the Center they'll know immediately, but not right now. I suspect that they had this made at some Master System location and flown in, using the festival to unobtrusively replace it. They don't know we're here, they just expect us sooner or later."

"What will you do, then?" Chow Dai asked, sounding worried in spite of the reassurances. Master System wasn't the only one who could get overconfident. They had been caught long ago in China Center because they committed that sin. They also understood full well that Vulture was even now in less danger than they; it would take far more than even laser pistols to stop him, and in a pinch he could simply become someone else.

"We will need some time to let things blow over," he told them. "You know the plan. The festival is winding down but there are still many people out there, and Center is still on a holiday schedule. It will take them quite some time to track down everyone who lives here permanently and count heads to discover who is missing and who they are after. By that time we must be well away, overland, and if possible at the first of the hideouts I have prepared. Make your way down to the service entrance and wait for me. I must get a few things to cover our exit."

Sabir looked at him hard. "And what is to prevent you from hanging us out to take the punishment? You have what you want."

He gave the Janipurian grin, tossed the ring up, and caught it again in his hand, then flipped it to Sabir. Keeping the liner with its track device, he headed off toward the security section.

His first task was to switch off the recordings that had hidden them from the gaze of security central. The more time they had, the better it would be, and if one of those watchers down there happened to get disturbed that the sun was coming up but their monitors still showed darkness, or if one or more of the guards got off shift and showed up down there to watch himself on the monitor, it was all over as well. He had prepared for all this well in advance; he'd had months to get ready and the aid of Star Eagle's maintenance robots and data base. He wished that he could just check out a flyer as usual, load the others in it, and head for the fighter still hidden in the hills, but that was no way out. It would take more than four hours to fly there, during the whole of which he would be at the mercy of anyone should the theft be discovered. Even if he got down, SPF troops would know his location and could get there quickly, mobilizing local guard as well. They would never make it that way.

He cut the recordings out in sequence, hoping that they would be as ignored as their emplacement had been, then set a large explosive device at the small crawlway he'd used to tap in and hold his equipment. Once he left and shut the door, anyone opening it would blow up the device and themselves as well—and probably cut off security center from its monitors for some time. Then, using the audio link for the last time, he called *Thunder*.

"This is Vulture. No time to talk. We have the prize, no casualties. Am proceeding to Pickup One with the group. Will risk brief five-second transmission from there on arrival, five seconds on permanent departure from that point for Pickup Two. Hope to see you sooner than later."

He signed off, not waiting for a reply, crawled back out, and closed the door, feeling somewhat relieved when it hadn't exploded on him right then and there. He headed back to his quarters, thinking all the time. He had anticipated that they might try some sort of tracking device and had prepared for it. His secret weapon, Durga, was sound asleep, but that was fine with Vulture. It made the great black falcon easier to carry.

Falconry was a popular sport among the security people, although most Janipurians considered it barbarous since the falcons hunted and killed living animals. The security men, with their own spiritual leaders, merely saw it as a close study of natural order. The bird made a few loud protests when it was moved to a portable case and the case strapped around Vulture's middle so it would ride on the Janipurian's back, but this was the way it usually traveled, and it soon settled down. With her hood on, Durga wasn't very wide awake.

Vulture went down to join the others who, he hoped, had already exited and were awaiting him outside. It was now approaching four-thirty; the sun would be up in less than ninety minutes, and the museum staff would arrive in three and a half hours or less. He wanted to be well away from the crowd and the company of Center people by dawn, even though they would have to make some of the distance in daylight.

There was no one on duty at the entrance at this hour, and they all had valid access cards for the computer, except Ikira, who would be in her defensive mode atop Chow Dai's back. He inserted his card and gave his handprint, and the doors slid back. He walked out into the night.

The night was a fearsome time for a Janipurian, so the records of the exits would be noted, and the Peshwar family, at least, would come under suspicion. But Center wouldn't *know* until they did a head count later and made a real effort to find the four missing ones.

They waited in the shadows just beyond the light reflecting from the Center entrance. The area immediately around them was dimly illuminated by the glow from the great dome, but once beyond the encampment they would be effectively blind and that didn't make for good speed. Vulture had covered this route a hundred times in the dark, though; he felt he knew it as well as any, and he had a set of eyes along to help guide him and the others.

But first he set Durga down, removed the bird from its cage in the semidarkness, and set her on her perch. He prepared a banded holder and strapped the ring lining with its locator to her leg, then freed her of all restraints, even removing the hood.

The bird seemed puzzled and tried to look around for a moment, before settling back and seeming to go to sleep. There wasn't much difference to the falcon between the real darkness and the darkness produced by the hood.

"There!" he said. "At sunup she will awaken and decide to fly and find to her amazement and pleasure that there is no tether tied to her. I don't know where she will go—perhaps only to the top of the roof, perhaps half a continent away, but where she goes, so goes the tracker."

Next came a very long coil of silk cord. He tied it around his thickly muscled neck and then around Chow Dai, Chow Mai, and Sabir. "Keep the cord relatively tight and keep a pace that maintains that, if you can," he instructed. "Do not worry about where you step, focus only on the person ahead of you. Captain, you come to my back and be my eyes. I know the route by touch, feel, and scent, but you never know what surprises might come up."

It was a peculiarity of the way a Janipurian brain processed information that the entire world seemed to be nothing but darkness, yet if they looked directly and only at the one in front of them they saw the whole column in shimmering infrared. There was some Janipurian instinct to follow the leader when this occurred, and match the pace of the group, temporarily imposing a herd mentality. The instinct could be ignored if necessary, but in this case, it meant survival.

Once they were into the darkness beyond the encampment, Vulture stepped up the pace to a trot, which was about as fast as he dared risk. He would have liked to have made twelve kilometers or more by first light, but he would settle for six to eight.

The predawn light revealed a desolate landscape: barren mountains, rocky desert, and only occasional scrub brush. They were all tired, hungry, and thirsty—particularly thirsty—but only Ikira could see and appreciate the entirety of the landscape. A small gully about nine kilometers from Cochin Center had shallow water in it, and Vulture risked allowing them all to stop and drink. In spite of their protestations, though, he told them, "We cannot linger or rest, and there is little to eat here. All that we need is in a cave in the low Yiabinnas to the southwest. Draw upon your inner strength. Say your *mantras* and follow."

"But I am Chinese," Chow Dai grumpily reminded him. "A Hindu body does not make a Hindu mind."

They all groaned but they followed him through the stream and off into the distance. Within a few minutes, though, it was light enough for them to dispense with the rope, and Vulture took the precise time to curl it back up and stuff it into a pack. The ground was barren, but hard, and there would be no tracks from this point on, and he wanted to leave no artifacts, either. Durga would be up and about by now, and if there was any sort of automatic monitoring of that tracking device, the alarm would even now be going up, and they were painfully exposed and without cover. There was no way around it. Short of the actual theft itself, this was to Vulture the most dangerous part of the entire exercise, and, with light, he could pick up the pace.

By eight in the morning, when the curators would be opening the museum, they were over thirty kilometers from Cochin Center. Entirely on all fours, even when pregnant, Janipurians could really make time. The last part, however, was slow and involved some climbing. It was not difficult, but they were dead tired and missteps could still happen.

Suddenly there was an increasingly loud sound, like that of an incredibly huge flying insect, gaining on them. They all heard it, but Vulture called out, "Lie down on your bellies and flatten out and be still! That's a flyer!"

Soon there was not just one flyer, but two, looking to Ikira like huge dragonflies. She had rolled off of Vulture and lay face up at a slight angle, watching the sky. The Janipurian bodies blended well with the gray-white of the hills, and she could be whatever coloration she had to be.

"They are criss-crossing most of the plain," she told them. "I think we left it just in time."

"Do you think they will see us?" Chow Dai asked worriedly.

"I would doubt it. I have done aerial surveillance myself and it is very, very difficult to spot anything from the air that does not panic or want to be spotted. Often it is difficult to see people who are *trying* to be noticed. Just lie still. How far is your cave, Vulture?"

"Not far now. Just a kilometer or so over the crest, no more."

"We may have a long wait before getting to it." She was looking at an angle from the rising sun and the bright light was nearly blinding her, forcing her to shut her eyes. "Just relax and wait it out. We might as well get some rest."

One of the flyers approached and flew almost directly

over them at an altitude of perhaps a hundred meters, but it was going very fast.

"Think they saw us?" Sabir asked.

"Just relax," Ikira said again. "They do not know where we are or even if we are here. They are trying to panic us just in case."

It seemed as if she were right, for after twenty minutes, the flyers began to move away, first parallel to the ridge line, then back in a reversal of their initial search pattern. When they had gone far enough that the noise of their engines were but a faint echo, Vulture decided to move. "Let's try for the cave. We need it."

It was definitely more than a kilometer, over terrain not well suited to the Janipurians, but at last they arrived.

The place didn't look like much from the outside. In fact, it was difficult to tell that there was a cave there at all; some fair-sized rocks masked the entrance.

The area immediately inside wasn't much to look at, and they had to go to the back to discover that there was a small passage off to the right that led farther. It was pitch-dark inside but there was no danger of getting lost; if the passage didn't open up into a larger cave, there would be no way to even turn around.

It *did* open up, of course, although Vulture had to feel for some lanterns and then light them before they could tell where they were. Even Ikira hadn't been able to see anything until then; there had been no light at all.

The cave was irregular, about six by nine meters, and it was cool and seemed somewhat damp, incongruously so considering the desert they were in. Almost half of the space was covered with straw mats and blanketing; the rest was piled high with boxes and barrels, each of which was small enough to fit the passage but had obviously been carted in one at a time. Other than the matting and containers, there were just gourd cups and bowls and very little else.

"I stumbled on the geological survey of the region," he told them. "I saw that there were a number of caves in these hills and checked them out until I found this one. It's not great but it's the best of the lot. This chamber and a few others showed up on the early surveys—no way to tell the size, though—but weren't connected to the outside. I dug the passage here, bit by bit, with an industrial laser. It was a pain to get all this stuff in here—a pain just to get it without somebody noticing in the first place—but the passage is nearly impossible to see from the outside and it's strictly one at a time in and out."

Sabir looked it over. "Yes, and it is also a very neat trap should they discover us."

"Uh uh. I've interconnected this cave with several other passages including some that lead upward, and covered the drilled openings with wood and mats. The idea is that if they come at us from the entrance, it'll take only one person to hold 'em off while we duck out, and I can blow the whole entrance with explosives if I have to. It's not very comfortable, and the cuisine will be strictly raw and natural, but it'll do. The barrels mostly contain water, but a few are *soma* and a couple of cheap but palatable wines. The boxes are airtight containers with basic foodstuffs. Sorry, no spices, and we can't risk fires. Captain, I'm sorry but I couldn't plan for you months ago, and I couldn't risk coming back here with extra supplies in the last couple of weeks. There is a box of *ava* fruit there, similar to apples, that we'll have to dedicate to you."

Sukotae shrugged. "Does anything live in these rocks?"

"Oh, yes. A fair number of insects, some small rodents that I was concerned about with the stores here, and things like that. Also you may have noticed that some birds nest in these rocky crags."

She nodded. "I'll forage, then. I think I can avoid their detectors, and, if need be, I have other defenses that might work on anything short of a Val. I'll manage."

Sabir stared at the tiny captain. "You eat . . . birds?"

"Oh, yes. Or rodents or insects. So long as they're alive or freshly killed."

"You are a—carnivore?" He made the term sound like something very unpleasant, like a vampire or ghoul.

"Omnivore, but I cannot survive forever without meat. The women of my world are not hunters, but when you're freebooting you learn survival skills. There hasn't been a freebooter freighter since the start that didn't somehow pick up some kind of rats or roaches. I've been getting by with decent synthetics on the *Thunder*, and I'll survive here."

The sudden thought of this tiny woman prowling the corridors of Cochin Center and then catching and eating rats and insects turned Sabir's stomach. It just showed how deceiving appearances were. The Janipurians looked very alien to Earth-humans, and Ikira Sukotae looked like a tiny human, yet inside, where it mattered, the captain was far less human than they. Sabir had always been pretty much of a vegetarian, but he understood and accepted those who bought or hunted and then prepared and cooked meat, but catching and eating raw, perhaps squirming, bloody animals . . .

Vulture unsealed a box of fruit and another of what looked like a variety of oats or barley, and tapped a barrel at random. It was red wine, and everyone had some. "I think you should eat and drink as much as needed, then get as much sleep as you can," he told them. "I'm going to do the same, but first I have something to take care of." He rooted around in the stockpile and came up with a small rectangular box with an antenna and connectors. "We can receive and send, within limits, and I must risk sending a five-second tone. That is the only way *Thunder* will know that we're at this position. I doubt that it'll be intercepted. None of the others have been, and my main equipment back at Center's now a mass of molten junk."

He took the transceiver and went out into the forward cave to do it. Chow Dai watched him, then looked over at the stores. "There is enough here for many weeks," she noted. "And I wonder how many more of these he has set up elsewhere?"

"Sometime tonight *Thunder*'s gonna issue a recall on that fighter he's been using out in the sticks," Ikira told them. "It'll almost surely get blasted out of the sky or else it's gonna lure a bunch of the enemy into a nasty little trap. If they don't blow it away, they'll track it to *Pirate One*, which will punch as soon as it's aboard. If they follow, they'll punch out into most of the fleet. The hope is that they'll think that's us and wind down the search parties here. Our job is just to hang on and stay clear until our people can come in and get us."

"And if they don't 'buy it,' as you say?" Sabir responded nervously. "What then?"

She sighed. "Then they have to bring in the whole fleet to get us, and that will cost." She paused a moment. "Ship-to-ship combat. Now *that* would be something! And here I am stuck down here!"

That, too, was disconcerting for a moment, sounding more like Manka Warlock, but they let it pass. The tiny captain was, after all, a freebooter. She might sneak up and kill small rodents or birds if they were smaller than she, but if one of the Janipurians just rolled over on her, she'd be crushed. She was, in fact, in a position of little power and it must have grated on her all along.

Outside, Vulture first listened carefully, then tested the air, but found nothing close by. He connected the transceiver and pushed the *send* button for five seconds, then released it. In a few minutes he'd know if their communications frequency had been discovered. He settled back to listen.

"*Thunder* to Vulture. Good work. All hell is popping loose down there from what our monitors tell us. Troops and security are out scouring the area, so lay very low. A Val ship is now in orbit, and we believe the Val is down as well. There are also two automated fighters that punched in out of nowhere. Hold tight for at least three days. Repeat, three days. We will broadcast after that at nine at night and three in the morning your time. Do not attempt to make Pickup Two unless we so instruct. Good luck."

Vulture sighed and came back into the cave. He didn't like being the hunted, not a bit, but for now he could only sit and wait.

The Val ordered a series of new satellites placed into orbit in interlockinig geosynchronous orbits, giving the SPF and Cochin Center a complete and instantly updated map of the entire continent. The continent, however, was thickly populated a hundred and fifty kilometers or so from the Center, and individual surveillance was simply not possible or practical. The searchers showed up the same as the quarry.

At two-seventeen in the morning, the fighter that had served Vulture so well as a supply and support system powered up and immediately rose into the sky. It was instantly noted by the new satellite network and tracked, and the automated fighters were placed on instant call. They reconized the craft and realized that it most likely could not contain the people they sought, but it might contain the ring. The Master System craft never even allowed *Pirate One* to show itself; they blasted the tiny pirate ship as soon as it cleared the atmosphere.

Master System's logic was clear. Transmuters required

murylium, and murylium could be detected by the satellite net. Since none had been, the odds were that even if the tiny craft carried a transmuter, it was not used, nor was there any ship in orbit that could have received such a transmission—it would have been easily detected from the start and dealt with. Therefore, the fighter was a diversion or an attempt to get the ring away. Either way, it wouldn't lead the searchers where they wanted to go.

The Val back at Cochin Center now faced Colonel Privi, the commander of the Janipurian SPF detachment.

"The three locals I can accept," the Val said icily. "Two of them pregnant yet! What a bold stroke! I forgive you missing them. Did you know that the sister, Sedowa, does not even exist? Her records are all very complete and very thorough—I can tell you her whole life's story—but when the family is asked, they acknowledge no such daughter?"

"I have heard. They are clever."

"I suspect, then, that the two females are probably Chow Mai and Chow Dai, on the original list. We will update our data on them to reflect that they are now Janipurians. Certainly the best choice—ignorant peasants, not even with very high IQs, but they have one of those inexplicable inborn talents for locks. Very well. The male could have been any one of them. It doesn't matter. For all that, they have succeeded! And in the one way you did not anticipate, Colonel. A leak, a mole, right here in security!"

"Yes, but Deputy Chief Boil! The second in command of security here for the past five years! How did they do it? How did they even get to such a man, let alone corrupt him like this? The others might be switched, duplicates, but none of it would have been possible without the aid of a known and established official of the highest rank. They did not switch him, I will stake my life on it! As is the case of many high officials including myself, Boil could not be mindprinted without an elaborate code known only to the chief administrator and Master System. It would have killed him instantly otherwise. Also, he is a lifelong friend of the chief of security and many others of the highest levels here and continued to socialize with them. That *was* Boil!"

"Impossible. Boil was always in and out of here, often for long periods and often alone. Who knows how long he has been setting this all up? They could have pulled the switch at any point. How they got around the codes and the nuances is disturbing, but it is the only possible explanation. Men like Boil do not simply go over any more than SPF officers could! Why, to even harbor such a thought would be to undermine the very basis by which our system of civilization operates! No, there had to be a switch, and early on. His duties often took him out alone before they could possibly have targeted him. They just took a man with a flyer assuming he was high echelon and got lucky, that's all."

"As you say," the colonel responded in a tone that indicated that he did indeed continue to harbor such thoughts. "However, I wish it on the official record that I recommended that we substitute a duplicate for the ring, and I was overruled."

The Val sighed a very human-sounding sigh. "Colonel, what is on the record is beside the point. You feel yourself blameless and your advice untaken and you wish to defend your reputation and that of your men. I accept that. The fact is, we could not substitute a false ring for the real one. It is impossible. Please don't ask me why, but it is. Otherwise I'd have all the other rings rounded up and locked inside Master System itself. We *did* think the tracker would do the job."

"We weren't even fully set up to monitor it. Damn it, we only just put it in! Boil stuck it on his pet falcon. We shot it down more than two hundred kilometers east of there thinking it might be trained to transport the ring, but it was only the lining. That sort of trick wouldn't fool someone for ten seconds if he could pull off a crime of this enormity in the first place. Imposter or not, this Boil is highly competent and dangerous."

"I agree, and it is good that we must face him only here; I would not like such a one planning future operations. From the start we have vastly underestimated these people. Ten people with little combined space experience break out of a maximum security prison on an asteroid and somehow get around all the automatic defenses, commandeer, then steal a universe ship. The head of security of the prison gives chase and vanishes with them. Months later he appears leading the escapees. They are cornered in space by one of my brethren, and manage to outmaneuver and vanquish him. They escape a second by a cleverness approaching the diabolical. They manage to find and then seize a hundred tons of murylium and the ship carrying it, and now this. It leads to startling conclusions."

"It certainly means that these are the most extraordinary people we have come across in centuries," the colonel agreed. "And the most dangerous."

"True, but it is more than that. It appeared at first to be a petty plot by Earth's chief administrator. We suspect it but can not prove it, and we prefer to keep him in place as he has a ring himself."

"Ah!"

"It is now clearly more than that. Somewhere out here, and it cannot be by accident, all of them met a higher power, someone who saw their tremendous genius and elaborated on Chen's plot to make it very possible and very real. The system has met its first worthy opponent. The first one that can give us a real challenge. We must assume that they are now fully in league with the enemy no matter whether they did it voluntarily or not."

"I have been aware of an enemy and a war, but the SPF was never committed to it, so I know nothing else about it."

"Nor I. It is being fought on a plane and in places where such as you and I are useless. Clearly up to now it has been a stalemate, and the enemy is trying to get around the stalemate using humanity. Whether this whole business was instigated by the enemy from the start or merely co-opted as a target of opportunity is beside the point. We are now in the war, and the enemy has discovered a weak link in our armor. Colonel, we must have these people. Any and all resources are at the disposal of the SPF, and all Vals have been redirected to this task."

The colonel threw his hands in the air. "Take a look at the maps. It's been three days now. Even assuming no ground transportation—and considering the skill of these people, I would not be shocked to find a continental railway system buried deep underground just for their use—they could be anywhere in a ten-thousand-square-kilometer grid from here. That begins to include some relatively dense population areas, and they will most certainly be in disguise and following a prescribed route."

"You forget that the two women are pregnant. Increasingly so. There is good reason to deduce that they acted when they did becaue in a few weeks neither of the Chows would have been in any condition to help."

"A Janipurian woman can move quite well even when extremely pregnant. And it's no special thing here. The average colonial world has a population of a half to three quarters of a billion people, many much less. This one has a higher death rate than average—and the inhabitants a shorter life span—and nonetheless it has almost two billion people. About one in six Janipurian women of child-bearing years seems to be pregnant at any given time."

The Val had not been briefed to this degree, and it startled the great hunting machine. "Well, they are Brahmans, a very small percentage in the field. That narrows it somewhat."

The colonel sighed again. "Sir, may we assume that none of these people were born and raised in the Hindu faith, and none have accepted it?"

"A reasonable assumption. If the Chows are anything they're Buddhists, and we have no idea who the other two are, but there were no Hindus in the group."

"Then I submit that anyone this clever would store away a supply of hair dye sufficient to treat all four. Change their caste and you change everything."

"Hmmm... A point well taken. And what caste would you suspect they became?"

"Offhand I would make myself a Ksatriya—the secular leadership, with a fair amount of freedom of actions and movement. However, they could just as easily be Vaisyas, which would have them as skilled laborers or artisans. If they wanted to blend in and had good cover and information, even a Sudra would do. In short—any color but black."

"I see. Then you are saying it is hopeless?"

"Not at all. We will keep up the search for a while just in case, but I have little hope here. However, we can keep them bottled up on this world until they settle down and grow old and die. I would wager, however, that that fighter was nothing more than the ship they used to get in here and contained nothing of value. I would bet they still have the ring. If the pirates had the ring they might be content to leave them here—they are, after all, permanently fixed as Janipurians. But I don't think the ring has left Janipur. If not, then we need only sit and wait for however long their patience lasts, and my troops have nothing else to do. If we wait, sooner or later they will have to make a move, either down here or from space. We don't have to find them. We need only wait until they are forced to expose themselves."

4. It's the Little Things That Get You

THE GROUND SEEMED TO VIBRATE, AS IF SOME DISTANT rockslide had rumbled down the side of the hills. A few minutes later it began to shake harder, then harder yet, and they began to be concerned.

"What is that?" Ikira Sukotae asked.

"I don't know," Vulture replied, "but I don't like it."

"Could be one last trick to drive us out," Sabir suggested.

"I'm going out to see." Ikira said. "I know this hill pretty well now—they won't see me. Wait here." And, with that, she scampered past them and out the passage.

The vibrations continued, getting a little stronger each time, and they waited for a report. Vulture had already decided that if the captain wasn't back in five minutes he was going after her.

She ran back in, out of breath. "They're going along both sides of the ridge in squads and tossing explosives into the caves they find. Then they look inside and go on to the next. They'll be here in maybe ten minutes."

"Roll back the mats and open the escape route!" Vulture ordered sharply. He got his gun and tossed another to Sabir. "How far into the caves are they coming?" he asked the captain.

"Not far. They're moving too fast. I think this is just a routine exercise. If we're in one they'll either stun or kill us or scratch it off their list. They aren't taking enough time to do more than shine a light in when the dust clears."

He thought furiously for a moment. "We should stick it out. When the explosions get very close everybody open their mouths and cover their ears and keep quiet! I'll cover the passage just in case—Sabir, you cover the escape tunnel. If I shoot, everybody get down there as fast as you can and keep going. I'll catch up—but they won't."

They waited, agonizingly, as the vibrations and the sounds of explosions came to them, the vibrations much stronger than the sounds. Finally they heard the distant voices of troopers shouting to one another, then there was a silence, quickly broken by three very loud explosions. The air moved forcefully down the passage and brought with it dust and dirt, and it was all they could do to keep from coughing, but they managed. The troops evidently waited for the dust to settle and then shined floodlights into the cave itself but did not enter. Everyone inside the inner cave held their breath, and then there was the sound of more men shouting and then an explosion a bit more distant and on the other side. Within minutes it was clear that the force had moved on, but they kept quiet and on guard until all sounds ceased.

Some of the crates had been knocked over and a few gourd dishes had been disturbed and cracked but nothing else seemed damaged. Finally Ikira whispered, "I'm going to check."

"But you're unarmed! If they left a guard . . ." Vulture left it unfinished.

"I can take care of myself. I'm a lot less obvious than any of you. They don't even know a creature like me exists."

She wasn't out very long. "It's getting close to sundown and I think they were just in a hurry to get it done. It sounds like they're running flyers up and down the ridge, probably with sophisticated infrared and other detectors to see if anyone pops out, but they can't keep that up for long."

Vulture nodded. "It's their last gasp, I think."

"Then—we will finally be moving out of this hole?" Chow Dai asked hopefully.

"Yes. I think it is time. I had several different plans for escape and set up a number of pickup points. I also have some elaborate disguises that would probably work. Twenty percent of the young females on this world are pregnant anyway. But I hadn't counted on having Captain Sukotae with us."

"You'd be surprised how well I can stay hidden," she assured him. "I have no natural weapons, but you would be surprised how well my defenses work. They were bred on a far more hostile world than this one, and they have served through the worst of occasions."

"Admirable, and probably true," he admitted, "but it isn't Janipur I'm worried about, nor those troopers, although they're more of a problem with their sophisticated devices and sensors. You wouldn't fool a Val for a moment—it knows all the colonial races and automatically senses them, or so I'm assured, and having gotten this far, a Val will come whenever we are spotted. Even I am powerless against a Val unless I can get the drop on it."

"No one can take a Val one on one," Sabir asserted. "It just isn't possible. Everybody knows that. A whole group with the best of weapons could, certainly, but as soon as the loss was sensed by Master System, there would be two Vals following, and more after that, with whatever added forces and weapons were needed."

Vulture smiled. "If I had a Val with its back to me, ignorant of my presence, and I had a common military laser like those here, I think I could take it. As for the loss sensors, it seems to be some kind of small device with its own punch power and capable of independent action and great speed. Nagy and I saw the module exit when we blew the Val ship. I don't know what sort of tiny mechanism it is, but it's at least the size of a fist and must power up and exit the Val when it's dead."

The idea was unnerving. "A Val soul," Sabir whispered.

"A Val is a thing of metals and plastics and other artificial parts. It is a machine, nothing more, although a great one and a thinking one. Its soul, as you call it, is also just a mechanical device, a recorder with whatever power it needs to get it to where it can report, nothing more. I can not see or sense your soul, if such a thing exists, but this is solid, material, and manufactured. What is solid and tangible can be destroyed."

"So? And if you do? What then? There is still the SPF, and that Val might not be the only one in the area, considering what we did."

He nodded. "There are two Vals. One has been alternating between the command ship and Cochin Center ever since the Troopers arrived. The other is acting as a sort of messenger boy and consultant going among SPF General Staff, the Janipur command ship, and Master System itself. So, that's two Vals, the command ship, and the two automated fighters—a hell of a good force, even against us. We can assume they have a few other automated pieces of nastiness waiting for the signal to come in as well. The troopers here are the Janipurian Division, racially the same as us and therefore of only marginal use elsewhere. They can stay here forever if they have to, and SPF won't miss them. The Vals and fighters are machines, and machines have infinite patience. They will simply wait for us to be drawn into a fight."

"What you are saying," put in Ikira Sukotae, "is that the only way we can get out is by playing their game, doing exactly what they want in the first place—forcing all of us into a head-to-head battle. That's fine planning!"

"If we didn't get the ring, the rest didn't matter," he responded defensively. "Frankly, we knew it'd be tough getting out, but we didn't really think it was a problem we couldn't solve when we saw the forces against us. Now I am considering the alternatives. We can go on as planned to Pickup Two, Three, and so on, until we tire of it or settle down and rot—or get desperate and call for that battle. Or we can have the fight sooner and eliminate all that wasted time."

"And lose," Sabir commented gloomily.

"Perhaps, but we have a few things on our side. We will pick the time. If we are willing to take some risks, we can also even the odds a bit."

"Risks," Sabir repeated. "What sort of risks?"

"Capture. Imprisonment, perhaps. They would not interrogate you here, you realize. We all know too much about the rings and their purpose. They would remove you to the command ship. The local Val and the local commander, a fellow named Colonel Privi, would handle it personally. They would have to . . ."

"I don't mind risks, but I don't like that 'you' stuff," Ikira said. "Us, not you?"

"Oh, I would be there with you all the way. That's the beauty of it. The problem is, I would have to have extensive communications with *Thunder* for it to work, and I don't think even now that I can risk any long-term transmissions from here. It is less than a day's trot from here to the edges of civilization. Two days southwest of here I have another hideout, better situated and more comfortable. With a bit of disguising, I think we can all make it to that one. I have the materials here for the disguises and the necessary maps, even some currency."

"There's bound to be a hue and cry over us," Chow Dai pointed out. "Wanted—two men traveling with identical twin sisters, both pregnant."

"We will not travel together. We are two males and two females so we pair up naturally, and no one will notice identical twins if they are not next to each other. Each pair will take a slightly different route to avoid any smart people getting wrong thoughts. I am unconcerned about the pregnancy aspect; there are close to a billion and a quarter people on this continent and growing rapidly in spite of a fairly high infant mortality rate. Maybe one in six women are pregnant at any one time on the average. Once we are in some sort of civilization, we will blend in and the searchers know it. If we make the real world from here, they won't get us. They will wait for us to make a move. Come—Sabir, help me with this black barrel. The applicators are over in that box."

They got out the barrel and the box, and the lids were removed. Sabir shook his head and sighed. "Vaisya. Must you step us down so much?" The dye color was a reddish brown.

"We can't go as Brahman. That would be like transmitting our presence and we could never move unobtrusively. Ksatriyas, as the political and professional leaders, have friends, higher education, and they stand out. They will be expecting us to use Ksatriya, and so it won't be long until the first slip brings them down on us. Sudra is simply too low and lacks mobility, although it's the largest caste and would provide the greatest invisibility. Captain Sukotae,

you will travel with me but you'll have to forage and fend
for yourself. We will work something out. Chow Dai, you
will go with Sabir; Chow Mai with me. We will go sepa-
rately at intervals as soon as we seem ready."

Sabir stared at Vulture. "You are enjoying this, aren't
you? You are really enjoying this."

"It is the most fun I have had in my whole life," he
admitted unapologetically.

Sabir and Chow Dai walked slowly down a road that
was little more than a dirt track between fields of grain
planted across very low rolling terrain. Here and there
would be a small Sudra village, its modest adobelike
houses made from the inhabitants' own dung and baked
and formed as bricks. The hordes of insects, particularly
flies, filled even a quiet time with a low buzz that changed
in pitch now and again. The villages were based around
communal wells, the wells usually being located in the
center of the settlement and creating a broad town square
that was filled with women getting water and often just
talking as young children romped and laughed and played
all about, looking more like four-footed animals with
strange heads than anything else.

The odors were the hardest to get used to after the clean
and filtered air of the Center and, before that, the even
more purified air of the spaceships, but they were starting
to adapt to it. The peasant organization itself was quite
familiar to Chow Dai, although her people lived in small
homes of bamboo, wood, and straw. Her *old* people, she
thought, almost longingly. These were her people now.

Her primary thoughts were of the child within, which
moved and kicked from time to time. She had never really
thought of becoming a mother since she'd been fairly
small, but now it seemed very important to her, the most
important thing in the world. She could still stand if she

had to, but she no longer wanted to do so and feared that it would risk undue pressure on the child. She was becoming more and more dependent on Sabir as a result, but this didn't really bother her. Other than giving the seed, the only real purpose she saw for Janipurian males was to protect the women during this period and through birth and the first month. She did not think of it as being subordinate, but rather as her due.

They had been given a bag of coins by Vulture that was more than adequate for anything they might need; indeed, it was the equivalent of a half a year's average income for these people. Sabir had more common sense than to show it or the pistol around, and kept them in a backpack. He kept just two coins, medium denominations with an incarnation of Vishnu on one side and a stylized Janipurian hairy elephant on the other, in the waist pouch for normal purchases. Many of the people in this small town were so poor that any more than a small amount would be an open invitation to thievery.

At first the proprietor had denied there were any rooms, but the sight of both coins, worth about four times the regular rental rate, caused her to change her mind and find something out back. It was a small, dung-adobe one-room cottage with straw for a floor and some well-worn mats for furnishings, but it was adequate. The inn's large outhouse was but a few meters away and the inn had piped-in well water with a "guest pump" just out back. A small alcohol lamp was the only illumination.

Sabir unpacked and removed the purse, removed two more coins, then stuck the purse in his pack. "I'm going to have to go out and get us something to eat," he told her. "I shouldn't be long. I don't like to leave the pack unguarded and I think we should just relax here and get some rest for the journey tomorrow. We are still far too close to take any risks. You saw how they looked at us just because we were strangers."

Chow Dai nodded. "Go ahead. I will be all right here."

They had not started until midday and now it was close to sundown in the town. The marketplace itself was officially closed now, but there were still enough vendors open to assemble some food. Although Sabir had had a harder time learning to be a Janipurian than the sisters, he had almost completely assimilated his thinking to the native culture in a way the sisters had not. Also, he felt very comfortable as a male, something the Chows could never comprehend. The Chows had been born peasants of peasant stock in a Chinese village no higher in culture than this one; a society that was protective, safe, and where everything was clearly structured. Sabir had a rougher upbringing and had always envied her brothers their freedom of movement and their confidence. Sabir had always been small and somewhat frail and had always felt a level of fear and vulnerability to those strange places and practically naked and defenseless on a dark street. There was no such feeling now.

There was more trouble getting change than finding things to eat at the marketplace, even though it was shutting down. Few patrons here used money; it was mostly a barter economy, with money something out-of-towners brought now and again. For a five-rupee coin, he was able to arrange not only to purchase decent food but to have a local woman prepare it and then bring it to the cottage. It was significant only that no one asked any questions, and that no one seemed particularly interested in his features as if comparing them to, say, a wanted poster.

The local dishes, when they arrived, were not the best cuisine, but they would do, particularly when washed down with some rather potent local Janipurian beer that eased fears, aches, and pains. It most likely had some mild herbal drug mixed in that made one feel happy and content after a hard day working the fields, but it was not of great concern. If any alarms were raised, there was nothing either of them could do about it, so there seemed little purpose in worrying or standing guard. It made Chow Dai relaxed and somewhat softer, gentler, even romantic. Sabir found himself fantasizing about having a mindprinter to himself for just a little while and removing Chow Dai's rough past and making her like this always. Deep down, he knew he should be ashamed of himself for thinking that way, but the fact was that was his ideal way to live the rest of his life. Chow Dai would probably have been appalled at this had she known, but as she did not, both slept better than they had since this whole business started.

It was near the end of the third day out when they reached their destination. They had not rushed, first because there seemed no need and second because it was pleasant to be out and not feel, for the moment, in imminent jeopardy of their lives. Chow Dai took the opportunity to talk with some of the more experienced mothers in the small villages, not only to find out what to expect as the pregnancy progressed but also to pick up some sense of what she would be dealing with in a Janipurian baby. She was also delighted when Sabir stopped at a local marketplace and bought her some small jewelry and trinkets. It was crude, peasant stuff, but to her it was like diamonds.

Pickup Two was a small cottage in a forest near a stream and well off the roads. The land was technically owned by a local maharajah, who, like most, was an absentee landlord. This was the edge of the jungle and not a place where people usually came; the trail was partly overgrown and difficult to negotiate. They had expected to find the others already there, but it was clear from both the condition of the trail and the state of the little cottage that no one had preceded them. The cottage itself was barren-looking and uninviting, and no one who didn't know could guess that the floor was false and under it was another cache of Vulture's supplies. It was adequate, although far smaller a store than Pickup One.

"I am worried," Chow Dai said. "I think I would know if something really bad had happened to my sister, but that means little. Could they have run into trouble, do you think?"

"I don't know," Sabir replied honestly. "The best we can do is settle in and keep out of sight and wait. They might have taken a longer route, or the weather could have delayed them, or a hundred other things. They had to keep the tiny captain hidden and supplied, as well, remember, so they were camping out and using the markets only sparingly. We will wait until they arrive or we are more certain something is wrong. There is enough here to last us a week, perhaps two."

"And if they do not come? What then?" Neither of them had the ring.

"If that comes, we will face it then."

The others did not come that night, and the next day Sabir took inventory of Vulture's stores. There was a lot more equipment here—some nastier weapons, a sophisticated communications link, and even a portable mind-printer from Janipurian security. There were a number of cartridges with it, mostly of the security type, including one marked "hypno," a security staple. Unlike the other cartridges, it wasn't a permanent program—although it could be made so with larger and more complex lab mind-printers and computers or by long-term consecutive treatments—but anyone put under with it and given suggestions would then obey those suggestions for a good five to seven days, staunchly maintaining that black was white and the sky was on the floor if that's what they were told.

And if they do not come? What then? Oddly, almost ashamedly, the question was a turn-on. Chow Dai was familiar with the uses of mindprinters and was now quite trusting of Sabir, but she couldn't operate or read the names on the cartridges. Repeated treatments as long as the power pack lasted . . . No! That was evil. It was one thing to fantasize, another to contemplate actually doing something of that nature. Vulture had called him selfish and that was certainly true, but selfish did not necessarily have to mean evil. Two more days, and then he would string the communications net among the trees and attempt to call *Thunder*.

Chow Dai stirred, then awoke. It was quite dark, far too dark to see anything, but her ears and her old sixth sense sounded a warning that something was not quite right. For a moment she wondered if it was just her imagination, but her keen Janipurian ears strained and caught what had awakened her and she stirred.

"Sabir! Wake up!" she hissed.

"Huh? Wa—?"

"Someone is coming! I can hear the sounds of steps crushing twigs and leaves along the path!"

Suddenly Sabir was fully awake and reached for the pistol, then moved around and got up on his feet. He stood, facing the door, not quite knowing what to do. He was totally blind in the darkness, but if he risked lighting the lantern, he might betray their presence to someone who otherwise might not know they were there. If he shot when and if the door opened, he might cut down those for whom they waited, but if he didn't, he might have no chance to avoid capture in case it was someone else. He thought quickly, then decided that while Vulture had prepared a number of things in this cabin just right, he had certainly neglected to provide any back exit that Sabir had been able to discover. The gun might prove an intimidator or even an equalizer, but there was no purpose in shooting unless there was some way to escape.

"You—you think it's them?" Chow Dai whispered.

"Shhhhh . . . Quiet." In fact, he did not think it was Vulture and the others. The footsteps, getting quite close now, had a far different sound than a Janipurian would make, and if it was Sakotae, she had gained a hundred or more kilograms someplace.

The footsteps ceased at the door and they both held their breath. This was not anyone friendly; they knew that now. Vulture would have sent Sukotae to check in silence, then come in boldly himself through the front door.

The door opened slowly, and both Sabir and Chow Dai expected to see the strange, illuminated form of a living being through their infrared abilities, but the picture they received was a strange one, with great heat coming from two glowing eyes and otherwise only in spots along a very tall humanoid torso.

"You might wish to light the lamp for yourself," the Val said calmly. It spoke Janipurian Hindi flawlessly and in a calm, clear male voice. "I can see you perfectly well but there is no reason to have you at a disadvantage."

Sabir was less surprised than let down as his worst fears were realized, a sinking feeling setting in that the inevitable had finally happened. You couldn't escape a Val. Everybody knew that. And here they had been taking on not just one but two. Sure, they'd nailed one ship-to-ship, but it had killed Arnold Nagy in the process and was no sure thing until it was already over. More a one-of-a-kind freak than a sure victory. He considered for a moment trying to shoot Chow Dai and then himself to at least keep the information out of Master System's hands, but even that was folly. He might get her, or himself, if the Val wasn't expecting it—and it probably was—but not both, and what good would one death do?

He put down the pistol, fumbled, found the match, and with some difficulty, lit the lamp. He was surprised at how calm and steady his hand was, however, once he could see. It was almost as if a great burden had been lifted from his soul.

"You have captured the others?" he asked the Val.

"Alas, no, but we will, sooner or later. We staked you out here the last two days hoping to net the whole crew, but it was decided that they were not coming, that they had probably seen our stakeout in spite of all our precautions and been scared away."

"Then—you were not on to us from the start. You discovered *us*, not the whole group."

"Yes. Brahman in Cochin Center have little use for money, as you know, so a small amount is kept in security just in case it should be needed. The coins are newly minted. Your accomplice Boil took seven hundred and sixteen rupees, a considerable sum, but they were of a larger than usual denomination for poor places such as the ones you went through and all, I fear, have slight defects in them. That is why they were sent to security from the mint rather than placed in general circulation. Not even the chief administrator himself knew this—it was a simple economy move by the mint. We had paid agents about, of course, looking for any stranger within a few hundred kilometers of Cochin Center who might be spending newly minted coins of large denominations. We really didn't expect to net anyone that way—although we thought we might be able to locate you later wherever in the world you turned up. Uh—I assume the lady is one of the Chows, but who might I be speaking to?"

He sighed. "I was Sabira, a freebooter crew member.

Now I am what you see, without a proper name or identity of my own."

"A freebooter! So they have freebooters on their side now," the Val responded, sounding very human and seeming to talk aloud only to himself. "I knew that breaking the covenant would cause a price to be paid. Master System eliminated a nuisance and appears to have created an army. How many, I wonder? Don't answer—that's for later. We decided that two of you in hand with information we desperately need was worth blowing this probably eternal stakeout. Uh—I don't suppose you have the ring, do you?"

"No. I had it, but I returned it. That's the truth, too."

"Oh, I believe you," the Val assured him. "There is no reason to lie now, is there?"

"Would it be too much to ask," Chow Dai interjected, "what is to become of us?"

"Well, that depends," the creature replied, still keeping that friendly, conversational tone. "For a while, you will be useful to us, I think. We will return to Cochin Center at first, then take a little trip up to a ship we have in orbit. Then we will find out what you know and evaluate that data. After that, you might be of further service to us and you might not. If so, we might do a little attitudinal adjusting to set you back on the true path to harmony and stability. When you are of no further use, our skilled technicians will erase your current memories and create new, permanent identities for you with, of course, some slight genetic manipulation to you and your offspring that will be consistent with, shall we say, a lowered status. But you, and your child, will be here, happy, for the rest of your days if you give no trouble. Of that I assure you. I will not promise you more than a Sudra's life, but if you are cooperative and cause no problems I assure you that your child will not be born Untouchable."

It was a powerful threat, more powerful than threatening

either of them with bodily harm. Even Chow Dai, who thought of the Untouchables as just unfortunates and irrational outcasts in this system, knew what price a child would pay in that class. The Sudras were serfs, but that had been her origin on Earth and it was honorable and without shame. Sabir was prouder and of higher birth, but he understood and accepted the offer as the price of failure and perhaps the punishment of God that he had changed sex and form from what had been ordained. Thinking that way, and being a fervent believer in reincarnation, it was not a horrible fate, but it was severe enough for him to feel that the Val was not just playing along with them but was really sincere.

"We might as well get this over with, then," Sabir said with a sigh. "At least it will not mean any more nights sleeping here."

"Move over in the corner," the Val instructed. "I want to see what you have here."

They complied, and the huge, black creature moved to the items Sabir had brought from the cache under the floor. "Hmmm . . . A communications system. Long range, too. Encoded subcarrier via one of our own satellites, I'll bet. We will not underestimate your people again. And one of security's mindprinters, too! I could use that on you—but I shall not. We should make this as honorable as possible. Worthy foes deserve respect, and we get very few of them." It turned back to the door. "Sergeant!"

A Janipurian with the uniform of the SPF entered. He was wearing some sort of headgear and goggles that apparently gave him limited vision in the darkness. "Sir!"

"You have called for the flyer?"

"It cannot land in here. We must move back toward the road for safe clearance. Not far—a kilometer or so. It should be here in fifteen to twenty minutes. They are not well designed for night flying, you know."

"Very good. Now, everyone out of here, please. Sergeant, see that this is sealed and then join us."

The sergeant looked dubiously at the prisoners. "Are you sure, sir? All but one of my men are down at the landing site right now . . ."

The Val chuckled. "Don't worry, sergeant. They won't escape me. Carry on."

The Val switched on a light that seemed to grow from someplace inside of it and afforded them a measure of visibility. They walked in front of it, the whole forest eerily illuminated. Suddenly the Val said, "Halt! Freeze! There is something here, something not right . . ."

Both Sabir and Chow Dai felt it, too. There was a sudden, deadly silence in the darkness and then, from forward and to their right a young girl's voice came to them ghostly in the night, a playful voice singing, and in English!

> "Ring around the rosy,
> pocket full of posey,
> Ashes, ashes,
> All fall down!

Sabir and Chow Dai were confused and frightened, but they were old hands enough to take the hint. Both dropped immediately to the ground. Almost instantly, there was the crack and flash of multiple laser pistols from behind; purplish beams shot out and struck the Val—who had turned and directed its sensors toward the chanting—directly in the small of the back, just above where its rectum should have been. Twin beams, criss-crossing rapidly, and doing damage.

The Val made a terrible, inhuman sound and tried to turn, but it seemed frozen at the waist, unable to move. It was not defenseless; return laser fire shot from its back, but the fire wasn't directed or locked on to the incoming fire as

it was designed to be but rather wild and random. Sparks
flew as its wild beams struck trees and leaves and started a
few small fires.

Chow Dai decided it was safer to take chances than to
continue there. She got quickly to all four feet and
screamed "Run" as she kicked off. Sabir was slower but
followed. The Val ignored them and began flailing around
violently, continuing its wild and undirected fire. A second
set of beams now struck it from the front, concentrating on
the lower abdomen.

The Val stopped shooting and began simply gyrating
about. The light flickered and died, and in the darkness the
great shape began to go mad. Tentacles shot from it and
groped around wildly in the dark at fantastic speed; small
balls of energy were launched and struck nearby trees and
exploded with incredible force, the concussions deafening.
The sound it made, both metallic and at the same time that
of a mortally wounded beast, rose in pitch as the fire continued to pour in from both directions. Suddenly there was
a horrible, grating sound of metal against metal; the great,
glowing crimson eyes flickered, faded, and died, and, as if
in slow motion, the gyrations and convulsions ceased, and
it quivered, then fell with a crash to the forest floor. The
firing continued for a few more seconds, then stopped.

"Stay away!" called the voice of the sergeant. "I want
that escape module, as well! Switch to wide disruptor setting like I showed you!"

Inside the Val, the independent automatic circuits determined that the unit was no longer functional. Automatic
backup of the memory core had commenced with the first
assault, and was now completed. Draining all remaining
power from the Val's circuits, the information module
powered up and began to bore its way through the Val's
structure, its normal route of escape blocked. The heat

generated by the friction in doing this was a dead giveaway to someone who could see in the infrared.

"Wait for it, but don't let it fly!" the sergeant warned.

It was out now: a bright, glowing ball of shining crystal a bit larger than an average man's fist. It glowed with such intensity that it hurt their eyes to watch it, but they immediately opened fire.

The ball shimmered from the assault, then began to rise slowly as they kept their beams trained on it. For a moment it looked as if it were going to get away, but it seemed to be having problems and began to wobble, then vibrate violently.

The explosion was so intense that it deafened all those nearby and knocked them down; trees snapped and there was a rain of debris, and the noise echoed off into the distance.

As soon as he regained his wits, the sergeant got to his feet, holstered his pistols, and kicked off down the trail, running right past the still-smoldering remains of the Val. A bit farther down, Chow Mai met him and they both raced out of the now-burning forest and into the fields. Ikira Sukotae waited atop Chow Dai; only a few meters away the charred bodies of four SPF troopers lay where they had fallen.

"Let's hit it!" the sergeant yelled, still deaf from the last explosion. "We want to be as far away from here as we can as soon as possible! Just key on Chow Dai and keep going!"

They had gotten only a few hundred meters when, behind them in the burning forest, there was a second massive explosion and a fireball that reached above the treetops. Investigators would get very little of use from Pickup Two.

With adrenaline flowing and thought too confused to be worthwhile, they ran into the night as fast as they could.

* * *

Sabir stared at the man who rescued them and shook his head. "I still cannot believe that we actually got away. I cannot even believe that you are the Vulture. How?"

"The Vulture can be whatever he wants to be," was the reply. "The Chows know it. You were told that I was not —human. In a sense, I am less human than that Val back there."

They camped in the trees well away from the previous night's actions. There were massive searches underway for them, of course, but they were random and haphazard. Nobody seemed to be able to understand even how such a thing could have happened, and the SPF was more concerned with covering up the demise of a Val at the hands of mere mortals than in immediately finding the perpetrators.

The trio had taken a more circuitous, less comfortable route to Pickup Two and had arrived hours after Sabir and Chow Dai. Coming overland, they had, more by luck than anything else, discovered a spotter on a hill with monitoring gear and knew that the duo below had been compromised. It was not a large force—four enlisted men led by the sergeant and the Val—but it was more than enough had they simply walked into the trap. It had been Vulture's decision to wait and see what would happen.

The previous night, it became clear that the Val had lost patience and was going to go in. It left the three men to guard the approaches and took the sergeant and one soldier up the road, positioning them on both sides of the cabin to cover any possible surprise exits. Vulture and Chow Mai, who proved quite adept with a pistol from a braced position, easily hit the men in the open field, silhouetted as they were against the darkness by their body heat. Then Chow Mai had taken up a fixed position to one side while Ikira Sukotae had gone into the trees above the cabin to watch, warn, and guide Vulture to the first of the two troopers. The timing was delicate, but Vulture had come up behind the sergeant and consumed him while the Val was still approaching the cabin. It was a silent operation, but it took seven minutes to accomplish. Vulture wasn't certain they had the time, but figured that if the Val emerged before the process was completed, it would have been up to Vulture to suddenly catch up and play the sergeant. It had been even harder because Vulture had had to get the uniform off the sergeant while beginning the process. A naked sergeant would have had much explaining to do.

Fortunately, the Val had been in a casual, talkative mood; Vulture not only had time to become the sergeant and redon the uniform, but also to lure and then strangle the remaining trooper.

"Arnold Nagy told me how to take a Val one on one, almost with his dying breath," Vulture told them. "Of course, I had only his word for it, but it was the only chance. I admit I did weigh just riding back with you and managing things later, but I figured the dead troopers in the field would go away with just the two of you leaving the sergeant in charge of finding the killers. I have to be honest—I wasn't sure if I could keep either of you from being hurt or killed, but that just couldn't be a consideration. It sounds callous and cruel, I know, but you were better dead than captured, isolated, and interrogated for information about the others."

"I understand that," Sabir told him. "I had considered whether or not I could kill the both of us prior to that."

"I hoped that you were clever and quick enough to understand my diversion," Ikira said. "I figured that if it was in the English used on *Thunder* you would take the hint and drop."

"That allowed Chow Mai to add her fire to mine," Vulture went on. "The weak point is in the operating core of the Val—the equivalent of a brain—and that's not where you'd think it would be. The casing is well protected even against the strength we were firing, but Nagy told us to shoot at the abdominal region, front and back, and give quick back-and-forth passes. The shots jolted and disoriented it for precious seconds, and in that time the back-and-front cutting motion burned out a huge amount of the embedded neurological system. Sort of like damaging or cutting the spinal column. The brain functions but the messages don't go where they should. Those suckers are *damned* hard to kill. Even at that, we didn't so much kill it as wreck it. When it lost control the real Val, that crystal ball that was its brain and more, and which wore that body like a suit of armor, got out of its own power and quite possibly could have gotten clean away. Only when we destroyed it did we truly kill a Val."

"And now what?" Sabir sighed. "We can't use the money, they're still combing the countryside for us, and there will be more Vals. We can't keep this up forever. Sooner or later they will find us."

"I agree, and we must hurry before Master System brings in God knows what else. Still, they really don't know who or what they're dealing with and that puts them at a great disadvantage. We have proven able to massacre them, or so it will look, but they will still have orders to take us alive if they possibly can. Considering we wiped out a Val and a squad of SPF troopers, they won't be certain how many are actually here or just who they can really trust. We've got to move. We'll live off the land and avoid human contact unless absolutely necessary, choosing the harder and rougher route and avoiding the roads. We must get to Pickup Three where I can call *Thunder*. Only then will we be able to get off this planet, although I fear that it will not be without cost."

Vulture was certainly correct about the disarray of their pursuers. There was evidence in the days ahead of some heavy-handed tactics and mass arrests by the SPF that showed desperation but also were violations of all that Master System stood for. The masses of Janipur were not simply outside the reality of interstellar wars and scientific marvels, they were quite deliberately kept ignorant of it. At first the mere display of many of the tools and weapons of the SPF caused great fear and confusion, but after a little while it turned from that into anger. Master Systems' principles of colonial maintenance were well founded and based upon a long-term common sense. Security and peace equals ignorance. It was difficult enough for the Centers to weed out the budding geniuses and suppress bright new ideas that might change the status quo; now troopers marched through towns using mass communication and information systems the people had never dreamed existed. One does not show such wonders as even simple flashlights and then tell the people that they are forbidden them and should forget them. Or, rather, you can tell them, but the seed will have been planted. Nor can you wipe out such knowledge when it is shown to masses of people.

The mere fact that such things were happenng at all showed a total lack of direction and firm leadership at the top. Colonel Privi was born to be a soldier, not a diplomat or planner. It was the Vals and higher command that used such men as weapons in their arsenals, with care and caution. Left alone with a major problem and no one to temporize, the colonel was doing what he considered his greater duty without regard to cost. Either Master System was out of touch or, more chilling to Sukotae, Vulture, and the others, it no longer cared.

Nor were such methods effective. Although there were some close calls and occasional long hours hiding out, the group reached the remote and crumbling area where Pickup Three had been established without detection.

It had been one of the very first settlements, but it had

not worked out over the long centuries that followed. Weather and agriculture were far better on the plains and in the rolling hills elsewhere, and it had been abandoned and now mostly overgrown. It was the third of the four places Vulture had chosen and set up as refuges, and the fourth was over a thousand kilometers away in the mountain region where Vulture had first landed on Janipur. Vulture wasted no time in setting up his communications network and uttering a silent prayer that the channel was still open.

Thunder was delighted to hear from them and that all were safe, but their tribulations were sobering to those who waited and the news not all good.

"Another Val has come in, although they don't seem very sure of themselves any more. The Val has remained in orbit, docked to the command ship. There is no clear indication that more forces are being brought in, but it's nearly impossible to tell for sure," Hawks reported. "Now that we know where you are, I think we ought to try a probing action to see just what reserves might pop out of thin air before committing all our forces. What is the condition of your people?"

"Chow Dai is well advanced on her metamorphosis toward motherhood. Although still bright and alert, her horns measure more than a meter and she no longer has effective use of hands and feet. In effect, she is a four-legged animal with human intelligence. She is even sleeping standing up at this point, and she's still got months to go before delivery. Chow Mai is a bit behind her, but her horns are long, and any standing or use of hands is uncomfortable and limited now. They both eat a lot, almost constantly it seems, and Chow Dai tires easily and will not, I suspect, be in much condition for a long run. Have you thought about my plan for allowing our capture? If I am lucky, I might even get to eat Colonel Privi himself."

"We rate it as too dangerous," Hawks told him. "Once

captured, it is likely you all would be separated and no matter who you become, Vulture, you couldn't watch over them all. First priority would be to get a complete mind-print that would tell them your own nature and betray our best weapon, which is their ignorance of your existence. No, sit tight, unless you are discovered, and wait. Within twenty-four hours we will know if we can get you out of there or not. If not, then your plan might be the only open course."

Hawks was clearly worried, and the council of captains was no more reassured, but they were all sick of waiting.

"I tire of skulking about in the uncharted regions!" Chun Wo Har exclaimed. The freebooter colonial captain with the shiny exoskeleton and inhuman eyes was not often given to emotional outbursts. "Let us strike! My ancestors came from the same China that bred the Chows, a fountain of civilization and culture that was tramped upon by lessers because it was often too civilized to defend itself. I am of rougher stock. It is more honorable to die than to rot. I say we go get them and the hell with the cost!"

Hawks looked around. "Everybody agreed?" There was no response, but a number of nods. "Very well then." He sighed. "I just wish we had someone more experienced in naval battles."

China, who often sat in on these discussions, cleared her throat. "There is no substitute for experience," she admitted, "but common sense and good information are ninety percent of any victory. The best admirals can do little without them. We monitor the command ship, the two fighters, and the Val. The command ship is also a troop carrier; it is deadly but slow and not much of a threat. I believe we can assume that it depends, like *Thunder*, mostly on its fighters and that its own armaments are basically defensive in nature."

"I have no idea how many actual fighters such a ship

might have," Star Eagle put in, "but I feel that there are more than just the two we know about, even though they are larger and more formidable than my own. Still, I wonder. I carry twenty-four, but this ship was built in a rougher time when external enemies were the likely threat. The SPF is not used to having real enemies and in effect is as inexperienced as we are in actual ship-to-ship combat, perhaps more—since we have had to do it several times while they are probably entirely dependent on simulations. They have fought some limited ship-to-ship engagements against the freebooters but it wasn't this command that was involved. To find out if there are any more surprises waiting for us, though, we will have to commit a convincing force. They will detect any feint. Clearly any force we send in must be theoretically large enough and good enough to win or they have no incentive to bring in any reserves. At the minimum, then, it means three of our better ships along with some supplemental *Thunder* fighters. I respectfully submit that we have only six ships useful in such a fight, *Pirate One* not being fast enough to compete, and while *Espiritu Luzon* may be well armed, it's better suited to fast getaways than head-to-head combat."

Captain Paschittawal of the *Indrus* nodded to himself, a grave expression on his face. "Then you are telling us that if our feint is large enough to be credible, we cannot afford to have it defeated because we would not be strong enough to try it again."

"Essentially, yes."

Hawks sighed. "Then it's all or nothing and to hell with the reserves."

They all absorbed that in stony silence. Finally Raven said, "Chief, I ain't on this council, but it's my ass, too, and I think you got the priorities ass-backward here. Suppose we could cripple, maybe knock out that command ship? That'd leave the fighters on strictly automatic programming, and if we weren't lucky enough to nail the Val, it would still be the only one big threat but acting pretty much on its own. I mean, what kind of reserves we talkin' about? Probably more fighters, right? They wouldn't even care about human-piloted craft—this is Master System we're talkin' about—and I ain't sure they got enough Vals to have 'em sittin' dead in the water, so to speak, waitin' for some theoretical attack. I don't care if they got a hundred fighters off someplace—if there's no command ship to call 'em, then they're gonna sit."

"The Val could call them in," China noted.

"Maybe, but maybe not. The Vals are just damned machines, not gods. We already proved that twice. They're made one way 'cause that's the only way Master System makes 'em. They're arrogant, egomaniacal, and loners. Most of all, they're loners. They use people, but they're always on top and contemptuous of any of 'em. They ain't got no experience in this sort of thing, either. Now I ain't sayin' we can work this trick twice, but I bet we can pull it off this once."

They were all interested. "What do you have in mind, Raven?" Hawks asked.

"Well, first you tell them down there that we're shootin' the wad on this one, and then you tell 'em they hav'ta sit tight a little longer than we said. This'll take some doin'. It ain't gonna be easy, but a few real old tricks might do the job . . ."

5. BATTLES AND WOUNDS

THE DUTY OFFICER ABOARD THE SPF COMMAND SHIP was irritated at having been hailed by the communications CQ, and decided that it had better be really important or somebody was going to get the chewing-out of her life.

"What is it?" he growled, still asleep.

"Freighter coming in, sir."

The officer frowned. "We aren't due for a supply ship." He was suddenly very suspicious. "ID checks out?"

"Yes, sir. Special shipment from Master System itself. Large-scale transmuters and heavy processing equipment along with a fair amount of murylium ore. I guess the rumors about us being ordered to abolish the Center form of supervision are true."

The duty officer nodded, having heard those rumors himself. He knew for a fact that it had been done elsewhere and was being contemplated as a system-wide policy, but he'd also heard that those plans had been put on hold pending resolution of the current crisis. Still, it made sense here. The prey below had done an impossible amount of damage but had now slipped completely from sight and could be anywhere in the billion-plus population by now. It seemed a bit drastic to destroy an entire civilization just to nab a few rebels, no matter how brilliant or dangerous they might have been. Orders, however, were orders.

"Did you scan the ship?" he asked. The pirates were known to have an operating freighter and they all looked alike. He wanted to take no chances, even though he had the firepower to blast something as lumbering as a freighter to atoms before it could get close enough to do any damage.

"Yes, sir. Murylium count abnormally high, as would be expected, and a great deal of inert cargo. No life forms aboard."

He sighed. "What are the instructions?"

"Dock with us and offload using service robots through both cargo bays. It's all containerized, so it shouldn't take more than a couple of hours. It is diverted from a deadhead run back to its normal pickup point and has instructions to offload and be away as quickly as possible in order to keep to its normal schedule."

"Very well. Call it in to the colonel's office below and if they have no objection, give the ship immediate clearance to dock and dispatch our service robots to the offloading bays."

"Aye aye, sir."

The colonel himself was not contacted, of course, but the SPF chief of security drew the same sad conclusions as the duty officer and saw no objections. The freighter was signaled in and ordered to proceed. It approached to within forty kilometers of the orbiting command ship and then slowly eased its way closer, a maneuver that took about seventy minutes.

The command ship itself, like the freighters, was never

designed for planetfall; the freighters were loaded by transmuter transmission and, for some specialized times, by
barges and tugs from the surface of whichever planet it
happened to be orbiting. Because of this, the command
ship was designed to be supplied by just such ships, and
maneuvers like this were routine, with the pilots of both
ships using centuries-old automatic procedures. The timing
involved in the docking and equalization of pressure was
precise. With that equalization, the two large ships were
locked together as firmly as if they were welded, although
if necessary they could be separated almost instantly.

The service robots waited for the cargo-bay doors to
open, then moved forward toward the now-gaping holds of
the freighter.

In the vacuum of space, the enormous explosion, and
the subsequent explosions that followed took place in
deathly silence, but were spectacular to look at. *Pirate One*
had been packed with all the explosives Star Eagle's transmuters could crank out and *Thunder*'s robots could pack
solidly in. With the pressurization and open holds, the tremendous force of the explosions was directed primarily
into the command ship, ripping into its very heart. Yet Star
Eagle had taken no chances; the first explosions were
merely a trigger for a murylium fusion bomb of a size
never before seen; in less than three seconds both ships had
been almost totally converted to energy in an explosion so
intense that, from below, it lit up the sky and could be seen
easily with the naked eye even in daylight.

The fighters, stationed in other orbits, immediately
came to life and searched for their mother ship, but found
nothing. They were not allowed time to be confused, however; their response switched immediately to automatic and
they powered up and headed out toward the punch-points
their sensors were even now detecting.

Raven and Warlock punched in in *Lightning*, followed

almost immediately by *Kaotan, Indrus, Chunhoifan*, and *San Cristobal* in a rough V formation.

They had practiced acting as a unit, but they were still basically a collection of individual ships rather than a tightly coordinated group. The captains were experienced pilots, but none had really captained a ship going into a head-to-head battle. They were linked by an interconnection that gave them almost speed-of-thought broadcast capability at short range.

"Mother of God!" swore Maria Santiago of *San Cristobal*. "Will you look at that! My readings are off the scale!"

"Yeah, we certainly plastered that bastard," Raven agreed, "but let's not get cocky now. We still have a bunch of bad guys around and who knows what in the shadows."

"Watch it!" came the steely voice of Captain Chun. "Both fighters just did short punches. I—"

There was hardly time to calculate the punch before the fighters emerged just behind the group and fired a series of rapid bursts from their aft systems, then looped in opposite spirals and came back at the pirate fleet firing.

"I'm hit!" called Dura Panoshaka, temporarily captaining *Kaotan*. "Nothing serious but the bastards are coming back in at me!"

The V broke apart as each ship went in a different direction in broad loops. Raven brought *Lightning* up and around as Warlock was targeting the lead fighter. She allowed the automatics to begin beam fire and concentrated on trajectories for the torpedoes. "*Kaotan*! *Cristobal*! Key on the lead fighter with all you've got!" she instructed. "All others key on trailing fighter with torpedoes."

At that moment the lead fighter launched its own torpedoes, more than a dozen in a spread pattern, each obviously instructed to key in on the easiest single target. *Chunhoifan* and *Lightning* opened up on them with concentrated beam fire, but two slipped through, curled around, and went for the stern of *Indrus*. Paschittawal shifted all shielding power to the stern and broke away in a high arc. Both torpedoes exploded on or near the tail, and the ship shuddered but still seemed to be operable.

"*Kaotan*! *Cristobal*! Keep keying in on the lead fighter!" Warlock instructed, sounding very calm and very much in control. "*Kaotan*, take a spread of six at the stern, *Cristobal* amidships! *Now!*"

The fighter noted three spreads coming from three different directions, and shifted most of its shielding to its stern, which was always the most vulnerable area of a ship, but it was also forced to shoot from its bow and side guns at the onrushing torpedoes. No shield operating at anything less than maximum strength could withstand direct hits by that many torpedoes, but a ship's weapons system couldn't fire outward if the shield was on full. The fighter was doing a good job of picking off the incoming missiles, but it missed seven out of eighteen in the three groups, each of which was now headed for a different area of the ship.

Kaotan's stern shots were going to hit first, so it shifted more power to its rear shield, but at the same time, three of *Cristobal*'s shots struck weakened shields amidships and the fighter shook and trembled. *Lightning*'s two surviving torpedoes landed on the undefended bow, and the whole forward quarter of the fighter became a mass of twisted metal. With no bow, the fighter was defenseless as long as the enemy kept coming dead on, and though it tried to take evasive action, *Kaotan* poured six torpedoes straight into the guts of the ship from the bow angle. The fighter shook and then disappeared from the pirate's sensors.

The second fighter was bearing down on the shaken *Indrus*, and *Chunhoifan* was in turn bearing down on the fighter.

"All ships key in on the other fighter!" Warlock ordered. "Concentrated fire. Pour it in! Pour it in!"

"There's something else coming in at high speed," Captain Chun warned. "I can't make it out."

"Worry about it later!"

There was a limit to a shield's abilities, since shielding had never really been designed for combat situations but to protect a ship from space debris. In this case, superior numbers meant inevitable victory. A vast amount of firepower raked all parts of the remaining fighter until it exploded.

"Damage reports!" Warlock called.

"Just some bruises for us, but we have limited mobility at the moment. Right now we're seeing what we can do to make repairs," Paschittawal reported. Damage to the other ships was even more minor.

"Unknown closing in," Chun reported. "I cannot make it out, and I don't like it."

"*Chunhoifan* and we will intercept," Warlock responded. "*San Cristobal*, you stay with *Indrus*. *Kaotan*, you are to go for Pickup Three as soon as we engage. *Thunder* command, stand by to commit reserves. I don't know what this is coming in, but it's definitely the surprise they had planned."

The mysterious object continued to close and the two ships went to meet it. Its configuration indicated a multi-drive vessel that should have made it large, but it was compact—too large for a Val ship or fighter and too small for anything else. As they closed on it, the shape changed; the new enemy actually split apart and was instantly recognizable.

"Holy shit!" Raven exclaimed. "It's *two* Val ships in tandem!"

One of the Vals continued straight on, while the other peeled off and headed for *San Cristobal* and the crippled *Indrus*. These were no mere fighters; there was intelligence behind these two ships as well as great weaponry. The effect was clear from the start; the Val ship closing on *Lightning* and *Chunhoifan* suddenly executed a series of maneuvers that would have killed any humans aboard, firing off salvos and launching a spiral pattern of torpedoes at the same time with deadly accuracy. The automatics aboard *Lightning* and *Chunhoifan* were simply not prepared for things like this, and both ships were slower than the Val's, *Chunhoifan* markedly so. Both human-controlled ships were forced to take direct control of their weapons systems —but humans thought far slower than Vals even if their orders could be carried out instantly. At one against two, the Val actually had a slight advantage.

"Commit reserves! Repeat, commit reserves! Key your punch location on *Indrus*! We will—holy shit!"

The Val had suddenly changed position, almost instantaneously. By the time they realized that the enemy was using punches mere milliseconds in duration, the Val had gotten beneath them and was coming straight up between the two ships, firing heavily, counting on them to hold fire for fear of hitting each other with their rounds. The distance between the ships was enormous, but not for the weapons involved.

Warlock targeted everything she could bring to bear on a point just a hair above *Chunhoifan*'s elevation and let it fly as the Val was just coming up between them. Both *Lightning* and *Chunhoifan* shook and shuddered, and behind Raven and Warlock there was a groaning sound.

"Oh, boy! I heard that one before," he said grumpily. "We're still intact, but I don't know what's holding us together."

The Val had, however, taken a risk itself. Its speed allowed no way to avoid the salvos fired by Warlock Chun. The Val had concentrated all its fire on the two ships as it spiraled upward, and was unable to pick off the torpedoes, six of which locked on and struck home. *Lightning* was hurt, but the Val was hurt worse.

"I'm stopped in place," Captain Chun reported. "All system and drive power lost. Three dead, with a gaping hole just forward of my stern tubes."

"I've got about half power, and I'm steering a bit wobbly, but I'm serviceable," Raven responded. "We'll stick with you and give you what firepower we can, *Chunhoifan*. By the time I got back up to the *Indrus* it'd be over anyway. Where's that damned Val?"

"Forty-two degrees off the orbital plane and about twenty thousand kilometers out," Chun replied. "Looks like he's dead in space, too. That's something. If he'd made it out with even minimal drive power, we'd be finished."

"Yeah, I got him now. Maybe playing possum, maybe not. I'm going after him. Stand by your guns."

The second Val ship was having great success, as well. It had entirely ignored *Indrus* and concentrated on *San Cristobal*, scoring some solid hits while remaining untouched itself. Santiago maneuvered as close to *Indrus* as she dared to combine their firepower, but she was definitely still in trouble.

When *Bahakatan* and *Espiritu Luzon* punched in, the Val was caught by surprise, not expecting this group to have the numbers to afford reserves. It abandoned *San

Cristobal and *Indrus*, both crippled but with weapon systems still functional, and headed straight for the two newcomers. Neither of the crippled ships were going anywhere it couldn't follow, but it wanted to take on the new threat before it became trapped between the two.

It attempted an in-between spiral maneuver, similar to the one that its companion had used on *Lightning* and *Chunhoifan*, but with an added twist. It released its salvo just beneath the two ships, executed a preplanned minipunch, and came out just above and let loose a second bombardment. The trick completely fooled *Espiritu Luzon*, but Captain ben Suda of *Bahakatan* hadn't waited and launched at the high position while the Val ship was still spiraling upward. All three ships took damaging hits, although none of them was completely knocked out.

The Val assessed the results and determined that it had lost its punch ability and some of its speed and maneuverability, but it was in better shape than any of its four victims. Its main problem, though, was that it was running low on torpedoes and none of the four enemy ships had lost shielding.

Below, Vulture could hear the whine of flyers coming in, and one was already landing within sight. Ikira and the Chows were already up, and Sabir was about to step into the fighter as small-arms fire erupted all around. "Go on! Move! I'll hold them if I can or get out another way!" He took up a position behind some crumbling bricks and opened fire.

Raven closed on the crippled Val, which still had its shields up and clearly had weapons control. He could only guess that the enemy ship really was hurt—otherwise why not come back and just finish them?—and that the Val within was trying desperately to jury-rig repairs. That was exactly what he had to try to stop it.

Warlock launched a six-torpedo salvo and had the same returned to her. Each ship easily destroyed the other's missiles with beam weapons. "No good." She sighed. "We are too evenly matched."

"Keep giving it all you've got," Raven growled. "It'll keep the thing from making repairs and at least buy time. Maybe we'll run it out of torpedoes before we're empty."

"It thought of that, too. It's just picked off the second salvo but fired none back. Why should it?"

"Good point. Lay off, then, and we'll try a standoff for a while. If that thing looks like it's gonna get back to full steam, I'll ram the bastard before I'll let it go."

The second Val, although crippled, was in better shape than its mate, but it was worried. It knew that there was one ship missing, and long-range sensors showed it in orbit around Janipur. No matter how satisfying blowing up enemy ships might be, a successful defense was not measured in casualties inflicted but in denying the enemy its objective. The Val understood that principle well, and turned and made its best speed toward Janipur.

"It's going after *Kaotan*!" Maria Santiago reported. "Can anyone pursue?"

"We can't afford another hit," responded Midi, Savaphoong's chief pilot on the *Espiritu Luzon*. "Best we cover you."

"I will give chase" came ben Suda's voice. "This one has made me very angry." His ship didn't appear to be in much better shape than the others, but he sounded as if he could track the Val by sheer willpower.

Aboard *Kaotan*, Ikira Sukotae was back in her element and very glad to be there.

"Break off!" Dura Panoshka said urgently. "There's a Val bearing down on us and it'll be in range in under four minutes. We're sitting ducks here in geostationary orbit!"

"No," the tiny captain responded. "Shields full along the flanks and watch out that he doesn't go under and come up on the planet side. Bring the throttle up full but do not release. I'm gonna give Vulture those four minutes."

Well away from the action, Raven was getting worried. "I'm registering energy flares on the Val ship. I think he's going to be operational again in just a couple of minutes, and there's nothing we can do about it." He opened a common carrier channel. "This is *Lightning* to damaged Val ship. Cease repairs and maintain standoff or I will be forced to ram."

"You wish to commit suicide?" came a response in a low, pleasant baritone.

"I do not, but if I let you get going again, I'm dead meat anyway. Might as well take you with me."

The Val was disconcerted and sensed that reasonable argument wouldn't meet with much success. It stopped testing its repaired lines, but it knew it could not accept such a standoff. A stalemate was as good as a defeat since the remaining ships would still be there, and with only one operable Val left in service there would be little chance of victory. It knew from its companion that the other ships were all damaged to some degree, but that made little difference. While the companion was chasing after *Kaotan*, the other four renegades would have time to make repairs of their own. There was little choice.

The instant the Val ship moved, Raven took a deep mental breath and pushed the throttle. Gaining speed with every second, he followed a course straight for the Val, while Warlock began firing with every available weapon, forcing their opponent to abandon its defense and get to full throttle.

The Val ship flared into brilliance, then winked out.

It took a second for Warlock to react, and then she was initially puzzled. "Did it get away or did we get it?"

"Whew!" Raven sighed. "I thought I was going to the land of my ancestors there. It blew up. I have lots of scattered debris in the scan, almost all small. One down, one to go. *Kaotan*, you get the hell out of there!"

The transmuter receiver installed on *Kaotan* hummed, and Vulture more fell than stepped off the plate. He was a bloody mess, and it looked as if he'd taken numerous shots to the body, but he was alive. Sabir and the Chows crowded around him and Takya Mudabur knelt beside him. "No one could survive such wounds," she said sorrowfully.

Ikira Sukotae didn't wait for a medical report. She released the engines and moved at flank speed out of orbit at an angle that took the ship away from the Val. Reacting instantly, the Val changed course to pursue and let loose a pattern of fire that did not quite reach *Kaotan*. It was clear that even damaged the Val had an edge in speed and maneuverability over the old freebooter freighter. And Sukotae could not depend on *Bahakatan* for help; it simply couldn't catch up.

Kaotan, however, was undamaged, and Sukotae was not about to take on the Val alone. She had the ring aboard and the rest of the people from Janipur; her first duty was to safeguard them. She didn't have speed for a really big punch, but it wouldn't matter; clearly the Val had lost its punch power and could not follow. *Kaotan* punched just as the Val closed to within range.

The Val wasted no time on lost opportunities. If it could not stop the getaway, then the least it could do was cost the enemy as much as possible. It turned and headed back at full throttle toward *Indrus* and *San Cristobal*.

"It's coming back in!" Santiago reported. "E.T.A. five minutes twenty-five seconds. *Indrus* cannot move and my shielding is completely gone. Can you move in, *Espiritu Luzon*?"

"Negative! This thing handles worse than a freighter at the best of times and I have damage. I will try to get in some good shots if I can, but all it has to do is skim to within your range opposite my position and I won't be able to stop it. The best I can do is position myself so we'll know where its best shooting position is. That will allow you to concentrate your fire on its salvos."

"*Bahakatan* here. I can't get back in time, but I noticed in its pursuit of *Kaotan* that it used no beam weapons at all. I believe the Val has been forced to divert all energy to its engines in order to maintain speed, maneuverability, and shielding. If someone could get in behind it, it might be vulnerable."

"Here we go!" Santiago called. "Angle is right where we figured. No vector to the ship, but we might be able to hit most or all of the torpedoes. We'll see."

The Val came in on an arc that placed it within range for only three seconds, not enough to be worth firing at, but it loosed its full complement of twelve torpedoes in a zigzag spread pattern at the two crippled ships. Three got through the withering fire; two of those hit *Indrus* but failed to penetrate the shields. The third, however, came straight into *San Cristobal*'s midsection, nearly tearing the ship in half and knocking out all power.

The Val looped and came back for a second run, its tubes reloaded. The last pattern, so perfect yet so erratic, indicated that the Val was leaving the ship on preprogrammed automatic pilot and guiding in the torpedoes itself. It let loose the whole series aimed at *Indrus*, following the same pattern as before. With *Espiritu Luzon* laying off and *San Cristobal* as good as destroyed, there was little chance for *Indrus* to pick off more than half the incoming missiles.

The Val, unlike humans, could consciously perform many functions at the same time, but guiding twelve missiles under fire was stretching itself to its limit. It noticed the sensor call of another punch, but so many of the torpedoes were getting through, it didn't dare stop and look.

Indrus' guns had done a good job, but four missiles got through, all converging on a single spot near the tail section where the engines were. The ship reeled and began spinning; its entire aft section in one direction, the rest of it in another. Noting this, the Val turned to take on its new attacker, and immediately fired its entire forward battery. It was to no avail.

Thunder's huge ram scoops were open wide like the jaws of a mighty beast, and before the Val could react, its entire ship was engulfed in the ram and processed by the great converters into energy. No other ship in service could have accomplished that feat; *Thunder* was so enormous that it ate asteroids larger than the Val ship just to feed its mighty engines.

"Everyone remain where you are," Star Eagle called. "I will come to you. The most badly damaged to the cargo bays, the ones with any real power to the outside docks. *Espiritu Luzon* and *Bahakatan* approach and look for survivors. I will go and collect *Lightning* and *Chunhoifan* first, then return here. I want the wreckage, too—and any bodies that might be found. The battle is over."

Raven sighed. "Yeah, and, just think. This was supposed to be the *easy* one."

The losses were large, but in many ways not as bad as they had feared. Maria Santiago and the two centauroids survived in their pressure suits, although the ship and the other three members of the crew were lost. Raven in particular regretted the loss of the one he thought of as the rock monster; it never was very sociable or communicative but it played a mean game of cards.

On the *Indrus* only Lalla Paschittawal and Suni Banderesh, wife of Ravi's weapons officer, survived, ironically because both had been in the tail section trying to repair the engines. Although they had been banged around and had a few broken bones, the fact that they had been there, tethered, and in spacesuits saved them. Ravi Paschittawal never wore one unless he had to, and his weapons officer generally followed this lead. Santiago, on the other hand, had put everyone in suits from the start just in case. It hadn't saved everyone, but it saved her.

So the cost had been five lives from their small company and two ships. "At this rate we will be unable to muster any strength for the fourth ring and we haven't even gotten the second yet," Hawks noted dourly.

"All our losses were in the escape, not the operation," China noted. "The next time we determine our methods before we commit our people, and that's that. We simply cannot afford any more of this. This time they underestimated our numbers and strength—they will not do so again. We paid a sad price, but it is the price of learning. If we use this experience, we should be able to do it better and with less cost next time."

One they did not lose was Vulture, much to Takya Mudabur's shock and dismay. She had seen a laser hole through his heart and another through a part of his brain. Now, only a day later, he was walking around with no sign of any wounds except for some bloodstains that wouldn't come out of the fur.

"And what about our prize?" Hawks asked the group.

Isaac Clayben cleared his throat. "It is a most fascinating device. As we expected it is passive, so once stolen it is impossible to locate. The 'stone,' as we might call it, is made of a highly conductive synthetic substance that has the electronics embedded in it—in fact, the electronics are mostly formed out of the substance itself! The design is actually somewhat primitive, and I have no idea what the material is and couldn't duplicate it now if I wanted to."

"But it is definitely what the papers said it was?" Hawks pressed.

"Who knows? I have no way of accessing the code inside of it, which might be incredibly complex, nor any way to read it if I could since it is early code—most likely direct assembly language to the original Master System core. The only thing I can say for sure, and probably the only thing I can say until we try to use it, is that it is definitely a module intended to interface with some sort of direct receptor. In other words, it is probably exactly what we think it is. The override and direct access to Master System's core was deliberately divided into five parts, possibly not so much due to fear of the computer as to insure that no one of its designers could gain independent access to such power nor could even form a majority cabal. It took the consent and direct action of all five, no dissent allowed, to even do minor modification work. I suspect it was a safety device by agreement so that no one person could make himself a god. I will wager that if we see the receptors, they will be spaced far enough apart from one another that it will take five individuals to insert them and hold them there."

"Interesting," China said. "The implication is that even with all five inserted it would only give the ability and authority to modify. It is entirely possible that it would take the agreement of all five people to do just about anything. Chen would only be one among equals. Even if he plans on the other four being henchmen under his control, each would have an absolute veto power. That's if the computer could be effectively accessed at all."

Hawks looked up at her. "Huh? What do you mean?"

"These might only unlock five terminals or some direct

interface by which the Master System core language could be fed in or read out. We might not know the language."

"We'll know," Clayben assured them. "First of all, Master System would not be so persistent against us if we had no chance of access, and, secondly, the original Master System would be far smaller and more primitive than the one we face now. The rings are more than a mechanical method of access—they are the passwords and the instructions to the computer on how it interacts with the ring owners. I would bet on some sort of direct access, possibly even simple speech. Why would they make it hard on themselves? They had to use this just about every day. However, she is correct about one thing—it will require unanimity to alter the core. Of course, hypnos and mindprinters could change this, but who can be certain? Suppose the interfaces were something like those of the spaceships? If they had mindprinters or similar techniques in those days, and primitive methods of mind control were available long before there were even computers, then the designers would have built a failsafe into the access instructions to allow for that possibility. Such an interface could also give Master System access to the mind of the human interfacer. They were top-security people in top-security posts. They would have to have allowed for it."

"Well, that makes me feel a little better," Hawks admitted, "but it doesn't solve the basic problem. At least this time we knew just who owned the ring and where it was. We have far less to go on with the next two, and we still don't know where the fourth one even is."

"I am equally concerned about the performance, or lack of it, in our own people," China noted. "I talked to Maria and to the two *Indrus* women, and Star Eagle has made a preliminary check of *Espiritu Luzon* and found very little damage. They had full operational power including punch power—they were just jolted around a little and had to rush to fix some minor damage inside—and they have almost their full complement of weapons still aboard. They falsified their on-site damage report and did almost no fighting. They were close enough and in good enough shape to give that Val hell but they begged off and let those two ships and those five people die. In the right position and with a full field of fire, they could have forced that Val to dodge torpedoes instead of guiding them."

Hawks nodded slightly, mostly to himself. "All right, I have the reports from the others myself. They did the bare minimum and they want a free ride. Well, it isn't going to wash. There's no use confronting them with it now or attempting any disciplinary action—I think they'll get some cold treatment from the rest as it is, and I'd rather not listen to any of their excuses or give them any cause to try to leave our band or deliver it into the hands of the enemy. For now, we let them get away with it, but they move to the top of the priority list. Individually they are going to put up or they're all going under the doctor's mindprinter. Now, they're going to have to put in for repairs or their story will be totally shot, and I suspect we'll find something major to be fixed even if it wasn't damaged during the battle. Star Eagle, while it's in, reprogram the pilot core to allow for both override from *Thunder* and self-destruct. None of that crew is to have the ability or authority to operate that ship without someone else there with a key password and override. Can you do that?"

"I can and will. But why go through the charade?"

"Because if we press it, Savaphoong will have somebody set up to take the fall all by him- or herself. It'll be more complicated than it's worth. But if *Espiritu Luzon* goes out again, it will be with somebody else there. Somebody without a ship—like Maria Santiago or one of the *Indrus* survivors. Let them relax and congratulate themselves in their lap of luxury. We know them now, and we have them on a list. It might not be right away, but sooner or later all those aboard that ship who can think for themselves are going to wish they'd risked death back there off Janipur. Nobody here gets off without sacrifice and risk."

That seemed to satisfy them for the moment.

Over the many days that followed, the damage was repaired and weaknesses identified and reinforced. Hawks was feeling somewhat impatient now that they had been blooded and the real work had begun. He began to look at the two other worlds known to have rings. Before the battle of Janipur, these worlds had been looked at as closely as could be allowed without actually landing.

"Chanchuk follows the usual Center pattern," he told Vulture. "We don't know their form or culture, but intercepted transmissions indicate that they speak a dialect of Chinese no longer used on Earth. China could read it but almost went nuts trying to understand it when spoken. The grammar and pronunciation are all very different; so different that a phrase like 'the writing pen is on the table' could be heard as 'the lead pipe is freezing up my ass.' We don't have any equivalent mindprinter modules for it."

"I'm not surprised by the Chinese. About half the colonial worlds are Chinese or Indian in origin because they comprised half the human race when the whole split happened. The language doesn't worry me, though. I can learn it by osmosis, as it were," Vulture noted.

"I'm aware of that, but it also means that we'd have to pick you back up, bring you up here, take a mindprinter reading of it, do comparison matching and eventually create our own new records. I'm also concerned about doing a second job so similar in some ways to the first— using Center security and the like. This time we'll probably have to break into the chief administrator's bedroom. There's an SPF command ship in orbit there, so you know they're just as much involved down there as they were on Janipur, only they'll have taken the lessons they just learned to heart. We just can't afford another one like we just had. Master System is probably even now making Vals to replace the ones it lost every bit as good and as tough as those were, and the fate the SPF on Janipur will have will be a real incentive to the ones on Chanchuk, you can bet on that. I think we have to be much better prepared the next time."

"I agree. So what if we bypass Chanchuk for now while we study the problem some more and maybe build ourselves back up? What's the other one like?"

"Bizarre. That's the only word for it. There are no Centers that we can detect. There is, in fact, no sign of any sort of artificial energy generation on the planet stronger than fire making. The world is rough. Lots of active volcanic activity, earthquakes, that sort of thing. The storms are extremely violent and they're huge. Much of the planet is shrouded in clouds most of the time, and better than sixty percent of the landmass is covered with jungle—the kind of vegetation that looks like it'll eat you instead of you eating it. You remember that world you stuck us on at the start of all this?"

"Yeah. Sorry about that. It was the only noncolonical world Koll knew about that could support people. How was I to know?"

"Well, this one's worse. It's hot. Thirty to forty-five degrees Celsius in the regions of vegetation and human habitation. Lots of islands with no clear signs of habitation and two main continents. It's got animals, but God knows what they eat except each other."

"Water civilization, then?"

"No, land. Mammalian. Quite a lot of them, all things considered, although I suspect they don't have long life-spans. They appear to be hunter-gatherers with social organization at the tribal level, and small at that, but there's several million of them spread out on both continents and a couple of the larger islands. You can look at the survey and also at the photos we managed to get through the infrequent cloud breaks. The lack of Centers bothers me, but the lack of cities or any large tribal culture bothers me even more. A 'human with authority' on Matriyeh would have to be no more than a tribal chief. With an average tribe numbering about a hundred, and with several million people on all that land, how the hell will we ever find the right one? It's a needle-in-a-haystack problem."

"SPF and Master System?"

"They have a fair number of warning satellites and the like around—far more than you'd expect for a place nobody would ever want to visit—but no command ship. You can be pretty damned sure that one will come running along with Vals and a whole division of troops if they get wind we're working down there, though. If I were them, I wouldn't bother wasting resources there right now, either." He sighed. "In a way, I wish we had the strength to mount two expeditions simultaneously. That way we'd probably have Matriyeh to ourselves while they bore in on Chanchuk. The fact is, though, that I don't think we have a prayer of doing both."

Vulture looked over all the data and was as concerned as Hawks about the lack of any clear centers of power. It just didn't fit. Master System tended to do pretty much the same thing place after place—except here.

If anything, Hawks was understating the looks of both the jungle and the blasted volcanic plains. The animal life looked even less appetizing. There were large flying things with brown and black leathery wings and strange, thin tails; and other creatures that looked like flying plates with thin, long membranes for tails. He couldn't imagine where

Master System had dreamed them up, unless they were there to begin with.

The land animals were less clearly defined, and though some of them were overly large for a jungle that dense, most seemed to have the same coloration as their habitats. Even the older volcanic areas seemed riddled with holes that served as dens for things that might be worms, snakes, or something worse, all man-sized or larger. No clear cut herbivore candidates for the ecological niche of prey seemed obvious, unless it was humans, and that wasn't a pleasant thought.

This world was almost any civilized person's vision of hell. There were, however, some high-resolution photographs of the people, and even though they were grainy and the close-ups in poor focus, Vulture was able to identify a variety of tribes from various areas of both continents. He noted with a touch of sadness and some guilt that the photos had been taken by the *Indrus*.

The natives actually looked Earth-human, although he knew better than to accept that at face value. They had tough, very dark brown skin nearly black in color, with huge manes of woolly black hair. Their faces, however, did not have any clear racial antecedents from Earth's old cultures that he could tell, but were surprisingly quite attractive, even delicate in a way, with small but prominent noses and thin lips. They wore no clothing but did seem to paint or brand their faces and parts of their body with delicate, intricate designs, and many wore crude necklaces or bracelets and anklets. Jewelry, probably of bone, dangled from their ears, was placed in the hair, and apparently inserted in the nose. Most carried stone-tipped spears and what might have been blow guns and other primitive weapons. They all seemed quite young.

He went back, looking again at picture after picture, and

frowned. "But where're the men?" he muttered. "There are no men in these shots. Not anywhere. It's all women!"

Hawks joined him. "You see how ugly the place is."

"Yes, yet there is a certain beauty to it, as well. I am puzzled, though. All those pictures, and not one male in the entire series. Where are the men? Is it a unisexual race?"

"I have no idea, although that struck me as well. As with Janipur and the others, there are some things we cannot know until we discover it for ourselves."

"I suppose. I also notice that none of the artifacts they wear or carry is metal. While it is possible that useful metals might be difficult to extract by primitive people down there, I find it curious. It is almost like a look into the earliest past of humanity. Stone axes, stone spears, reed blow guns, no signs of cultivation even with a volcanic soil. They are tough, though, these women. Virtually all the hunting parties contained pregnant ones, as well."

"The lack of any Centers bothered me more, but I have a possible explanation both for that and for much else of what you see," Hawks told him. "Theory only, of course. But Lazlo Chen told us that Master System had the idea of reducing Earth to this level of civilization and culture and abolishing the Center system because Master System is finally realizing that it is not in complete control that way. It took the ancestors of humanity tens of thousands of years, perhaps longer than that, to rise up from the primitive to anything near what we think of as civilization. With satellites doing surveys almost constantly, it's possible that when signs of large settlements and cultivated agriculture appear Master System's forces could be brought in to reduce them once again. Simpler, cheaper, more efficient than the current system, although terrible for humanity."

"And you think this was done here?"

"The number of monitoring satellites and their type suggest it was. Look, they are close enough to Earth-human, in appearance at any rate, and the population was probably never very advanced on a world such as this. It would be far easier to do it here and see how practical and manageable an idea it might be. And, of course, it is a world with a ring. Master System would think of the needle-in-the-haystack problem, as well."

"A prototype, then."

"Yes, I fear so. We used a similar scenario to get *Pirate One* docked to the command ship at Janipur and none of the SPF or their computers thought it the least odd, so they know of it. Still, something bothered me and it was only later when I dragged these out for you to look at and got to looking at them again myself that I finally was struck by something. Master System is a prisoner of its core program. A chief of some tribe measuring a hundred simply wouldn't do. Life is obviously short down there—for chiefs, as well, and perhaps for chiefs in particular. There would be no control, and no assurance that the ring would remain where it is mandated to be. Also, in a society like that, such a ring would have incredible magical properties, perhaps even be an object of worship. It is worked metal with intricate designs, far beyond their knowledge and powers. It would obviously be taken as something of the gods and would be treated accordingly."

Vulture nodded. "I see what you mean. Such an object would be sufficient to generate, perhaps, a priesthood. Maybe even an entire theology."

"That led me to begin comparing both the designs they paint on themselves and on their totems, as best we can make them out. My own people use face-painting, charms, and amulets both for religious purposes and to denote, say, rank and position in a hunt or in battle. My tribe is quite small, yet its markings are distinctive; so much so that there is little or no chance to mistake a Hyiakutt for a Sioux or Sauk or Manitwoc. In all our photos of southern continent people I found what I would expect—some basic similarities, but overall quite distinctive color and design even between small groups living close together. But in the north—well, look for yourself."

The picture that came up on the monitor was somewhat fuzzy but still showed painted markings of distinctive design on faces and bodies, the variations small enough to be those of rank or assignment. A second picture showed a different tribe, but the markings were quite similar, differing only in minor details.

"The two tribes you see live a thousand kilometers apart," Hawks told him. "The tribal groups tend to be territorial and there is little trade because there is little *to* trade. Yet the markings are pretty consistent, as are the shapes of some of the bond charms. Unfortunately, the resolution isn't perfect, but there is a consistency in the patterns. They all seem to be bone or wood carved into the shape of stylized birds and basic trees—but the things that fly down there aren't birds, I can assure you."

"A consistent theology, then. One that probably justifies their existence and seeks to maintain the status quo. Very clever. So there are religious leaders within the tribes, and perhaps a priesthood surrounding the ring, as well. Then there *is* a chief administrator down there, and a supporting staff! They just don't know what they are!"

Hawks nodded. "Exactly."

"But why only the northern continent? It would seem to me that it would work best if all of them were unified at least in a basic set of beliefs."

"Perhaps. Perhaps this is an ongoing experiment and the south is the control group. Which is more dangerous—a diffuse culture with no strong common cultural base, or one that has a religion that tells them that life is but a test for the hereafter, progress is blasphemy, invention is demonic, and has the totem to prove their divine authority? Master System knows human history but it's the first to ever be able to run experiments on human social behavior. Although it fascinates me as a historian, it is beside the point for our purposes. The fact is that we have clear evidence of a unitary theological base in the north and all that implies. Somewhere down there is a religious center with a high priest—or priestess, as it looks—who is protected and pampered is the ultimate authority because he or she speaks to the gods—and has the ring to prove it."

Vulture stared at the maps. It was a big continent. "But where? It need not be very large, but it would have to have some kind of support system so that the priesthood would be freed from the daily grind of hunting and gathering. And there would be a single permanent settlement of sorts."

Hawks shrugged. "Right now we can't find it. It might just be too small to be noticeable on these survey photos. You can bet it's an austere priesthood, living a hard, monastic life. The only way to know would be to have some surface operative who could guide us there. Surely someone down there knows the way. Someone must relay the theology, exercise the power down the social chain. The tribal priest must be instructed, trained, and kept to the straight and narrow. I suspect that the culture is far more complex than it looks from a distance."

Vulture nodded. "And, as usual, I provide the intelligence. What about getting in and out?"

"Ever since the problem on Janipur surfaced, we have been working on ways to do that. We were able to get into orbit and take a survey because of some of our experimental work. I think we can jam the satellites sufficiently to move rather freely in that system without an alarm going out. There's all sorts of cosmic interference going on, especially with so many devices. Getting in and getting you supplied and supported, even getting you out, would not be a major problem so long as they don't send a force to the system. My concern is, for all its complexities, it's too easy."

"Huh? What do you mean?"

"They know we're after the rings. They know we have to have all of them. They have access to better tools than we do, and they aren't hampered by any moral or ethical considerations. They have the ability to create true believers who won't question even the illogical or irrational and will think when they use the magic to speak to Heaven they are talking to God and not Master System. It can't afford to entrust the ring to savages, yet it can't do otherwise without violating its experiment. Somewhere, down there, they've set a trap for us, Vulture, and I bet it's a whopper. If we don't find it, then we're going to be faced with a battle as ugly as the one we survived and that might just cripple us for years. Still, until we can work out alternate exit methods for Chanchuk, this is our best bet. Go down there. Spot the trap. Then and only then will we be able to take the ring."

6. PLAYING PICKUP STICKS IN A MINEFIELD

TIME PASSED SLOWLY ABOARD THE *THUNDER* AS IT always did, but shipboard life continued to change. Children were born, expanding the colony even more; children of two races with different physiologies and needs. Hawks himself was now a proud father. For a man of his cultural background he did not seem at all disappointed or upset that his first child was a girl, whom he and Cloud Dancer named Chaudiqua, a combination of their Hyiakutt names which meant Night Dancer.

Clayben, China, and Star Eagle continued to work on easier methods of penetrating the closed colonial worlds in Master System's domain, and had some real success. Long-range reconnaissance indicated that Master System had finally managed to process all of its ships so that the access codes were different, and could be altered far more easily and quickly in the future. But with so vast an area and so many ships, stations, Centers, and satellites, it simply was impossible for Master System to change the entire surveillance and communications system, and thus the new challenge was not to feed the systems false information, as had been done with *Pirate One*, but rather to deflect or confuse those sensors so they would not report an intruder at all.

Thunder was moved to a system off the charts with no habitable worlds for a larger project of Star Eagle's that was quite ambitious: nothing less than the construction of a small shipyard, entirely robotized, in which ships of new design—small but fast, well armed, and possibly piloted by only one or two people—could be constructed in modular sections using the larger transmuters and then assembled and tested. Part of the idea was not only to match the speed and maneuverability of the Val ships, as well as their firepower, but also to do so without killing any human pilots. Mechanisms had to be created to shield and protect those pilots from the incredible forces of acceleration and battle. The automated fighters of *Thunder* provided the basic outline for the type of craft they wanted, but did not have punch capability. The required mechanisms added weight and complexity to the new design and caused some problems they were still hammering out.

In the meantime, Vulture had been down on Matriyeh for many months, and there had been no communication with him for most of that period. As before, they had been forced to set him down in a remote and unpopulated area where he, as a Janipurian, had to make his way to civilization and then blend in as only he could. Hawks and the others often thought that they could see Clayben's point in the great experiment that created Vulture. With a mere five or six Vultures there would be no problem in getting the rings; without one, it would be next to impossible.

As the time dragged on, though, with no word from the strange creature, Hawks began to harbor dark thoughts that

they might have to go on without him. Vulture had so
many strengths that it was quite natural that he felt himself
invulnerable and therefore could become careless. But
Vulture would be as helpless as any if surprised by a Val:
there were a number of ways to destroy even such a thing
as he, including incineration, disintegration, cellular
disruption, and chemical baths. Like the werewolves and
vampires of ancient legends, Vulture was fearsome—but,
like them, he could still be killed. The key so far had been
the ignorance of Master System and its minions that such a
creature even existed. The records on Vulture had been
destroyed, Clayben was on *Thunder*, and the few surviving
scientists who had known about the project had long ago
had their memories altered for their own protection. Their
luck, however, could not last forever.

It was a great relief, then, when word came that Vulture
had at last activated the signaling devices and was request-
ing a pickup from the surface of Matriyeh. It had been over
eight months. Unlike the Janipur mission, they needed to
bring Vulture back aboard and analyze both the new mind
and new body he had taken on when he had absorbed his
native persona, and they also needed first-hand consulta-
tion.

The body was that of a tall, thin woman with long,
muscular legs and small, firm breasts. The arms, too, were
muscular when flexed, showing surprising power. The skin
was a very dark brown, so dark as to be almost black, the
color extending not just to the skin but to the palms and
soles of the feet and other such areas, as well. The black
hair was thick and woolly, but the natural curls were much
larger than those of an Earth-human of one of the sub-
Saharan African races or Melanesians, and the features
were delicate and more European than anything else. Save
in the the groin, brows, and the underarms, there was no
other hair on the body. The large eyes were jet black, and

seemed slightly puffy or swollen and protruded more than was natural for an Earth-human. She was naked except for a thin, tough-looking vine hanging on her hips, but wore loose bracelets and anklets made of some vegetable material and dyed green and blue, and she wore earrings and a necklace of carved bones and thin wirelike vines.

She also had body markings on her cheeks, forehead, and around the breasts and groin. These were simple designs that seemed burned or tattooed in, although instead of the lighter discolorations one might expect the outlines were simply a lighter brown, and some, but not all, had been filled with various colors of paint or dye. Aside from that, the skin was remarkably smooth, without the kind of scars that might be expected. The thin, dark vine on her hips proved to be an intricately woven ropelike belt with loops to hold a blow gun fashioned of reeds, a small pouch made of some fibrous material, and she held in her left hand a long spear that was made of a stick or branch, carved straight, on which was mounted a smooth, sharp-pointed stone held on with more of the thin, wirelike vines that fitted into notches in the shaft.

"You must bear with me," Vulture said apologetically in a firm, husky soprano, "but it is more difficult to readjust from this form than from the others. Let us go to the village where I won't feel so—closed in."

Many of the others crowded around as she entered the central area of *Thunder*, and at one point she gestured menacingly with the spear and said something unintelligible but obviously threatening. They backed off.

Someone brought her some water and she drank it and sank down on the grass. Hawks approached and sat opposite, and after a while Vulture was able to shake off enough of the native personality to seem almost her old self.

"We were right," she told him. "The people are subject to an experiment and they are not *quite* as human as they appear. It is a brutal place, but disorganized enough that some independent movement and actions are possible even over large distances. It is sobering to see an entire society reprogrammed and their works wiped out. Their true colonial past exists in occasional ruins and odd artifacts here and there, and in vaguely remembered legends and half-truths, but not as a personal sort of thing. Their very language, while expressive, is clearly artificial, and as we expected, the north, at least, is more complex than it appeared."

Slowly, but with professional thoroughness, Vulture sketched the basic structure of the society and its people.

They called themselves just the People, and no memories remained that any other people, or types of people, or other worlds even existed. There were the great gods who lived in the heavens and created and judged, the sun being the greatest and the two small moons the lesser; the stars were reflections of the lights in the villages of the gods at night. The world itself was filled with spirits; there were spirits of air, and water, and trees, and demons in the volcanoes. The People were entirely subject to the whims and occasional mercies of these spirits and while they were always praying to or attempting to please or placate them, they expected little. Life was a constant series of tests by the gods, a nearly endless cycle, lasting until the gods or some spirits had mercy and removed them to the heavenly realm, which was thought to be much like Matriyeh but with abundant food and eternal good health. To fail the tests of life set by the gods, spirits, and demons was to suffer; to succeed did not guarantee any reward. To rebel against the system, to question it or to try to make life easier, was a heresy that was punished with a slow, agonizing, tortuous death.

"The point is, you can't even invent or introduce a more efficient weapon, nor plant a seed, although such things might occur to them. It would make things easier and change the tests of the gods and would be a heresy. There *is* food, of course, or they couldn't survive, but they must spend their whole day searching for it. They can eat pretty much anything, but they are constantly on the move. The children are carried on the backs of their mothers in rope carriers, sometimes two or three at a time, and guarded communally during hunts. There is a high infant mortality rate anyway, so they have lots of kids almost constantly to make up for it. Pregnant people do the same work as ones that aren't even when it's well advanced, as food goes first to the hunters and gatherers, then to the children. These brands are tribal markings; the colorations indicate rank and position. In times or areas of plenty, there's no problem with other tribes, but in hard times or when a territory is depleted they might war with one another.

"They have nothing but their weapons and what ornaments they can find time and material to make for themselves. They carry nothing with them on their endless journeys and camp wherever they wind up with enough food for the day or when darkness falls. It is far more deserted and desolate than you would think—a million or less on a continent perhaps thirty million square kilometers. One might go for days or even weeks without seeing a member of another tribe, but there's a lot of ground to cover each day. The territories aren't well defined; you go where you have to and hope you don't have to fight somebody for it."

Hawks nodded grimly as the others listened in hushed silence. "It sounds truly primitive, but you said it was complex."

"It is. But before you can understand it, and all the bad news, you have to understand the basic biological differences between them and you. They are partially unisexual, which is why there are no men. I contain within me both sets of sexual equipment, as do they all, but all but one in a tribal group is biologically female. That one is the most aggressive, the nastiest, the most commanding personality, and hormones trigger the development of male characteristics, including a half-octave dip in the voice, and the growth of some sparse body hair, and male sex organs. That one then becomes the tribal group's only male and its leader. However, if he loses the respect of the tribe—such as by cowardice or incompetence—the leader loses those characteristics, becomes fully female again, and is chased away into the bush. Within days another will take on the leader characteristics, sometimes by sheer force of will. There is occasionally a conflict that must be settled by force, but that's rare. Only one can rule at at time, and the gender change seems to be triggered mentally in both directions. Naturally, if the leader dies another takes his place, and leaders have short lifespans because they have to be in the forefront and take the real responsibility."

"That certainly explains that mystery," Hawks agreed.

"As with most very primitive people, sex is a dominant part of their lives. Some of these charms are sexual totems, and phallic symbols are an all-consuming passion. Even rocks of the right shape take on mystical connotations. The tribal loyalty is more than just cultural, though—it's chemical. Once you've had sex with the leader you simply don't want to have sex with anybody else, though it's no blind love or slavelike submission. You might hate the son of a bitch—which is not uncommon—but he's the only one you want. In fact, if a tribe is in danger of depletion, the only way to increase its numbers is to stalk members of another tribe, capture them, and have the leader rape them. I told you it was a brutal place."

Raven, the cynical commentator of the group, had been standing there listening with the others. "I see you don't have the male characteristics," he noted. "That's not your style."

"I couldn't afford to. Too much responsibility and visibility. Besides, I don't think I could maintain it very long. I duplicate a victim cell for cell, but they are false cells—duplicates with a difference beyond the ability of most analyzers to measure, but still false. I can neither bear nor father children of a race I am merely imitating, nor replicate myself. Not bearing children can be an advantage down there, although it's the lowest status and likely to get you the job of scout or of testing rope and log bridges to see if they're safe, but not fathering children is an unforgivable sin in a leader. I couldn't maintain the male aspect very long, so it wasn't worth trying."

"Such a life," China commented, shaking her head. "I think I would kill myself."

"That is the cultural difference. You are not an individual down there, at least not in the greater sense—you are the component of a group. Racial survival depends on group survival. There is not a one there who would consider not sacrificing herself for the group. Bad luck is attributed to the will or capriciousness of the gods. To fail the tribe, however, is the only major dishonor. They would turn on anyone who did and that one would wish she had chosen death long before she actually died. Even a captive from another tribe turned to the new tribe would submerge herself in the new tribe and dismiss the old. It's not the way we think, but it's the only pragmatic means to survival. Suicide would weaken the group and is therefore a terrible crime, the worst kind of crime."

"And what of those crippled, permanently injured, or deformed?" Hawks asked. "Are they simply killed?"

"Those who can't contribute or keep up can't be afforded. The people are pretty tough—this skin has the thickness of aged leather, the major bones are very hard to break, and the toleration level for pain is incredible—but accidents do happen, of course. When they do, in honorable service, there is a ritual done at night. Some of the plants down there produce powerful drugs that can be given to the crippled and that kill without pain or agony. Then . . ." She stopped and sighed, not quite knowing how they would take it.

"Yes?" Hawks urged gently.

"Then the tribe eats them, so they always remain with the group. A valiant enemy may also be treated that way, as a mark of honor and respect. Little is wasted." She fingered her necklace. "Some of these were carved from human bones."

"So that's what Master System plans for our future," somebody growled, and there were lots of other murmurings, mostly angry. Hawks put a stop to it.

"Those of you who find this horrifying are ignorant of the cultures of some of your own ancestors. Nor is it any more terrible than some of the things some of us supposedly civilized and cultured people have inflicted on others with our technology. It is not right when our own kind practices such barbarism, but I think I understand this culture. I do not like it, but I understand it. Still, those of you sickened and repulsed by this should remember why we are doing what we are doing and against whom. We are not here to approve or disapprove. Each of us, I suspect, has things in their own culture they consider normal, proper, and civilized that would horrify others standing around here now. We need to know about this place. There is a ring there. Did I guess right about the unified theology?"

Vulture nodded. "Yes. Oh, there are minor differences but the whole culture is held together by a common set of gods and beliefs. The firebearer, which is the oldest female in the tribe—age is a mark of extreme respect down there, as you might imagine—and who has the flint stones to make fires, is the spiritual leader and gets training from the only nontribal people on the planet. They are quite easy to spot—they shave their heads and are almost as heavily marked as Silent Woman. They are called *wassun*, which basically means 'truth-bearer.' They are celibate females— no leader would dare touch one—and they are the authority. They remain with a tribe for short periods, and even participate in tribal activities, but mainly they teach theology to the firebringer and all others who are interested. They remain with a tribe until that tribe interacts with another, and then they cross over and go with the next one. That means their stay might be days or weeks or longer."

"Ah!" Hawks said. "And where do *they* come from?"

"Well, they don't officially come from anywhere— they're regarded as always there, like the rest of nature. I only had encounters with two, but it took some time to determine that it was two, not one. They look and sound remarkably alike—like identical twins, almost—and are generally regarded as the same person. I was really tempted to become one of them but I could never get alone with one of them long enough to do it. They do more than counsel, though—they almost interrogate, only so smoothly and professionally you hardly realize it. They're looking for any signs of heresies, deviations from the norm. And they have *power*. I realized what they were almost immediately—field agents, although they don't realize it. They really believe this guff, too—I'm convinced of that. But when they talk to the gods, the gods sometimes answer back, in holy places prohibited to all but the *wassun*."

"Oho! Now we're getting someplace! So somewhere there's a central authority with at least some access to technology," Hawks said. "Could it be automated? A computer buried and self-maintained, for example?"

"I think not. The *wassun* come from some specific place

and they report back there. I had a crazy idea that makes a lopsided kind of sense."

"Go on."

"Now, the SPF has a division for each race, right?"

"So we are told."

"But what good are Matriyehans when their parent world is reduced like this? Not much. So what if that division were processed to become essentially the priesthood on Matriyeh? Make 'em all look the same, act the same, spout same stuff. Any good psycho lab could do that and Master System could use the best. Make their commanders the high priestesses someplace, not necessarily large or fancy—give 'em just enough technology that they regard as magic to do the job, and take the reports."

"Logical, but to what end? And how would they replicate themselves if they are celibate?"

"Well, celibate doesn't mean barren. If the racial bond is chemical—and I can assure you from personal experience, it is—then maybe theirs is permanent or periodic, such as one year on, one year off. Who would notice? You'd have a closed hierarchy dedicated to maintaining the established order. In other words, everything you need in a Center without all a Center implies. The important part is that they seem to have access to technology. They couldn't wait months for word to get back that something was going wrong, and they'd have to have the power to restore order. Not all the big devices like flyers and lasers, but mystical tools regarded as god-given devices for maintaining the natural order.

"But now comes the kicker. The system's fragile. Do you realize what just one freebooter landing there would do to it? And it's at least a century old, maybe more, so that would have to be taken into account. I kept asking myself why a world that *they* know and *we* know has a ring would be that undefended."

"I think I can see where you're going. I wouldn't have wiped the minds of those troopers. There would have to be a control someplace. A monitoring computer with access to all the latest tools, able to mindprint the young priestesses with all the supernatural theology and monitor them. *That's* why there are still survey satellites. If they get any hint of an alien presence or unauthorized technology, the priesshood will become a fully operative SPF division again, with the knowledge of their own grandparents' experience to draw upon and whatever technology and support they need to either deal with the alien menace or call in all the help they need." He stopped a moment. *"Whew!* You realize what that means?"

"I think so. Stealing the ring would certainly trigger the system, so they must never know it's stolen. We can't use more than limited technology on the surface because that's what all the monitors, human and mechanical, are looking for. The mere sight or report of anything out of the ordinary might be enough, we'd be suddenly faced with who knows what in the way of automated defenses plus a full SPF division. They'd call in every ship within reach, and this time they *won't* underestimate our strength. Another battle like the last one could set us back *years*."

"Pickup sticks," Isaac Clayben said, and they all turned to him in puzzlement. "An ancient children's game in my native land. Nothing more than a bundle of thin, straight sticks dropped in a heap from a small distance. The object is to remove each stick without moving or collapsing the rest of the pile. The one who removes most is the winner. This is like playing pickup sticks in an enemy minefield, except we don't know the nature of the minefield or what will trigger it, so we must be extremely careful. They must not be permitted even an accidental chance to learn that we are there or ever were there."

Vulture shrugged. "So I get in, and I get the ring somehow. The moment it leaves its home or somebody important turns up missing, the alarms ring and it's all over. You'd never get me out."

"Exactly. And I must frankly state that if the alarms go, those down there would have to be abandoned for the sake of the rest of us. If they came in full strength, they would easily locate the fighter and destroy it and install permanent monitors. Contact would be lost, perhaps for years, perhaps forever. It must be done right the first time."

Vulture stared at her creator and all could sense the hatred there. When and if they had the rings, Clayben would be the new project for the strange creature, but for now Vulture would keep her word.

"There is simply no way to do this. We don't know where it is, or what we're facing. And, down there, as one of them, I react as a native. It's impossible."

"Maybe not," Star Eagle put in through the speaker. "For one thing, I know where it must be."

That startled all of them. "What? How?" Hawks asked.

"One satellite is geostationary, all its channels beamed to a single location. There can be no other reason for this than to allow an open channel of communication to the outside. It is in an area almost eleven hundred kilometers from our fighter station, and it's quite central to the continent. It is logical that it is the religious center, and therefore the one with the ring. It is probably held by the highest-ranking priestess."

"Big deal," Hawks responded. "We don't know what's in there, or who, and we can't land anybody even remotely close to that place. To escape detection we had to set that fighter down in one of the rare holes in the satellite surveillance, and the other locations are farther away. So Vulture's got to be dropped down with nothing but what she's got now, traverse eleven hundred kilometers of that hell without being noticed, scout out the whole place and become one of the high priestesses with access to the ring the first time, because anybody who mysteriously disappears will be missed. Then she takes the ring—and triggers the alarm."

"We have one ring," China pointed out. "Those of us who have seen another state that ours seems identical in all ways except the design on the face. If we knew the design on the ring below, we could use ours as a prototype for weight and feel, manufacture a dummy, and make a switch. I will wager that they do not put this ring under a microscope."

Vulture nodded. "I thought of that. I believe I know the basic design, since it's on everything owned by the truth-bearers that I saw. Anybody have paper and pencil? None of my incarnations has been an artist, but I'll see what I can do."

The only pads and pencils available were in the children's nursery, and were quickly rushed in. Vulture made several attempts, drawing left-handed, before she finally got one that was approximately correct. A stylized, spindly tree with a tiny figure of a bird in it. "Damn! That's just not quite right!"

"It will do," Clayben responded. "If their markings were more exact and you studied them closely enough, we can pick it up in a mindprint. The whole stone area is only about three square centimeters, and we know the style and workmanship of the rings. It could be done. Not well enough to fool a full-fledged analysis, but certainly, I think, well enough to fool even someone who wears it daily. One rarely looks at rings; they are taken for granted. If they eventually notice, the thieves will be long gone. It is certainly worth a try."

Vulture sighed. "Even if true, this is a situation where my . . . talents . . . will be of limited use. If we are correct, then I can eventually waylay and become a truth-bearer, but I will have to remain that person until the ring is well away. We just can't have someone come in and later turn up missing, without triggering everything. If they *are* programmed SPF troopers, then we can't pick one up and use her as a prototype either. As I discovered when I became the sergeant, they all have latent triggers. Mindprobe one and the subject dies unless a specific computer code is entered, unique to each individual. We'd get nothing."

"Then what would you need?" Hawks asked, wondering if this would be the one theft they couldn't work.

"To even attempt it, I have to go along with the restrictions set by the system. We'd have to go down, cross all that distance and survive, and we'd all have to be programmed so that we *couldn't* betray ourselves. We might just pick up a truth-bearer anywhere along the line, or we might lose someone to another tribe looking to build itself up, and without proper programming, each of us would be a loaded bomb ready to go off. To do it convincingly, and unobtrusively, I'd need a tribe. More important, I'd need a tribe with someone else as leader, since I couldn't maintain the post. When we got to that main installation, I'd have to go in as a truth-bearer returning for leave or whatever it might be called, scout the place, locate the ring, and figure out a way to make the switch. It might well take more people than just me, too. We can't know until we get there. We can't even know if it's possible."

"You expect us to be the tribe?" Hawks asked. "We can't spare people like that. We have ships to staff and only a few who can really qualify."

"I don't need a large group. Too conspicuous and hard to support anyway. What do you expect to do? Go down there, knock a whole tribe senseless, ship 'em up here one at a time, and mindprint them? I'm proposing the ultimate heresy in this den of gods—when push comes to shove I've got to have a group of atheists. I could go back down and try to track down, isolate, and sedate four or five natives, but that just increases the risk, and I'd have a small tribe that still wouldn't know a Val from a god. Maybe we can't take high-tech stuff in, but we might be able to use what they have if we can recognize it, and we sure have to figure how to avoid tripping the booby traps. I'm not sure that installation is gonna be any more advanced that the rest of this world, as far as the people there are concerned, but we'll be hip-deep in people all of whom will suddenly become full-fledged SPF if a slip is made."

"We can't have them all looking like you," China pointed out.

"True, but there's a fair variety down there in spite of in-breeding. Just keep the basic racial characteristics the same. Hell, we have those photos. As for the mind print, I can become my native persona, Uraa, so completely for that purpose that only she will come out on the print. Ask Clayben. He designed it that way."

The doctor nodded. "It's true."

"Plus we've got China's experience in psychogenetics, psychochemistry, attitudinal programming—the works. I can work with her and Star Eagle to create what is necessary to survive down there, avoid exposure, and still get things done." She looked at their faces and saw their hesitancy, their doubts.

"Surely," Ikira Sukotae said, "there must be some alternative."

"Sure. I'll sneak in, somehow manage to become the big cheese if I can—and it might take a year or two—then steal the ring, and make a run for it as the whole security force is awakened and the alarm goes out to an orbital defense system designed to destroy anything trying to get on or off the planet."

The silence that followed was such that they could hear the air filtration system.

"The odds for success in this attempt are quite low," Star Eagle reported after a lull. "The highest probability is that the attempt will be judged impossible and the party will have to trek back and return empty-handed."

"Permanently stuck in that form for nothing," China noted.

"Yes, although I'd say the odds of escaping detection are even. A truth-bearer missing at the center would be noticed; one who vanished in the field would be simply written off as a routine casualty. At least we would have people toughened by the harsh experience down there and better equipped for a later try, and we would know just what we were facing and could figure out an alternative plan while we went after another ring. There are so many unknowns and variables here, the odds are astronomical that if an attempt were made it would either be unsuccessful or would trigger the response we do not want. In that case, those on the planet would be stuck down there, perhaps permanently. Vulture might get out by becoming a trooper, but no one else would, and accomplishing a safe pickup, assuming they avoided capture, would be next to impossible for a year or more. The odds of actually stealing the ring undetected without the use of computer aids, massive intelligence, interpretation, and analysis are pretty slim. That's assuming the group survived in that environment long enough to get to the installation and back in the first place."

Hawks thought for a moment, then said, "This may be a great blow to your ego, Star Eagle, but human beings existed in great numbers at a high level of culture and civilization long before computers. The big trick here is to keep our operation on the level of the culture of Matriyeh—all the way—while being aware enough not to step in any of the technological and anachronistic traps. You may be right. This might only be an intelligence mission, or it might fail. The risks are certainly great. But right now I'd say it's the better of the two choices open to us. There is a lot of activity now around Chanchuk, and we're sending out ships on long-range surveys trying to find if there is any other unusual activity that might tip us off as to the whereabouts of the fourth ring. *Here* is where they're overconfident. *Here* is where they are convinced that the odds are so much against us we won't even make the attempt until we have to. I say we give it a try."

Raven looked around and gave everyone a thin, humorless smile. "Any volunteers?" he asked.

Hawks, in fact, was not looking for any volunteers, at least not yet. There was a lot of research and technical data to accumulate first, plus work with Vulture to computer-model the sort of mindprint he wanted and determine just what the best attributes of survival might be. In the meantime, Hawks dispatched *Kaotan* to supplement *Bahakatan* and *Chunhoifan* in surveying the known colonial worlds for any signs of unusual activity there. Without the fourth ring the first three were nothing, and he would have liked nothing better than to go after number four before tackling Chanchuk. If they had three, Master System would know just where to expect them, and if he had to fight one more major battle anyway, it might as well be in the spot where he probably had to fight one anyway.

By the time they had to, he hoped they might figure out a way to win.

Although Clayben could put ideas into programs better than any of them, Vulture worked mostly with China and Star Eagle on the aims. The creature had no desire to ever be subject to Clayben's control again, and didn't trust him a bit. And of all the things to fear in all this, Clayben feared his creation most of all.

By the time Star Eagle had read, picked, probed, and

analyzed the Uraa personality as much as was possible, and chose and modeled the genetic information, Hawks had a pretty good idea of who he wanted to go and why. He discussed it all with Raven first, and was very much surprised to find that the Crow was in agreement.

"She's the logical choice. The *only* choice for leader among this group for a place like that," Raven said simply.

"I just thought you and she . . ."

"Look, they tinkered a little with her head on Melchior, but that was just to give her some kind of loyalty so she could be kept under control. Nobody I know of messed with *my* noggin. She ain't even good in bed. More like fightin' a war and tryin' not to get hurt. The only thing I wanted to always make sure of is that she was always on my side. No, I can get—satisfied—here if I feel the need, Chief. Tell the honest truth, if Ikira was a meter taller or me a meter shorter and she had a little more liking for men and a lot less for women, she'd be my choice of this lot."

"You sure you wouldn't like this one yourself? You were a field agent by choice all those years and you were in some pretty tough scrapes over the years."

He sighed. "Chief, there ain't no question this is Manka's meat. The kind of world just made for somebody with her personality and charm. She *has* to go. I think she already figured that. And under this kind of setup, I tell you she'll be the leader and therefore the male in the pack. Now, I ain't got nothin' against bein' a woman—face it, everybody's always damned curious how it'd be to be the other way, and I'm gettin' on in years and have nothin' much to lose—but under that system, I'd be physically bound to Manka as my lord and master. If we got to put more down to pull them out or reinforce them, I'll do it. I won't like it, but I'll do it. But that second part's just askin' too much."

Hawks nodded sympathetically. "All right. Accepted. I

just kind of figured you were used to working as a team and, besides, this is probably the closest race to our own we're going to have to deal with."

"I know, and it's tempting for that reason. But she's much too mean to die, Chief, and I'll be damned if I'll spend the rest of my days as one of her harem. Otherwise, you're right. This is my meat. Any ideas on the others?"

"Yes. It might surprise you to know I have a couple of volunteers."

"Huh?"

"Lalla Paschittawal and Suni Banderesh. They're pretty tough characters but they've lost their husbands and their ship and they are like fish out of water around here. I thought of them as pilots for some of the smaller ships we're building, but this doesn't necessarily preclude that. They took hits right off and never really got their licks in. They want to get even. They want to thumb their noses at Master System. Most of all, I think they want release from the unremitting boredom they've had since the battle."

"Okay, that's four. Is that enough?"

"If nobody died down there, yeah, but you and I know the odds of even getting to the damned place, let alone back, in one piece. Vulture wants seven, herself included."

"Seven! But who else is nutty enough for this one?"

"Let's call in Warlock and ask her."

Raven's sense had been correct. Manka Warlock had been expecting to be summoned, and she was not adverse to the idea. "Judging from Vulture, I won't even have to change my appearance much," she noted. "A little blacker, a lot tougher."

"It's far more alien on the inside, but you're probably right." He told her about the two *Indrus* widows' offer.

"They have motivation, but I wonder if they are too civilized. We will check them out and see. Anybody else?" She looked at Raven, and Hawks got her thought.

"I'd rather save Raven. You two have unique qualifications as experienced field agents. I'm willing to risk one of you but not both." There. That got the Crow off the hook, and he could see the gratitude in the field agent's eyes. Hawks decided he was owed a favor.

Warlock sounded disappointed, but accepted the logic of it. "Very well, then, who else?"

"You tell me."

She thought a moment. "If we will not have Raven, then I think we should have Captain Santiago."

"Maria? Why?"

"She is without a command or crew, she has reason to want revenge as much as the others, and she is tough. I have learned through this that no one gets to be captain of a freebooter ship without being tough, and she was the undisputed mistress over two big men and two different colonial life forms. She may need to unlearn some of her dependence on high-tech weapons, but I believe she can be taught. She is a survivor. If anything happens to me, she is capable of command."

"All right, I'll talk to her about it, anyway. Anybody else?"

"Let us summon her now and see if she has the will. Perhaps she will have some suggestions."

It was done. Hawks hated these kind of sessions, but there was no getting around them. At least Sabir and the Chows seemed to have adjusted and accepted their forms, although it was true they still tended to socialize more with the Earth-humans aboard than with the Janipurian refugees they'd impersonated.

Captain Santiago was not exactly thrilled with the idea, but she realized why she had been nominated. She asked for time to think it over, but within hours returned and agreed. "On one condition, though."

"Yes?" Hawks was willing to go to any lengths within reason.

"You need a couple more, right?"

"Yes. We could go with you five, but if you have any ideas, let's hear them."

"Midi Ng, at least, and hopefully the rest of that crew of cowards." Ng was the pilot who commanded *Espiritu Luzon* in the engagement that cost Santiago her ship and crew. "It's about time they paid up."

Warlock grinned, showing she shared the sentiments.

Hawks sighed. "I wish we could send the whole batch. Savaphoong gave the orders, but he also gave us the murylium shipment and you and the other freebooters. You owe him for that, but we'll do it anyway—my way. Those five brainless beauties would be nice for this, but they're transmutees. We can't change them, only reprogram them—which I will do if I need warm bodies. I'd also ask for Autoro but I wouldn't want to take any chance that he'd wind up in command down there, even by accident." Autoro was Savaphoong's bodyguard and enforcer and the only other free man he'd taken out of Halinachi with him. "Midi's girlfriend, Tae-Jin Chun, however, is proud of her martial arts abilities and was the *Espiritu*'s weapons officer. Anybody as small as she is who can act as a bar bouncer is somebody who'll be very useful down there."

"They're gonna say no," Raven said flatly.

Hawks shrugged. "I'm going to talk with Savaphoong first. I think by the time we're through, they'll realize that they don't have a choice. They owe him their lives, and he owes for the *Indrus* and the *San Cristobal*. I think he knows it."

Savaphoong wasn't buying at all, and he was quite miffed that anyone would even consider using anything of his again. "We did our part, and we continue to support you," he said, sipping a drink mixed in his luxurious bar by his personal slaves on the *Espiritu Luzon*, where he had lived in luxury since coming aboard. "I know what the others think, but we took damage in that battle and did the only prudent thing we could to save at least one ship out of three."

Hawks settled back in the comfortable chair he'd been given and looked squarely at the old entrepreneur. "You force me to put my cards on the table early. Up to now you've been acting like you have some kind of special privilege or position here, and up to now, thanks to your previous help, I've been willing to go along. No more. Then, I didn't need you, but after the battle, I considered you a potential risk as well as an ally. I know about the small explosion you rigged in the stern tubes to show real damage rather than just the shaking up you actually got. Don't bother denying, I have the battle recordings recovered from the wreck of the *Indrus* and the sensor readings from *Kaotan* and *Thunder*. An explosion, even a very small one, is difficult to control. It affected your port steering mechanism."

"Indeed, that was part of our problem. So what?"

"You couldn't have moved into the position you took opposite *Indrus* and *San Cristobal* if that mechanism had been damaged before the Val attacked. You couldn't have steered that way. You could have gotten there, but it would have taken many complex maneuvers you didn't make. I'm no pilot, but Santiago is an experienced captain, and Star Eagle is nothing else but. Once I saw that, I had no hesitancy in approving Star Eagle's request that when this ship was inside for repairs, we make a few adjustments. You take off without Star Eagle's codes, and you explode. You try something even then, and Star Eagle can assume remote command, including life support."

Savaphoong almost dropped his drink. "By what right . . ."

"*I* am the commander of this fleet. Me. I was elected, and then affirmed by the council of which you are only one member. I command every ship and every person in this community. *Every* ship. *Every* person. Would you like to put this to a vote of the captains when they come in? *They've* all seen the recordings, too. At this point, the only thing that is saving you from the mob, the mindprinter, and maybe the transmuter, is me. I'm doing so out of pragmatism and past considerations, but you used up most of that reservoir when you cost me two ships and five good lives. Now you're getting the rest of it, and the scales are even. Either you and another of your choice go down there, or you get to remain here in luxury by giving me the two people we want. I may need you or the others or the ship later on, but not now. If I do, I'll have them—and you— or you will not be there for the payoff if there is one. Which is it? You? Or them?"

Savaphoong sank back into his chair, visibly shaken. For a moment, he just stared off into space, oblivious to his company. Finally he said, "You do not pull your punches, do you?"

"I can't afford to. We—all of us—are living on borrowed time. I told you when you signed on that it would be permanent—once in, nobody gets out. It is a luxury we can't afford. As long as it doesn't jeopardize this mission or its people, I allow what I can, but don't overestimate your importance or power."

"I've had men shot for far less than this, you know," Savaphoong said, not threateningly but actually rather casually.

"That was Halinachi and the hard climb up to build it."

"I didn't build it. I took it. Jamie, there," he said,

pointing to one of the slaves, "is the old owner. I keep him around because it amuses me to do so."

"You try to take this from us—" Hawks responded in the same sort of tone. "Go ahead. You might even get me, and perhaps a few others, but in the end you will envy Jamie his brainless happiness. I have far too many deadlier things to worry about than you, Savaphoong. I do not lose sleep over you, but perhaps you should lose some sleep over me."

"I might very well. All right, you can have them. Enjoy yourself, señor. I admit that you have me, but I have not exhausted all my bargaining chips yet."

Hawks stared at him. "What do you mean by that?"

"Nothing. Now. It is not yet the time to need them, and if I use them now I will have no further reason for existence, will I? Do not worry. It is all locked up in here," he said, tapping his head, "and while it might be destroyed, even our friend Clayben could not get it out of me. You just let me be, and you will not regret it, my friend. When it is time, I have things you still need."

It was Hawks' turn to rise from his chair. "You know where the fourth ring is?"

Savaphoong just smiled, satisfied to win at least a minor round. "I do not say what I know. I will, my friend, when it is time."

Hawks wanted to throttle the man, and promised himself later vengeance, but he had more important things on his mind now. He went below to see the two women who shared a luxurious cabin and found that they had already been tipped. He suspected they were listening in to the conversation.

"We will not do it!" Midi said firmly, always the spokeswoman for the pair. "He does not own us! We are not his slaves!"

"Yes you will," Hawks responded icily. "And I'll ex-

plain why very simply. He saved your neck and we saved
your skin. You're experienced pilots but you've contributed nothing—except following his orders and letting two
ships be smashed. He's disowned you. You know what
went on. He's throwing you to the wolves to save his own
skin, just like he threw those ships to the wolves to save
his. Why should he care about you any more than he did
about them? You're just employees—and you've been
fired. You're being thrown out of this cozy little love nest,
and the only place you can come is *Thunder*. I am telling
him that he will either present himself tomorrow morning
at oh seven hundred to Manka Warlock on the common in
Thunder or present you. No other ship will take you. Now,
you *do* have choices. You can report. You can commit mutual suicide—no one will grieve for you, I assure you. Or
you can leave, but taking no equipment with you. I've just
explained to your ex-employer that everything here is common property. You report, or kill yourselves, or you will
both be thrown stark naked out the nearest airlock."

He turned and left the cabin, then got on his spacesuit
and exited the ship, walking down to the airlock entry port
of *Thunder* and back inside. He was slightly ashamed of
himself for feeling so, but by *god* he felt good!

Manka Warlock had volunteered to be the test case for
the transmuter template Star Eagle had worked out using
the genetic information from Vulture. Outwardly, the
change was noticeable but far less extreme than in any of
the others who had or would undergo the process. Her
creamy brown skin was now much darker, and her mane of
woolly hair changed from tiny curls to large ones. She had
been tall and muscular and was still tall and muscular, if
more so than before. Her features had always been fine and
delicate, a mixture of French and Ashanti ancestors, and
these needed no changes. They did add the brands, mathe-

matically chosen to be consistent with Matriyehan practice yet unique, as well as filling most of them with colored dyes consistent with local culture and chemically identical to those on Vulture. It gave Warlock a fiercer appearance she liked, but, she looked and sounded much like the old Manka. Some bone and local twine jewelry and ropelike bracelets and anklets also taken from Vulture's patterns completed her appearance.

One major difference was her skin, which looked and felt normal to her but was hard and tough, almost like hide, to anyone else. She held a finger over a lighted match and barely noticed it, and when she pinched it out with her fingers, she did not get burned. The most marked difference, however, was in her apparent physical age. Manka Warlock had been good-looking in her forties; she was a stunning sixteen. She did not, however, take the Matriyeh mindprint program they had worked out. That would be last.

Decked out as she was in her Matriyehan fierceness, she met with the others who would be her team. "Those of you who volunteered or got talked into this may reconsider," she told them. "Otherwise, by tonight, there will be no turning back. I want you in Matriyehan bodies, getting used to them, and feeling their power and potential as soon as possible. We have prepared a very large room in the office section and we will go there and remain there, cut off from the rest, while you train and learn the things that will keep you alive down there. On Matriyeh there will be no margin for error, and the lives of others might depend on the actions or inactions of any one of you. The mind-printer can give you all the information you need, but it cannot give you skills or increase your reaction times or fine-tune your reflexes. Partly it will be a case of unlearning what you take for granted. Pistols and rifles, computers and data banks, armor and shields—and even the little things, like food acquisition and preparation in a primitive environment, medicines and medical kits, and even such basic things as matches. I am going to train you until you think and act as one. I am going to try to make certain you stay alive because that is how *I* will stay alive." She paused. "Anyone have second thoughts?"

"Many," Maria Santiago said, "but as a captain, I have never asked anyone to do anything that I, myself, was unwilling to do nor turned from my responsibility. Besides," she added, "it is not, thank God, some four-footed beast or whatever else they might be on Chanchuk or the other place. I worked hard climbing up to be a captain. If I can survive down there, I can survive anywhere and be captain again."

Warlock nodded, liking the captain immediately. She would be a valuable ally. She turned to the *Indrus* widows. "And you?"

"We have only one goal," Suni Banderesh said for the both of them. "We wish no more like us from the ruins of *Chunhoifan* or *Bahakatan* or even *Thunder*. Perhaps we exist to help in this. Neither of us look forward to it, but we believe in it."

"Very good." Warlock turned to the last two, the ones who had been forced to come. "I asked for you two, because you're tough, sassy bitches with a killer's instinct. I know you don't feel any guilt at what you did, but that is beside the point. In this, you will atone or you will die. If you do not die, it will be because you have shaken your selfishness and become full members of the team, in which case you might even become full human beings someday."

"I am surprised you want us, considering your opinion," Midi Ng replied sourly. "You think we failed your company once. What if we fail you again?"

Warlock grinned evilly. "You see, that is the thing. If you fail us, it will also mean your own lives. If you *delib-*

erately fail any of us, I promise you that you will truly be in hell. If any of the others of us survives your actions, or lack of them, you will not. If they do not—then you better have the ring, or you will be left down there to live out the remainder of your miserably short lives."

The transmuting process was a swift one. Since Star Eagle could subtract but not add mass, all five would remain shorter than Warlock, some by a fair amount. Only Santiago, who was chunky and wide thighed, gave the pilot any room to play; her 157 centimeters could become 164 using that excess mass while also slimming her down, making her the second tallest but still almost a head shorter than Warlock. Star Eagle retained the best of their original features, flattering them wherever possible, within the racial limits set by the Matriyehan genetic code. Only Ng and Chun, whose features were strongly Asian, needed any substantial makeover, and they were the only ones who could not be recognized on sight by any who had known them before. Their physical ages ranged from fourteen to sixteen, and the only thing that really disturbed any of them was the branding marks that to them defaced their faces and bodies.

"Now we will go and begin our training," Warlock said. "None but Vulture and I wear the colors of rank and the ornaments of honor. Those you will have to earn, and we alone will decide them. From this point on we will see only one person from the outside until we are ready to go down —and when that will be is when Vulture and I say it shall be."

The one and only outsider allowed, at Warlock's request, was Silent Woman. It seemed an odd choice at the start, and both Hawks and Cloud Dancer had initially objected. "We do not even know if she really understands any of this," Cloud Dancer said. "Nor do we know how she will take to you all, like that, in there."

"She understands what is necessary," Warlock replied. "At the moment, she is the most valuable one on this ship to us. She survived a culture and an environment gentler only by degrees than the one we must go to, and she has shown skills in those areas where modern folk are weakest. It was you who told us of the unerring knife throws back on Earth, and the silent, animallike way she managed to approach and then kill two men. I need someone to teach those skills. I do not propose she join us, just teach us."

Hawks thought of the small, fat, middle-aged woman of unknown tribe who was colorfully tattooed from the neck down and who had spent her life in slavery, her tongue cut out to stop her screaming as they killed her malformed only child in front of her. She had been mostly bewildered by all this, but seemed to have found her place in the nursery caring for the young children of others. But she *had* been deadly and cunning in an almost animallike way when she had chosen to make her escape with Hawks and Cloud Dancer. It was easy to forget that.

She *did* seem bewildered and perhaps a bit frightened at first by the seven strange women, but she knew and recognized Warlock and seemed to understand what she was to do, not so much by words as by patient illustration. Even Hawks had to admit the brilliance of using her in the end. She knew far more than knives; she knew how to exist with what was on hand, to weave vines into useful things, to patiently select and shape stone and bone into anything from weapons to ornaments. Within a week she was acting very apologetic to Cloud Dancer about neglecting the kids and spending almost all her time in Manka Warlock's training room.

According to China, who could interface with Star Eagle and tap into the great ship's communications and monitors, Silent Woman was doing very well in there while most of the others were suffering badly. Tae-Jin Chun, for example, was very proud of her black belts in some of the more esoteric martial arts, but eventually Warlock had badly beaten the former bouncer while barely getting bruised herself. There was clearly more than one mistress of those arts, as later lessons were to show, and Warlock's only problem was that she needed Vulture and Silent Woman to keep her from killing rather than forcefully demonstrating to her pupils.

There was no getting around the fact that Manka Warlock liked hurting people and if she gave a damn about being hurt, it never showed. If she ever got tired or weak or frustrated, that never showed, either. She did everything they did, and took everything they took, and she did it better. It was a mark of her strength that after seven weeks, they hated her so much that not one of them broke.

It was about this time that Silent Woman approached Hawks. She still could only communicate in a basic sign language; there was no way to know what language was hers. Even mindprinters with language programs seemed to have only slight effect, since they cross-referenced ideas from the language you knew, and it was by no means certain that in her mental state Silent Woman really had a language as the rest thought of one. Even now, Hawks had some problems understanding her, but finally he figured it out. By his own code of honor, she was as much his wife as Cloud Dancer was, and it was clear suddenly what she had in mind.

In very basic terms, she wanted a divorce.

Once he go that idea, he could guess the rest. "You want to go, don't you?" he said aloud, then signed it as best he could.

She nodded. She made cradling motions, then pointed in the general direction of Warlock's lair. For a moment he thought she wanted to care for any babies they might have, or perhaps she understood the change in the others, and that perhaps, she, too, could be restored to function and youth, but finally he realized that it was a more basic, uncomplicated idea.

They need me, she was saying. She seemed to understand that they were being prepared to go into very primitive areas, and while they had learned well, she was unsure that they would all have a good chance unless she were there to help and reinforce the lessons.

In fact, ever since the true potential of the transmutters was known to him, Hawks had been tempted to use them on her, to give her a new tongue and perhaps beauty and fertility, but he had no real way of conveying that to her or finding out what she really wanted and Clayben and the others had been very nervous about doing anything to or with someone who was, in Clayben's words, "clearly a functioning psychotic." Now she was asking for it and Hawks didn't know what to do. He did, of course, what he always did when he was in such a dilemma: he called in Cloud Dancer.

"I believe we should let her," Cloud Dancer said without much hesitation. "Although I love her and am frightened for her, it is what she wants and perhaps what she was born to do. Perhaps she could save some lives down there —and perhaps, live or die, she might have her only chance of regaining her soul."

Hawks sighed. "And the hellish thing is, we might never really know if we're doing the right thing. But, all right. If Warlock and Vulture agree and Clayben is willing, we'll give it a try."

Since being taken prisoner with Hawks and Cloud Dancer, Silent Woman had lived in a world totally of magic and incomprehensible mystery and she hated it as much as she loved the people around her. Now she expected that magic to reward her for loyal service and suffering and give her purpose once again.

Clayben was nervous about it. Not the physical part—that was easy. It would be the mindprinting at the end that would be the problem. "Still," he said, "whatever language she uses, primitive and basic thought it may be, should provide reasonable matches for this Matriyehan tongue. It's my guess that she will function better down there than here."

Warlock was delighted, and Vulture relieved. Oddly, the changeling's one concern was that, once down, it would be Silent Woman in charge. He only hoped they could make her understand that the object of it all wasn't just to survive down there, but to steal something.

She was quite fat, which gave Star Eagle a great deal of mass to work with. He understood how she had suffered and how hard this all was, and he made her almost a primal sixteen-year-old Matriyehan goddess. When she first stepped down from the transmuter, looking in a mirror, and saw herself, she traced the whole outline of her body on the mirror, felt her whole body, and then she cried.

Silently.

There was no longer a single thing physically wrong with her, and she almost choked on the tongue a few times, but Silent Woman remained as mute and almost as enigmatic as ever.

7. THE ETERNAL TESTS OF THE MOTHER

AT THE END OF NINE AND A HALF WEEKS, MANKA Warlock felt as if she'd done as much as she could.

To properly complete the group's training she needed more than the poor simulations that Star Eagle had managed to conjure up, she needed to be in the field where she would be no more experienced than the rest of them. There was no practical way, however, to take everyone down to the surface for a few days and bring them back; each time someone was inserted into the world or withdrawn from it, they ran the risk of detection no matter what the safeguards and timing. Silent Woman's very presence had suggested one thing to her, though, which she carried out and imposed during the last two weeks. She worked out a series of codes involving finger snaps and clicks made with the mouth that could convey basic information, and then imposed a rule of absolute silence. Everything was by gesture and sign, with even the audibles used only when necessary.

It was difficult at the start for all except Silent Woman, but after two weeks they hardly needed speech to function efficiently.

It was Vulture finally who emerged from isolation. "We are as ready as we can be," she told Hawks. "I'm still a bit nervous about the *Indrus* women, who are tough enough but perhaps still too civilized, and the two from *Espiritu Luzon*, who have done well but who I'm not sure I want to depend on in a crisis and may have to. But we can go no further here."

Hawks nodded. "All right, then. Are you really sure you need so many of us, though? Even at this stage it looks like we are committing a large number to unknown risk for no purpose except covering you."

"I need covering," she assured him. "We all do. In the end, this caper might be as intricate as Janipur's. The only way to know is to go in and find out. Do we have the duplicate ring?"

Hawks nodded. "It's the same size, shape, weight, and general composition as the Janipur ring, and we have placed on its face the consistent design taken from your mindprinted memories of the carvings on the truth-bearer's charms and staff. It's to scale and in the same style, but there is no way to know for certain if it's able to fool anyone until the two are physically compared. We've made a housing for it inside a bone charm so it looks like a single piece. We'll show you how to get it apart. Don't lose it, or you're going to have to come all the way back for a new one."

"I'll take good care of it. Anything else you want to say to them before we go ahead with the mindprinting?"

"We'll cover the details when it's done. Good luck."

"We'll need it," Vulture responded.

* * *

They stood there in silence, already looking the part of a savage band. All now had colored dye markings in their brands indicating the pecking order; Silent Woman wore the marks of firebearer. The most marked change was an expected one; Warlock had developed some woolly facial and body hair, and while her body was still female in shape there was a definite difference even in how she moved or carried herself. When she said, "We are ready. Let's get it over with," her voice was still Warlock's, Caribe accent and all, but a half octave lower and definitely male.

Only Warlock and Vulture did not plainly show that they were nervous, even a little scared.

Star Eagle would handle the process automatically, but it was decided that China would give the basic briefing. Although Clayben had been the major human participant in creating the programs, it was thought best to leave him out of the actual performance of the printing process for political reasons.

"Basically, we took the information and experience of Uraa's life and analyzed it," China told them. "You will all receive the same basic print, minus some of the more personal items that would have no bearing on you down there. We don't know what might trigger the activation of the defenses, but if it is keyed to alienness, then just hearing a non-Matriyehan tongue would be enough and we want no slips, but we also want you to have full memories and knowledge. As a result, we have instituted a filter of sorts. The Matriyehan tongue is simple and not geared to the creation of new words or concepts, but it is adequate even if you might have to use approximations and fifteen words to describe one thing. The filter will simply not permit you to vocalize anything except the native tongue. It will be your primary language. You will think in it and it will take effort to access another, even internally, and impossible vocally. You will, however, still understand all the languages you know now, so you would still understand me. Language shapes a culture more than anything else. Master System knows this, which is why this was imposed. The more you relax, don't fight, and use this language exclusively, the more native you will become. The terms are holographically linked. When you hear *'daka'* for example, you will instantly think of the huge lava snakes."

The language was in fact compact, but relatively versatile. There were no ambiguities allowed, and every term had just one meaning; most words, like the names, were no more than two syllables. The native name for the world, mystical and important because it contained three syllables, was pronounced "Mah-treh-yeh."

"You will respond only to the names we give you," China continued. "That is also for security. People's names are also legitimate words and might be descriptives of personalities, but there don't seem to be any hard and fast rules, so we tried to keep it close if we could. Maka means 'high tree,' for example, so we can use that for you, Manka. Similarly, Mari means 'pretty dirt.' Not a great name but close to Maria. Suni is 'Gray Rock,' Midi is a kind of plant, Taeg, which is close, is—sorry—a kind of bug, and we chose Euno for Silent Woman because it means 'quiet hand.' Lalla, your name is unpronounceable in Matriyehan, so we selected Aesa, which means 'strong branch.'"

She paused a moment, then continued. "We also must take a number of security precautions considering the close call on Janipur. You won't have laser pistols and you'll be practically defenseless against something like a Val. We doubt one is there now, but if anything goes wrong, you can be sure one will show up faster than we could. Now, listen well. Any attempt to probe your mind, hypno you, or in any way gain information about us will trigger an automatic dormant program in your mind. It will block off any knowledge, any memories, not Matriyehan. For all intents and purposes, it will erase anything not in the programming we are about to give you. Only we know the code that will erase the so-called worm program instead of triggering it. Only the machine that creates it can remove it. It's an idea we took from the SPF, and we'll be using it from this point on in the field. If you get separated from the group for any reason, try to retrace the route to the fighter. It will be there unless it is discovered and destroyed by the enemy. Just give your name. It will recognize you and then notify us to set up transmission and reception. If you return for any reason and it is not there, use the map references that will be imprinted in your mind to go to the alternate points where pickup might be made in order. That's all there is, except, good fortune guide you all."

Only Vulture did not need the mindprobe; she already had an identity and experience below, and had been designed to fool and be impervious to any of the standard devices. This also made her valuable in one other respect: she alone would not be bound by the limitations of the program.

Unlike transmutation, the mindprobe process was neither quick nor without some difficulty, and it took several hours to process them all.

Maria Santiago, like the others, awoke with a headache and slight dizziness that took awhile to go away. She felt —strange. Strange memories and stranger landscapes filled her mind, and she felt oddly cramped, closed in, and threatened by the room. In the back of her mind she knew who she was, who the others were, where they were and why, but it seemed suddenly remote, even alien, and hard to grasp all the complexities of it. She tried not to think of those things; thinking of them confused her and frightened her still more. There was only the tribe, only the People, her wife-sisters and their chief. Security lay only in the tribe, and so long as she was one with them she had nothing to fear.

Maka led them down to the place where they would return to open and the People, and they followed, eager to be away. Uraa went first, to scout the way, then the rest followed with Maka last. They were transferred first to *Lightning*, with Raven piloting, and made the short jump from no-space to the carefully precalculated angle and orbit that would bring them in at the "dead" spot, where the ship could attain geostationary orbit long enough for them to transmit down to the fighter without being picked up by the monitors.

One by one, they stepped out on the surface of Matriyeh and formed up. They carried the crude stone-tipped spears, and stone axes and blow guns hung from their vine belts.

Although they all had memory-pictures of the Earth-Mother, they all knew that, except for Uraa, they were seeing it for the first time. The heat was great, the humidity almost as bad, and the air had the faint smell of sulfur and sulfuric compounds that took some getting used to.

The landscape was rough, barren of life, and filled with grotesque rocky forms; black lava frozen in place like a great wave locked forever in stone, and beyond, a burnt wasteland of reds and oranges and gray ash like thick sand. The place had great beauty to it, but it was dead and threatening, as well, and no place for people to live. The sky above was thick with clouds swirling in demonic dances, and here and there in the distance thin fingers of lightning lashed out and struck far off, bringing occasional distant explosions to their ears.

Maka, too, was affected for a moment by all this, but she knew she had the responsibility and that the day was more than half gone. She nodded to Uraa, the scout, and she turned and led them down from the burnt and black-ened side of the great volcano, its cone invisible in the clouds, and finally on to the gray sands. They set off at a run, the only sounds those of distant thunder and the sharp breathing of the others. They ran for more than an hour without a break, until they were within sight of the edge of the ash field and the first green growth, which began abruptly. Now they slowed, but still Maka kept them to silent speech.

The jungle floor was quite dark and filled with vegeta-tion; the great fronds far above captured most of the light and rain, but enough trickled down to the floor or was stored as excess in the great trees to support a variety of lower plant life—mostly vines and creepers and spindly bushes with sharp, thorny leaves, and various mosses, algae, and fungi. The jungle also teemed with insects of all types, but there was no sign of birds or animals. They reached a swift-flowing, shallow river, in the center of which rough water rolled about protruding rocks. Uraa took them down one side of the muddy bank for almost a kilometer until they came to a bend in the river where the water flowed more quietly through transitory islands of silt. There they were permitted to kneel in the mud and drink, and then Uraa spoke, breaking the silence.

"Maka tribe spear fish in river," she said. "Else eat bugs. Uraa show," She picked up her spear, examined it, then walked very slowly into the water at a quiet point and out near one of the mud spits. As they watched, she stood there, absolutely motionless, spear ready, eyes only on the water. She remained there in hip-deep water, like a statue, for what seemed like forever, but then, suddenly became a blur of motion, bringing the spear down swiftly and force-fully, plunging it all the way down, twisting, then lifting it up with both hands. On the end, neatly speared but still wriggling, was a large fish. She waded back to them, looking very satisfied, as indeed she was. Her biggest concern with this show was that there would either be no fish in the area or that she would miss.

The creature was certainly ugly, with a wide mouth, enormous feelers all around it, smooth purple-and-white skin rather than scales, and two large fins that seemed almost like protoarms. Silent Woman suddenly grinned, nodded, and waded out into the river. It took her even less time than it had taken Vulture, and it was clear that it wasn't the first time she'd done this sort of thing.

Now it was the others' turn to try.

They didn't do nearly so well, although both Uraa and Silent Woman tried to show them how. Absolute stillness was required in this water, and the position in the water was also critical. These fish did not so much swim as walk along the bottom rooting through the mud, but no matter how muddy the water became they gave off small, telltale bubbles as they cleared themselves of river-bottom debris. Ultimately, Suni and Midi each caught one, after several failures, but the rest came up empty. Uraa and Silent Woman made up for it as darkness began to creep onto the surface.

The fish were gutted and expertly skewered by Uraa and Silent Woman. It might have been possible to gather enough dead wood from the nearby forest floor to make fire, but it was forbidden. This was not uninhabited territory. No place that could provide food with little physical danger, even for amateurs and novices like them, would be unclaimed.

It was very difficult for some of them to face eating the bloody meat raw, and Maria and both of the *Indrus* women looked distinctly nauseated, but they choked it down all the same. Manka Warlock didn't like it but ate her share, and

Midi and Taeg had less problems. Uraa and Silent Woman
ate with unreserved relish.

"Camp here to Great God's light," Maka told them.
"Uraa know this place?"

Vulture nodded. "If other not here, will not come in
dark. This place of big tribe. Many more than Maka tribe.
Must go far next light. No bad things near. Safe camp to
light." Demon-things prowled the darkness looking for
lives and souls; Matriyehans moved in darkness only when
forced to do so.

Tonight there would be little need for a guard; later on
there would be, and it was understood that those who
didn't pull their weight in food gathering by day would not
sleep much by night. For now, until they were fully
blooded and well experienced in living here and had
learned the practical means of survival, allowances would
be made.

They cleared a dry but protected area near the river and
lay down close together to sleep. There would be better,
less austere camps later, when they had made what was
necessary, but for now a spartan camp was all they could
manage. Highly uncomfortable, and with the tension creating somewhat sour stomachs, sleep was not easy to come
by. So far, though, it hadn't been as bad as they had feared
it might be, but there were memories from the mindprinter
of harsher things and harder places on this world and they
had a long distance to travel, much of it in areas that even
Vulture had never seen or heard about.

Isaac Clayben frowned. He'd called Hawks and Cloud
Dancer to his lab, and China was already there. The blind
woman looked slightly shaken.

"I've been analyzing these mindprinter recordings of the
group we sent down," he told them, "using Star Eagle's
capabilities and some proprietary programs I developed

from analyzing what Master System did with the records it took from all of us periodically. No major surprises, although I don't think anyone would ever like to sample Warlock's sadomasochistic fantasies, which are a bit hard to take even in data form. Although she's probably the one best able to keep them alive and maintain success, I feel sorry for the other poor women down there whenever she gets in the mood for sex, which I think will be often. No surprises, that is, until I get to Silent Woman. We took her print routinely on Melchior, and I vaguely remember being given a report that the results were highly unusual, but there were so many other things to occupy me that she didn't rate a very high priority. The data was simply overridden by shock and psychosis, looped back over and over, so it was just meaningless garbage. China tried to read it with the printer and almost went mad herself."

"An endless loop, over and over," she said weakly. "Incredible horror and sadness, the same terrible images again and again, and through it all a chilling scream of her soul. I know they're your people, but to me, those medicine men set a new standard of human cruelty. I never imagined that such as they existed. It wasn't just a necessity—they *enjoyed* it. They *forced* her to watch . . ." She trembled and choked up for a moment. "To watch . . . the ritual disemboweling of her baby while it was still alive. To be held close, your face pushed into your baby's wounds . . . I was kept intellectually distant, a watcher in her mind, and still I will have nightmares forever."

Cloud Dancer shivered, as well, and even Hawks felt the horror. "They are not our people," he said defensively. "The same race, yes, but they are not our people. They are of a different nation, and religion, although this does not sound like Illinois work, either. It smacks of demon worship in the way it was carried out, although it was still policy."

China's head snapped up. "Policy? Whose?"

"The child was deformed—"

"The child was *not* deformed! It was a perfect baby girl!"

There was shocked silence at that, and Cloud Dancer gripped Hawks' hand and squeezed it hard. Hawks thought of the fat pig of an Illinois pirate chief telling him that story, knowing it made perfect sense and had the full ring of truth to it and thus saved his miserable life.

"There is more to this, then, than cultural beliefs and practices. Can you get beyond it? Can you filter it out?"

"What do you think we've been trying to do? It isn't easy with a trauma of this magnitude," Clayben responded, "and I'm no psychiatrist. *Thunder*'s computers are good, but they aren't specialized for this sort of thing. You know how many cross-referenced memory bytes there are in the average forty-year-old brain? Quadrillions. The human brain is an incredible natural indexing system we can only approximate in Star Eagles and Vals and the rest. The combinations create both data flows and holographic images. What we have here is basically a self-imposed worm program. I know she didn't know it or think of it that way, but that's what it is. The trauma was so great that she shut off access to everything preceding a period of perhaps a couple of weeks after they cut out her tongue. Any attempt to access anything prior to that runs into the trauma loop and there is instant recoil. After a while it's like electric shock conditioning. You just don't go there any more."

"The language that she has is her own," China explained. "It was created in her mind after the trauma. The very *concept* of language is in the blocked-off regions. She thinks in ideographs, much like a deaf-mute would. She simply doesn't have a self-image; it must be supplied by those around her. Even her dreams are mundane things about what she did the day before. She does, however, retain many basic skills that indicate that she once led something of a wilderness life. It is incredible that she survives at all, given the strength of the trauma. Suicide or catatonia would be more likely. What it really comes down to is that she is a very strong person—perhaps the strongest among us."

"The thing is, we've suddenly given her cause for developing a totally new self-image. She cannot totally escape the old one—she is still the prisoner of her past in that—but we gave her one hell of a body and good looks. In face, at Vulture's urging we strongly emphasized the female sexual attributes and added some additional nerve links to increase the intensity of feeling there. He was afraid of her psychosis coming out very strongly and violently in a setting more like she was used to and, with her wilderness skills, taking command from Warlock. Not knowing what we were dealing with, we went along. I think we struck the right balance, anyway. Warlock, of course, had intercourse with her in order to establish Matriyehan chemical bonding, and I suspect that will be sufficient to control her. But she is still a strong and violent personality, which of course, we need down there. If she is redeveloping a whole new internal personal image, that's probably fine, but we must know more about her past. If the violence and cruelty down below begin to trigger the old traumas—we don't know what she might become."

"It seems to me you're a little late thinking of this," Cloud Dancer noted acidly.

"Huh? What?"

"Suppose you discover that she might become a raging

homicidal maniac who can be stopped only by death? How could we warn them? What could we do about it?"

They had been on Matriyeh for seven weeks, and if their harsh existence wasn't getting any easier, at least it was becoming more routine. They were always busy, hunting for food and tools, and all the while moving slowly and cautiously toward their goal. They avoided the many dangers by being ever alert, surviving by thinking only of the moment at hand. There were snakes large enough to swallow people, and leathery-winged beasts with sharp teeth that could dive at any moment on unsuspecting prey; there were vines that could trip the unwary, and twists and turns in the ground that might break an ankle.

And even when at rest they were always tense, listening for potential dangers. The only real pleasure came late at night or just before dawn, for the lucky one favored by Maka's attentions. The coupling was animalistic—raw lust and gratification—but the tensions built up to the point where they all craved relief.

And because only Maka could give this pleasure, all behavior was aimed toward pleasing Maka, serving Maka, obeying Maka. If they'd had the opportunity and the motivation to think about it, they all would have been shocked at how quickly the veneer of civilization and their own diverse cultural standards had been stripped away. They all were killers, bound to each other and their leader—literally no one or nothing else counted.

At dawn, they preened one another, washed themselves if some water was available, finished off anything left to eat from the night before, and the cycle started all over again.

Manka Warlock was comfortable with her role, although the overall responsibility for them all was a heavy burden.

At the start, when she'd first studied the system, she had been upset that a male figure dominated packs of women, but she'd come to realize the logic in it. It was, after all, democratic; any Matriyehan had the potential to be chief, if they had the will and the personality to do so and a vacancy came their way, and only one male figure was biologically necessary in the system. She often wondered, though, how many women a chief could serve in a day. Some of the tribes here were a hundred or more strong.

Warlock was also pleased if somewhat surprised that as yet they had not suffered any serious casualties: some sprains, a number of bruises, and a number of near-serious incidents, but nothing really severe. She knew, though, that the luck wouldn't last forever even though they were skilled at primitive living. They were getting so proficient at hunting the *tuka*, an animal resembling a green-haired wild boar but with a long snout, razor-sharp teeth, long tusks, and the temper of a shrew, that when they found one, it seldom escaped. Both Suni and Mari had been slightly gored by one when they first tried to catch one, and Silent Woman still had teeth marks on her right arm, but they hadn't been crippling injuries. Unless it received a mortal blow or a major compound fracture, the Matriyehan body had a tremendous capacity for self-repair equaled only by its enormous toleration for pain. They did, of course, have the knowledge to set simple fractures if necessary and use certain jungle herbs and leaves as medicines. That had been included in the program.

But for the landmark-based maps in their heads, they would have had no idea how far they had traveled, and even that was an approximate measure. The Matriyehan language had only the concepts of short and far, and the definition of far translated out as "horizon." Nor was there any long-term sense of time; the day was measured by light and shadow because it was necessary to know where you stood compared to what was left to do; no other time was relevant. Even now it was impossible for them to tell how long they had been living this life, and every day it seemed more and more their only reality, that existence before some kind of wild dream or vague religious view of heaven.

Vulture, however, could tell that they were averaging less than six kilometers a day, counting the amount of time they would spend having to find bearings when lost and the necessary diversions for hunting and gathering, which almost always took them in the wrong direction. This meant that they had covered, at most, a quarter of the distance. The life and the absolute requirements that her form imitate a Matriyehan exactly were also taking their toll, more, in fact, than they had the first time. She was as chemically bound and devoted to Maka as the rest, and if Maka suddenly proclaimed that they would build the tribe, remain, and forget the mission, it would have been instantly accepted. That devotion, and the collective mind-set of the tribe, had almost trapped Vulture here the last time.

Already Maka had fallen prey to one of the potential traps in the Uraa-based program and the language. She had begun first to refer to, then to pray to the various spirits and demons of the world. These had been left in the programming because to edit them out would have marked them as somehow different and could have betrayed them; now the theology was taking on a shadowy reality of its own.

About nine weeks out, they had taken shelter in a lushly overgrown lava tube against one of the incredibly frequent and very violent storms that swept the world. They had caught a *tuka* early and had drunk its blood for strength, and so were well prepared to sit out the rest of the day. Often they had seen, but managed to avoid being seen, by other tribes, although sometimes that had meant hiding in

deep water using the blow guns to breathe or covering
themselves in mud and lying very still. In spite of the complications that would result, Maka would have been impossible to stop from taking a smaller group than they, but
these were all much larger—which, at least, made them
easier to detect.

In the cave, considering the storm, they had risked a
small fire to cook the meat, a rare luxury in this life. Fires
caused smoke, of course, but in that sort of storm it was a
reasonable risk.

But a lone figure did approach through the roar of the
storm, and Midi, who was on guard at the mouth of the
tube, didn't see her until the stranger was almost inside.
Then she leaped upon the figure and wrestled it to the
ground in the rain, while barking a single word of warning
to her wife-sisters within. They responded instantly, drop-
ping whatever they were doing and running to Midi's aid.

Midi had the stranger well in check, arm around her
throat and stone ax poised to bash in a head if any resis-
tance was offered. None was, and it was soon clear why
when Maka arrived, looked down, and ordered Midi to
release the prisoner.

"Hold, sisters!" The newcomer gasped, rubbing her
throat. "Truth-bearers serve all tribes."

She was quickly offered a hand up and taken inside the
cave. Maka was undecided just what to do and looked to
Vulture for advice, but got none. The leader decided that it
was a good, and perhaps inevitable, test, and that the traveling priestess could always be killed later if she proved a
problem.

So they offered some *tuka* and examined the stranger.
Truth-bearers were the only Matriyehans who wore any
sort of real clothing, although it was more of a great cape
than a robe or true garment, made out of what looked like
tuka hide dyed a dark red. Her face and her entire body

were covered with tattoos of varying colors and designs, although a bird and tree seemed to recur in many themes and variations. She also had a polished bone ring in her nose running through a perforation and with no visible break, and similar earrings, although a carved charm hanging from the left earring was a tree and the one from the right, the bird. She had no hair save eyebrows; the head didn't look shaved, either. It genuinely appeared that no hair had ever grown there.

When Silent Woman saw the incredible tattoos covering the newcomer's body she gave something of a gasp, and thereafter couldn't take her eyes off the truth-bearer. Warlock saw it and was unnerved by it, but could do nothing. "What spirits bring truth-bearer to Maka tribe in storm?" she asked. This was, after all, decidedly not the normal way you got one.

"Maka tribe near spirit ground next hill," the stranger explained. "We go to spirits to get strength, storm come, know cave, Maka tribe here." It was as simple as that.

Matriyehan society wasn't really made for small talk, and there was little to talk about. The truth-bearer asked about the unusually small size of the tribe and Maka gave the official story, that she and two others had been separated in a storm from a larger tribe far to the south—Uraa's tribe, which was real and where they said it was—and had not been able to contact the tribe. They managed to survive, and Maka began developing the chief's aspects stimulated by the mental acceptance that they would not again find their chief. She then "took" the other two, and they began to wander, picking up other isolated people from various tribes until they had the current eight. Neither Maka nor Vulture liked the skillful interrogation, although the individual cover stories seemed to stand up. The mute Silent Woman was not considered all that odd; this sort of mental withdrawal was relatively common, particularly among individuals of a tribe separated from it and their children for great lengths of time. It was attributed to being alone against an onslaught of demons; no single person was strong enough to ward them off for long.

Vulture glanced uneasily at Silent Woman, who continued to stare at the visitor and show no other expression. What was going through the strange woman's mind when she saw someone rather ugly and tattooed in a way that had to bring back memories of her old self? But Vulture also continued to check Maka for a signal. Here was a gift from the gods—a truth-bearer alone and close to one of the holy places, the sort of place Vulture would love to get a look at. She suspected that Maka believed the gift too good to be true; that this might be some sort of trap. Vulture hoped her suspicion was true. The other alternative was that Manka Warlock had gone so native that she could not bring herself to order a mortal sin and ultimate heresy. That could be a real problem, since in this form, Vulture was commited to obedience and service, yet because it was not a mindprint, she also was more aware than the others of their true nature and mission and was thus more critical of their current situation.

"Good spirits guide truth-bearer to Maka tribe," the truth-bearer was saying. She took out her magic sack, which was wet and muddied but appeared dry inside, and brought out a handful of what looked like volcanic sand and ground leaves. "No danger here," she said. "Truth-bearer protect Maka tribe. Bring wonder of gods." Without waiting, the priestess sprinkled the material in her hand slowly in the small fire. Smoke billowed forth, which startled them all at first, but which they could not avoid breathing in the closeness of the cave. It was neither acrid nor unpleasant; indeed, breathing it in brought a sudden rush of great pleasure, and after the first inhalation, they settled down and wanted only to breathe in more. All pain was gone, all cares, all thought—they felt as normal as before, but knew the joy of the gods.

They rose out of their bodies, and their souls stood upon the face of the Earth-Mother and became aware of all the spirits and demons of the Testing Place. The Earth-Mother was below them, holding them with mystical bonds that were beautiful and erotic to the touch, and above them the Great God's hand could be dimly seen, wearing a great and mystical ring with the symbol of life—the bird in the tree. Through Her light of glory, and only dimly perceived, was Her smaller firebearer *Topakana*, and the lesser gods of heaven, whom the People called stars, looking down on them. It was so wondrous, so exactly like the teachings, so exactly as it should be.

And then the Earth-Mother spoke, a gentle whisper that sent chills of ecstasy through them all.

"We show Maka tribe this because tribe fail to doubt demons," she said. "Maka tribe not believe truth. Maka tribe not worship us."

No, no. Earth-Mother! Maka tribe believe. Maka tribe good, holy!

"Now you see truth. All but this be false. All else be demon thought. Throw demon thought from soul. Clean soul. Be born as new baby. Grow as new tribe, no demon thought, no doubt, only truth. Only then be all with us."

Oh, we will, we will!

The vision faded, but not the pleasant feeling and the wonderful glow of the experience. Truth was Matriyeh; there was nothing else. Truth was touching the Earth-Mother and the spirits at all times and taking the tests of life. All else was false, lies from clever demons seeking to make the strong fail. There, in the dark, damp cave, as the storm died down and darkness fell, they believed.

Of them all, only Silent Woman had not seen the visions nor heard the talk. She had heard talk, but it was the chatter of the tattooed stranger and meant nothing to her. The smoke had made her feel good, though, and she did not question what had happened, although she was not aware of what the others believed they saw and experienced.

The truth-bearer could not stay; she had to answer the summons of the spirits and they understood, but they allowed themselves to be blessed at dawn and then watched her depart. They did not follow; that area was holy ground, forbidden. But each received a small amount of the magic sand for their pouches, with instructions to smoke, inhale, or eat it if they ever found themselves beset by doubts or their way invaded by demon thoughts. They were told what to chant as they took it, since such chanting would reinforce the truth and drive away the demons and close their ears to demon speech.

The change in the tribe was immediate. They no longer spoke of strange things and all seemed to have lost their drive to journey someplace. They still had their memories, but they no longer believed them; here, on Matriyeh, which was the only place there was other than heaven, such strange and bizarre concepts could only have come from the minds of demons. They had been failing the life-tests, but now the Earth-Mother had shown mercy upon them and corrected their descent into demonic heresy. But if they were no longer on a journey or quest, then they had to find a territory in which to live, and that meant building their strength, creating a true tribe that could hold its own.

Now, instead of avoiding other tribes, they began to seek them out, but silently and in stealth. Then, when they could, sometimes with great daring, they would take the wife-sister of another tribe and bring her to Maka where the new one would be tied down with vines and taken in the rite of transfer. Within a week they were twelve, and within three they were twenty strong. Some of the new-

comers were pregnant, and by now it was clear that of the
original tribe all save Uraa were pregnant, too.

It had been so easy to simply let the Matriyehan personality take over, so exhilarating to build the tribe that little
of the magic sand had been used, save by Uraa, who felt
somehow cursed because she alone was not with child and
therefore not fully contributing. There were many more
wife-sisters for Maka to take now, and her favors to Uraa
had almost ceased, which was another reason for her to use
the magic sand.

Silent Woman, on the other hand, was very confused.
The slight bulge in her belly filled her with enormous joy
and excitement, but she also knew something was wrong.
The chiefs of the heaven-ship village had not sent them
down here for this, and watching Uraa with the magic
sand, she seemed to grasp that the sand was at the heart of
what was going wrong. She had no power to make it right,
but Uraa did. Among all the others, there was something
very different about Uraa, something she sensed but could
not define.

She knew, however, that there were poisons, like the old
chief's firewater back in the river village, that could do
strange things to people, and there were certainly machines
that could do the same. She loved these women, even
strange Uraa, and it was almost a duty to her to protect
them if they could not protect themselves. Such a thing
would not go against Maka's wishes, for Maka wasn't
using the magic sand anyway.

It was very simple to pick up some sand the next time
they were near a volcanic area and put it in her pouch
unobserved, then add a pinch here and there of leaves to
make it look just right. And then, in the dead of night, it
was almost a thrill to remove what was left of the magic
sand from Uraa's pouch and scatter it in the forest and
replace it with her mixture. Uraa would be angry the next

time she used it, but Silent Woman was experienced enough to know that she would be the last to be suspected, and that Maka would find it funny. They had all contributed some to Uraa out of sisterly sympathy and respect for her as a warrior, but they would part with no more. It was a gift from the gods, after all.

The first time Uraa took some of the ersatz magic sand out of her pouch and popped it into her mouth, she immediately spit it out, gasping and choking, and headed for water. She was very angry, but because of her lowered status within the tribe there was nothing she could do about it.

It took another two weeks for the effects to completely wear off, and even then it was in Uraa's dreams that the demon-thoughts came and would not be denied, no matter how she tried. Again and again, she could see the face of the demon, leering, grinning at her from in back of some dark shield, laughing as he made her inhuman and horrible and monstrous . . .

And, one night, in the middle of the late watch, Vulture suddenly sat up, wide awake, and said the name of the demon.

"Clayben," she whispered.

Because Vulture was not mindprinted but had become Uraa through a process even she could not understand, the shock of Clayben's image had jolted her mostly free of the hold the truth-bearer's drug had on her mind. It took many nights of thinking and concentrating to bring her submerged memories out and put them all together.

The first problem Vulture had to consider was whether the truth-bearer had really suspected them or had simply happened on them by accident as she'd claimed. It *had* to be the latter; they would have known if anyone had been spying on them all this time.

All this time . . . How much time? Midi and Suni were

farthest along in their pregnancies, so they had probably gotten pregnant while still aboard ship. They looked to be in their seventh month now; Taeg, Mari, and Aesa looked to be a month behind, give or take, while Silent Woman was just beginning to show, reflecting her later start.

And suddenly it was clear what had triggered the truth-bearer's suspicions. None of them had stretch marks save Uraa who had no children with her. That's twice now pregnancy has complicated a mission, she thought sourly, although this time it was unavoidable. If they were to be down for a very long period of time then it was necessary. Any wife-sister would wonder at a tribe that had no children and no sign that it had ever had any. Well, since they hadn't had a program to work from, they'd had to write one from Uraa's genetic code. Even the greatest of computers made mistakes. Because Vulture was by nature sterile, fertility had been interpolated—and wrongly.

She wondered, though, about the magic sand. Truth-bearers had appeared in the tribe she'd joined on her reconnaissance and no such drug had been used that she was aware of. Insurance? A new tool for keeping the People on the straight and narrow? Was the static system not quite as static as it was supposed to be? Or was Master System playing the long odds? It knew they had transmuters; such a campaign would help the faithful and reinforce the system even if none of the rebels came here as Matriyehans; however, it might just catch anybody who did—and it had.

The problem was rescuing the rest of them from the drug's influence. They already had a larger group than was manageable—twenty-six now—and Maka was insatiable about gaining more. The upward limit was around a hundred, but the average tribe was usually fifty or sixty. Maka was in fact building her strength while searching for another smaller tribe, one that could be conquered and absorbed to give her real power while also gaining that

smaller tribe's territory. That meant a war and a war was
not in their best interest. They had already lost three
members—fortunately, none of the pirates—as Maka's
greater strength made her seek bigger and more dangerous
game, and the chief seemed willing to take more risks and
even risk herself needlessly to demonstrate her bravery and
right to leadership. A war might well cause the deaths of
Maka and the other eight, and, just as bad, they might lose
and the survivors be absorbed into the other tribe.

When Vulture had become part of Uraa's tribe, it had
been incredibly hard to exert free will, to break away when
the time was right, to get back to the fighter and to
Thunder. How to wrench the others back to their senses
again? And Maka—could she be brought around, or would
she have to die? Vulture wondered if she could force herself against all the instincts of a Matriyehan to take and
become Maka. She didn't want to do it, not only for those
reasons but also because it would reduce their number by
one and a key one at that. Still, it would be only months
until Vulture had to feed once more—or begin to die. It
was a two-year cycle that could not be changed, much as
she hated the idea. It was the onset, the slight beginnings,
of that need which helped Vulture to regain almost complete mastery over the Uraa personality.

And with that came the realization that Maka tribe
wasn't going to roam from this territory, and was still
within a week's walk of that lava cave area where the
problem had started. She knew this tribe well; she most
certainly could find it again if she was not taken by another
tribe. The question was, could she find that forbidden holy
place where truth-bearers might come for whatever it was
they got in such places? Could she stand being alone and
eating at what might be starvation levels until one of them
showed up?

Curiously, of all the tribe, it was Silent Woman who

seemed to sense the change in Uraa, the return of Vulture, and her torment. Vulture was shocked to realize this, and even more shocked when she realized that only Silent Woman could have brought her out. She had checked all the others and there was no glimmer of their old selves there. Now at last she understood. By the very nature of her trauma Silent Woman had been immune. That was easy to understand from the beginning. The fact that she had realized that something was wrong and picked the only one capable of overcoming it was astonishing. Just how much *did* go on in that mind?

Vulture only hoped Silent Woman would understand that if Uraa vanished it was not desertion, but hope.

During the next several days Vulture prepared, weaving a net out of the strong vines that were the staple of this culture's primitive technology then waiting until they camped near a *bis* grove. The *bis* fruit grew very high in its trees and had a hard, smooth shell, but inside were seeds and a pulpy yellow mass that was extremely filling. So long as the shell was not cracked they traveled well and were one of the few food staples that could be harvested and carried for several days by tribes. That harvesting wasn't easy, though; *bis* on the ground were already over-ripe and spoiled. The only way to get them was to climb a smooth-barked ten-meter-tall tree and select only the ones that were ripe. This was not only very dangerous in its own right but the harvesters were effectively alone and defenseless and were sometimes targeted by the leathery-winged *misum*, which were all teeth and tentacles.

Harvesting *bis*, however, allowed Vulture to get her bearings and also to survey the land. She intended to take no more *bis* fruit than she had harvested herself, but she knew she had to move quickly. This small valley between two volcanic ranges was the home of Sosa tribe, with about thirty-five adults and fifteen children. Sosa knew that

Maka tribe was in its territory but was large enough that so far there hadn't been a confrontation. Now Maka was being faced with a possible showdown as Sosa tribe searched for them. Maka would have preferred at least equal numbers, and Vulture felt that she would avoid the fight as long as she could but she saw no advantage to moving on. Vulture very much wanted to act before such a battle took place. The idea of Maka losing her male attributes and the tribe becoming absorbed into Sosa tribe was only slightly more daunting than the idea of having to deal with the mission and a tribe of seventy.

It was still difficult to leave. The darkness itself was threatening on this world, and safety lay only in numbers, but the sudden, overpowering feeling of loneliness, of being somehow incomplete and empty, was just as bad. She had picked her route for maximum safety and did not intend to go far. The fact was, Vulture wasn't sure what would happen if she were snared by a strangler vine or attacked by some of the animals that might prowl at night. Could she eat the animal and, if so, would she then no longer have human reasoning, or could she be digested by the strangler plants and die? Falling into some pit or mud hole would be just as bad. It was not until Matriyeh that she had ever had a sense of her own possible mortality.

Early the next day she began the climb over the mountains. It was treacherous going, the landscape hostile enough that it had kept the valley pretty well isolated from other marauding tribes. Hot fumeroles hissed at her, spewing foul gases, and there was the strong stench of sulfur and occasional hot spots in the rocks. A steady rain made much of the lava field slippery and dangerous. She was relieved to finally make it to older rock, and she could see a small pass ahead, perhaps another two or three hundred meters up the mountainside. She stopped for a moment and sat, trying to muster enough strength to make it to the top.

The lava snake was not in the ideal position but when prey stopped, it moved fast. Most of the time it lived in its lava tube, head pointed so that only the eyes, set in the skull then but capable of protruding on stalks when needed, looked out.

Lava snakes could live on rock, particularly high-sulfur rock, but they preferred supplementing their diet with living meat. At more than ten meters long, and all mouth at one end, they could anchor themselves in their dens and shoot out straight ahead with enough speed to snare an unwary *misum* and sometimes an unwary person as well. There had been a few the tribe had faced when crossing into the valley. They had been lucky because they'd come down between two dens; the lava snakes had attacked at about the same time and it had been quick reflexes that saved them, causing the two snakes to go after each other instead.

Vulture heard it and rolled away just in time. The great jaws snapped shut less than a meter from her. There was no time to prepare weapons, and none of the weapons she had would be much use singly against such a beast. She rolled, came up on her feet, spear ready, all supplies tossed away, and quickly eyed an area about ten meters away that was out of range of the snake if it kept itself anchored but which ended in a sheer drop. The snakes were single-minded eating machines and she depended on that. She'd probably kill the monster if it ate her, but that wouldn't do her much good.

The field became suddenly alive with great, angry hisses and roars, and several more snakes revealed themselves but did not emerge from their lairs. Anchored, the snakes could lunge at an incredible speed, but if forced to move freely and crawl they were slow and ponderous. She could outrun one, but it would do little good if she just ran into the jaws of another. The easiest way to the top was past the first creature's lair, and now it was her task to empty it or die.

She stood almost on the edge of the precipice and held her spear high in defiance. "Ho! Snake! Come! Uraa be snake dinner! Easy meat! Come!"

The snake roared in anger and began to emerge from its hole. Its back end was quite small, almost tentaclelike, good for gripping, but useless now that it was free of the lair and slowly coming toward her. The rock actually hissed as the beast traveled, thanks to a secretion it left as it moved.

She was suddenly afraid she had miscalculated, and fear of death was not something she was used to. The great Vulture, the creature that could become anyone and could fool even Master System, was, here, no different from the most ordinary of Matriyehan women.

The snake approached but stopped five meters short, one eye stalk on the spear. Clearly this one was an experienced hunter. Vulture saw the small, tentaclelike rear gyrating back and forth, trying to find something to grip. If it did, she was dead meat, so she had to force the issue.

With a fierce, steady scream she ran straight for the head of the snake, spear ready. The action confused the snake, which did nothing for a moment, and she let the spear go with full force. It struck the head area and sank in a bit; a superficial wound, but painful. The snake roared in fury and lunged at full speed at Vulture, who jumped to her left and rolled flat. The snake in its fury had forgotten it didn't yet have an anchor, and it went straight on past her and over the edge of the cliff. Its hind end, however, managed to catch a jagged edge of a lava outcrop, and it hung there for a moment, then slowly tried pulling itself back up.

Vulture wasn't going to give it a chance. She ran

straight past the now-empty lair and made the top before she dared stop and look back.

The great snake was indeed pulling itself back up, but its relative helplessness had not gone unnoticed by its kin, who were converging on the spot where the great head was oozing back onto solid ground. She decided to let them fight it out.

The exhilaration of surviving the encounter quickly gave way to concern. *What am I celebrating?* she asked herself. *That I'm smarter than a damned snake?* Of more concern now was that she had no reserve food supply, no spear, and not much else except a sharp knife-stone, the blow gun, and a supply of dart thorns. It was a long and dangerous trek down the other side, and there were more snakes and other dangers. She would be easy prey should a *misum* pass by and get curious. Worse, she would have to cross dozens of tribal territories, perhaps more, to reach the point where she wanted to be, and she would be in no condition to resist warriors if one of those tribes found and then adopted her.

It was her worst nightmare. The mission was in shambles before it even had a chance to begin, and she was alone and relatively defenseless on the surface of the cruel planet Matriyeh.

8. A NEARLY PERFECT TRAP

VISIONS FILTERED THROUGH THE SCREAM... A HAND-some race living in a primitive village by the side of a small, swift-flowing river... The village is more a part of than carved out of the surrounding jungle... It is very hot all the time; the people wear lots of jewelry, trinkets, but no clothes, yet they do not appear naked, their bodies covered with intricate, multicolored tattoos that have personal meanings... The men even have designs tattooed on their faces, but the women do not, instead wearing rings and bone ornaments from their ears and their noses and in their long, black hair...

Reflections in a pool... a young girl's face—very young, but already a woman, with sensual features and good figure. Her intricate body tattoos that mark her a woman are still fresh and bright, not worn and faded, and she is proud of them and what they say. She has not yet had a man, but it is being arranged, and she is both excited and scared by that idea . . .

It is a simple world if a hard one, and a simple life in which everybody knew their place in their small universe. It was a life of personal doubts and triumphs, but one in which there were no great questions. They knew there were other tribes, much like them, scattered in the region, but they were few and far between and there was almost no contact. Strangers were always considered dangerous and dealt with accordingly.

Thus, when the warriors had caught in their territory the stranger who did not look quite human, they had not asked questions but simply killed him. He wore multiple layers of cloth in the tropical heat and thick things of hide on his feet, which baffled them, although they salvaged it all and turned it into more practical things. The great knife of metal and some kind of strange colored bone they had never seen before was tough and sharp and finely polished; the chief would make good use of it. The contents of his pack contained more cloth of impossibly fine weave and design and other things that were unusual or inexplicable. They tried melting down the things made of the strange metal but more often there would be an explosion or a roar or it would simply collapse into a gruesome puddle giving off thick, acrid smoke that choked them.

The hair on his face and body made him almost resemble a monkey, but after much debate they decided he was indeed some sort of person and deserved final respect, so they ate him.

And, later, the evil spirits had come from the air, shooting fire from their hands that caused people to fall over, while spears and arrows and darts seemed to just bounce off them. She had run in panic into the woods but they had pursued and she felt a sudden shock as if she had run into a tree and remembered no more.

And always, in the forests and in her mind, was the scream . . .

"That's all I've been able to sort out through the trauma and weave into a kind of sense," Star Eagle explained. "There's much more, but even getting those images, you could still feel the singular horror of the event, and this has taken me much time and effort."

Hawks nodded. Of the company, he was the only one likely to be able to interpret the disjointed scenes, and he was impressed by the results so far.

"They always said Silent Woman came from a southern tribe," he said, "but I doubt if anyone realized how southern. The type of landscape indicates northern South America, deep in the jungle. Throughout known history, that has been the dwelling place for some of the most primitive people in the western hemisphere. Just where, we can't be certain—that region could be under Caribe Center or Amazon Center, but the stranger they killed looked to be Brazilian, although it was hard to tell. Some of the artifacts they took off him were pretty sophisticated stuff, though. A field agent, most likely, although what he was doing up in there will probably forever be a mystery. Possibly they had heard rumors of a tech cult working in there—it's so dense and so remote that you could almost build a Center in there if you had the resources, and no one would know. He was most certainly wearing a tracking device because they located the spot so quickly." He gave a grim chuckle. "They were searching for enemies of the system and wound up tackling a group that probably never knew there *was* a system. It is entirely possible that they lived through the last thousand years without Master System even knowing of their existence."

Cloud Dancer, who was becoming a bit more sophisticated in modern ways, asked, "Is that possible?"

"Oh, yes, but only in remote and primitive areas. Parts of Borneo, and the Philippines, a few remote places in Asia and Africa, and in the northern part of South America. They were so primitive and so ignorant that they simply weren't worth going after. They were already at the level Master System wanted." He sighed. "You know, in spite of the tattoos and the obvious mental filtering we all do, she was quite a pretty young girl. You would never think of that face and form and Silent Woman in the same context, yet if you stared closely enough you could see how it *might* be the same person, ravaged, and older."

"But how did she wind up a slave of the Illinois?"

Star Eagle answered. "I'm working on that. I can't give you specific scenes but I have some data. They were taken to Amazon Center and put through the usual mill and found to be just what they appeared to be. Most of them had all memories of the incident erased and were put right back in their village, but not her. Somebody important took to her. Since she couldn't understand anything of what was being said nor even comprehend where she was, it's impossible to tell who. One thing is for certain—they went to great pains to isolate her from the wonders of Center and to keep her ignorant. They kept her outside in a caged-off area that was very primitive. Then there are big gaps, and the next thing I can find, she's being paddled up the Mississippi on a trader canoe. You figure it out. She couldn't."

"I keep going back to that baby," Hawks muttered. "That makes no sense unless . . ." Suddenly he snapped his fingers. "Get Raven. I know he'll just *love* this, but I want him to get the trauma scene."

"But it's—horrible," Cloud Dancer protested.

"Uh huh. But I want an experienced field agent to get a good look at those two medicine men. A really *good* look."

Raven was shaken by the experience as they all had been, but he nodded sourly. "Medicine men, my ass," he muttered. "If I ever get my hands on Bends With the Wind or Jonny Motoia I'll personally take pleasure in snapping their necks real slow."

"You know them, then?" Hawks thought he had the key now.

"Yeah. Bends With the Wind looked and sounded real authentic there, but he's no Illinois. He's a Huron without the haircut. Field agent for the upper lakes. They must have imported him special and given him a good mind-print. The other one's Motoia—from one of them screwy California tribes, but not a field man. Deputy chief of security at Center, that's who. This was big, whatever it was."

"We may never really know, but I think I can guess what happened," Hawks told them. "You remember China's father—the experiment to breed a race of superhumans under Master System's nose? I think this was something like that. Somebody else's project, of course, totally independent. They needed guinea pigs for their tests and experiments before they risked it on anybody important. She probably was far from the only one, but word leaked out to Master System. The heat was on, and they had to get them out quickly and quietly. They could have just killed them, but that would have wasted a valuable experiment. To disperse them, though, using contacts in North America, would make sense. Later on they could be tracked down and analyzed after everything blew over. It probably sounded like a good bargain to a younger Roaring Bull or his predecessor. She's your slave, do anything you want with her, but you can't kill her or sell her. Otherwise, no charge."

"Yeah, but she was capped off, Chief," Raven said.

"Mindprinter, probably. Strictly for security. She was stuck with her native language and no other. Couldn't learn more'n a few words, most likely. That way she'd never be able to tell anything about her past or blow the cover. She also changed too fast. Got fat, got dumpy, got gray and faded and worn and saggy. Clayben might be able to tell more, but it was probably side effects of whatever was done to her. One thing's for sure—you'll never be able to find it out from the guy who did it. They tracked 'em down, found she was pregnant, waited for the birth, and then did in the kid real nasty. Why? That was orders. Why that way—well, it made a better cover to declare the child born with birth defects and have a public ceremony. They were a little too enthusiastic about it, though, the bastards. That extra cruelty wasn't necessary."

"But why the child?" Cloud Dancer asked. "Why not just kill or take her and avoid all that needless suffering?"

"I doubt if we'll ever know the whole story," Hawks told her, "but I suspect whatever was done to these women was a one-shot thing. They were to have one child only. Roaring Bull said she was barren after. If they came in and just took Silent Woman, there would have been resentment. Better to simply wait, kill the child as Master System ordered under the guise of the religious codes, and let it go. They knew the women involved were innocent dupes. I wish I knew what the experiment was. What did they see in that child that warranted such a thing?"

"Beats me," Raven said, "but they didn't have to go to those lengths. Maybe they were a bunch of little potential Vultures, or something just as nuts. Speaking of which, any word?"

Hawks shook his head. "No, none, and it's been a long time. The sheer primitiveness of the place frustrates me. I think sometimes that the fleet off Chanchuk would have been easier. We are good at fighting modern battles, technology against technology, and that sort of problem solving. We've gotten the probes in and around Chanchuk in spite of all their efforts."

"You know we don't have the strength to go head-to-head with them again. Not for a while. I got to admit I'm gettin' antsy, too, Chief. We depend on Vulture too much. Still, it's damn near impossible to do this without an inside man, and there's just no way to infiltrate these places otherwise. I'd like to get a couple of people down on Chanchuk buildin' up information, casing the joint, but there's no way we could get anybody down with access to a Center. We could send some people in and have 'em live the field life, maybe, but they'd be stalled and stuck there until we had our inside man with inside information."

"There have *got* to be other ways to do it," Hawks responded. "Got to be. Suppose the Matriyeh business takes years? Suppose we don't hear from them even then? Raven, I want to assemble a study team. Some of our experienced people and Star Eagle to work out alternate methods. I don't want to bite off more than we can chew, but if there are ways, I want to know them. We're not even halfway yet. Use Savaphoong, too. That bastard knows a lot he isn't telling us, but I think he'll be anxious to show he's valuable. For years he bought and sold information from just about every freebooter ship around. He can access that information the way Clayben did with his programs. Remember, it isn't just infiltrating. We have to get them out under pressure with minimum cost—and even if we managed all four rings we might have a hell of a fight when we go for Chen."

Raven shrugged. "I'll see what if anything we come up with. But our best chance is still Vulture, you know."

"If Vulture is even alive..."

* * *

It had been a harrowing ten days for Vulture, but now it was going to pay off. The forbidden holy area was a deep cleft in the rock where two lava flows had almost, but not quite, merged. The bird and tree symbols were etched into the rock on both sides of the entrance, which then turned sharply, blocking any view of what lay beyond. The symbols were slightly worn but impressively carved in the rock, certainly by some technical means and not by hand. They were too uniform. The detail was quite good, and she couldn't resist removing the dummy ring from her necklace and comparing the design on it with the ones etched in the rock.

The tree was stylized, but had two clear branches under its canopy, one on the right hanging down a bit more than the one on the left, and on that branch was the figure of an impressive if stylized bird. The ring and the design matched pretty well; to the trained eye there were minor differences, but if they weren't carefully compared, it was impossible to tell the ring was false. The ring's image was so much smaller it compensated for some of the flaws.

She carefully replaced the ring in its holder and tried to decide what to do. She could find out what was in there, of course, but there was a strong possibility that it was booby trapped. It was even remotely possible that there was some visual connection with the computer at the main installation, and it wouldn't do to have a common native show up on those sensors. It might bring a force far too large to deal with.

That had been the problem with this assignment. Limits. Vulture didn't like to think she had limits; none of the weapons here could really harm her, and she could eat anyone and become them with all their knowledge and memories. But enough of her could be ripped apart or consumed to make it impossible to effect self-repair, and she was the only one of her kind. If they knew, if they even suspected that one such as she existed, they'd pull out all the stops to capture or kill her. Disruptor fire had allowed her to kill a Val; disruptor fire from a Val could kill her.

She had been here a couple of days. It might be weeks or even months before a truth-bearer happened to be in the area again alone, and she knew from her previous experience as Uraa that within a tribe the truth-bearer was never alone or isolated enough to eat. Eating took time, and in this instance demanded privacy. There was ample food here and shelter, too, but the large tribe that controlled the area was also nearby. She had seen them more than once, and they appeared to be on the verge of splitting, having become too numerous to be manageable by a single chief. Then would come the ritual of the culling, in which the chief would choose a group and essentially divorce them; these would be the ones who didn't pull their own weight or had in some way irritated the chief. They and their children would be remarked, branded, and sent away. Within days, one would develop into a new chief, and they would have to find a new area to live. The ritual was unusual here only because this was a prosperous area, rich in food and shelter and with fewer dangers. This indicated a far higher survival rate than the racial norm.

It also meant a stranger was more likely to be killed than taken in if found by the larger tribe.

The process, however, was not automatic. Chiefs were aggressive and ambitious and wouldn't mind their tribe growing as large as they could feed and control, but to get too large could lead to new ideas, like planting crops and building permanent settlements, and that was heresy. It was the truth-bearers who forced the ritual culling on the tribes, and so a truth-bearer had to be with them. Vulture thought it unlikely that a priestess in this area wouldn't take time to drop by the holy place. There would, after all, have to be a report.

It was six more days before something happened, and then Vulture almost missed it. Bored, impatient, and half starved, she'd carved out a hiding place with good shelter against storms and other irritants and just waited. Only her incredibly keen senses woke her to the sound of someone walking through the forest. At first she had trouble locating the sound, and then was very cautious, making certain it was someone alone and not a scout or castaway or some lost individual from a hunting party.

The truth-bearer might have been the same one who caused them all the problems, since they all looked and sounded pretty much alike, but it didn't matter. The priestess stopped suddenly and tilted her bald head, obviously sensing Vulture's presence. Vulture was too desperate to care about risks at this point; she removed her necklace and belt and then walked out into the clearing and approached the truth-bearer boldly, then bent on one knee.

"Lost sister?" the priestess asked, confused but hardly frightened. "What be sister name? Why sister be here?"

"Uraa be lost, alone, long time," she responded. "Uraa beg just . . . touch truth-bearer." She rose and before the priestess could react, Vulture put her arms around the priestess and hugged.

The truth-bearer stiffened, then froze, mouth agape, eyes wide, unable to move. The process had begun; Vulture began to feed almost immediately.

The two bodies merged together and seemed to flow, to mix into a single mass in which only vague remnants of the human forms were visible. They became a single, bubbling, seething mass; the truth-bearer's cloak was suddenly freed as the last of the head melted into the great, pulsating mass, and it was caught in a breeze and blew away, catching in a tree. Nothing happened for several minutes, and then from the center of the mass, the top of a head appeared, unfinished, ill-formed, like a new casting of wax around a skull. Slowly, more and more of a human body emerged, with long stringy bits of goo peeling off and collapsing back into the pool. Now it was a full figure, stuck like a plant growing out of the still-pulsating mass, and then the details began to develop. The face, the breasts, the navel, everything began to take shape as if fading into the blank mold from nowhere, until, at last, the naked form of the truth-bearer stood there, while the skin turned the proper dark shade and the bold tattoos came in.

Finally she opened her eyes and looked around, and then stepped from the mass, whole. While the new figure seemed dizzy and uncertain of itself, it forced itself to reach down into the still-seething muck of blood and slime and find first the staff and then the necklace, pouch, and belt of the truth-bearer. They were covered with the muck, but the figure didn't seem to care. She turned, spotted the cape, which had escaped most of the process, and walked unsteadily to it, picking it up but not putting it on. Then she walked, still unsteady, back into the jungle until she found a place that felt safe and afforded some shelter. Then and only then did she sink down and collapsed into a near-comatose sleep.

When Vulture again opened her eyes, it was very dark, with no way to tell through the dense clouds if it was early in the night or late. It didn't matter. The new data was already settling in and sorting out in her mind. The memories of Uraa were joining the memories of the others who she had taken over the years, while new memories existed in the duplicated brain of the truth-bearer, the memories and personality of someone quite different.

It seemed that truth-bearers had both names and ratings, although such things were not for the masses. The masses were ignorant, and must be kept so, lest they overpopulate themselves and grow and destroy their people and their world. The Chosen Ones were the discipline and guardians of the masses, and theirs was a sacred duty. She was Omaqua, Flower of the Spirits, a Guardian Third Rank. Even the truth-bearers didn't have much long-term time sense, but Vulture made her out to be perhaps nineteen or twenty.

She had been born and raised in the land of the Chosen Ones in the Middle Country, which was forbidden to the masses and guarded by steep mountains, the way in and out known to only a few. There, below the Great Temple carved out of the side of an inner mountain, was a valley containing something unique on Matriyeh—a village with cultivated land. It was not much of a village, really—huts made out of straw and bamboolike materials, the land carefully tended by the young who lived there—but compared to the rest of the continent it was remarkable.

The permanent residents were few; these were the elder priestesses, the leaders of the whole religion and its authority and inspiration, who had survived long years in the field and shown their devotion and their toughness. That was the first rank.

The second rank was the long-experienced truth-bearers, those who had been out in the field for a long time and knew the land and tribes and people and had undergone much. They supervised broad territories and correlated reports from the subordinates, and returned to the village at regular intervals to teach the young.

When each of the young reached puberty, they were then put through a purifying ritual in the Great Temple, and were given drugs so that each was for a period the male and for a period the female, until all were impregnated.

Each was expected to bear and nurse two children; by this time they would be fifteen or sixteen, and would then undergo a second and far more dramatic ritual. To Omaqua, they were hazy but wondrous memories of the Great

God and the Earth-Mother taking her into their spiritual tribe. Out of this would come the tattoos, small variations in which made each look unique, and a new name, and they became physically neuter. They lost all their hair, even pubic hair, save only their brows and lashes, and became hard, lean, and muscular, and their appearance was now the same as all the other truth-bearers. They even lost interest in their children; the masses were their children now.

Then began what must have been a year of training, including field trips to some tribes outside, to ease the new truth-bearer into the job. Second-rank priestesses taught them, often forcing harsh decisions on the young ones, drilling them constantly and punishing them unmercifully until they all thought the same and all knew the same. When they were perfect, and only when they were perfect, did the second rank send them out, the only loners in a world of collectives, to administer the truth and guard the masses from heresy.

Vulture almost felt sorry for them. They spent all their time chanting and reciting the creed and law to themselves over and over, performing every ritual, and acting according to procedure in all cases when with tribes. They were the most thoroughly brainwashed individuals she'd ever seen, and lived lives where the only joy was living almost entirely in the spiritual world they had been taught to believe as real. Omaqua had not been the one who had visited them in the cave, but the truth drug, a hypnotic to which the priestesses were immune, was one tool that could be used in some cases. There were many other drugs, as well, and they could be drawn from the holy places.

Things were both good and bad. No longer subject to biochemical whims and linkages and trained to operate as a loner and individual, she was now far better suited for the mission and would find it easier to operate as Vulture. She could also literally protect a tribe if she wanted, since they would not be attacked with a truth-bearer in the way, and she could mediate between two groups with great authority. She also had imprinted in her memory the specifics and locations of more than forty tribes, as well as their territories and the best routes for safely getting between them. Unfortunately, natural hazards and lava snakes and *misum* didn't know the privileged role of truth-bearers, which was why longevity in the field was the primary prerequisite for advancement to second rank—that and not making mistakes.

Basically, third-rankers couldn't go home again—ever. They had to be promoted. Well, she thought, that wouldn't be an insurmountable problem in the long run. Sooner or later one of the Holy Sisters would have to show up for a report, and, if alone, could provide a quick promotion for Vulture. If not alone, well, terrible things happened to people in the field.

It was a good thing she hadn't tried the holy place earlier; it was more than just booby trapped, it was first a psychological and then a physical horror. Such things, however, no longer concerned her. She waited three hours until dawn, then sought out the stream and washed the cloak, herself, and peeled off the now-putrid goo from the staff and necklace. The bag she did the best she could with; she couldn't really clean it completely and save all the stuff in the compartments inside.

Finally she was ready. She checked where the mass that had given birth to her had been, and it was now rotten, smelling of carrion and overrun by insects. Such was the remains of Uraa, let her rest. She almost forgot Uraa's artifacts, but remembered and went back for them. They weren't worth much, but the necklace contained a very large charm of particular importance. Eventually she'd have to figure out a way to put it permanently on her new necklace, which had the intricately carved religious totems, but for now she just put it in the bag.

Almost immediately after she entered the passage beyond the symbols of bird and tree, she was assaulted by demonic noises, terrible howls and shrieks, and visions of terrible monsters looming ghostly in front of her. She said the required prayers and made the proper signs almost habitually; the demon guardians didn't worry her since she was used to them, but they would have scared even the toughest chief on Matriyeh half to death. Beyond them was the Wall None Can See But Kills. Again, it was simply a matter of standing in a particular spot and saying the holy prayers of supplication to make it vanish, but only truth-bearers knew those prayers and those symbols and exactly where to stand. Vulture knew that she would have easily walked straight into that lethally charged forcefield if she'd tried it earlier, and something like that might well have killed even her.

Finally she reached the shrine. All the forbidden places looked different but were actually quite uniform, with the same demonic horrors, forcefield, and the shrine. They were always at sources of fresh water—this one had a small waterfall—and they all had a small gardenlike area at the center of which was a stone tree that looked just like the symbol. On its right branch was a large stone bird unlike anything on Matriyeh. For the first time the symbol was made large enough to see that the tree bore some odd kind of fruit, but she couldn't make out what it was. Vulture submerged her mind and became completely Omaqua. She removed her belt and bag, her cape, and all necklaces and other ornaments and was totally nude. She walked to the stone tree and bird, and prostrated herself in front of it.

"Spirit of Holy Place, hear Omaqua the Low Ranked. Give Omaqua spirit blessing."

And a voice, a male voice that was gentle and quiet yet had great power within it, said, "Speak."

And Omaqua spoke, and told everything that had happened to her since her last report. She confessed every doubt and error, she told of everyone she met, of all the things she observed, the disputes settled, the rituals performed—everything. Omaqua truly felt that she was in the presence of a great spirit, and that compared to it, she was less than a bug. She truly worshipped and wanted only to be commanded.

"Omaqua imperfect," the voice responded when she'd finished. "Need to purify. Rise. Embrace tree."

She trembled and did as instructed, wrapping her arms and legs around the trunk of the stone carving. Suddenly she was drawn and stuck to it as if by some great and powerful magnet and could not move. What followed was a strange and terrible afternoon, as one after the other every one of her confessed sins, doubts, and errors was paraded before her mind and dealt with over and over again with painful shocks. At first she cried out, but even that brought punishment.

There was no instruction, no admonition. As each guilty thought was presented, she had to welcome the pain and work out for herself what was wrong and why, and then it was eliminated from the sequence. Finally, when all errors and sins were dealt with, the range of mental emotions was played. Mercy, compassion, even guilt were sins that had to be banished from the soul. One had to be cold, unfeeling, totally objective in all things, and devout and obedient only to the spirit world.

Vulture had the ability to cut herself off from this, to bury herself in a dark corner while it went on. It was this same ability that would allow her to pass a stringent mind-probe from the most skillful psychophysicist, even a computer. The mechanism for the "cleansing," however, was far easier to understand and elude. The tattoos themselves were some sort of conductors through which other remote devices could operate directly on the nervous system and pain centers. It was clear that the ritual that made a girl a priestess was similar to the conditioning process that *Thunder* used to make its own Matriyehans or Janipurians.

It ended, however, in a rush of religious ecstasy for Omaqua, in which the pleasure centers were directly tapped and every physical sensation of pleasure was released at once. No wonder they went through it without complaint, even with excitement—the payoff was extraordinary.

Eventually it was so much, she passed out from sheer pleasure.

The recovery was rather slow; she gradually woke up with all her pleasure cells tingling, not even able to think, and she lay there and let it slowly fade over several hours. There was a deep longing for it to return, of course, but mostly there was a feeling of gratitude that such an experience had been permitted. There was near rapture at being the lowest slave of the lowest of spirits. Eventually she would attain perfection, a time when there was no punishment, no cleansing, needed, and that was what every truth-bearer strived for.

Vulture worried that perhaps a total mindprint could be taken this way. If so, hers would be seamless until she met this strange girl near the gates of this shrine and then there would be only the memory of waking up, bathing, and cleaning, and then coming here—a gap that a computer would notice. She doubted, though, that anything that elaborate could be done without a complete mindprinter being present. More likely this was just a preprogrammed sequence the truth-bearers could trigger. They did it— pain, pleasure, and judgment—to themselves in response to the proper signals.

It sure as hell kept the priesthood honest.

The next morning, she ritually bathed in the pool and then spent the whole day in prayer and supplication. On the third morning, the spirit revealed to her the cache that was always there, with fresh drugs and other things, as well, such as the purification vessel. She undid the stopper and poured a measure into a gourd cup and then drank it while sitting in front of the tree. It put her almost at once into a stupor, and Vulture had to act fast to keep from being trapped as she had been with the magic sand. That, however, had been inhaled; this was drunk, and took longer. Knowing it was coming and how it worked, she had been able to prepare for it.

Vulture thought that it was going to be simply another recitation of the drills of truth-seeking, since Omaqua had no memories of anything else in past shrines, but it was not. It was a command in a language Omaqua didn't even realize she knew. Vulture, however, did know it, although in a different form. It was spoken in a crisp, sexless voice —and it was French.

"We believe that demons from the stars might be here in our own form. These demons will be very difficult to tell from normal people, but we are particularly concerned about their chief. Continue administering the compulsive hypnotics to all chiefs and be alert for anything odd or unusual, any heresies of even the slightest degree, in anyone. Anyone expressing curiosity about the location or even the existence of the Holy Temple is to be immediately reported and tracked. They are dangerous and will kill even a priestess so if they cannot be contained with drugs do nothing overt or suspicious, but report immediately. Until further notice, you are to do a cleansing whenever you are within one day of a shrine, even if the two are very close together. All strays are to be drugged and interrogated. Second-rank personnel are deployed in the area surrounding the accesses to the Holy Temple. You are to obey their orders without question as if they came from the gods themselves. Any command given in the Holy Tongue is to be obeyed instantly. Condition Orange. Repeat, Condition Orange."

"Oui, mon commandant," Omaqua responded.

"You will not consciously remember this message or this tongue, but you will obey all instructions. Now, you will put all that is past out of your mind, and you will go away as new and spread the truth and live in perfection. Upholding the truth and the guard, attaining personal perfection, and absolute obedience are your sole reasons for living. Now, awaken, and go!"

She awoke, feeling newly born and wonderful. Vulture was startled, as well, by the transformation; even she couldn't access that message nor anything at all in French from anywhere in Omaqua's memory. That was one hell of a mindprinter program. Only the fact that she had been monitoring from her external memory outside Omaqua's mind made the experience real at all. But several suspicions had been confirmed and new knowledge gained.

There were two people, two personalities, in each priestess' body. One the humble and ever-vigilant Matriyehan truth-bearer, the other a dedicated soldier in the SPF. Somewhere back in there, an entire third personality was possibly submerged. Could it be, perhaps, a mindprint of the first members, the ones trained and raised in space as soldiers? Possible. At least it confirmed that every fear the rebels had had was true, including the fact that they were already suspected of being on Matriyen.

It had to be driving Master System mad that such a long time had passed after *Thunder*'s big success without any sign of an attempt on another ring. The more that passed, the more paranoid the big master machine would become that it was missing something obvious. Of course, it was also a bit ironic. Because of its own elaborate plan, there wasn't much it could do to this world that it hadn't already done.

Vulture left the shrine feeling much more in control again, although it still wasn't going to be easy surviving in this place nor even getting back to the valley, something which, after provisioning herself, was absolutely essential. Too much time had been wasted, but she now had some of the tools and authority needed to get the job done. At least the way back would be relatively open; no more dangerous diversions into lava-snake country to avoid being spotted. Truth-bearers came and went as they pleased and explained to no one, and if she got into trouble this time she would not hesitate for a moment to yell for help.

Still, it was a journey of many days, and not for the first time did Vulture curse the fact that the culture here didn't even allow for domesticated animals of the sort one could ride in a hurry.

It was a stormy day when Vulture reached the main pass into the valley. The swirling clouds above were matched by solid clouds below; the only clearing was the space, perhaps two or three hundred meters, between lower and upper cloud layers that was the region of the pass. The cruel, dangerous, and spectacular Matriyeh lightning was everywhere, going from upper to lower layer and, finally, beneath the impenetrable lower fog.

Not far away she could hear the deep hisses and roars of lava snakes disturbed and frightened by the lightning, and she stopped short of the start of the fog-shrouded area, wondering if it was safe or even good sense to continue. If visibility waned all the way to the valley, then it would be a dangerous descent and not one to be attempted now. Still, the storm looked stationary; the pattern was circular and when that happened it might last for days. She decided to risk it, at least for a ways. The trail was reasonably marked by the impressions even bare feet made on rocks over the years.

Even so, it was a nerve-wracking descent, with visibility quickly decreasing to less than a meter, and the trail more identifiable by feel than by sight. At just about the point where she was deciding to go back up and wait for the fog to lift, it began to thin, but that was only a slight improvement as now the rain began. Below her the dark-green forest was swept by wind and rain while patches of white and gray fog churned above. Here and there the yellow-orange fingers of lightning snaked down and struck, accompanied by thunderous roars that echoed up and down the valley and bounced off mountain walls, often starting rock slides that began slowly and then gathered force as they crashed down into the valley below.

I must be an idiot to be out wandering in this stuff, Vulture thought sourly. Even the toughest tribe members down there were under shelter someplace and praying to appease the storm demons. She knew she, too, had to find shelter and food and wait it out herself; there was no chance of finding her old tribe while this went on except through sheer luck, and that luck had already been pressed far enough.

Once under the relative shelter of the forest canopy, she set about finding that shelter, eventually settling on a deep depression inside a rocky outcrop. The area showed signs of recent use, but there was no one there now. Food would have to wait for the rain to stop.

It took two and a half days for Vulture to find Manka tribe, and the only reason it was easy was because of the large amount of smoke rising from its midst. She was too late; the battle had already happened, and now the dead were being tended to. It appeared to have been quite bloody; numerous corpses were being piled up beside the makeshift pyre for the firebearer's attention. There was no way to tell who had won or how many the new tribe contained without getting in close enough to identify individuals. *Well*, Vulture thought sadly, *if there's any good time for a priestess to show up it's now.* Except on a personal level it was almost irrelevant who'd won. This was now a major tribe and not one that could move unobtrusively into forbidden territory.

First things first, Vulture decided. *First we find out who won and how many survivors of our original band are left, then we go from there.* She walked boldly past the perimeter guards and into the gathering, toward the fire.

She estimated the group to be about fifty adults, many of whom were sullen and on their knees, hands and feet bound, under the watch of a few guards. Those would be the losers waiting to be made members of the new tribe.

The arrival of a truth-bearer stirred more excitement than concern. It would be taken as a sign by the victor that the gods blessed their ascension to the top in this valley.

The sight of Silent Woman standing as firebearer reassured Vulture a little, although it didn't mean victory for Manka. The other firebearer might have been killed, for example. There were signs of fresh wounds on several of the women, and even Silent Woman had a deep gash on her arm and another along her left thigh. This had been no picnic. Such warfare was not at all rare on this world and only the toughest, most vicious members would survive.

A very young looking woman wearing a couple of *sisu*-leaf bandages and with a number of freshly healed scars on one cheek came up to Vulture and kneeled. "Oosa greet Truth-bearer," she said softly, as if Vulture were expected. "Wait. Oosa bring chief."

"What chief Oosa bring?" the new truth-bearer asked. "This be what tribe?"

"Maka tribe, holy truth-bearer."

"Sosa?"

The girl gestured slightly to the pile of corpses.

"Go. Bring great Maka chief," Vulture instructed, and Oosa was off. So at least Warlock and Silent Woman remained, but how many more of the original eight survived?

Manka Warlock had been in one hell of a fight and it showed. She had several wounds under treatment and she was limping, although not badly. It was clear from her bearing, though, that she was mighty pleased with herself. The day's work, for all its cost, was probably the most fun the bloodthirsty security agent had had in years, and it must have been quite impressive—the kind of stuff you tell and embellish over evening fires for years to come. Before, the tribe members had mostly looked upon her as anyone does on their boss or leader; now the looks were absolutely radiant, adoring. She did not kneel but merely said, "Maka greets truth-bearer at time of great victory."

Vulture recognized Maria Santiago and Midi in the adoring retinue, and a couple of others added to the tribe before she'd left, but those plus Silent Woman were the only familiar faces.

For the time being, Vulture had to suppress everything but the truth-bearer persona and say all the right things, do all the right rituals and prayers, and preside over a most unpleasant banquet of human flesh. From their point of view, it was not as barbaric as it seemed, of course; it was the highest honor to a foe who had fought valiantly and hard, and it was believed to transfer the finest attributes of a dead warrior to the victors. Fortunately for Vulture's sense of propriety, though, truth-bearers never partook of such fare, being blessed of the gods and above need of that sort of thing.

The ritual was a natural conclusion to the biochemical trigger Maka was even now experiencing, wherein she would become sexually insatiable for several days, bringing all the losing survivors into her tribe and under her control and reasserting supremacy among her own. It would die down quickly, but from that point they would be one tribe, one unit.

Finally, when all the victors had partaken of the cannibal feast, the rest of the remains were thrown into the fire. The next day, the survivors of the losing side would sift through that pile and find bones from which new totems would be fashioned for Maka tribe.

Vulture decided that information was what was needed first, and picked Maria Santiago to isolate. She was tough and smart and the best one to start with. One did not question a truth-bearer's actions; it was unthinkable. Only Maka could object, and Maka was preoccupied with other duties. Thus it was easy to isolate Mari one night and induce some magic from the substances in the truth-bearer's bag of chemical tricks.

Vulture figured that any hypnotic drug strong enough to push them all over the line was strong enough to bring them back. To insure privacy, it would also all be done in an alien tongue, which only the *Thunder* team could understand although not speak themselves. Thanks to the dozen or so people the creature had been before, it had command of many languages and was not inhibited by any mindprinter program. Vulture chose Spanish because it was Santiago's native tongue, the one in which she thought when not mind-altered, and therefore the one probably easiest to reach. When Santiago was clearly under the drug, seated near a tree and far from the rest of the tribe, Vulture began.

"Mari feel good," she started in Matriyehan. "Mari feel safe. Mari not see, hear, smell, feel but truth-bearer. Just Mari and truth-bearer be. No other. No tribe. No Earth-Mother. Nothing."

Mari smiled, eyes closed, completely relaxed. Vulture switched to Spanish. It might not have been Mari's dialect, but it was closer than anything else. Any responses, of course, would have to be in Matriyehan.

"Who are you?" Vulture asked.

"Mari Maka," breathed the girl.

"Where was Mari Maka born?"

"Earth-Mother bear Mari Maka."

"Who is Maria Santiago?"

She frowned, then looked confused, eyes still closed. "Mari—not—know," she responded, but the inner conflict was already clear.

"*Capitan* Maria Santiago, commander of the spaceship *San Cristobal*, freebooter and leader, come forth! The *Thunder* calls you!"

Her face twisted up; she was clearly confused and fighting Vulture's command. "All dead," she responded. "Maria tribe all dead. Be Maka tribe now."

Vulture was no psychiatrist; she was not really human at all, but all those minds inside her, all those memories, male and female, professional and commoner, gave her a unique understanding of the human mind. Suddenly she realized why it had been so easy for them to go native, to fall into this trap.

Maria had lost her ship; she'd lost her command. Was there guilt there, even though it hadn't been her fault? Was this the punishment of a commander who'd lost her ship and somehow survived while many of the crew did not? Did she somehow feel she had to be punished for not joining them? Or was it a combination of things? On Matriyeh, any defeat of a chief meant death or abject subjugation. Had, somehow, the Matriyehan values bridged the cultures, so that she had begun to look upon, even dwell upon, the loss of her ship and some of the crew in totally Matriyehan terms? How could it be otherwise, since she was forced to think Matriyehan?

And the others? The two *Indrus* women had lost everything, too. In Matriyehan terms they were nothing unless they were members of a tribe, and here they were. And with the biochemical link, Matriyehans of a previous tribe had an obligation to put any previous tribe and loyalty and friendships from their minds. They had been made members of a new tribe, with new loyalties, and everyone else was gone from the old life anyway. It had taken only that slight hypnotic push to allow them to do what their impulses and inner voices were urging them to do all along. It removed that veneer of civilization that had kept them fighting to retain control.

Had they underestimated Master System? Was this the trap of Matriyeh, in which the very language, values, and biochemistry worked to make any alien a true member of this violent society? They were on the edge of control as it was, and it took only the single act of the drug to cut the last link, the last intellectual fight between alien and native. It was the power of that very pull, which Vulture hadn't really understood, that caused her to want more people down with her on this mission. It was insidious. If you came as an alien, you tripped every damned alarm in the quadrant. If you came as a Matriyehan, the whole thing was designed to make you totally Matriyehan.

Warlock? She never much believed in missions and causes anyway. She just liked to hurt and kill people; she always had been a sadomasochist. To her, as chief, Matriyeh must be a fantasy come true. As for Midi and Taeg —they'd been cast out by their boss, threatened with death unless they joined up and came down, and they were at the mercy of ones they had betrayed up in space. They had no stake in the mission—they'd just gotten out of Halinachi when they could with their boss—and had nowhere else to go. All things considered, they were better off and more secure down here in this hell than they were anywhere else.

And that left Vulture out on a limb. Could any of them

be brought back? It was far easier for the first truth-bearer to cut the thread, giving them what every fiber of their being was craving, than to retie it.

"You can have a new ship, Maria Santiago," Vulture whispered soothingly. "You can have your revenge on the whole system of evil that caused you to lose the first. You are strong. You are tough. You can fight the great evil or you can run from it and be Mari forever. Will you fight or will you run away?"

It was a difficult struggle within her, for she had locked out the past willingly but now it was being forced through the doorways of her mind. The response, when it came, was frustratingly Matriyehan.

"Not Mari place choose fight or run. Chief say fight, Mari fight. Chief say run, Mari run. Mari no chief no more."

Vulture spat in frustration, growing angrier by the moment. "Look up, Mari. Look at the sky. Look *beyond* the sky to the stars, to space, to many suns and many worlds. It is your birthplace. You loved it once, and were willing to fight and die for it. To be free among the stars, almost a goddess. No holds, nothing but the stars and love and adventure. Feel the thrill of first thinking of this as a young girl. Think of *San Cristobal* not as something lost but as something gained. If it meant so little to you that you can snuff it out, then why was it important at all? *Remember your loves, Maria Santiago! Remember your dreams!*"

And she looked up, and her eyes grew wide, and she remembered. Had Vulture used Matriyehan or Maria been limited so that she could not even understand any language but that one, it might have been a lost cause, but the old tongue and the strong, evocative images it could create in its melodic, poetic tones touched something that was always there inside her. Forty years could not be so shut out when it had to be confronted in that frame and context. She saw, and remembered; remembered the poverty, the early struggles, the sense of accomplishment and achievement, the romance of the stars as well as the work involved. Why was it worthwhile? Why was it important? Was not the struggle, the fight to get what she had attained, and to keep it, equally important?

Fight it ... Fight it ... Did you work all that time, all that hard, to be chief or slave? Fight it ...

She was still under the drug, but suddenly Vulture heard her utter, "Wha—what happen? What Mari do? . . ."

"I am truth-bearer, and I am Vulture," said the other, sighing with relief. "Vulture and truth are one. Now, say —what happened to the others?"

"Taeg . . . two spears in chest . . . gone. Dead. Aesa . . . have no heart to fight. Act, not do when kill or be killed . . . Midi . . . first no fight . . . then fight like demon . . . Suni first no fight, then see Aesa fall. Go crazy—kill, kill, kill. Still crazy in head, like animal. Euno . . . when first spear nick belly with child . . . become like wounded *kutu*, kill many, many Sosa tribe . . . They break . . . run. We chase . . ."

Vulture nodded. And now there were six, she thought, and one of those is power drunk, another is still a psychotic mute, the third has gone violently mad, and a fourth was most likely worshipping her chief and figuring she finally had a replacement for Savaphoong.

Maria Santiago suddenly went wide-eyed in horror, staring at the tattooed, bald visage that was now Vulture, thinking much the same.

"*Now* what can sky tribe do?" she asked plaintively.

Vulture wished she knew. "Would Mari go back to sky now?"

She shook her head slowly from side to side. "No. Go back with finger bracelet or not go back ever."

Even at a time like this, it was damned good to hear that again. No matter what, when her personal frenzy died down, it would be most convenient and necessary to have a little private talk with Manka Warlock.

꓿꓿꓿꓿꓿꓿꓿꓿꓿꓿꓿꓿꓿꓿꓿꓿꓿꓿꓿꓿꓿꓿꓿꓿꓿꓿꓿

9. THE HOLY COMMAND

IT WAS A SHOCK TO VULTURE TO DISCOVER THAT MANKA
Warlock was not nearly as lost as the rest of them, nor even
surprised to find Vulture returning as a truth-bearer.

"Maka play Maka game instead of *Thunder* game,"
Vulture said disgustedly.

The chief stood up and glared at the truth-bearer, who
was considerably smaller. "*Is* no game but Maka game.
Never no game but Maka game. Not *ever*!"

"Maka no care with sky tribe? No care sky tribe need
Maka to battle evil demon-god?"

Warlock spat. "To fire god with sky tribe! Long life
Maka slave to big chiefs. Do this, do that. Then mess with
Maka thoughts. Make fat bird Maka chief. No more. No
more. *Maka* chief now. Think clear, be strong. Tribe do
what Maka say, think what Maka think. If demon-god say
people be this way then maybe demon-god right. Power,
strength always chief. Then. Now. Best Maka be chief here

than belong to *Thunder* chief or demon-god chief or secret chief."

"What of sky tribe people here?"

"*No* sky tribe people here but false truth-bearer. Only Maka tribe."

Vulture had just about enough of this psychotic. "False truth-bearer is not people. Maka know," she said menacingly. "False truth-bearer need just touch great Maka chief. No more Maka chief. Then *Vulture* chief," she noted, using the foreign word deliberately.

Warlock was mad but not suicidal. Her eyes went wide and she seemed to inch back a bit from the small figure.

Vulture smiled grimly. "That not help Maka. Can run, but great chief not run. Not and keep body of chief. But, if so—chief must touch people. Chief must mate with tribe. Which tribe people be *Vulture*? Not know. Not even know. Is Oona? Tabu? Midi? Maka not know. But Maka know now. Fear in eyes of great Maka chief. No can have fear, Maka chief. Fear turn Maka chief to just property. Common tribe. Great god-demon create Matriyeh to trap any tribe that can do harm, but great god-demon not know *Vulture*. Maka chief do." Suddenly she lapsed into English. "You aren't free, Manka Warlock," she said coldly. "I've got you between a rock and a hard place."

Warlock understood this well now, but she wasn't through yet. "No can steal finger bracelet if finger bracelet could be steal anyway. Maka tribe big tribe. Earth-Mother born, not sky tribe born. False truth-bearer can kill Maka, be Maka . . . but *then* what?"

Then what indeed? Vulture had been pondering this, somewhat with the help of Maria Santiago, and they had decided that now was the time for big risks.

"God-demon make one mistake," Vulture told her. "Matriyeh created to trap sky tribe people. Good trap; clever trap. But to make trap work had to make tribe stronger than beliefs. Sky tribe finished with hiding. Finished with god-demon traps. Maka like Matriyeh? Maka want be great chief? If Maka have courage to risk tribe, life, all things—then Maka can get what Maka want and sky tribe what sky tribe want. No more tribes play god-demons's game. Now god-demon play new game. Maka game. Sky tribe game."

This was more like it, and a way out. "Maka listens," she said seriously.

It really wasn't either Vulture or Maria who came up with it, but rather both of them discussing their experiences and their problem. The world was a nearly perfect trap. If you came in with weapons and high-tech devices, you would trigger a wholesale invasion of Vals, SPF forces, and planetary defenses. If you came in Matriyehan but with modern things and different tongues, then sooner or later a truth-bearer would smoke you out, and the closer you got to the holy place or the more dangerous you seemed, the more likely you would bring down all the truth-bearers in the region upon you. Star Eagle had pegged it correctly: the only way in safely and quietly was to come in as a true Matriyehan, as they had come in. But Matriyehan society was engineered, even to its language and its biochemical bonding, to trap anyone who came in that way, as well. Invulnerable. Impenetrable. On Janipur and perhaps elsewhere the ring had been guarded by technology and open displays of force, and those had been beaten. On Matriyeh, the ring was guarded by a total absence of those things. It was insidious. Whoever attained one type would be unlikely to fail to be trapped by their own ego and self-confidence in the other.

But the system was quite fragile, depending as it did on the absolute adherence by the people of Matriyeh to the religious codes and beliefs of the priestesshood, reinforced by third-rank truth-bearers. But because of the structure the system couldn't use any of the high-tech mechanisms that Master System had elsewhere. To bring out legions of SPF would destroy the system in the act of preserving it.

The only thing the religion could do would be to rally large numbers of tribes to fight the demon-dominated rebels, overwhelming them by sheer force of numbers. But the rebel tribe would fight to the last, since its members were not only culturally but also biologically linked to their chief. Maria Santiago had said it in her drugged state. Her job was not to think but to obey. The king's religion was the religion of the nation, even if that nation numbered only sixty-one.

Guards were posted at the few easy entrances to the valley. Anyone was to be allowed in, but none were allowed out, not even truth-bearers of whatever rank. Raiding parties of the best warriors would be sent out to capture and haul back any strays, to build strength wherever possible. The valley could easily feed a hundred or more for a long time, if they were careful, and with new training and new ideas they might be enough to become the most formidable army in the recent history of Matriyeh.

The bow and arrow were easily fabricated, but were on the forbidden list. It wouldn't take many archers to decimate a tribe like Sosa tribe. Salt preserved food for long periods and there were a number of salt outcroppings in the region. Sledges could be rigged to carry what was needed over long distances. Santiago knew how to construct the bolo, a weapon so obscure it hadn't even made the forbidden list. Obscure, but damned effective.

Vulture was getting tired of skulking around. Now it was time to bring revolution to Matriyeh and bring down this terrible and cruel experiment—but subtly. If it were done right, and the weapons and tactics properly chosen, it might not even appear than any of it was of alien origin. Master System was also about to learn a lesson in evolution. If you keep an environment soft and comfortable, the people are pushovers; if you have them in continual conflict, danger, and under constant pressure just to remain alive, you are going to get only the smartest, strongest, and toughest surviving.

Without the tribal bonds that were the heart of the trap, the tribes themselves would have disposed of a chief committing such heresy. Not here. Here the people belonged to the chief. It was a gaping hole in Master System's otherwise perfect defense, but it also remained untested. Surely innovation and invention was not uncommon on this world; chiefs were of the personality to put self above religious restrictions when power was available. The normal control procedure was to administer one of the drug compounds in the truth-bearer's bag of tricks. So far, it had been effective; certainly nothing in Omaqua's experience indicated a major failure.

Now Vulture and Warlock intended to rock the very foundations of that system and see just what they could shake out. The risk was that the protectors would have to break out the heavy artillery or technical defenses, but that would mean some folks in the holy place knew a lot more than the rest, and it would require bringing those people to the scene.

The campaign had been going well, carefully taking on selected contiguous tribes whose numbers were within the reach of Warlock's band. Within weeks they numbered more than two hundred, the most powerful organized force on the planet outside the priestesshood, but it was almost immediately clear why no action had yet been taken against them.

A band that size was simply unmanageable by the system of Matriyeh. It was not sufficient for Warlock to take each tribe member once; the chemical bond only held strong, it seemed, if each member were taken every few weeks at most or was made pregnant, and the numbers were against Warlock from the start. Most Matriyehans were no more oversexed than most Earth-humans, but none were celibate. Here the urge for sex was far more biochemical, a survival mechanism for the race. Warlock's capacity was great but not infinite; certainly no more than four in a day and that was exhausting enough. That was a hundred and twenty a month, once a month. Already that left eight and loss of control began perhaps eight to ten days after a period. Those would find what relief they could among themselves, and that would inevitably trigger the sexual sea change in one or more of them.

Warlock felt frustrated and incensed by it, but Vulture simply decided on a change in tactics. Warlock didn't like it one bit, but she was smart enough to see that there was no real alternative; she was more frightened of Vulture than of diluting her power. It was time to halt, take stock, and let the truth-bearer pharmacy grind into action.

Another truth-bearer was attracted by all the action, though, and was quite startled to find one of her own already there. Omaqua suggested they go off someplace quiet and discuss things first. They looked so much alike that few could even tell that the one who returned wasn't the one who left, but Vulture had a better briefing on the situation, a new perspective, and a whole second set of drugs and aids that would be badly needed.

Warlock's movements had indeed attracted attention, but the truth-bearer's instructions had been pretty limited toward what Vulture and Warlock thought of as a major movement. Wait until it splits and new chiefs fight the old, then move in and take one of the new tribes and eliminate the innovations. There was a definite implication that more truth-bearers would be heading this way to take care of the others, but there didn't seem to be any hurry or sense of urgency. This was routine stuff; it was their job.

There *was* a flaw in Master System's defense, of that Vulture was certain, but it wasn't the fear of empire. It was obvious now that that route had been effectively fore-closed. The weakest route was the one thing the very culture and background and biochemistry and system provided against. One chief for each tribe, and that tribe was a maximum of a hundred, but the chiefs would see other chiefs, other tribes, as rivals for food, territory, and resources. They fought each other during fallow times and otherwise avoided one another; they would never think of banding together.

As soon as Maria and Midi had borne their children, and a small amount of time had been allowed to rebalance their biochemistries, Vulture began the program. It was none too soon; after using her chemicals to restrain the development of spontaneous chiefs in the mob, she was running low on material in spite of the double supply and did not want to risk hitting another sacred place to replen-ish her stock. She hoped another priestess would show up soon, but as of yet none had.

Although both the alien women were tough and aggres-sive, neither had the fire to be chief nor the self-ego to desire the sexual trappings that went with it. It was neces-sary, even with their understanding, to use the hypnotic powders to ease the way. Vulture only hoped that both, who would have far preferred to remain as they were and nurture their children, would have enough sense of loyalty and mission to become what was required and stay that way.

Suni lost her child, possibly as a consequence of her wounds, and did not really seem to care. Vulture under-stood, but it was tough going to reach her. When Suni had seen Aesa fall after being unable to join the battle carnage

out of beliefs far deeper than even the mindprinter program, something in Suni had snapped. She was now the
last of the *Indrus* crew; she had no one and no status here,
and she felt horribly alone and very, very scared. She had
the same background and philosophy and personal religion
as Aesa, but it had suddenly seemed not enough. She'd
waded in, wanting only revenge, seeing only Aesa'a
bloody body savaged and ripped again and again, and she
had killed like a maniac.

Afterward had come sanity of a sort and the realization
of what she had done during that period. She felt that her
soul had either fled or died in that moment and that she was
now no more than an empty shell without purpose, living
beyond its time. She had wanted to die in that battle and
she had survived. Just how deeply the shock had gone
amazed even Vulture, who tried with her hypnotics and
what reasoning powers she could to enlist the aid of the
woman. She understood Suni's basic Hindu beliefs and
knew Janipurian Hindi, close enough to be understood by
her even with its bizarre pronunciations and odd terminol-
ogy.

"We have a duty higher than ourselves," she told Suni
urgently. "We have a duty to humanity, to all those who
call themselves human. We may fail, but if we do, let it not
be because we did it to ourselves, that we quit. Your husband was committed to it, as was Captain Paschittawal and
Lalla. You must not let them have died in vain. You must
not let us fail because you fail. If we fail, let it be because
the task is too great, or because others were too weak, but
not because you were. Fate has placed you here. You must
not refuse your destiny, for in that there is surely damna-
tion."

For a while she had said nothing, but then she said, in
ancient Hindi, as if the mindprinter and its powers and its

filters did not exist, "For I am death, the destroyer of worlds . . ."

Vulture was shocked, although she knew that the powers of the mind were potentially greater than any program or any machine and that if anyone could prove it so, it would be one of the Hindu faith. "Suni . . ."

The voice that replied was so strange, so utterly inhuman in accent and intonation, that it gave even Vulture chills. "Suni is no more," the voice said, as if from someplace other than a human throat, someplace distant and very, very unpleasant. "Her soul has gone on, as it should."

Vulture swallowed hard, not quite sure what she had here. "Then who are you? *What* are you?"

"Do you not know me? I am the true goddess of this place, the one whom they serve without knowing. I am the one who follows you about the universe. I am death. I am the void and the nothingness. I am Kali."

Vulture sighed. All they needed right now was another wacko. Still, there was something unearthly, unreal about the woman, something not a little bit frightening.

"Most mighty and fearsome one, will you then for a time stop following and aid us in our struggle?"

"Those who worship me and serve me shall gain my favors," she responded coldly. "If those conditions are met, I will participate, but not because I care about your cause."

"Then—why?"

"Because it might be amusing. Because the places that follow the enlightened faith nonetheless do me no service any longer. I am here, this world is here, because I require a world of my own. The death of the child has given me power and incarnation. Now we will remove the sham religion from this place. Now shall this be my world."

Vulture wasn't quite certain what she had to deal with now, except that insanity seemed an added trap of this place, but pragmatism had to rule. If sheer biology limited a tribe to a hundred or so, then an alliance of chiefs could create a formidable force. With Vulture as go-between and councilor to the tribes, easing the automatic dislike and suspicion between chiefs, it just might work.

In the days after it began, and aided by the drugs of the truth-bearers, Santiago and Midi took on the male aspect and began carving out sections of the larger tribe, being selective for balance of skills and burdens. It tore Manka Warlock up to see this and she had a hard time repressing her desire to fight, to challenge these new ones, but she kept away with her own, comforted that she still had the largest tribe, and understanding the need as no native child could.

Suni seemed to throw off all drugs and assumed the chief's aspects rapidly on her own. There was a change in her that madness brought, a level of callous violence and cruelty that even Warlock would be hard-pressed to match. The next step was to move on other tribes as they also proceeded on their march in toward the center and flesh out the new tribes to full strength if possible. Working in concert, this proved relatively easy although not without losses; still, these were blooded, experienced tribes now, and after initial problems in coordination they began to function less as a tribe than as an army.

Vulture had a number of objectives, the first of which was to draw more important people from the holy places. So far they continued to be sent low-echelon truth-bearers who could conceive of such an alliance in theory, but who were ill prepared for chiefs who had no more regard for truth-bearers than for the lowest of their tribe and disposed of them as enemies.

In a matter of weeks all four tribes were at maximum strength. Using sledges and litters and salt packs, they were able to gather large quantities of food and preserve some of it to take with them. Such a force could even take on lava snakes.

Vulture's goal was not the holy seat but a region about two hundred kilometers south and east of it—a broad valley located on the topographic maps burned into her mind at the confluence of three rivers into one mighty one, well away from the great volcanoes but lush from their bounty. What the volcanoes took in danger and sudden death they also paid for in rich soil. If properly managed, such a valley could support a population far in excess of their combined forces. That would be the point of challenge, the place where the priestesses would have to deal with them, on their own ground. And the people of this new nation would have a real stake in fighting for it.

While still on the way there, Silent Woman had her child. Vulture had been concerned that should the child be born dead, as many were here, or have problems that would mean its death, Suni's madness would be as nothing compared to Silent Woman's, but it didn't happen. The child was normal and possessed a loud, strong pair of lungs, and she doted over it and protected it with a fierce loyalty beyond Matriyehan norms.

In the process, the levels and numbers of third-rank truth-bearers had to be priestesses of the false religion. Vulture kept wondering when they would either send one or more of higher rank or make a bolder move in force, but so far they seemed unwilling or unable to comprehend the idea that things were really getting out of hand. Like the system itself, the priestesses were too used to dealing with things in a normal fashion and no longer ready or well suited to grapple with radical departures. They would soon be forced to, however. If there was some kind of computer brain at the heart of this system, it would now be getting very concerned. The new movement struck at the very heart of the religion, a more radical revolution than any

political or technological idea. If chiefs could learn to co-
operate with one another, to divide the spoils and work
together when need be, there was the threat of a real rebellion here. Its very success might even inspire other chiefs
who merely heard about it to try it, as difficult as it might
be. Deep down, no one really liked the constant struggle
and quick and early death of the life here, not if there was
an alternative. In many regions they would be forced to
remain so by geography, but much of this world was rich
and bountiful and could be organized.

Even the people of the tribes felt that they were a part of
something new and good. The security of such a massive
force with cooperating allies on all sides rather than enemies fed on their need for such security and groups. The
chiefs could never be friends; the situation made it next to
impossible for them even to meet without the urge to challenge and come to deadly blows exploding inside them, but
no such constraints were on the firebearers, who carried the
messages between the chiefs and faithfully represented
their own leaders to the others. Only Silent Woman was
useless in this, but the birth of her child had become the
only thing in her mind of importance and she easily relin-
quished the post to Oona, a sycophant with some intelligence and a near worship of Manka Warlock.

Vulture was most nervous, waiting always for the
priestesses to make their move, but she ultimately guessed
that it wouldn't happen until the tribes had attained their
initial objective of securing the valley. Vulture's aim was to
keep them guessing. This might be a native rebellion, or it
might be alien inspired and led. If native, it could be dealt
with once it could be seen where all this was leading. If
alien, then the alarms could be sounded before they
reached the holy seat. Once the apparent objective of the
new force was achieved, the priestesses would act. The
only question was how.

The heretic army had reached the edge of the river valley and had looked down on the promised land before the first new move occurred. They strode boldly into the large encampments looking unworried and unafraid; seven third-rank priestesses led by an eighth who was most definitely different.

She had the same basic appearance, but the holy tattoos covered every square centimeter of her body and she wore a cape of skin and fur. Her necklace held not only the usual totems but also a shiny metal charm: the bird in the tree. Her staff was metal-tipped with what looked like gold dulled by age and use, and she had the arrogant look and swagger of someone who knew the gods were on her side.

They had finally sent someone of the second rank to have a firsthand look at the situation.

Vulture hurried over to Warlock, who was watching the parade. "What now?" the chief asked.

"Truth-bearer need be alone with truth-bearer chief. Separate, delay others. If cause trouble send to Suni tribe."

"Truth-bearer chief not stupid. Must know others come, no go. What if truth-bearer chief no want one-talk?"

"Then truth-bearer do change right here before all if have to. Manka tribe take others."

Warlock nodded and gestured to Oona, making the orders plain, then stepped back, not wanting to have a direct confrontation now. There was no telling what nastiness a truth-bearer chief might carry with her. That was why a separation was vital as early as possible. Take the second-rank official, and the others were irrelevant. Any attempt to take them immediately and by force might bring out some surprises they neither wanted nor needed.

Warlock was right; the old girl was no fool even if she had placed herself in a precarious position. The mere fact that she had indicated the presence of some weapon, or other way of dealing with a group this large, meant trouble. She was, however, very surprised to see a third-rank priestess here, in this camp, apparently alive and unharmed. Vulture approached reverently, bent down and kissed the hand of the second-rank priestess, and waited.

"Stand," she commanded. She looked around at the large assembly of tribes present, then back directly into Vulture's eyes. "Explain this."

"If imperfect truth-bearer can talk to Holy Mother beyond other ears . . ."

"Talk here. Look around. See heresy. See blasphemy. *Explain!*"

"If Holy Mother can . . ."

Vulture was suddenly stunned as the holy mother brought up her staff and struck the other hard, hard enough to cause Vulture to fall to the ground with blood trickling from the side of her mouth. Vulture wiped it away with her hand as best she could but did not immediately rise. She was getting pretty damned mad fast, and the smirks on the seven third-rankers' faces did nothing to calm her down.

"Truth?"

"Always," the holy mother responded.

"Spirit sent by sun god come. Command this. Say truth-bearer chiefs not talk for gods, talk for demons. Tribes obey command of sun god."

"*Liar!* Holy fire come down from sky and strike blasphemers! Cook whole tribes in fire of purity! Show this spirit! Holy Mother will show demon, not god!"

Vulture looked around, made eye contact with Oona, and nodded. Oona didn't know what was coming, but she had her orders and she certainly wanted to remove these people before they went through with their threat. Then Vulture got up and stood straight before the holy mother. "Power against power!" she screamed suddenly so all could hear. "Faith against faith! Truth against lie! Truth-bearers stand back!" She gave the holy mother a bloody grin, and saw the other's hand groping for something concealed in the great cape. Vulture reached out, and the holy mother stepped back a pace. All work had stopped now; all eyes were on the pair save a few well-chosen warriors whose spears were directed at the seven lesser priestesses, who didn't seem to know it.

Vulture smiled grimly. "Faith against faith. Might truth-bearer not kiss the hand of Holy Mother first?"

"What stand before Holy Mother is no truth-bearer!" the older one said nervously. "Are demon!" The movement back into the cape was quick, but Vulture was quicker. Not knowing quite what to expect, but having only to make full skin contact, she lunged forward, and her palm touched the exposed chest of the high priestess even as that worthy was bringing from the cape a small, slender object that was unfamiliar to Vulture but which had a trigger. The holy mother stiffened in a look of extreme surprise, and the process began.

Warlock was quick to move forward even as it happened. "If Maka tribe truth-bearer be demon and Holy Mother be of gods, then Holy Mother win. If Maka tribe truth-bearer be of gods, then truth-bearer soul will enter Holy Mother! Watch! Bearers make sure no help either one!"

That last was unnecessary; the seven truth-bearers were as appalled by what they were seeing, and as transfixed, as most of the tribal onlookers. Warlock, however, was more concerned about them afterward, since this show would certainly betray alien origins. She was fairly confident that they could not escape no matter what, but they might do a great deal of damage.

The gun slipped from the hand of the holy mother as Vulture's body moved, enveloped, and merged with the older woman's. It was ugly, grotesque, and unpleasant to

watch, but Warlock was a pro. She darted in and snatched
up the gun and examined it. It seemed to be molded out of
a single piece of medium-red synthetic, except for the trigger, which was merely a long, thick rod with no trigger
guard. The barrel mouth indicated a beam rather than a
projectile, but the lack of sights or aiming devices suggested that the gun packed enough power, it didn't need
much expertise to use effectively. The damned "eating"
process took fifteen or twenty minutes, and then Vulture
wouldn't be any good for a while except for show. For just
a moment she considered firing into that writhing mass of
flesh or whatever it was, ridding herself of Vulture and the
holy mother at one and the same time. With a gun, a chief
could go very far indeed. The problem was, she didn't
know what the gun really did, nor could she be certain it
would kill Vulture. She was not unmindful that the creature
had killed dozens in the high-tech labyrinth of Melchior
before being not killed but merely stunned.

It no longer really mattered, either. At the moment her
interests were Vulture's interests were *Thunder*'s interest.
Without *Thunder* she could lead a savage band until she
died; with it on her side, the role of empress in a rebuilt
Matriyeh was not out of reach.

"*Etranger*," she heard someone whisper, and several
other voices whispered the same. "*Prenez garde!*"

Warlock whirled, gun in hand, and her look and her
gestures motioned everyone else back from the seven
priestesses. "*Prenez garde, Maka's ass!*" she shouted, and
fired at them.

There was a burst of light, and five of the seven were
suddenly in flames; the guards were startled but not startled
enough not to trip the other two as they began to run. They
were caught by the crowd even as the others screamed and
burned, and a blood cry went up as the two untouched
priestesses were torn to bits by the mob. They were seeing

miracles here; great power beyond their comprehension, but they knew who was wielding that power and who was its victim.

Warlock watched the five women burn; they were already dead, but they made a very nice line of bonfires. She'd been right about the gun: it had been quite effective, and would have been more so had that Holy Mother pulled it out, screamed for god's curse on Vulture, and burned her on the spot.

By the time it was over a new holy mother was stepping unsteadily out of the mass of goo that represented Vulture's old body. She was concentrating mightily to keep control and bring off the show. She pointed to the mass of still-writhing, bubbling goo and said, in a loud if croaking voice, "That be soul of Holy Mother and demon! Behold Maka truth-bearer in body of enemy!"

That started a rumbling that became a roar and then a cheer as warriors raised their weapons and shook their fists and rejoiced that they and their great chief was truly in the right. Vulture raised her arms to show appreciation, but saw Warlock out of the corner of her eyes. "Better get me someplace so I can lie down," she hissed in English. "I feel like hell, and I can't keep this up very long."

"They're getting pretty worried," Vulture told Warlock, using English rather than the more limited Matriyehan Warlock was forced to speak. "The command structure is far more like a Center than we thought. The experiment here might be radical and on a large scale, but the organization is still very much along familiar, if more primitive, lines. The old Holy Mother was still fairly ignorant, but she knew a pistol when she saw it and what it could do, and she didn't think of it so much in mystical terms but rather as a pragmatic tool for keeping the faithful in line."

"How many fire spears they got?" Warlock was getting

worried. It wouldn't take many of these things to wipe out the whole assembly.

"A lot. A whole arms cache. They aren't very well versed on how to use them, though, which is why they're more of the blow-everything-to-hell kind. There're enough of those, and more powerful weapons, for the higher priestesses, but the third rank is kept ignorant of them and as fearful as the tribes might be."

"Until truth-bearer become warrior."

"Yeah, maybe—but I'm not sure about that. It's been over a hundred years since they started this system. None of the original troopers are left, I'm sure of that, and their descendants are given basic information in mindprinter programs buried deep—but a mindprinter can only tell you how to use a weapon, not give you the skill to use it expertly. You and I would be able to handle anything they have a hundred times better than they would, but you put hundreds of those in the hands of the most unskilled people, and they'll take out everybody from horizon to horizon."

Warlock thought for a moment. "So they be no more good than warrior with same flame spear. Where they keep these flame spears?"

"Huh? Oh, I see what you mean. An interesting idea, but I'm not sure I like the idea of hundreds of warriors running around with those blowtorches. Even if we won, I'm not sure this world is ready for the consequences of that. More interesting is the idea of keeping them from using them."

Vulture sighed, then picked up a stick and began to sketch a crude diagram in the earth as she talked. "The holy seat is in a broad valley ringed by very high mountains. They're volcanic, but that area's very old and inactive. The heights reach to twenty thousand kilometers, and at that latitude they're snowcapped almost all the time. The melt comes down and is collected in a bowl-shaped depression that is probably a glacial cirque. That provides year-round fresh water, and during the warmest months it overflows and feeds a large river. The river provides the only outlet—here, at a great waterfall. Steps have been cut into the rock behind the falls providing the only way in or out with any ease. Those are both human and device guarded. The magical stuff is probably computer driven but designed, like the holy places around here, mostly to keep people out, not in. Still, between the high mountains and the guards and traps, it's pretty nasty getting in and out."

"And inside valley?"

"It's a rough life for the truth-bearer tribe. They spend all day tending fields and crops and doing backbreaking labor to feed and maintain the area, then spend whatever time is left training for their destinies as priestesses. No wonder they're anxious to get out of there! Unlike the tribes, the truth-bearers in the field don't do much work or any fighting and they have a privileged spot wherever they go. Caves and depressions in the rock provide the storage facilities, but they live in the open like the tribes do. Dug into the rock at the far end of the valley is the Great Temple itself, which is a pretty impressive structure. Huge reliefs of the great and lesser gods looking down on the Earth-Mother are carved into it so they also symbolically look down on the valley. Inside is the Inner Temple, with a huge statue of the Great God—and the Great God not only listens, it talks and even shows pictures. A real miracle idol. The second rank maintains the whole area, and the very small first rank, all of whom are pretty old for anyplace and ancient for this world, do all the talking and ordering. They're considered divine, infallible, and without sin or fault—goddesses in human form. It's a sin for any thirdranker even to look at them as they pass, and death to walk in their footsteps."

Warlock nodded. "Do great chiefs believe own perfection?"

"Huh? Oh, I see what you mean. It's hard to say—as a field supervisor and part-time teacher, I've never actually laid eyes on one. They're not ignorant, though. I bet they know all the automatic systems and nasty stuff they need even without stimuli. Knowledge only the gods possess. Whether that's made them corrupt cynics or whether they feel they really are demigods we can't know. The ultimate leader is the Earth-daughter, who is said to be eternally young and beautiful—all knowing and immortal. If she's real, or how they work it if she is, I don't know."

"Then Earth-daughter wear ring."

Vulture frowned and gazed off into the darkness for a moment, looking puzzled. "No, I don't think so. She's the ultimate chief, judge, general, whatever, but as all chiefs have firebearers, she has a ring bearer. That would be the adjutant, the executive officer, the one who runs the day-to-day operations."

"Human with power."

"What?"

"Ring must be with human power. That be ring bearer. Why not Earth-daughter? Maka wonder . . ."

"Good point." She looked up. "Unless the Earth-daughter is either mythical or—nonhuman. Either one explains why I never met anyone who saw her. I've met people who know people who say they saw her, but that's possibly bragging or exaggerating to look important. Even within the second rank there are the ins and the outs—those in the temple look down on those in the field. Buck sergeants versus top sergeants. But what if she *is* real?"

"If ring bearer got ring, then ring bearer be Matriyeh chief. Should be top."

"Yeah, I see what you mean. If the ring bearer's the chief administrator, the highest-ranking human with power on this world, then who would be over her? Immortal—hmmm—could we have a Val in there keeping the Center honest?"

Warlock held up the gun and looked at it. "No flame spear like this could kill metal demon."

Vulture nodded. "Yeah, I did one in, but with a heavy-duty laser at point-blank range. A Val and a master computer with satellite links. This is getting a bit complicated. *Damn*! I wish I could talk to *Thunder* now! We've come so far—I'd hate to have to do this all over again, but it'd take many weeks to get back to the blind zone, call up there, then get back here. They won't wait that long. We have two separate problems, though. First, we have to take the ring without them knowing about it, and, second, we have to negate religious control without the computer calling in the SPF. Damn it! I am fifteen people, yet I need China's expertise, Hawks' way of approaching a problem, and Star Eagle's analytical skills and data. I'm the only one who could give you any information and protection, yet I'm the only one who could possibly make the distance and discuss the problem."

"Truth-bearer chief got no magic here," Warlock said "Send Holy Mother and truth-bearers. Will make war if Holy Mother no report. But if Holy Mother report trouble ended..."

Vulture's jaw dropped slightly. "What an interesting, devious idea. There aren't any Vals out here, and not much else. Most of the stuff they know is word of mouth and reports taken from the truth-bearers at the holy places. Okay, so I go in there and I tell 'em my seven truth-bearers are taking care of the job, that it was all indigenous, and that the tribes are separating and returning to the old ways. Fine. I have the ability within me to create whatever experiences are necessary or expected, even under the mind-printer. That was my original function, remember. But will they accept that? Sooner or later that computer is going to notice that none of the seven report in to holy places. Other truth-bearers may come and report otherwise. How long can we maintain the fiction? If they find out my lie, then they'll know somebody can beat their mindprinter, and that will trigger the alarms."

"So? What if tribes go back old way? Go far to south, far from holy place. Find new rich territory, much food. Wait."

"You've forgotten the effects of those drugs. I haven't. And for all four tribes to settle in the same area, to take the same territories, will mean war with whatever tribes are there now. More death, more risk—but also in the end more people. Maybe several more tribes' worth. And we're fresh out of *Thunder* chiefs."

Warlock spun around and stared at Vulture. "Matriyehans not animals! Humans! Think! Sky demons want make Matriyehans animals! Not stupid. Many warriors see, like, what Maka tribe and other tribes do. Wonder, doubt, question old ways, old beliefs. Would keep talk."

"I wonder. You can't even be within eyesight of another chief without an irresistible urge to fight. It's in the biology."

"Chiefs speak through firebearers, like now. No can have tribe but so big. Only fight then for food. Plenty food here. Holy Mother take many seasons if need to. Chiefs still be ready."

"And the drugs and inevitable other truth-bearers?"

"Got two pouches magic dusts from dead truth-bearers. Holy Mother teach. Maka do magic on truth-bearers! Big joke! If no work—truth-bearers die just like warriors each day. Fire-bearers, other chiefs watch, too. Protect others. Whole life Maka fool great chiefs. Maka fool these, too.

Warriors will obey long as Holy Mother takes. Mean better life for children if not them."

Vulture sighed. "All right—I'll see each of the other chiefs and explain it. If they agree, then that's the way it'll be. I just hope I can find you again."

"Tribes stay close. Not hard to find. Good land to south. Twenty days, maybe more. Come here, go south. Tribes not be hard to find."

Within the next two days the plan was discussed with the other chiefs in turn, and Vulture was surprised to find agreement with all of them. Suni, or *Dakuminifar*—goddess—as she now insisted she be called—actually thought she'd commanded it, since great magic was needed to counter great magic. After some initial reservations, Midi was now clearly enjoying the chief's role and in no hurry to give it up. And Mari, the most reluctant of all, had come to terms with herself.

"Matriyehans be good people," she said. "*Thunder* people be only hope tribes have. Mari teach much—learn, too. Mari was chief in stars and beaten. Mari chief again. This time no get beat. Have chance do great thing here. Not know, understand, but this be where Mari belong. Mari needed here."

And so Vulture taught what she could, and wished them well, and started out, not back toward the fighters but in toward the holy seat only a hundred kilometers away. She wondered, idly, even if this operation was successful, if any of them would go back aboard the *Thunder*. It was difficult to see Manka Warlock as a revolutionary and social organizer, let alone a visionary, but history tended to glamorize the visionaries and heroes. How many had been egomaniacal and psychopathic to boot and still done their great deeds?

Maria Santiago had lost her ship and much of her crew, and all she'd done was wallow in guilt at that loss and dream of a new ship. Now she was captain of a new organization with a much larger crew and dedicated to their welfare. She had a new command, and hope. If they broke the grip of Master System she could do wonders for this world. If they didn't, she might just as well remain as she was.

Midi, too, had new responsibility, new commands, and she had nothing to go back to. She might well be less visionary and more selfish than the others, but she had more here than she had anywhere else. As for Suni—if she survived at all, better a self-deluded goddess here than a sane and lonely character up there.

And Silent Woman was back in her element once again and given back that which seemed lost forever.

Vulture could only wonder which of them would still be alive and in charge when she finally made it back to them —and what their mental condition and commitment would be if and when that happened.

And, most of all, she wondered what she would say and do if *Thunder* went after the ring at the expense of helping its people.

The holy seat was as good as invisible from the plain leading up to it. As far as any eye could tell, a wall of great mountains simply rose up into and beyond the almost omnipresent clouds. To find the entrance, one followed the river—now flowing fairly fast although not nearly filling its eroded bed as it might in other seasons—to the waterfall that fed it from perhaps three hundred meters straight up. Only up close could you see that there were the mystic signs and warnings and then a stone stair carved sideways in the gray rock going up toward the source of the falls.

It was also nearly impossible to see the small guard posts, cut as they were out of the mountain and disguised so that only eyes and weapons need betray themselves. As in the holy places that were the prime information source for this theocratic leadership, there were also effective automated guardians that required passwords and recognitions and at least one that appeared to read footprints from two plates set in the rock. One was expected to climb the stairs without hesitation, saying or doing what was required routinely, even automatically, and pausing for nothing else. Anything else was a sign of weakness, and would cause suspicion.

The valley itself was a great gouge in the rock, roughly five kilometers wide by more than twenty long. It had been well planned, with one area set aside for fruit- and nut-bearing trees. Another for bushes of the same type, yet another for the growing of grains. The diet was well balanced but generally uniform and totally vegetarian.

At the far end of the well-worn river trail loomed the temple itself, with its dramatic carvings above and below the inverted crescent-shaped opening. They were so huge they could be seen even from the top of the stairs, although as one approached, the detail and sheer scale of them became evident and overwhelming. Most startling to someone like Vulture was that they did not seem to have been cut by machine, but rather hand-carved by who knew what talents and numbers and over a very long period of time.

It took almost the whole day to get to the temple, a task made even harder by the seemingly incessant requirement to stop every time a junior was encountered and have them kneel and kiss her hand. She was not allowed to eat or drink during this period; total fasting was required until after the report was delivered.

It was dark by the time she reached the temple itself, its entrance all the more eerie, lit by the glow of internal torches, and here again there was another falls, grander still but not nearly so great as it was in the hottest season. Now she removed her cape and put down her staff and the rest and stepped into the pool and under the icy-cold falls.

The Matriyehan body had a tremendous temperature tolerance, but cold was cold.

All that she had remained behind save the necklace and other crude jewelry. Those, too, were washed and put back on. Then, stepping from the pool, she allowed the breeze to dry her, and then proceeded up the stairs and into the temple itself.

It was unclear whether the temple had been developed out of a natural cave, or whether it had been human-made, but it was enormous—a great cavern adorned with multi-colored pillars and also with stalactites and stalagmites, indicating rock layers of other than volcanic origin somewhere above. The statue of the Great God, rising twenty meters in the main cavern and still not touching the curved ceiling, looked down upon her and others within, all of whom she ignored, prostrating herself on the cold, damp floor and saying the prayer-chants to the statue.

When Clayben and his team designed Vulture, they knew that their creation would be useless if it could not pass a mindprinter test and reject imprints. In effect, Vulture could create her own mindprint program, using the holy mother's memories until they were no longer convenient and then writing whatever ending was necessary. It was a complex process but she did it automatically when desired and had no idea how she did it. Vulture could remain a passive observer, its own memory stored elsewhere and in a way that no mindprinter was ever designed to detect. In effect, the form and mind there now was that of the holy mother—as edited and rewritten—and no one else, although Vulture could reassert control at any time.

When they'd been trapped by that first truth-bearer with the hypnotics, Vulture had been in full command of Uraa, and there had been no time to sever the connection. It was a sobering lesson on yet another vulnerability, and one she had no intention of repeating.

And now it was time to go down a long side tunnel and report to the duty officer, another second-ranker like herself. The fact that the duty officer wore a finely woven cape with the bird and tree design in gold and wore metal jewelry marked her as the upper temple rank, but technically they were equals and there was no deference, no bowing or hand-kissing.

"Holy Mother Francine Yvonne reports from the field," she said simply and firmly in the temple tongue—which was French.

"We have been waiting anxiously for you," the duty officer responded. "Speak your preliminary report to me now. Then you will be sent up for a full debriefing."

"It was a major heresy, the worst I have ever seen or heard about. I am filled with great joy that I was adequate to the challenge."

"You have dealt with it, then?"

"It is in the process of being dealt with. Some chiefs needed replacement, others needed to be merely reminded of their sacred duty and all four tribes involved will have to undergo extensive reeducation. I feel that the sisters I brought with me are adequate for the task, but I will keep checking on the progress. At least we managed to break up the unit, and the tribes are moving to find other hunting grounds and in the ancient ways prescribed by our divine commands."

The duty officer looked pleased. "Nature of the heresy?"

"Two chiefs with little faith and much ego and cleverness managed to find a way to talk with and ally with one another. Their combined success took over other tribes, and they were able to place like-minded chiefs at the heads of those tribes. Innovation and alliance were encouraged, cooperation praised, and this was leading to the eventual attempt to seize the Muse Valley not far from here and establish there a permanent settlement."

"Grave indeed. And what of the other truth-bearers sent before you?"

"Most were killed, I think, although we might never be able to be certain of that, but two at least had been turned against the faith. I cannot conceive of such a thing, but somehow it happened. They were quite young and inexperienced, I think, and vulnerable."

"And what kept you and the others alive?"

She smiled sweetly. "The challenge, of course. I brought down the wrath of the Great Sun God upon them in full view of the tribes they were with. That and some other examples of the Great God's wrath set things straight."

"It always does," the duty officer noted, "but it's an ultimate defense, a last resort. Still, for something this huge, and among tribes who almost certainly have killed our sisters, I think it was the only way. This will look quite well on your record, Mother Francine. The only other question was demonic involvement. Was there any evidence of such?"

"None directly. At least, none of the chiefs and tribal elders I interrogated using the magic powders and potions betrayed any forbidden knowledge I could find. They were simply self-deluded. They found a new way that made things easier and then created a complex rationalization for it within our scheme of things."

"You are confident the situation will return to balance?"

Vulture shrugged. "I have no reason now to believe it will not. Naturally I will have to monitor them for some time to be sure."

"The Earth-goddesses have been very concerned about this one and will have to make the final decision," the duty officer said.

"Other than destroy them, what else could be done?"

"There is a potion that can be distributed to the people in great numbers. It is sweet to drink but later is quite painful, I'm told. It burns out all personal memories, all knowledge of self. It destroys identity and memory without destroying skills. One is like a newborn child, eager to be taught the truth. It is used only in extreme cases because it takes a fair-sized staff to manage them after for the period of readjustment and because it dulls the mind as well—a complex process. Still, such was the concern that it was talked of here in high places. Hopefully it will not be necessary." She sighed. "Very well—report to debriefing."

"Debriefing" was a carved wooden chair with straps and many vinelike things that were attached to the body. It looked primitive but was not: it was a full-blown mind-printer machine set to record. Vulture had expected it or something like it; there almost had to be one to double check reports like this and to capture any missing details or attempts to embellish the report for the sake of career advancement. The only worry Vulture had about the process was that her abilities had been tested only in the lab; this was her first time going head-to-head with a Master System computer.

If any alarms rang, though, they certainly weren't apparent. Afterward, she was given a strong, sweet liqueur to build strength, fed quite well, and given a place to sleep that actually contained a hard, thin mattress—although it felt odd after all this time sleeping on the ground.

The next day she was taken up to see the first rank for the first time.

There were seven of them, and they were all old and somewhat wrinkled, something almost never seen on Matriyeh. They looked, however, in good shape and their minds were clear, their eyes alert. They wore white, silk-like robes and headdresses of silver with large gems set in them, and more silver gems in rings and bracelets and necklaces and earrings. All but the one in the middle, whose headdress and jewelry were gold, and on whose left ring finger was a monstrous gold ring with a black stone setting. Kissing that ring was something that almost caused Vulture fits.

She had kissed the ring itself, the duplicate of which was still hidden in the charm around her neck. So close she could take it right off—it seemed a bit large for the Earth-goddess's finger. Take it, yes—but with no way to call in the guard for a getaway.

Still, it was interesting that the ring did not fit. The highest human authority on Matriyeh definitely took it off when not in public performance.

"We have analyzed your debriefing, Mother, and find much joy in it," the chief said in a low voice that was somehow both masculine and feminine at the same time. "We wonder, though, about the permanence of these reforms. Nothing poisons souls like the spread of evil ideas. The concepts such as the litter, the cultivation of crops, the bow and arrow—these are dangerous and far more difficult to stamp out. Such images linger in the mind and corrupt. We are talking of—what? Four hundred or so people, not counting the children too young to remember. We commend your evident skills and courage in this, but can seven novices with your advice contain this? Speak."

It was time for Vulture to be Vulture again. "I may be inadequate to the task, Holiness, but I have been told of the potion of forgetfulness, and I find it extreme and wasteful unless absolutely necessary. I would like to try the gentler ways first."

"There is division among us about that. You were there, we were not. Still, we have a sacred duty to their souls far beyond any regard for trouble and inconvenience on our part, and to the souls of others not yet corrupted. Dare we chance not doing it? Dare we chance not making an example to the other tribes who might have gotten ideas?"

"Holiness, your infinite wisdom and divine perfection is to my own poor self as the Great God whose glory brightens the world is to the lowest of worms. I cannot presume to do more than set my case and obey your commands."

"But? . . ."

Vulture hesitated a moment. "Holiness, if it were mine to decide, I would try the gentler way first. If the contagion has not been contained, it will be quickly obvious and can then be dealt with drastically, as you suggest, and at only a slight additional cost in human power and reserves. But if it can be contained without doing so, then it will save many innocents pain and our holy order much trouble."

"All contagion must be stamped out now, ruthlessly!" another of the Earth-goddesses snapped. "We cannot compromise with evil! One compromise, and it will destroy us!"

"No!" another responded just as firmly. "She's right. Such an operation with four tribes will strain us to the limit and even then can't be guaranteed."

The chief put up her hands and all quieted down. "Mother Francine, you are now privy to a great secret— that we are not omniscient in our decisions. I suspect that anyone of your rank probably guesses that anyway. I did when I was Mother. We have asked the Great God, but she does not clearly respond. Such an operation comes at a bad time, with lower than normal personnel and much to do here. We cannot afford to do it, and we cannot afford not to do it. We—"

Suddenly there was a feeling, a *presence*, that beat down on Vulture's back almost like radiation from the sun. Although still kneeling before the seven, and out of propriety not allowed to turn around, it was clear from the looks of the Earth-goddesses that someone else had just entered, someone powerful.

"*Turn and face me, Mother Francine*," commanded a voice that was very feminine, musical, even beautiful to hear, yet carried with it such confidence and power that one had to obey.

Vulture turned, head bowed, then looked up and gasped.

She was everything perfect in a Matriyehan, totally feminine yet conveying a sense of power and awe beyond that of any chief. She was totally nude, unblemished, unadorned in any way, and unmarked in a way no Matriyehan could be. She was not of the priestesshood; she had long hair that might never have been cut cascading down almost to her ankles—hair not dark brown but golden, as golden as the ring—and large, firm breasts and sensuous curves that were unbelievable. Thick lips, and large, dark, eyes that seemed to peer right inside you completed the picture, but there was something else.

She glowed. She gave off an actual, physical aura that shone and illuminated the chamber. Such a one could never have been born of human flesh; her perfection was too great, her glory supernatural in the extreme. In almost any terms this was truly a goddess, and there was no need for introductions. The aura of the Earth-daughter played across the whole room and carried with it also more subliminal commands. You didn't want to take your eyes away from her, ever, yet at the same time there was this overwhelming urge to lie flat upon the floor and grovel. It was the latter that was finally forced upon Vulture; it actually hurt to look upon her for very long, such was the glory.

"The Holy Mother seems quite capable, far more capable than any of you at making hard decisions, and more pragmatic as well," the Earth-daughter scolded. "Holy Mother, I shall grant you whatever you require to complete your mission. Ask and it will be yours. Eliminate this evil as you choose to do it. Purge their souls in my name. Do this for me and I shall cleanse you and raise you up. My mother gives me all power."

And, just like that, she was gone once again. You could feel her go, and feel the aching loss of that going. Even Vulture was hard-pressed to explain it in other than supernatural terms.

After a while she managed to rise to her knees and turn back to the seven, who all seemed somewhat relieved that the decision had been taken out of their hands. "What will you need?" asked the chief.

"Until I can return and assess the progress so far, I cannot say," Vulture responded, her throat dry and voice a bit shaky. "It will take time most of all."

"Then you shall have it, and whatever else is needed. We know you will not fail. No one can look upon a true goddess and hear Her commands and not obey." Her eyes were shining, as if fanaticism was commonplace, as indeed it was. What believer could fail to be a fanatic when her goddess shows up and speaks? Vulture knew that Mother Francine's eyes now showed the same sense of worship and devotion. "When do you wish to leave?"

"As soon as possible, Holiness," she responded firmly.

"You have the goddess within you now, forever," the chief told her. "She is with you and in you. Few ever are so honored. Therefore, we have no true secrets from you, for if you succeed you shall be raised up as she has promised. Come."

They gave her a new cloak and staff, much finer than the old, and then they took her down a long set of stairs that few knew existed, until it seemed as if they were descending into the very heart of the Earth-Mother.

Then, finally, they stood in the darkness, but there was wind and a sense of open space. The chief, who was never without the others—damn it—clapped her hands and suddenly lights came on, almost blinding them for a moment like the Earth-daughter's glory. But these lights you got used to, although what they revealed was something totally unexpected.

They were electric lights and they illuminated a modern, smooth area that looked for all the world like some sort of transport station.

రు

10. READJUSTMENTS IN THINKING

"**W**E HAD ABOUT GIVEN YOU ALL UP AS DEAD!" Hawks practically screamed when Vulture's call came in. "My god, what's been happening? It's been so long we're starting work on Chanchuk without you!"

"You might still be in the dark, but I lucked into something I never imagined on this world. I got here from the Center in under two hours. Would you believe that? After all this . . . two lousy hours."

"What? How?"

"Um . . . Would you believe I took the train?"

That got them almost as much as Vulture's unexpected contact. "Uh—you took the *what*?"

"The train. It's fascinating. Works on some kind of high-speed, magnetic principle, I think. Little cars, really, but there are couplers that indicate more could be added. I have much to tell you, but the first thing is I think we made a basic mistake with this world. I don't think this is a

283

century-old experiment at all, and I don't think it's the harbinger of things to come so much as the origin of the idea. Hawks—you're a historian. If this were a relatively new project, wouldn't there be artifacts someplace? Ruins, perhaps, or an overgrown road or statue of *something*? Even after almost a thousand years they're still all over Earth."

"And there are none there? None that you saw anywhere?"

"Uh uh, and if you think it out it's unlikely. The volcanoes around here are very active. The train tunnels are reinforced with the same synthetic linings used in jump propulsor motors on spaceships and rely as much on physics to keep them aligned as the rock they're in. You don't import lava snakes or the hundreds of other nasty creatures here, either, all well adapted to this place, but you also sure wouldn't have them if there had been long-term civilized settlement here. The church *is* a Center and its chief is the C.A. *This* was the system imposed by Master System from the start for these people. I think it's been going like this for centuries, maybe eight or nine. The kicker was the biology. I could see Master System transmuting a population but not an indigenous one. The very biology of the chiefs and the limits on the tribes makes it very unlikely there ever was a civilization here."

"And those . . . trains?"

"That's how it works. Until I was shown them—and only those who have seen the goddess firsthand and received her personal blessing know of them or can use them—I still couldn't figure it all out. How did they maintain control over so vast a region? How did they stamp out innovation? How did they supply and support those countless truth-bearers in the wild? When I went to my first holy place there was power support for a computer and a limited sort of a mindprinter system, sophisticated security programs, and fresh supplies. There's not, however, any indication of a direct communications grid. The train supplies them and also picks up the recordings and drops off new programs. Its power grid is fed by thermal stations deep below the surface and powers the holy places as well. They can cover an enormous area with the network and even shift supervisors around."

Star Eagle broke in. "Then these holy places—they are train stations?"

"Exactly. But let me tell you all the details in order and all the complications and problems. I need help badly but time is of the essence. We are in serious danger of losing what remains of our people and causing a lot more suffering."

As quickly but as thoroughly as possible, Vulture recounted the entire proceedings from their landing to the present situation.

"You actually *kissed* the ring." Hawks sighed. "Too bad one of your lives wasn't as a pickpocket. All right—after all this inactivity we have a radically changed situation and time pressure. Star Eagle?"

"I will need more information," the pilot responded. "I'm going to need a thorough mindprint. Vulture, you will have to be picked up and taken aboard."

Almost everyone aboard had been poring over the data bit by bit, trying to come up with a plan, or at least make sense of it all.

"I don't like the sound of that amnesia drug one bit," Raven commented. "I heard of stuff like that from my training days, though. Ten to one it's the same stuff they give to Center personnel when they flunk a mindprinter exam or get caught with their nose where it shouldn't be and are sent back to their people to live. Burn 'em out, give 'em a simple mindprinter program on living the old ways, and send them home to live and rot more ignorant than they were before they arrived. It's that kind of crap I think Master System has been tempted to use on whole populations."

"I'm more concerned right now about this Earth-daughter. Any idea what she might be? Or how?" Hawks asked any of them.

"The vision is quite graphic," Star Eagle responded. "She is not hologram or other illusion. Tiny details picked from the scene in Vulture's mind show consistent shadow, light breathing, moist lips, all indicating a living being. The radiation might be easy to fake, but I think she actually does glow. The subliminals indicate the use of a low-power hypnocaster but directionality emanates from her. It is almost as if she had the hypnocaster inside her."

"Is that possible?" Hawks asked.

"Not if you're human, even Matriyehan. The required power sources alone would be injurious to tissue. If we rely on the assumption that she does indeed glow and she has this sort of device inside her, she is not at all human. Yet all external evidence that I can extract indicate she is."

Raven sighed. "I been thinkin' about Nagy."

Hawks was startled. "Yes? What about him?"

"There was just something about him, something not right somehow. He was afraid only once that I saw, and that was when he thought his dead body might be ejected with a Val ship present. Now why would he be afraid of that if he's dead? No earthly use to nobody—I mean, you've seen what a vacuum does to a body anyway. And then there was that small power surge, almost exactly like the surge we recorded when that Val we blew up sent out its little module and that ran and jumped. Suppose... suppose Nagy wasn't human, either. Suppose he was something else, something transmuted to fool the best of man and machine but something a Val would discover anyway if it picked up the body—or maybe if it just scanned the body."

"I have his medical records and his mindprints," Star Eagle pointed out. "They show nothing unusual."

"Yeah, and neither does Vulture's. If we didn't have Vulture, if I hadn't seen the whole thing with my own eyes, I wouldn't believe such a creature could exist—no offense."

"That's all right. I *am* a creature," Vulture responded off-handedly.

Isaac Clayben was fascinated by the line of thought that Raven had kept to himself all this time. "You mean you think my Arnold Nagy was a creature, as well? Like Vulture?"

"Uh uh. Not like Vulture, but with the same purpose. To fool everybody, human and computer. To hide. Look, I know this sounds crazy, off the wall, but Vulture was there and heard and saw it all, too. The way Nagy talked in his last moments about the heavy price to be paid using the transmuter. Almost a sense of loss, or longing."

Vulture nodded. "Yes, that's it exactly. I hadn't thought of it much, though, but you're right."

"Doc, let me ask you—could you turn me into a horse? I mean a real, authentic horse, but with my memories?"

Clayben thought a moment. "There would be problems with memory storage and reinforced muscle controls, but it could be done using a modification of the memory storage system used on Vulture. Yes. Why?"

"What about a Val, Doc? Assuming you had the template for one, could you turn me into a living machine?"

"*If* I had the template, yes. The difficulties involved in control and reflexes and the like would be almost the opposite of the horse, but memory storage would be no problem, although you would literally no longer be human. Biochemistry would be replaced by programs, which are never as complex or complete as the natural thing. But, yes. What are you driving at?"

"Suppose you took a Val, for example, and tried to transmute it into a human being? Not human—but a perfect fake? One that would bleed and wheeze and drink booze and smoke cigars and tell dirty jokes and would be able to manipulate scanners to show the human insides you expect and would be able to make a mindprinter jump through the kind of hoops Vulture can?"

"It is—possible. Not with what we have here. It would take an incredibly complex computer with massive memory to do it, and possibly long periods of research and experimentation, but, yes, it could be done, I suppose. The price, however, would be quite high. As I said, you can only simulate so much. The creature would have to be half human, with biochemical responses, emotions, feelings of pleasure and pain, yet half machine, with a synthetic inner structure, power source, programmability—it would be an incredibly complex task, and it would create something that had the weaknesses of humans without the powers of the machines. Why would you create such a thing?"

Raven sat back and chewed on his cigar. "To replace a real human, to put your machine in a key place where it would never be suspected. As a spy, Doc. The perfect spy. I saw Nagy in action, Doc. He took on a Val head-to-head and he won. He thought as fast as the Val, and he outthought it in planning and maneuvering. And those languages. He knew every language, every damned dialect there was, while all the time he kept playin' the beer-drinkin', cigar-smokin', good old security boy."

"But—he even had *women*. He *enjoyed* sex," China pointed out. "He excelled at that, too," she added, "although I never had his child."

"You said it, Doc. Given a big enough machine to write a program that complicated and you can give your creature anything you want. Almost anything, anyway. He took his turn with China, and it didn't take. Why? He wasn't human. Now we have this goddess. Same thing. She's human but she can't be. More important, she gives the orders but she don't wear the ring. Only a real human can wear or possess that ring. She could have the power source and all the gadgets you could want built in."

"Hold on," Hawks said. "This is all fascinating, but if some sort of humanoid Val was the top authority down there, it would violate the core program, the very reason for the existence of Centers in the first place. Humans must rule the day-to-day affairs of a planetary civilization."

But Clayben was taken by the idea. "This is not necessarily a violation. It would be if she *did* rule, but she does not. She is rarely seen and then only by a few. Clearly she was not even a participant in the argument over how to handle the tribes. When authority must weigh alternatives and cannot decide on policy, it goes to its machines, its computers, and asks for advice. They were heavily, probably evenly, divided, and the chief administrator didn't want to alienate either side by making a firm decision. So they put it to the Great God—*their* decision to do so—and the Earth-daughter intervened and decided as requested. It is like making a compact with the devil. If one does not consider all the angles and close all the loopholes, the devil will take advantage. Humans can choose freely to abrogate their decisions to machines. We do it all the time right here on *Thunder*. Whenever a complex issue is beyond us we defer to Star Eagle's superior data, speed, and analytical skills. I can't believe it of Nagy even now, but Raven may be quite correct here."

Hawks sighed. "So we're dealing with some sort of powerful and unusual Val, whose loyalty, of course is to the system, working with a master computer through a re-

ligion. Vulture is now on the inside and in good graces—
maybe good enough to switch rings."

"If I am successful at stamping out all vestiges of crea-
tivity and progress," Vulture replied. "Let's face it—it
may already be too late, but probably not. Still, sooner or
later it's gonna fall apart. The data will be inconsistent, the
charade our people are playing down there will come undone, and that will be the end of it. If I don't do what the
Earth-daughter and the hard-liners on the council demand,
I'll never get close enough to that ring again to make a
switch. If I do, then I'll be destroying the minds and fu-
tures of four hundred or more people, not to mention five
very brave members of this company that I personally re-
cruited to go down there."

"Then the only logical solution," China said, "is to do
both."

They all turned to the blind girl expectantly, and she
seemed to sense it.

"We have been too conservative, I think. We were afraid
of activating a trained and fully equipped SPF unit. Now
we know they're all natives, and the bulk of our trooper
opposition is technically superior but ignorant and inexperienced even when their hidden mindprint programs are
triggered. We thought if we kept our raiding party at the
level of stones and spears, we'd only have to deal with the
same, but with this—goddess—and the trains and the rest,
it simply isn't so. Let's use our technology. We have very
little to lose at this stage and we're so close. *We* have psychogenetic chambers and mindprinters and biochemical
agents. And now we have access to the trains and the
Center. Vulture—you say the trains serve the holy places?
And that each and every one of the priestesses must go
there if near one?"

"That is true."

"Then the first thing we need, and pretty damned fast, is some truth-bearers of our own . . ."

"Wait a minute!" Raven replied. "That won't work. Remember the SPF have self-destructs if you try something like that."

"Sure, the SPF does—but these aren't SPF. Maybe their grandmothers were, or perhaps more to the point their ancestors, but not them. What kind of mindprinting do you think they give the third rank, anyway? The temple language, information on the technical weaponry and assets needed, and the chain of communications and command, I bet. Nothing more. They're Matriyehans, not born commandos! That's where we went wrong on this. You could give them the instructions on how to build an ion propulsor unit but they wouldn't be able to comprehend what the hell it was. No, first things first. Let's snatch a few and see. If I'm right, we can start turning this thing around in stages."

And she was right. The first two Vulture snatched by using the previously forbidden laser pistol proved relatively easy. Waiting for them had given Vulture time with modern sensors to find out just what was in those holy places and how they worked. The answer was simple—Master System's standard memory storage modules and a preprogrammed automatic computer sequence. The control computers were quite primitive and quite limited in what they could do. With that climate and level of volcanism it had probably been decided that simple and compact was best. For the same reason, long communications lines within the rail tunnels were ruled out. The structural fields needed for the train would wreak havoc with any hardwired system, and ground-to-satellite communications would require a lot of maintenance. Forced to choose between communications or transport, Master System had chosen transport.

"The change to truth-bearer is a transmuter function,"

Star Eagle reported. "They have quite a modern setup in the temple masked under that primitive mumbo-jumbo. They have to—to keep the system working. Reprogramming and reorienting them while letting them pass the mindprinter tests is not much of a problem, but other than changing their loyalties, don't expect much more than you see now. Their level of superstition and ignorance is appalling even by Master System's standards. They will obey your orders, Vulture, on coded commands. If you tell them the grass is black and all women are turtles, they will believe."

"Fair enough, but we need more," Hawks told them. "We need the people who pick up those modules."

"No go there, I think," Vulture replied. "They're on really tight schedules and they'll be missed. A few hours here or there wouldn't matter—the power's always erratic in the tunnels—but not the two days it'd take to nab 'em, bring 'em here, process them, and return them."

"Then we'll go with portables. We're going to have to do that with the other truth-bearers anyway."

"You can't run third-rank programs on them!" Vulture protested. "They're a lot more slick and sophisticated than that."

"Then knock one out, take a print, and make it look convincing so that when she wakes up she'll think she tripped and fell or something. You're creative. Give me one, and I can work up something that won't be a hundred percent, but will be general and generic enough to be useful."

Inside of seven days they had five truth-bearers and the first of the programs. Vulture decided they could wait no longer on the tribes; even now, using the transport system, it would be guesswork where they'd be and would take some time to track them down. She needed her truth-bearers in place right now. The rest would have to wait.

The nearest holy place to the last known position of the tribes was about forty kilometers south-southwest of where the large camp had been, which was a good starting point. Vulture and her five worshipful, obedient retinue spent another two or three days checking with locals for word of tribal movements. What they heard was disturbing. The four groups had split geographically much farther apart than had been the plan and were established in broad areas with other tribes in between. The land they had was not the best, and they would have more than the usual struggle to support themselves in those places.

Vulture headed for the nearest new tribe, wondering what the hell could have gone so wrong in just a few weeks with everybody on the alert. Maybe something hadn't seemed quite right to the computer at the holy seat right from the start. If so, that would be very bad luck.

The tribe welcomed them with the usual rituals and no sign of suspicion or hostility in spite of their numbers, which really wasn't good. They looked worn, tired out, and clearly had been through a rough time. Vulture recognized a few faces as belonging to Mari tribe, but the priestesses were being welcomed to Tura tribe, another bad sign. She stopped one of the old-timers and asked, "This used be Mari tribe. Where Mari now? Dead?"

The woman shook her head negatively, which was a relief. "No. Lose honor. Tura say it be for forbidden things Mari tell us do. Take tribe back to old ways. Mari now chief—of babies."

It was actually a relief to hear that Santiago was still alive and healthy, but Vulture understood the insult. Chiefs who lost their male attributes were in deepest disgrace; when there was nothing else, honor was everything. Now she would not even be a warrior but in effect a slave, not just of the new chief but of the entire tribe.

It was late in the day, though, after all the amenities

with the chief and firebearer had been settled and the news discussed, before Vulture could seek her out. She did look pretty miserable even though she seemed to enjoy playing with the young children, at least one of which was hers. They had used a slightly mismatched natural brown dye to cover over all her tattoos and badges of rank; she carried no spear nor wore pouch, belt, or adornments. When honor went, everything went.

The old Maria was still in there, though. She viewed the approach of the holy mother with mixed hope and fear, depending on who or what this one turned out to be.

The holy mother crouched low as Mari knelt and whispered, "Vulture has returned."

She gasped and grabbed Vulture's hand so strongly she threatened to wrench it from its socket. Finally Vulture was able to ask, "Why did this happen? And how?"

"Got word. Runner from Dakuminifar tribe. Truthbearer showed up. Bad fates, bad medicine." That meant rotten luck. "Suni strange, like demon. Holy Mother know. Worst tribe to pick. Truth-bearer saw heresy but not stupid. Play along with Suni so Suni no kill right off. Mix potion. Tell Suni potion make Suni body like rock, spears bounce off. Suni crazy, drink potion. Later scream all night. Next day Suni not chief, not crazy. Stupid, like child. Remember nothing, not even name or tribe. Nothing. Not know own face in stream. Big fight for new chief. Some of tribe sneak away, go to Maka, Midi, and Mari tribes. Tell all. Mari not wait. Remember Holy Mother teach drug for chief—no chief. Firebearer mix chief drug in Tura food. Tura never like new ways. Truth-bearer come, look at tribe, seem happy. Do nothing. Go away."

Vulture nodded. "It must be rough on you—like this. But better this way than Suni's way. Damn!" The only alternative Maria had in that time period was to flee, and that would mean loss of honor, reversion, and incorporation into a new tribe if she survived long enough in the wild. Better to wait here where Vulture could find her.

"Suni was always the weak link," she continued, as much to herself as to Mari. "I just hoped they'd give me more time before checking up. I smell a palace revolution here, from somebody on the council who doesn't like the idea that the chief administrator couldn't make the hard choice and had to defer to the Earth-daughter." She looked around. "All the truth-bearers here now are my people. Mindprinted. They're still ignorant but they're mine and you can trust them. Never mind how I pulled it off—now we have to reorient everything. What about Maka and Midi?"

"Midi do what Mari do. Same thing, but not as bad. Oona now chief. Made truth-bearer happy but then sent runners to talk Tura. Tura cut out tongues and send back. No more runners."

Vulture nodded. "All right, then, so Oona's learning real fast and that's good. Maka?" She could hardly imagine Manka Warlock as this lowly slave and nursemaid.

"Word come Maka flee with Euno, two, three favorites. Rest fight, Maba be chief. Not good as Oona but not bad as Tura. Like new ways but know of Suni. Truth-bearer take Suni around to other tribes, show as warning." She shivered. "Warning be real strong!"

"Uh huh. I bet. And what about this tribe? It seems to be totally back to the old ways."

Mari nodded. "Strict discipline. Most no like. Much grumbling. Hard life again. But tribe obey. Tura *is* chief. Many still not taken but obey with no other chief. But Tura take Mari—every day, since . . ."

And that would settle that, particularly with Tura strictly and punishingly enforcing a return to the old ways, and publicly and visibly—and probably violently—raping

Mari, the old chief, every day reinforced the change. No wonder she moved so tiredly and looked like hell.

"We'll take care of Tura if and when we have to. Right now I'll have to contact Midi and reassure her and somehow find Warlock and Silent Woman if I can. I'll see if I can spring you two from this to work with us. As soon as we can get organized things are going to start to pop around this dump."

She looked excited but nervous. "Mari's child . . ."

"Can come along, don't worry. This thing is getting too damned complicated as it is. For two rocks I'd just blow that damned holy seat to hell and fight the whole galaxy's fleets!"

It really wasn't much of a problem to spring Mari, although taking her child along took a bit more negotiating. Still, if you're going to return to the old ways then you always obey the truth-bearer. Springing Midi and *her* child was even easier. Although it was never said and all the actions were to the contrary, Vulture and Mari had the strongest impression that Oona not only knew who Vulture was but that the situation had changed once again. There was some question, though, as to just how much help the two could be. The trap of Matriyeh was that much of the culture was imposed physiologically. One who had lost honor also lost more than the male hormonally triggered attributes; they lost their aggressiveness, some strength, and actually became more submissive and dependent. If one was chief one died a chief or lived forever in dishonor. The fact that the pair were not native mitigated the change only slightly.

Still, a portable mindprinter made conversation far easier. They might have lost much, but not their intelligence or mental skills. Star Eagle had anticipated problems and provided a cartridge to remove the filter. It hardly seemed worth it any more. It made them educated and articulate

Matriyehans, but still Matriyehans of the lowest social order. They simply would not fight, even in defense, but they would carry the supplies no matter how heavy or complex. They would wear nothing, nor would they even eat until Vulture had finished. She argued with them on this over and over to no avail. It was a wrinkle outside Vulture's vast collective experience.

"Look, don't you think we *want* it?" Maria asked, almost pleadingly. "We were both captains and then chiefs. Independent leaders. We want to be again, but we *can't*. You must stop torturing us like this. It's like someone who is crippled. She wants to walk, but her brain, her muscles, her legs just do not respond. It's not fear. I'm still not afraid to die, and I'm surprised I'm still alive. And I don't want to die. Neither does Midi. But alone, out here, if we were alone, we *would* die, and our children, too. If something dangerous were to attack and there was no place to hide, even if I had a spear, I could not defend myself or the others. I just could not bring myself to do it."

"It's humiliating," Midi agreed. "It's like, well, you get muddled or confused and have no real confidence. You can't plan, you can't think straight. The result is you just can't make a decision. What was once clear isn't any more. That may sound nuts, but it just is, that's all. When you lose honor you lose your ability to lead. You can't do anything but follow." She sighed. "If I'd known, I'd have tried Warlock's way or killed myself first, I think. We both had tribal members who lost honor one way or another but you never thought of it as something that changed you, just some cultural thing."

Maria sighed. "Maybe you just should have left us with the tribes. At least we would not be a burden."

"Cut the guilt! We've misread this and played into the hands of Master System from the start," Vulture told them. "Maybe we can work with some of the psychochemistry when we have a chance to study this genetic system in detail, but, right now, if all you can do is haul stuff and make pleasant conversation and maybe orient me around here, that's more than enough. I'm mostly concerned about Warlock and her party. Technically, she lost her honor when she ran out on the tribe. I can't imagine Warlock reverting to your state without committing suicide, so maybe mental power can overcome its effects."

"I had not thought of that," Maria replied. "If she perceives herself, or is perceived by those she took with her, as having lost honor it will happen, and she will not kill herself. That would require a firm personal decision to act. I could not have come with you on my own, but you wished it, and the chief ordered it."

Midi nodded, thinking of the Warlock party. "It would be a small new tribe but it would be only a few smaller than we were at the start. I wonder which of them would become chief."

"One thing's sure," Vulture responded. "Any of the others would want to get as far away from here as fast as possible. We might just have lost them. For the time being, we'll be canvassing all the tribes we run into and if we get any word of them, fine. If not, we'll just have to move without them. I need more personnel now, and I need to get a complete picture of what we're dealing with here. You two just follow me and stay mute in the presence of any others, concentrating only on me."

She had hoped originally to use the tribes to do things more quickly and efficiently, but that was now out. Vulture's "girls"—the mindprinted truth-bearers—would be doing the real work without understanding what they were doing or why, but more was needed. Oona couldn't be a big help; how did you explain to a Matriyehan native who spoke and thought no other language and had no other experience that you were planning to knock off a goddess and reprogram an entire theocracy?

For several weeks Vulture and her pair of porters were busily seeking out the native tribes and gathering information. On occasion, using injectors or even a small stunner, Vulture was able to knock out and reprogram a truth-bearer or two, and once, at a train stop, she managed to knock out and record the mindprint of a second-rank priestess who maintained the places, making it convincing that she'd slipped on a wet spot and fallen and knocked herself out. It was a major victory.

"I don't want this to go to waste, and I think you two will be better off aboard *Thunder*, particularly with the kids," Vulture told the rebel women one day. "Besides, we'll let China and Clayben look at how these psychochemical processes function. Maybe there's some way out of this."

"Yes," they both agreed. "If you say so."

Thunder was more than agreeable. "But what will you be doing?" Hawks asked.

Vulture sighed. "I think it's time I became one of those courier priestesses," she told him. "I ate a couple of very good computer scientists back in the bad old days on Melchior. I think it's time I got an idea of just exactly what we're dealing with."

By the time Vulture reappeared to report again, weeks later, much progress had been made aboard.

"The changes in Santiago and Ng are permanent as far as their submissive nature goes," China reported. "Essentially, their bodies simply lose the ability to manufacture certain brain chemicals and hormones, reducing them to that. The solution, such as it is, is to administer chemical substitutes for what their bodies can no longer make on a day-to-day basis. The trouble is that the human being is such an adaptable animal. We learn to live on ice floes in the Arctic and in equatorial jungles. The longer they remain in that state, the more hardened their thinking will be to that type of behavior, and we can't do more than a tiny stabilization without risking their unborn children, since both are pregnant. Afterward—well, maybe with some mindprinter therapy and daily injections, they'll come back to their old selves. I can't help thinking that if I weren't blind Matriyeh might be a world for me. It seems as if everybody's pregnant all the time."

"Mostly," Vulture agreed, "but remember that maybe one in nine children will survive to adulthood. The biggest problem they'll have down here, if they can ever break this cycle and create a civilization, is that medicine, sanitation, and the lack of constant hunting and gathering will dramatically decrease infant mortality, but yet they'll keep having babies. I don't see how the southern continent keeps so primitive without this church-imposed system."

"We have a theory. It appears really brutal there. The average age of an adult is in the low teens, and they don't even seem to have control of fire. Clayben says they're in a prehuman state, more like smart apes, and doubts they even have what we would think of as a language. It's possible that whole southern continent overstepped the proscribed bounds and was given a good dose of that mind-destroying drug. It could be that some of the fruits peculiar to the south were bred to produce it naturally. We're not sure, but also it's possible that the south is the real experiment. Data suggests the geology there would make the north's transportation and communications network impossible to maintain. If anything, it's rougher geologically than the north, but has fewer large animals of prey. But enough of that. What do you have?"

"Plenty. The standard data packs retrieved from the holy places are brought to a smooth and obviously artificial chamber below the statue of the Great God. There are no controls, screens, speakers, or the like, but there is one wall composed entirely of slots. With proper ceremony you stick the cubes in the slots, wait until they turn from blue to red, then remove them and replace them in your pouch. Because there are chambers on all sides and the train below, I feel pretty certain that the computer console isn't very large and is possibly a modified starship core command module and data center. It looks to be about the same size as the one we have on *Thunder*. That's still one hell of a computer, though—but I get the very strong impression that it controls only the direct machines within the temple and the communications link to the satellite above. It's more a transfer station than a command center like the one on Janipur. It takes the raw data, sorts and correlates it, then beams it out to someplace far from this system, and gets its orders back from there. Its output is strictly through the modules, the mindprinter, and, of course, the Great God, who not only speaks but also moves a bit on occasion while giving commands. It's pretty impressive."

"Pretty limited," China agreed. "And it matches our thinking. The codes it uses to transmit to Master System are new, but the frequencies and methods are ancient. Instead of being one of the latest installations, Star Eagle now thinks this may have been one of the earliest colonies, when Master System was still experimenting. Maybe even the first and the origin of the Center concept, which was later refined. So Master System just left it that way, and stuck a ring there as well because it figured it would be damned impossible to lift it. Good. Then the master computer of Matriyeh only knows what is fed into it, not what it directly observes and measures, and is basically a simple device used to maintain a simple system. That explains the Earth-goddess, who was probably added later on, maybe much later, when the south got out of hand and needed direct action. She doesn't run the church—she is the guardian of that computer!"

"My thinking exactly. If she ran things, she'd make herself more visible. Nothing like an appearance by her to inspire the troops and send the new field agents out with fanatical devotion. But that's not her job, of course. That's the council's job."

"Yes. What is most significant in the matter of sending the truth-bearer independently to deal with your tribes is that it was against the direct orders of the Earth-goddess to let you give it a try first."

"There was something of a power struggle," Vulture agreed. "It's still the talk of the second rank. The chief held on to her job, but there was a shake-up on the council and the balance was changed. A couple of second-rank officers got the call to godhood, and a couple of the ones on the council passed on into the company of the Great God having attained absolute perfection. You get the idea."

"Yes. What else?"

"I've managed to make a pretty good guess at the layout of the entire temple. It's big, but not as big as you'd think by looking at it. One thing I hadn't noticed originally was how stagnant the air was. Torches burn straight up, and the place smells. The only reason it's not unbearable is the transport center beneath. Every time a car leaves there's a pull of air in from the entrance all the way through."

"It's that solid?"

"It seems like it. The first rank have large quarters higher up from the administrative areas. Hard to say how large they are but they're said to be straight up, and the curve of the rock at that point wouldn't indicate that they were very high up. It occurs to me that if you could block the train for a period, the air would just sit there, since the valley itself seems to have an almost permanent inversion. It rarely clears up there, but there're never any bad storms.

I think we have a pretty good chance that it's nearly a sealed air system there."

"Hmmm . . . Yes, and we have now some pretty extensive knowledge of Matriyehan biochemistry. Yes, this is coming together nicely. If it wasn't for that damned Earth-daughter, this would be ready to go. Still, we have some ideas on her, as well, although it's going to be very chancy in the end. You will have to face facts, Vulture. We can deal with her, but unless we guess right a hundred percent on slight knowledge, the master computer is eventually going to miss her and sound the alarm. If so, short of having all five rings and using them properly, there is no way in the universe that we can help or protect these people. But we will give it a try. That's all I can offer."

"It will have to do. I'll remain in this role until we're ready to go and continue intelligence-gathering. I'm supposed to be put on a route next week that might take me close to Oona. If I get the chance I'll check on her. She's a good kid."

"All right, but take no unnecessary risks. We were very lucky on the Janipur job, and we didn't realize it and got overconfident. Even without the Earth-daughter to deal with we are still going to have to make many educated guesses and suppositions and trust to luck for the fine details, and we haven't had much luck on this job so far."

"Yeah—I think luck owes us one."

Vulture took a chance going to Oona's territory. True, she wasn't due for a new set of rounds for a few days and was technically off duty, but she had no real authority to use the train for a personal mission, and there was great risk if it was found out she'd done so. She didn't care by this point. This time, too, Oona, who had been a witness to the startling transformation of truth-bearer into holy mother in that encounter that now seemed ages ago, was not kept in the dark as to who her high-ranking visitor was.

"Oona—Holy Mother must know. Do Oona believe real truth-bearers or new truth-bearers?"

The former firebearer, now chief, who'd been the only one to keep a few comforts in spite of constant observation, shrugged. "Oona not know. New truth-bearers have much magic, but old way has honor."

"If all Oona tribe had way to end old way, make tribes free to live as wanted, even if way much dangerous, much chance die or worse, small chance be free—then?"

"Oona no like live hard when tribe can live easier," she answered carefully. "But Oona no like there be no rules, no true belief. Each chief have own faith, own rules. Whole Earth-Mother break from cracks."

It was an understandable and quite sophisticated line of thinking for such a one as this, a native who knew nothing else. She no longer believed in the old church; if she ever had, the sight of truth-bearers being killed without some angry god striking dead the killer dissolved that. She understood that much of it was drugs and trickery, even if the trickery itself was magic. But this was the world and the life she knew, and she understood it and her place in it—and there was comfort in that. She was concerned that if the old order broke, it would collapse everything she knew and leave only a chaos worse than the life she now had. Hatred of unjust rule and oppression was balanced by fear of the unknown—fear, in fact, of freedom. The church was a hated evil—but it was all she had.

Vulture sighed and wondered if she wasn't right. They wanted an easier life, more freedom to make better tools and weapons and gain some shelter and protection and security, but their own racial preconditions and genetic makeup would make any real sort of civilization as others understood it next to impossible here. With settlement and agriculture would come that security, but with an exponentially expanding population that was nonetheless limited by biological imperatives to a hundred per chief, things would explode in violence and the losers would be slaughtered again and again. Perhaps over thousands of years a workable and unique system would develop, but just as likely they would descend back into permanent barbarism and remain there. The only other way would be to impose it through alien technology, and even then the amount of people involved would be enormous and the task long and daunting. It had seemed so simple when they had decided to join the four tribes—a few hundred out of a couple of million. They just hadn't understood the complexity of the problem.

Vulture could only change the subject. "Holy Mother still looks for Maka. Oona hear?"

The chief nodded. "Maka no chief now. In small tribe two day walk west. Soba tribe. Be captured long time. Oona scout see, no talk. Get word from truth-bearer. One of Holy Mother's. Not know which."

"Lose honor?"

"Not know. Should have, but Maka strange like Holy Mother."

"Not like Holy Mother but Holy Mother know what Oona mean. Thank you."

Finding the right truth-bearer in this whole area was a job for which she didn't have the time, but she felt she could find this Soba tribe and did so, although it took three days. Vulture was concerned at what she would find, since losing honor was not confined to chiefs. It was triggered by a mental attitude, a way of looking at oneself that precipitated permanent changes. If a whole tribe all thought of themselves as cowards, as running away from power and responsibility, then they might all be a bunch of submissive slaves, and that would be too bad. Vulture could particularly use Manka Warlock in what was to come.

What she found was not nearly as bad as she expected. The tribe was small, no more than twenty-five with perhaps nine children. Soba herself was almost tiny; unusually short for a Matriyehan and quite thin and wiry, she was almost dwarfed by her tribe. That showed her to be doubly dangerous and clever that she had managed to defeat or outwit the larger contenders. They had blundered into the tribe by chance less than three days after fleeing. Warlock had already lost her male aspects and, in spite of herself, Silent Woman had been taking them on, although slowly. The strange, mute woman had been the most independent and self-sufficient in the wild, and nature had started the process, but she had no will or desire to be chief. She quite literally led them into Soba's entire group and refused to challenge. Because the process had been involuntary and incomplete, and because Silent Woman simply did not know the Matriyehan standards for loss of honor, she had not suffered.

Warlock looked somewhat different—softer, with a tighter figure, but she still held the spear and wore the accoutrements of a warrior. She had taken on many of the traits that accompanied a loss of honor, but she could still fight. She seemed both relieved and chagrined to see Vulture.

"Maka fight two fights," she told the creature. "Fight enemies of Soba tribe, fight Maka." She was, in effect, at war with her body's own built-in instincts. She had run and thus lost honor, but she simply couldn't see it that way herself. Moreover, Warlock was a psychopath, someone who loved to kill. "Maka not quick as think. Get old. Make mistakes."

"Why didn't you just kill her and run with the tribe?"

"No chance. Most of tribe not obey Maka. Rebel. Think

truth-bearer one of Holy Mother's. Big mistake. Used magic, turned part of tribe with Maka not know. Saw too late. Enemy *cheat!*" she spat angrily. "Holy Mother say not come, only look, see. Holy Mother wrong. Now Maka not be chief again. Know this. *Not* lose honor. Betrayed. Now Maka fight self. Hard."

"Yeah, I know, I blew it. I didn't understand the way things really worked up there, and I admit it. But we're ready to move soon, and we need help." Quickly she sketched in the situation to Warlock. "Do you think you're up to helping?"

"Maka still good warrior. How long do not know. Soba good chief. Smart. Young. Know much. Ambitious. Holy Mother talk with Soba if need tribe to help. Soba still listen to Maka. Ask, take advice."

"Then we will both talk with her."

Warlock was right about Soba, a personality tough and hard but not at all cowed by her culture. When she was still a little girl she'd overheard two truth-bearers comparing notes, talking patronizingly about the tribes and discussing the tricks they pulled on this chief or that. She had never told—who would believe her?—but she had never again had any faith in the one true way. Soba very much believed in magic, but she had no such belief in Great Gods or testing places. Magic might be great, but behind magic were people who were the same as her. In a sense she was the ultimate cynic in a world not made for such people; even if faced with a moving, talking statue of the Great God, she would be less impressed than wary of its power while looking for the ones making it move. She had heard of the innovations the four tribes had briefly introduced: the bolo and bow and arrow, methods of storing food and perhaps concentrating and aiding its growth. She didn't believe in afterlives or heavenly rewards, and she was impatient for something better—nor was she alone. Many of the chiefs felt this way secretly, but they could never get along with each other for any coordinated action and the church's magic was far too strong.

Neither she nor the others would rebel because they did not believe they had a chance, but if they thought they did . . .

"*Thunder* tribe not gods but people. Look, act different than Matriyehans, but people. *Thunder* tribe has great magic and wants put end to church. Be many Earth-Mothers, many ruled by great chief of church." The ring was something Soba could understand. A master of power behind it all, with all the knowledge of magic, but with one weakness. With the five magic rings they could destroy the all-powerful chief. In the meantime, they might be able to help—if they had a sufficient number of local people to make it work.

She thought about it, believing some of it, probably not believing the rest, but she listened, and she deliberated, and she consulted her firebearer and others whom she trusted. Finally she said, "Tribe fights, dies, for honor, for food, for territory. No can stop. Fight, eat, make babies, sleep. Over and over, then die. Do this to stay same, do same, be same. If tribes must fight, if warriors, chiefs must die, why not fight, die, to get better? Tribe die anyway. If be one chance . . ." She looked at them. "Soba tribe help."

"If Soba live, Soba be greatest chief of all Matriyeh," said Manka Warlock.

"Not be long," Vulture told them. "Wait for call of *Thunder*."

11. WARRIORS OF THE STORM

A STORM WAS BREWING——ONE OF THOSE VIOLENT, swirling storms that broke large trees and blasted rock. Manka Warlock spotted the figures moving through the swirling fog and rain and gestured to other warriors to approach. There was no need for caution; no Matriyehans would be wearing such packs or carrying such equipment as these. Most were Vulture's third-rank truth-bearers, along with Vulture herself, but also along were Maria Santiago and Midi Ng, looking much stronger and better. Rather than wait the extra time before the children were born, China, working through Star Eagle, had developed supplements to replace what their own bodies did not make in proportions so close to normal that they had no chance of affecting the unborn. While both women were still having identity problems between their old and present selves, both felt so much better and more confident that they insisted on being a part of this, and Vulture needed them desperately. Both now carried far different spears than they had before—long-stock laser rifles with heavy wide-field charges.

The base camp was in a sheltered cleft partway up the mountains in back of the holy seat. The trains ran automatically according to a preset schedule and any variations of that would have triggered a computer alarm, but they had been quite useful for getting people and supplies to this point. Vulture and the planners on *Thunder* would have preferred to send the raiders into the temple by train but dared not risk it. They could only get a few in that way anyway, and the station was computer monitored and security codes were required. The objective was to be undetected to the last moment if possible, and, if luck really ran their way, perhaps win the whole game.

"That inversion around the holy seat makes the weather around even worse," Vulture griped. "This isn't going to be easy, but I doubt if they even considered this way in. Soba's been shown the charts and diagrams and understands the idea?"

A restored Warlock nodded. "I will work at her side entirely in Matriyehan. We have worked out a series of sounds based on the hunt. We've done some practice with the ropes and grappling hooks. I can tell you none of them are too confident that either the ropes or the hooks will hold, but even Silent Woman is getting pretty good with them. I still wish she could have been left with Oona and the children, but in her own way, she can be most insistent and it is her right as a warrior. At least she won't yell and give us away. The children are all right?"

Vulture nodded, noting to herself that Manka Warlock, up to a few months ago, would never even have considered that question. "Oona isn't any too confident of all this, but it wasn't hard to talk her into that much. If we make it, they'll be safe and we'll owe her. If not, her tribe will adopt them. We can't overstate the need for stealth and the equal need to follow the leaders of our team no matter what a chief takes it in her mind to do. I don't think the traps are very elaborate but we don't want to spring any if we can help it."

"They respect magic, so don't worry on that score. They also know the usual passwords, although Matriyehan is so unlike French they might not be able to manage them right. Last-resort stuff. That is, if the passwords haven't been changed."

"How could they be, with two-thirds of the priestesses spread all over the countryside? The other important thing is that you kill only if you have to. We need the higher-ups alive if we're to learn anything, and we can always work on the third rank later."

"I know, damn it," Warlock muttered disappointedly.

"I was going to give you a laser pistol and charge belt, but that belly bulge of yours rules that out. Better take one of the rifles."

Warlock nodded. "Who would ever think of me as a mommy? Not me, I can tell you. I'm glad I've got the rifle—I feel awkward as hell. Truth is, though, that part of me I keep pushed back kind of likes the idea. Both parts of me will be relieved when the little bugger's out. I will be all right so long as Soba keeps her own head. In a pinch, I would not disobey her, Vulture, except to save her life. Not for anything."

"I understand. Midi is going with part of the tribal group; I'm keeping Mari with me but she will be available if needed. Crazy world, this. Because they're pregnant by other chiefs, they aren't bound to Soba and can't be right now. They'll cover your backside. I suggest we all huddle —Soba, too, and her firebearer, and go over this as much as we can. I get the feeling we could wait forever for perfect weather, but if we get a good break we're going up."

Matriyehans were used to mountains and climbing over potentially slippery rock, but this was new territory and there were no passes here, no worn trail in the rock to show the safe way. Other than the remote geophysical survey *Lightning* had conducted, there was no way to know just what these cloud-shrouded mountains might hold.

The weather broke enough for them to dare a start two mornings after the arrival of the rest of the team. It was not an easy climb, and there were areas requiring the use of pitons and strong arms to toss grappling hooks more than once. Both concepts were fairly new to the natives, but there had been sufficient practice that they accepted the methods even if they didn't completely trust them.

There wasn't much living on these old, high mountains although this sort of terrain was a natural for lava snakes and other, smaller beasts. Either they were regularly cleaned out or the food sources just weren't right. It suggested that this complex might well have been created artificially rather than discovered and adapted.

More than once someone slipped or fell, and it was then that they learned how vital those uncomfortable ropes fitted through harnesses were. The natives in particular had balked at them from the start, fearing damage to themselves, but it hadn't taken more than one fall to make wearing the rope and harness an unquestioned duty.

Going through the cloud bank took a full day, with visibility negligible and every step treacherous. Just above it was an almost sheer rock wall that took the better part of another day just to plan on how to climb. Still, using power grapples and careful piton work, they managed it and reached a nearly level area. The air between the two cloud layers was remarkably clear and they could actually see the summit, although it would still be several days away. The winds, however, were blowing wild and unpredictable, and it most assuredly was not always so clear up there. They had reached the snow line.

Most of the natives had never really seen snow firsthand before and were scared of it. Not even the people from *Thunder* had any real experience with it, but they had mindprinter programs to teach them some of its treacheries. Clayben had calculated that the Matriyehan body could tolerate a wind chill to twenty below zero without permanent damage for a couple of days, but they knew they had to move fairly rapidly in spite of their experience. Above three thousand meters, they found even ordinary tasks became harder to do and strength seemed to ebb. Pills fabricated for the problem helped, but weren't a cure for the lack of oxygen.

They avoided as much of the snow field as they could, sticking to areas of exposed rock, heading not for the summit but for the lowest and closest visible point. By the time they got to it, they were nearly frozen and utterly exhausted, but they were ready, even eager, to go down. At least there would be no interior cloud cover to battle, as well, and the valley stretched out before them in miniature.

Still, the mere sight of it was enough to both cheer and enrage the natives. "Truth-bearers," Soba said, her voice dripping contempt. "Lie-bearers. Live in protection in ways forbidden tribes. Soba want cut out lying tongues of whole truth-bearer tribe. Make *truth-bearers* live like make tribes live."

The climb had not been without cost; four natives had been either killed or mortally injured. Still, the party was more than ample—if they could make it down into the valley undetected. The slope curved inward and in places was quite smooth, and the longest ropes they had were about forty meters, which would make the twenty-eight hundred meters descent long and dangerous.

With satellite monitors designed to detect energy surges

and so much sheer terrain to cover, it was little wonder that this route was simply rejected as a way in and left as a natural defense. The power grapplers alone had been a risk, although a minor one—the burst was basically a small explosion and lasted for only fractions of a second, not nearly long or powerful enough to allow a satellite fix.

"Hawks called this plan brilliantly insane," Mari noted, looking around and shivering. "A rag-tag bunch of primitive women, less than forty in all, nine pregnant, and only one with real mountaineering experience, tackling a rough and uncharted climb using limited equipment with the idea of overthrowing a system. It *is* absurd on its face—no wonder Master System never thought it could be done." She looked around at them. "This race may be primitive and strange, but no others could have done this. If we accomplish our mission, it is because Master System has done its job too well. Making a race that could survive under the most primitive of conditions on a world like this for a thousand years, perhaps, breeding the strongest and toughest and weeding out the rest. I don't know if these people will ever achieve a level of civilization as we understand it, but there is something truly great in them."

They weren't concerned with observation on the descent, but getting down was difficult and yet had to be done fairly quickly, hopefully between dawn and dusk. There just didn't seem to be anyplace a body of them could stop and camp for the night anywhere on the way down, nor even places where more than four or five could stand at a time. Once they started, it would have to be a continuous progression.

Many were still hanging from ropes as the sun set, but Midi was first down to the outcrop atop the temple proper shortly after, and they were all about to complete the descent using the ropes and guides set by the ones who went before. At least the near-stagnant air of the valley helped;

one good storm or gust of wind at any point would have undone them.

Finally, though, the thirty-five who'd made it all the way were atop the crag above the temple complex, about fifteen meters higher than the great statue over the temple entrance. Now would come a period almost as difficult as the journey had been: remaining up there all day, without making any noise or movement that could be detected by anyone below, and waiting. Sleep was necessary for all, and arrangements had to be complete before the raid could begin that night.

Vulture was busy throughout the afternoon and evening finishing her planning and preparations. At least they could risk energy tools and weapons, particularly in and around the temple area. No satellite or computer ever built could distinguish proper from improper energy use in a place where electronic sensors, booby traps, and computer and communications links were established.

They would have to take one big risk by using what Vulture had developed as a favorite trick on Janipur. The only subcarriers of the Center's computer-to-satellite link were too old and noisy for any real communication but would still carry a simple pulse tone if the transmitter were aimed at the correct angle toward the master transmitter.

A very slight breeze had been detected almost at the start, and Vulture relaxed. It was always a small breeze, always toward them, and always once an hour, just when one of the continually traveling cars of the internal magnetic railroad would come in to the temple station, stop for one minute, then pull out again. Timing here was vital; at least basic communications had to be risked. One tone up for thirty seconds, then another tone back down from the fighter hidden in orbit—not to them but to one of the mindprinted truth-bearers well away from the valley. This would be the second-rank field supervisor Vulture had managed to control through the generic program Star Eagle had created.

It was near midnight when they were rested, awake, and ready to act. Vulture aimed at the spirelike peak that was in fact the master transmitter and held down the button on her tiny transceiver for thirty anxious seconds, then released it and flipped a small switch. If there was any sort of answering tone they would have to wait, but after ten minutes they had none. If all was going well, their second-rank priestess was now either aboard a transport car or waiting for the next one.

Then, as the tribe watched in wonderment, the four from *Thunder* used small laser drills to bore into the rock with beams of dull, magical light. The rock was thicker than they had anticipated; they had to pierce perhaps a full meter before the first beam broke through and automatically cut off, more for the others.

Now the packs and equipment they had carried with great difficulty up the mountain and down again were transformed. Hoses were unreeled and pushed through the open slots. Vulture and her truth-bearers took rectangular canisters and made ready to descend to the temple entrance. They put on dark breathing masks after reminding the others, "Breathe through nose only. No mouth. Talk little." Although all had been injected with a chemical antidote before starting the climb, it was going to be very smoky inside, and the gas would still irritate their throats and lungs.

Vulture went straight down to the second-rank headquarters. No one was about in the main temple at this hour, but there was always a duty officer. She walked in, pistol in hand, and fired on stun. The duty officer stiffened but never saw what hit her, then slumped forward. Quietly now, the Vulture team fanned out, placing their packages in strategic locations and then pressing their activators. A second signal from Vulture's small hand-held transmitter would set them all off at once.

Satisfied, the team now waited near the entrance as most of Soba tribe descended to the temple opening and took up guard positions. Above, Maria Santiago waited as well, sitting on the remaining canisters.

There was no way to be absolutely positive that the next train car would be the one Vulture's mindprinted priestess had rigged, as nearly as she could figure it would arrive forty minutes from the time it had been loaded up by the agent in the field.

Although none of them could hear it, the car came in and stopped at the station far beneath the statue of the Great God. There was a significant airflow from the entrance through the temple complex. They waited one more minute; if there was a second breeze they would have to work quickly, in an hour or less. If more than a minute passed without it, then they knew that the car was the right one and had done its work.

The unoccupied car came in and stopped. The door opened, and as it did it drew back a triggering mechanism. There was a sharp report, and the converter in the car was exposed and began to spark. The car was unable to draw further power from the system and was effectively stalled. The same action also released the valves on an entire canister assembly. Above, the computer sensed the power outage and sent a signal by alternate routes to the automated repair facility in the station. Power outages were common, but the schedule had to be kept. Service robots popped out of walls, glided to the tracks, lifted the whole-egg-shaped car out, determined it was not immediately repairable, and went to get a spare. By the time they did, the canisters were empty.

By three minutes by Vulture's timer, and those of Mari

and Midi, there had been no second rush of air. At that exact moment, Mari and Vulture detonated their canisters.

The gas was slightly lighter than air at that altitude; it would rise, slowly, upward and permeate the structure whose system would now be fairly well sealed. Some might leak out the entrance but that didn't matter; what mattered was that the much cooler, heavier air inside the temple wasn't about to flow out very far into the warmer, lighter valley air. It would sit.

With gas entering all the levels from both above and below, everyone would get a good lungful of the stuff. It wouldn't kill, but, tailored as it was to the Matriyehan constitution, it would induce deep coma. The gas had been concocted after analysis of the biochemistry of Midi and Mari on *Thunder*, and the antidote tested on them. Without the antidote, the victims would continue to sleep until they starved to death. But there was the possibility that not everyone would be exposed enough in the forty minutes the gas had before it began to break down into harmless compounds; there might well be a few people in the temple who would still be awake—and dangerous.

And there was no chance that the Earth-daughter or the computer would even notice. They were prepared for the few who might not get the full dosage; that was one reason for all the people in the assault team. Vulture felt certain that the computer would know only what it was told; it might notice the lack of activity toward morning, but by then their work should be completed, and she doubted that the computer would be a problem. The real worry was its guardian, the goddess with the built-in hypnocaster, who could alert the computer and compromise the mission.

Vulture's immediate search was for the quarters of the council. They were not quite where she'd guessed they were, but they were not hard to find in the end. For Matriyeh, the rooms were about as comfortable as any she had seen, but the chief administrator, unfortunately, didn't seem to have a bigger or grander room than the others. It took a few minutes of checking still forms in comfortable-looking beds—with silken sheets and pillows—before the right one was found. The ring was not on the C.A.'s finger, and it took more precious minutes to search through the drawers and compartments of jewelry and ornaments, an impatient Vulture praying that it was not locked away in some safe.

It wasn't, but only a wild afterthought revealed its location. There was no reason to lock away anything in the inner sanctum of the temple but even these top-echelon leaders really *believed* in the religion, and the ring was the ultimate symbol of authority.

She kept it under her pillow.

Now, at last, Vulture twisted the necklace charm she'd carried from the start and removed the copy of the ring, then compared it to the original. It wasn't at all bad. Subjected to analysis it might have been revealed as a fake, but without that kind of precise inspection, no one would know. She quickly made the switch, then discovered that there was a slight but important difference in the two: the real ring didn't fit properly back in the charm. On impulse, Vulture tried the ring on her own finger and found that it fit—a bit too tight, but she left it there anyway.

They had been inside a full forty-six minutes by Vulture's timer, and so far they had not encountered a conscious enemy, let alone the Earth-daughter. Vulture was beginning to worry about the ease of it. She checked the computer access room and found Manka Warlock, Midi, and Maria Santiago pretty well set up. Silent Woman, looking proud of herself and them all, stood guard. Soba tribe was checking every room, nook, and cranny of the temple, while the team's truth-bearers guarded the entrance and the stairs to the train to head off any unexpected surprises.

The failure of the Earth-daughter to appear stood to foul up their plans. They couldn't really leave until she was dealt with. "Maybe she's more of a tool than the independent operator we thought," Maria suggested. "Maybe she only comes when she's summoned."

They felt a sudden rush of air. The transport system was operating again, and by this point most if not all of the gas had converted to harmless elements. They removed their breathing masks. Only a trace of the musty-smell odor remained. Those knocked out would stay out, but anyone new coming in would be no more affected than they.

"Well, we can't wait for her," Vulture replied. "I'm gonna pull four of my priestesses and start work off the main entrance. If our gorgeous goddess shows up, holler if you can."

The most they dared carry with them due to the weight had been two portable mindprinters; processing the temple priestesses with the generic reorientation program to fit the new order would take some time. There were between sixty and eighty people other than themselves in this place, and the process took at least ten minutes per person. Figuring the extra time for the setup and move, it would take about ten to fifteen hours nonstop to cover everybody. They could only try to get the ones who would be expected to be public and active right off; those could best maintain the fiction of a normally functioning temple.

Unfortunately, it would take years to recondition the entire third rank in the field, and there was no way they could edit the memory module information that the third rank would turn in to the holy places for pickup and insertion into the master computer for analysis. So far, Star Eagle had been unable to find any way to change the existing system without alerting the master computer. The team might escape, but the people of the northern continent could not and would not. So a temporary solution was settled on, until the dogs of Master System could be called off entirely. The second rank, treated here, would keep the portable mindprinters and go into the field to treat the third rank in the holy places. Then a simple code phrase uttered upon greeting a truth-bearer of any rank would erase from the mind of that priestess any memories of that tribe's existence. She would go on her way and even in her official reports, knowledge of that particular tribe would be omitted. The computer, then, would get no information on those tribes, and since tribes and chiefs changed all the time in this fluid society, the omission would not be noticed.

And these tribes would be free. *Satuuka moaba*. Warriors of the storm.

At the entrance to the computer room, Midi, Warlock, and Maria Santiago were feeling very good indeed, although still on watch for this mysterious creature only Vulture had seen. The Soba tribe was picking up morning entries into the temple and hauling them off for treatment, and it seemed that the worst was over. They were going to make it, and if they weren't going to revolutionize the world, at least the Soba and Oona tribes would be able develop a freer and easier life, which would also establish a good base when and if Master System was even vanquished.

As the four pirates waited in the computer room there was a *click* behind them and then the sound of a panel sliding back. They all turned as one, at the ready, and *she* stepped out of an opening in the wall opposite the computer. She was everything Vulture had said and more, the epitome of everything the word *goddess* implied. She glowed, and the glow filled the room and seemed warm when it enveloped them. She showed no fear and gave a slight smile as her huge, dark eyes looked at each of them in turn and seemed to be looking right through them. The quartet was ready, two with laser rifles, one with a laser pistol, and another with a spear, but they were frozen as if living statues.

Like a laser blast, there was no way to shield against a directed hypnocaster. One could only hope not to be in its path and thus able to avoid it. The Earth-daughter's power was not great—in the great hall it would be so dissipated it would be useless—but in a small room it was overwhelming. Matched specifically to Matriyehan psychochemistry, it worked on the most basic, empathic levels. They had known this and been expecting her, but they had been surprised by her entrance from behind. The radiation had an almost instantaneous effect in such a situation, blocking action and slowing thought, buying time for the subtle, almost orchestral play of waveform commands to induce the desired effect in the brains of the onlookers. Awe, love, devotion, an absence of fear or concern, an absence of thought, an urge to obedience.

"Come," she said in Matriyehan, in a voice so musical and supernatural that it sent shivers through them, and she gestured with her hand. "Sit at feet of Earth-daughter and guard." They obeyed instantly, even eagerly. Even Silent Woman seemed to understand her command. Then she switched, rather suddenly, to English, without once losing that musical quality.

"We will talk, and you will tell me all that I wish to know," she said softly, and they knew they would.

Vulture decided to check the computer room. It was getting about time for her to leave, and it was important that she know who might or might not be leaving with her. The work would go on here, perhaps for days, perhaps for weeks, but it was practically automatic now and did not require her or any other nonnative presence. Eventually Soba and the others would make their getaway, far easier than the entry, and runners would be sent to Oona tribe to fetch the children and spread the word. But not now; much of the future of this small band would have to be determined the way they preferred it—by themselves.

When no guard was apparent at the entrance to the computer room, Vulture became suspicious. She doused one of the torches close to her, and even though there was still plenty of light, what she feared she would see became visible. That glow, that golden glow from inside the computer room . . .

Their brains are not in their heads, Nagy had said. Aim just above the crotch, from the back if possible . . .

Sound advice that had worked once, but this wasn't the same sort of creature, not really. Where *was* her brain, her vulnerable spot? Not the usual place, certainly. Her waist was far too thin. The head, the chest, or the buttocks were the only possibilities, and Master System tended toward uniformity. But did she have other defenses, perhaps weapons, other than the hypnocaster? There was only the one entrance to the room, and the only people that really mattered to Vulture were already in there, obviously under her control. Had she already sent the warning out? Were squadrons of Master System's automated fighters and ships of SPF even now heading here?

Vulture was not immune to the hypnocaster if taken as they had been, by surprise, but now that she was able to feel it, measure it, she was able to adjust, controlling her body from those places that were remote from the mind. The hypno would still cause the usual chemical reactions in the brain, but they would be irrelevant. Still, she'd be walking right in, a sitting duck. The door was too small to have a real chance at surprise.

What could be done? Explosives? None around, and even if there were it would also kill the hostages. Gas? Obviously not. And her allies would be no help at all in that small a space.

"Is that you out there—Vulture, is that not what you are called?" the Earth-daughter called somewhat playfully. "Come in. It was a brilliant effort but it is done. Before you could flee, I could have all the entrances and exits sealed by simple command from here. And, even if you managed to escape, I could call in more force than you could deal with to insure you rotted here. Come—or must I have one of your friends here become a blood sacrifice to me at the hands of the others as you hear her screams?"

Could have all the entrances and exits sealed. *Could* call in more force . . . The situation was bleak, but it wasn't over yet.

"They're overconfident to the point of arrogance . . ."

Vulture eased to the doorway and peered cautiously inside. She was standing a bit out from the back wall, and the four warriors knelt in front of her, making a shield, the expressions on their faces showing that they were no longer in command of their minds.

Vulture drew her laser pistol, checked its charge, and stepped into the room. The laser weapons held by the trio all centered on her. If they were on narrow beam, the Earth-daughter might have a rude surprise, but if they were set on wide-field stun, it would knock Vulture helpless.

"Your tricks won't work with me," Vulture said dryly.

"Just put down the gun and give me the ring," the Earth-daughter responded.

"You cannot ask for the ring," Vulture said. "The ring must go to a human in authority. Whatever you are, you are not human and have no right to it."

The Earth-daughter smiled. "We have been having quite a discussion while waiting for you," she told Vulture. "You are quite right—I am not human, and I am bound by the core commands, but neither are *you* human, Vulture. You have no more right to it than I, and so it is my obligation to reassign the ring properly."

"And then what?"

"You, naturally, will have to be held somewhere until you can be picked up and taken for study and analysis. I'm sure you understand. As for the others—I will collect them, slowly and in good time. That which you do with your small mindprinters, we can undo with our fuller model. The local tribe will be allowed to drink the waters of forgetfulness in my presence, and these—at least the three that are useful to me—are special cases. After we have recorded all they know, we might well send them back to your friends up there, to set them up for the kill."

"You don't know exactly what I am or precisely how to deal with me," Vulture noted coolly. "You are as ignorant of me as I am of you." *She hasn't yet shown a weapon. She's using the warriors for protection. If I can just ease my thumb on to the right stud without her noticing . . .*

"You are mortal as I am not," the Earth-daughter responded just as coolly and confidently. "You may be difficult to kill, but we will keep firing until you are nothing but a burning pile of goo. Now—drop the gun."

She can't actually do that or she'd have done it from the start! It's the ring! She's afraid of damaging it! "No. I prefer the present standoff, for a while."

She smiled sweetly. "Maka, you must prove your love to me. Turn and shoot Silent Woman. Narrow beam, in the stomach, half power, so it is slow. Midi, Mari, if Vulture tries to interfere, burn her."

Silent Woman did not understand the words although she recognized her own name and Manka's, and turned, puzzled, to see Warlock grin evilly and bring the laser rifle around until it was pointing directly at Silent Woman's belly. At Silent Woman's child...

Silent Woman screamed the most terrible, anguished scream that any throat could utter; a scream so horrible that it rang and reverberated through the computer room and down the hall. At the same moment she moved her spear to knock Warlock's rifle up and out of the way. So horrible and penetrating was that scream that Maria and Midi turned toward it...

The goddess was taken completely by surprise. Vulture had suspected some action, but not this, but was in immediate control of the body. The finger flicked the stud, and even as Silent Woman leaped on Warlock Vulture fired— wide beam, maximum stun.

The four warriors collapsed into a tangled heap. The terrible scream stopped abruptly and brought on a dramatic, sudden silence. The Earth-daughter, unaffected by such a blast, now stood alone, looking first at the collapse of her defense and then at Vulture, who had dropped, rolled, and now rose again, pistol reset for full power. "I never dreamed you'd actually do that," Vulture said calmly, "although if you had to pick an example, she *was* the logical choice, being the most useless of the group."

"Do you think you can kill me with *that*?" the goddess responded arrogantly.

Vulture shrugged slightly. "Gee, I don't know. Let's find out." She fired a steady stream, up to the head and back down again.

The Earth-daughter was flung back against the wall by the force, but dropped and then recovered. Her glow was fading, and her flesh was blistered and gaping, but she was far from dead.

The Earth-daughter rose and launched herself at Vulture, who quickly stepped back and open fire once more. If she could have kept a continuous stream on the creature, it would have had no chance, but the Earth-daughter, like Vulture, knew the laser could fire for only ten seconds before it automatically cut off for a precious second or two to allow the weapon to cool down.

Vulture was not quick enough. The Earth-daughter was on her at the first opening, steely hands around Vulture's throat, squeezing with enormous pressure, until the eyes bulged from Vulture's head. The humanoid heard and felt the neck snap, saw the life drain out, and let Vulture's limp form fall to the floor. The Earth-daughter reached out, removed the ring from Vulture's limp finger.

The humanoid was no longer willing to play games and no longer supremely confident. The laser had severed vital connections; she had no glow, her body was severely charred, and, worse, she had no hypnocaster. She made her way uneasily to a wall panel near the slots for the information modules, entered a code, and waited as a small panel opened. She was about to press the activator when laser fire again raked her body, throwing her back and away from the panel. The fire was well concentrated now, back and forth along the hips, and she screamed an inhuman, electronic scream and tried to get up. Her blackened, burnt face looked up . . . and saw Vulture, still bloody, her head dangling crazily to one side, with a laser pistol in each hand now, firing, firing, coming on . . .

In a deep, strained voice that sounded about to break, the Earth-daughter said, *"What are you?"*

But the raking fire continued with no reply. There was a sudden crackling and then the Earth-daughter started moving, randomly, jerkily, hitting the two walls, then slowly grinding to a halt. There was a sound of someone at the door, but the horrible corpselike figure that had been Vulture ignored it, and the terrified scream and rapid sounds of panicky feet vanishing down the hall.

The Earth-daughter's chest twitched, then moved on its

own, cuing the waiting creature. There was a sudden burst of heat, and the module, shining and shimmering, emerged and floated out. It did not get far; Vulture bore in on it with both laser pistols, medium field, maximum intensity. The beams caught the module and held it, suspended in the air, but it vibrated rapidly and seemed to be trying to escape, to muster enough strength against the beams to dart past and out the door.

It exploded with a concussion that knocked Vulture flat; the heat seared not only her broken and bloodied body but also those of the four unconscious warriors. There was a smell of burnt flesh and singed hair, but it was over.

Vulture rose again, ignoring the mess, and made her way to the still form of the Earth-daughter. She knelt down, reached behind the smoldering ruin of beauty, and picked up the ring, then put it back on her own finger. She then made her way back to the wall opposite the computer interface, sat, and tried to rebuild as much of her body as possible before the others came to. It was quickly clear that while the Earth-daughter had not inflicted fatal damage, the scope of repairs was not worth the time and effort. Better, with the tribe in control of the temple, to find another. That, she reflected, would not be hard.

Still, it had been the Earth-daughter's last words that continued to echo in Vulture's mind. *What are you?* A collection of past minds? A new form of artificial life? What? She didn't know, not really. For the first time, she began to wonder if even her creator knew, either.

All that time, all the years of Vulture's existence, she had hated Clayben, but could Clayben really explain Vulture? Could the scientist even duplicate her, given all the means? That was now in doubt.

Arnold Nagy had worked for Master System's enemy, and Nagy had spent ten years on Melchior with access to almost everything. In fact, Nagy had spent just slightly longer there than Vulture had been alive. Coincidence? Raven had become convinced that Nagy was not human; now, seeing the Earth-daughter, that theory took on a lot more credence.

Vulture struggled to her feet. Enough was enough; a new body was mandated, and quickly. There was much to do. Still, she felt a bit better about it all now, somehow. She owed the Earth-daughter a debt, in spite of the problems the humanoid had caused.

Perhaps I am not the monster of a mad scientist after all. Perhaps, just perhaps, I am the weapon forged by the enemy for this very purpose and kept, preserved, until the time was right to act. Perhaps I am the deliberately created key player in this master plan.

And that feeling, for now, was enough.

Matriyehan skin was thick and tough; all four of them would show the burn marks of the explosion for some time to come, perhaps permanently, but the hair that was singed would grow back and there would be no lasting effects that would cripple their lives and performance.

Silent Woman seemed to have no memory of the attack; at least she didn't act any different around Warlock than before. Still, Vulture didn't think it a good idea to keep them close together. They could never be sure about Silent Woman.

Warlock looked at Maria and Midi. "You are going back—up?"

They nodded. "There is no medicine available here," Maria noted. "We would quickly lapse back into dishonor. It had gone too far for us; the physical changes are permanent, although China believes she might one day determine a psychochemistry program that will retrain the body and brain to release the proper chemicals naturally. As it stands, we have a chance at a ship again, particularly considering the losses each of these operations has caused so far. There will always be a lingering loneliness, I think. This world has changed us far more than merely physically. I will always be Matriyehan from now on, neither fully of the old way or the new, but our destinies lie elsewhere, and we can do more for this world, our world, our people, there than here."

Midi nodded. "I have never had a world or a people of my own before. Neither of us has. Each of us has a child and another on the way and those children are Matriyehan. Somebody has to make sure that we are not forgotten. When we face down Master System, Matriyeh must be there."

Warlock sighed and nodded. "I understand, but I cannot leave. Someone also must remain here, to help and protect these people. The raid has restored my honor and my confidence. I know I will never again be a chief, but I will remain a warrior, and being the chief's advisor and confidant is not a bad thing. Just as you must go, someone must stay."

Vulture couldn't help but wonder if part of Warlock's change was her added softness and her pregnancy; it would have been damned hard for her to face Raven and the others like this. She would be invaluable in helping connect the chosen tribes, the Warriors of the Storm who would know the secrets, and in protecting and guiding them. She would not be alone; Soba had proven the potential of Matriyehans to change if they could be freed from the grip of the system, and Oona had the same potential. The real trick would be keeping their lives remote and secret from the master computer as well as keeping the circle of tribes large enough to function. It was a risk, but, as

Soba had noted, all life on Matriyeh was constant risk, so you might as well risk things for a positive end.

"We shipped the remains of the Earth-daughter up with the ring, and they did an analysis," Vulture told them. "It's an amazing construct, half human and half robot. The hypnocaster survived mostly intact and it's of unfamiliar design, small and integrated into the bone structure. The glow was more than for effect—it was also a carrier mechanism designed to induce incredible subjectivity in anyone within the field. We can duplicate the mechanism quite well, although we can't duplicate the Earth-daughter. That level of technology is beyond us, and unless we were able to capture intact and analyze one of those master Val modules, we cannot even guess what her core was like. She had no other defenses, no other weapons, but against anyone but me, it still would have been more than enough—and even I wasn't sure until the last moment. If she had not given me the diversion I needed, or if, after strangling me, she'd turned one of those laser rifles on me—I would have lost. It's a sobering thought."

"But—so much of what might be done here depends on keeping the master computer ignorant," Warlock noted. "We can't replace her, and we can't explain her absence."

"We thought of that, almost from the start, but we had to see the remains to be sure. The Earth-goddess was a later addition to the system, a fail-safe backup in recognition of the limits of the master computer here. There was no direct interface, and, needless to say, a mindprinter is useless on any kind of robot. It served as a second, independent observer, not subordinate of the computer. It appears that what little contact she had with the computer was through a small control room off the computer center where she had direct access to the data banks. Any communication, however, appears to have been by voice or

keyboard. The computer was the manager; she was chief of
security. They were very confident, too. The computer access
is a standard setup without even rudimentary security
protection. After all, no one else could even get down
there, let alone operate the machinery. The appeal of having
our own goddess, with computer access and hypnotic
abilities, at the center of power here is nearly irresistible."

Maria gasped. "But you're talking about someone transmuted
into a creature who would be the only one of its kind
and under constant risk of exposure. There could never be
another."

"That is true," Vulture admitted, thinking of Nagy's
comment about willingness to pay the ultimate price, "but
there would be compensations. Using a duplicate of the
intricate nervous system and exterior skin from the original,
the wearer of the body would feel quite human but
have much more control over it than humans could. The
organic parts would be inside, extremely well protected
and monitored. While not immortal, she would never age
externally, be impervious to the elements and most things
humans are prey to, and she would be in charge. She
would be a living goddess incarnate without the limits or
programming of her predecessor. She'd run the whole
damn show. She would almost certainly be an activist goddess,
unlike her predecessor."

"Could they make such a creature?" Midi asked. "And,
if so, could they get anybody to actually take the job?"

"Isaac Clayben has a knack for building creatures,"
Vulture noted dryly. "As for appearance and behavior, in
addition to the remains, they have our mindprints of how
she looked, acted, and sounded. As for volunteers—it
might be very difficult for certain types to turn down. We
will see."

"Yes," Warlock said thoughtfully. "Raven, for one,

would love the power of it. It would be quite amusing to see him lock into the role of a stunningly beautiful goddess."

"Damn me if I ain't tempted," Raven said, puffing on his cigar. "Can't you just see me with that body, walkin' around like some naked virgin?" He chuckled. "But, with that power and that hypno and all, *damn* wouldn't it be fun!"

"I certainly hope so," Ikira Sukotae responded. "You can forget it, though, Raven. The job's been filled and it starts in a few hours."

His eyebrows went up. "Huh? Not *you*?" He stared at her, so tiny and yet so beautiful. "You don't have the mass for it."

"For most of our purposes, no, but I have more than enough to provide the organic portions. It's been checked out. I'm the logical one. All this time I've been a tiny person in a land of giants, and I've lived as one of a kind. And I have no problems looking or acting like that. I was born to do it. I understand the computers and technical material, and I'm as used to the politics of command. You have to play the games very well to get to a position of authority and respect in a universe of giants. And the challenge ... Overseeing the development of a whole new society and culture, uniquely female yet tough and self-reliant. I was born to be a goddess. I just never thought I'd get the chance. I don't have to wait for Master System to be destroyed to get what I want. I never really knew what I wanted, Raven, but when this came up, and I found that I could have it, I knew this was my chance. What do you want out of this, Raven—really? Do you know?"

He sighed. "No. But I'm gonna miss you, kid."

"I'll miss you, too, Raven. All of you. Drop down and worship me sometime."

"We're gonna get the rest of the rings."

She smiled. "I know. Maybe by then you'll know what you want to do with them."

EPILOGUE: DECEPTION AT OLYMPUS

T HE COUNCIL HAD NOT EXPECTED HER ENTRANCE, BUT, then, they never knew where the Earth-daughter might be nor when she would choose to appear. She came and went as befitted a goddess, with the same inscrutability as one might expect of the supernatural. Lately, it was said, she had departed from her cloistered life and actually gone out among the trainees in the valley, and even beyond, to visit tribes whose faith had been wavering.

"My master, whose glory illuminates the days and gives life to the world, commands your presence this night in the great hall," she told them. "Come now and follow me."

They arose and followed; one never questioned one's deities. They used the back ways forbidden to all others, and entered the huge cave with its statue of the Great God from the side. It was late; no others were about, and no rituals were performed at this time.

She knelt down before the great statue, and they, the

elders and leaders of the church, prostrated themselves and waited.

"Master, Your obedient and loving daughter who is part of you obeys Your holy commands. Command us, greatest God of all, who created us and the world."

Now sounds emanated from the great statue, as if, somehow, it had begun to breathe through enormous stone lungs. The head and torso took on a more fluid, plastic look, and the eyes moved. And then the Great God spoke, in a mighty, inhuman voice that instilled instant awe and fear in the hearts and minds of onlookers.

"A large amount of anomalous data has been sent to Us over the past weeks," it said. "They produce cause for concern, indicating increased demonic activity against Our people and Our will. We have sent Our daughter to investigate, but She had found nothing that could not be dealt with. We are reassured, but require a final confirmation before dismissing the matters. The ultimate goal of demons is to thwart Our holy and absolute will by taking from Us the Ring which We have given to you as a sign and symbol of our faith. If you have the Ring, hold it up so We may look upon it."

The chief administrator rose to a kneeling position, then, fumbling, removed the ring from her finger and held it high. Great eyes turned and focused on it.

"Very well, Guard it with your lives and souls and honor. The demon forces are strong and may make the most bold and outrageous attempts to get it. Our daughter will help you to protect it even more. Obey Her in all things when battling the greatest of demons, lest you lose not only your lives but your immortal souls. She is a part of Us, and Her glory a reflection of Our own. Go now and enact Our bidding and carry out Our sacred will. At all costs the tests must be run, the system must be preserved."

They groveled and made the responses and prayed for

mercy and wisdom, but the Great God's statue had already lost its fluidity, its life, and returned to being the statue it otherwise was.

The Earth-daughter rose and turned and looked down on them. Poor, simple creatures; slaves to do whatever bidding she commanded. The Great God had been wrong; the last important test had just been run.

She was now the goddess and mistress of all Matriyeh. Matriyeh . . . the first world and people freed from the system. With the computer's own help she'd analyzed the memory recording modules and now understood how they worked and what were their limitations. From now on the collectors would make two stops, not one, when they returned from the field. Using the more sophisticated portables, her priestess-slaves would first evaluate and then reprogram those modules so that the Great God heard only what She wished it to know. The modules going out to reprogram the third rank would also carry Her will and Her messages, not Master System's. It was already mostly done. The religion itself was being reprogrammed, the old beliefs crumbling before the new truth. Polytheism was dying, replaced with a different, almost monotheistic pantheon. There was only one deity for the masses and it was Her; there was only one system, and it was Hers to make. And if they doubted, or questioned, She would walk among them and even the biggest, toughest chiefs would grovel in the mud and worship Her.

Soon they would have more reason than magic tricks to do so. Soon the priestesses would be instructing them in the art of planting, of building, and the new doctrine of cooperation and alliance. It was a challenge, but one she welcomed, for nothing was beyond a goddess, and she was determined to be a great one and give them more reason for worship than most religions.

She wondered, idly, about the ones she'd left behind. If

they got all five rings, if they inserted them, if they gained collectively power far greater than even she could dream of, would they be worthy of worship?

It was irrelevant. This was Her world and Her people, and this was Her entire universe from this moment on. If those others attained their godhoods, they better damn well keep off Her back . . .

The Rings of the Master
continues with
Masks of the Martyrs
from Del Rey books.

ABOUT THE AUTHOR

JACK L. CHALKER was born in Norfolk, Virginia, on December 17, 1944, but was raised and has spent most of his life in Baltimore, Maryland. He learned to read almost from the moment of entering school, and by working odd jobs amassed a large book collection by the time he was in junior high school, a collection now too large for containment in his quarters. Science fiction, history, and geography all fascinated him early on, interests that continue.

Chalker joined the Washington Science Fiction Association in 1958 and began publishing an amateur SF journal, *Mirage*, in 1960. After high school he decided to be a trial lawyer, but money problems and the lack of a firm caused him to switch to teaching. He holds bachelor degrees in history and English, and an M.L.A. from Johns Hopkins University. He taught history and geography in the Baltimore public schools between 1966 and 1978 and now makes his living as a freelance writer. Additionally, out of the amateur journals he founded a publishing house, The Mirage Press, Ltd., devoted to nonfiction and bibliographic works on science fiction and fantasy. This company has produced more than twenty books in the last nine years. His hobbies include esoteric audio, travel, working on science-fiction convention committees, and guest lecturing on SF to institutions such as the Smithsonian. He is an active conservationist and National Parks supporter, and he has an intense love of ferryboats, with the avowed goal of riding every ferry in the world. In fact, in 1978 he was married to Eva Whitley on an ancient ferryboat in midriver. They live in Maryland with their son, David.

By the year 2000, 2 out of 3 Americans could be illiterate.

It's true.

Today, 75 million adults...about one American in three, can't read adequately. And by the year 2000, U.S. News & World Report envisions an America with a literacy rate of only 30%.

Before that America comes to be, you can stop it...by joining the fight against illiteracy today.

Call the Coalition for Literacy at toll-free **1-800-228-8813** and volunteer.

**Volunteer
Against Illiteracy.
The only degree you need
is a degree of caring.**

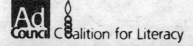

Ad Council   Coalition for Literacy

LV-2